A Real Daughter

Lynne McKelvey

Savant Books and Publications
Honolulu, HI, USA
2017

Published in the USA by Savant Books and Publications
2630 Kapiolani Blvd #1601
Honolulu, HI 96826
http://www.savantbooksandpublications.com

Printed in the USA

Edited by Eleonor Gardner
Cover by Ted Engelbart
    Cover photograph with permission by Michele Quattrin
    Cover Leaves @ istockphoto | javarman3
    Author photograph with permission by E. David Luria

13 digit ISBN: 978-0-9972472-5-1

First Edition: October 2017
Library of Congress Control Number: 2017913732

for Ellen, Jonathan, and Isaac

"Child, it is such a narrow house,"
The ghost cried; and the wind sighed.
"A narrow and a lonely house,"
The withering grass replied.

- Walter de la Mare

SPRING 1978

Lynne McKelvey

Chapter 1: Sarah

Every year since Sarah died, Claire had baked her daughter a birthday cake. Now, as she lifted a lemon-frosted cake from the bottom shelf of the refrigerator, the cold heft of the platter reassured her. She held the cake in front of her and admired the deep swirls in the frosting she'd sculpted with the back of a teaspoon the night before. The six candles ringing the top of the cake tipped slightly, but the all-important candle in the middle—the one to grow on—stood straight and tall.

She walked carefully to her tiny living room, footsteps echoing off the bare floor and walls, and set the cake on the coffee table. Rays from the dying sun shone through the windows, etching the cake with light. She scooped up a glob of frosting and sucked it off her finger, then drew the curtains and unplugged the phone. One by one, she lit the candles. While wax dripped onto the yellow frosting, she willed Sarah to come.

In her dreams, the child appeared uninvited, always

gasping in her crib, her tiny face contorted, the color of a bruise. In her dreams, Claire ran down the endless corridors, faster, faster, until her own lungs were bursting. She was never in time. But on her birthdays, Sarah ran to her—as now—hurtling through the doorway, cheeks aglow, eyes crammed with light. Frisky, her half-grown kitten, bounded in behind her, its gray and black striped tail with a crook in its tip held high. Sarah wore the dress Claire had made for her, a smocked yellow gingham that matched the cake's frosting and the child's hair. Sarah threw herself into her mother's lap and flung her arms around her neck, her knobby knees punching into Claire's abdomen. Claire buried her face in her daughter's hair, breathing in the smell of sunshine.

"Mommy," Sarah said, spinning off her mother's lap, twisting the skin on Claire's thighs. "I can't wait to open my presents." She was hopping in place, holding her ankle. Claire was a little surprised to see Sarah's bare feet were callused with wavy patterns carved into her heel, like rake lines in a tiny Japanese garden. She'd lost a tooth—the same one that had caused Claire to cry out with pain and pride when she'd nursed her daughter. But the bud of a splendid new tooth was in sight.

"Can I blow out my candles? Can I wish for anything? If I tell you my wish, will it still come true?"

Sarah whirled away—arms outstretched, head tipped

back—and spiraled to the floor.

Then she was gone. As the candles sputtered into the frosting, Claire peered around the living room, hoping to catch one more glimpse of her child. She thought she saw the striped flicker of the cat's tail disappearing through a doorway; but for now, Sarah was nowhere to be seen.

Lynne McKelvey

SUMMER 1978

Lynne McKelvey

Chapter 2: A Secret Daughter

It wasn't until after they'd made love for perhaps the twenti-eth time that Jake told her about Mandy. He lay next to Claire, a low warm wall in her narrow bed, his arm propping up his head. With his free hand, he traced the dark ring around her nipple, his finger catching ever so slightly on the tiny nodules. Without his glasses, his eyes seemed variegated, flecks of gray and yellow dappling the brown. He looked at her in silence. It had been a long time since anyone had looked at her the way Jake was looking at her then. "Claire," he said, removing his hand from her breast, there's someone I want you to meet."

She felt the sheet pull toward the indentation under his elbow. From the beginning, she'd known he was holding something back. But in the five weeks they'd been going out, she'd never questioned him about what it might be, never even asked him if he'd been married. Best to let him keep his secrets. The Lord knew she had hers. He took a breath and exhaled slowly.

"My daughter, Amanda," he said, his voice rising and falling with the name.

Claire was astonished. She'd expected him to say, "My wife."

"Why didn't you tell me before?" she asked, her voice sharp, almost as though he *had* said "wife."

He ran his eyes along her body as if memorizing each curve and plane. Did he think this might be the last time he would see them? She saw his throat muscles working under his beard.

"Guess I was afraid to," he said, his voice almost inaudible. "Guess I was afraid Mandy might complicate...us." He rolled onto his back and stared at the ceiling. "Mandy's with her mother for the summer," he continued, "but she lives with me." He emphasized the *me*. "She's just turned eight."

He went on, but the roaring in Claire's ears drowned out the rest. Sarah had just turned six—would have just turned six.

"Amanda," she said finally, her voice sounding hollow and far away.

She turned toward Jake and combed her fingers through his beard. It felt dry and springy, like peat moss in the fall. Had *he* picked his daughter's name? She decided he probably had. It was a beautiful name, but slightly showy, like the floribunda roses he'd told her he grew.

"Amanda," she said again, thinking not of the name now, but of a little girl. She couldn't see her yet, but in her mind she was already stroking the child's soft cheeks. Claire fit her body against Jake's side. Her breasts felt full and tender, the way they had in the months when Sarah was alive.

Lynne McKelvey

Chapter 3: Reflections

Claire rolled to a stop in front of her cottage and parked her pickup truck. Her shirt was drenched, and her skin felt gritty with soil and salt. She'd spent the long day working in her San Fernando Valley client's garden, where Santa Ana winds spun around her like a hot cocoon. She liked the way her work made her feel: hot, sore, sweaty, and physically spent. It was what saved her after Sarah died.

She opened the cab door and slid to the pavement. Now that she was near the coast, the temperature had dropped precipitously—one of the city's many anomalies that still startled her. She stepped onto the curb and headed toward a tiny house with white clapboard siding and an asphalt tile roof. She'd found the cottage the day after she'd arrived in L.A. from Vermont. Wedged improbably between two mid-sized apartment buildings, it appeared not much bigger than a child's playhouse and lacked common amenities—no dishwasher, no microwave oven; but Claire had been struck by how it stood alone.

She opened the front door, pausing at the threshold to take in the Spartan living room: bare floor, blank walls, nondescript coffee table and sofa. Except for the workbench with her drawing board on top and a four-legged stool underneath, the room might belong to anyone. Or no one. When Claire first moved in, she'd planned to acquire rugs and pictures, extra chairs, and knick-knacks; but as the years went by, she'd grown accustomed to the empty rooms. They contained nothing to remind her of the past; nothing to distract her from it.

She slipped off her mud-caked shoes and set them by the door. Barefoot, she shuffled to the kitchen where she removed a plastic water pitcher from the chunky Coldspot and drank deeply from the spout. She returned to the living room and flopped onto the sofa, propping her feet on the coffee table. She was doing what she always did after work. Usually, the routine soothed her. Today, though, she was agitated. Her house seemed different—noisy, inhabited. The air felt charged. Infinitesimal particles—billions of them—seemed to be rushing all around her. She pictured them pulling away from their centers, colliding, recombining, then splitting apart again. She stood up and, with quick strides, began to pace the room. A daughter. Jake had a daughter. An eight-year-old daughter who lived with him. A single fact, but one that filled the cottage. All day long she'd had to push the fact away for fear it might consume her. But she was home now; she could surrender.

She stopped pacing and sat down again. In the weeks she and Jake had been seeing each other, Claire had wondered why he'd never asked her to his house. He mentioned it frequently—the leaky roof he'd fixed, a window he'd glazed, shelves he was building—and he talked about his garden, especially about the roses. But he'd never invited her over. From time to time she amused herself wondering what he might be hiding there. Blue-lit closets filled with plants in trays? Manacles chained to the bedposts? Corpses in the basement? Now that he'd divulged it, his real secret seemed hardly less astonishing. Mandy's dolls and toys, of course, would be scattered throughout the house, offering clues to, if not proof of, her existence. The real mystery was why he'd waited so long—five weeks and some—to tell her. "I was afraid I'd lose you," he'd said.

Lose her?

In the years since Jake had been divorced, surely there'd been other women in his life. Yet none had stayed with him. Was Mandy the reason? Now that Claire knew about his daughter, a daughter who lived with *him*, to Claire, he seemed more attractive than ever.

She leaned back and recalled their first meeting. One of

her garden client's leucadendrons was ailing, and she'd stopped by Armstrong's Home Improvement Center to pick up a forty-pound sack of Gro-Power 5-3-1. As she squatted beside the fertilizer stack to read the ingredients, she'd heard a voice rumble above her head.

"So, what do you think? Will Whitney Farms do it for my floribunda?"

She'd put her finger under *soluble potash* and let her gaze slide to the edge of the sack. The man was kneading the corner tab where the thread started with his fingers. It was a hard and callused hand—at odds with his speech, which hinted at college and maybe more. She looked up, curious about the contradiction, but the man was pretty much what she expected—denim cut-offs, a neatly trimmed beard. The store lights reflecting off his glasses, wire-rimmed and flecked with paint, kept her from seeing his eyes. But she felt them looking at her—looking and looking.

"It depends on your soil," she'd said, wishing he'd move his head so she could see his eyes. Eye color mattered to Claire—perhaps because she'd never had the chance to find out whether Sarah's eyes would turn brown like her father's or stay blue like hers.

"Acidic," Jake said, with an emphatic nod. As he moved his head, she saw that his eyes were brown—not a rich loamy brown or the light flat brown of clay, but an ordinary, medium brown.

"Definitely acidic" he replied. "The pH is 6.5," he added, head bobbing as though he'd just scored a winning point.

"That *is* acidic," Claire agreed, thinking, here was a man who liked to be sure of his facts. "Should be perfect for roses. The compounds have to be soluble, you know, so the sulfur can be released."

She'd gone on about the chemistry. As she spoke, she felt her cheeks grow warm. This wasn't how she usually talked about plants, as if she believed facts and figures could ever explain why some thrived and others didn't. But she liked the way Jake kept looking at her, so she kept going, preening as if she were one of his roses.

When he asked her out a week later, she agreed, telling herself it would be a one-time thing. They'd arrive in their own cars, have dinner in a strip mall, she'd give him some pointers on his roses, and then they'd go their separate ways. Since her child died and Claire had moved to Los Angeles, she lived without desire. Gardens. Sarah. They balanced one another. The scale might tip if anything was added.

She burrowed deeper into the sofa cushions and let her thoughts drift back to that evening—so different from the one she'd intended to have.

When she pushed through the red lacquered door at the

Chinese restaurant, smells of garlic, sesame oil, and faraway spices greeted her. Jake waved from a booth at the far end of the room. He stood when she joined him, appearing taller than she remembered, and the courtesy pleased her. Over plates of glossy vegetables and steaming bowls of rice, he told her he taught tenth grade history. She said she planted gardens; she didn't like the word *design*. He wanted to know about her, but didn't dig too deeply, asking only if she'd always lived in L.A. or was she a "transplant" like him. He smiled at his joke and tapped his chest with his middle finger. "Pittsburgh," he said with an eye roll.

She described growing up in Vermont without naming the town: father, a dentist; mother, a "mother"; one older brother. Nothing much to report. After college, she worked as a children's librarian, she told him, stumbling on *children's*, but he didn't seem to notice.

"Then one day," she continued, vaulting over Scott, their marriage, and...the rest, "on impulse"—for how else could she explain it?—"I decided to try something completely new."

"Just like that?" Jake had asked, his eyebrows lifting.

She nodded. "So I came out here," she hurried on, hoping he wouldn't urge her to say more and wondering what to tell him if he did.

"Gutsy," he'd said. "Takes guts to pull up stakes."

She was pleased with his admiration, however misplaced. She was no bold explorer that winter afternoon when she flung her clothes into the brown tweed suitcase, placed Sarah's things—carefully selected items—in her grandmother's hatbox, and headed west into the pale sun. She was a fugitive, fleeing.

"And you?" she asked, both to shift the focus and because she was curious. "What brought you out here?"

"College, at first," he told her, reaching for his cup and taking a swallow of tea. "Then graduate school. Ancient history," he added, anticipating her question. "Rome." As he unrolled the word, he stared into the middle distance. "Although," he lowered his eyes, "I never quite got my degree." He paused, his fingers tight around the porcelain cup. She wondered what had prevented him from finishing, but didn't ask. Perhaps, like her, he kept the past contained. "When I was offered a job teaching history at Venice High, I grabbed it," he said, looking up again. "And it's been good."

He went on to regale her with stories about his students and asked for her opinion on various plants. They riffed on these themes until the waiter, clearing his throat, removed the teapot. Claire looked around the restaurant and found, to her surprise, it was nearly empty. As they got up to leave, Jake caught her hand and pressed it to his lips, igniting nerves long dormant. She looked away.

"May I see you home?" he asked. His voice rumbled through her body. He kept hold of her hand, his beard grazing her knuckles. His breath was warm. *May I see you home?* An old-fashioned phrase—one her grandfather might have used when he was young. Still, she was about to demur when the bright lantern lights overhead were suddenly extinguished, leaving the room in a dim, sourceless glow—and the image of a white pine cabinet with three drawers stacked on top of one another arose in her mind: gardens, Sarah, Jake. Perhaps she could have all three. She took a breath, pressed his hand with hers, nodded, and exhaled.

When they arrived at her cottage, Jake parked his Mustang behind her blue truck and followed her to the front door. Her hand trembled as she reached for her key. It wasn't too late to end the evening, she remembered thinking. She could open the door partway, exclaim about the lateness of the hour, and slip inside. And then? Her life would go on in its predictable pattern—imagining Sarah, planning gardens—the way it had for years.

Jake stood behind her not touching her, giving her space. Still, she felt his heat. She thought of his eyes—their particular safe shade of brown—and, as she slid the key into the lock, she let the door swing wide. Again, the image of the cabinet with its stacked drawers came into her mind. She would keep the three drawers separate, opening only one at a time.

She shoved the sofa cushions aside, sat up straight, staring at the empty wall in front of her, and wondered yet again what Mandy looked like. "I don't need pictures," Jake had said when Claire asked to see one. "I have *her*."

Have her? The phrase was vaguely troubling, but she'd let it pass. "Why doesn't Mandy live with her mother?" she asked instead. Jake's mouth had tightened. Rita never wanted a child, he told Claire. She'd only gotten pregnant because she wanted him. After the baby was born, it was Jake who fed and bathed and changed her. "I loved it," he said, his voice thick and deep. She seemed so tiny, so helpless, so exactly right."

Was this how Scott had felt about *his* baby daughter? Claire wondered now. In those golden months when Sarah was still alive, Claire knew she hadn't given her husband much chance to care for someone so tiny, so helpless, so exactly right. Sarah was almost always in Claire's arms—except at night when she laid the baby in her crib. Darkness beat above Claire's head. She ducked and hid her eyes.

What if she'd let Scott put Sarah to bed that night? Would he have noticed the damp spot on the sheet? And if he had, would he have changed the bed before he laid the baby down? Or, like Claire, would he have covered over the damp sheet with a blanket? The fluffy one hung so handily on the rocking chair beside the crib. The jostling particles were getting louder, shriller. Claire dropped to the sofa and clapped her hands over her ears.

For a while, she took the pills they'd given her—red ones shaped like bullets with tiny green letters printed on the side. They dulled the pain, but also the memories. She could no longer feel Sarah's weight on her left shoulder, the little shudder the baby gave before her gums clamped onto Claire's nipple. She couldn't hear the hollow plucking sound Sarah made when she burped. The pills seemed to double Claire's loss. She stopped swallowing them and hoarded them instead, hiding the brown plastic bottles behind the laundry soap where Scott wouldn't find them. She kept the razor blades there too. Backup.

The noise subsided. Claire lowered her hands to her lap. What, she wondered, had Scott been feeling throughout those terrible weeks? Had she even asked him? She assumed he was mourning Sarah, but maybe he was mourning Claire. Nothing he did or said made any difference to her. He became discouraged, then angry. Finally, he left. She didn't blame him.

Claire dropped her head and closed her eyes. She could hear the clock ticking in the bedroom. Now that Jake had told his secret, wasn't it time to tell him hers? A dead daughter for the living one? Her jaw tensed. No, she told herself. The two secrets had nothing to do with each other. There was no reason for them to be exchanged.

Lynne McKelvey

Chapter 4: Plants and Piñatas

Claire peered down the line of stalls that spilled onto the gum-stained sidewalks of *Avenida de la Revolución*. As she searched for the medicinal herb stand, the light stench of the *Río Tijuana* wafted toward her and mariachi music blared from bootlegged tapes.

She'd discovered Tijuana soon after she moved to Los Angeles. Nora, the owner of the plant nursery where Claire was working at the time, had asked her to check out the native plant sale at the Quail Botanical Gardens a few miles north of San Diego. "Don't rush back," Nora had told her. "Take the day off. San Diego's only minutes away. You could poke around Old Town and wait for the traffic to calm down."

But it was Tijuana that Claire chose to visit instead. Apart from her family's trips to Canada when she was small, she'd never been to a foreign country. After she'd admired the stateside gardens and bought some plants at the sale, she'd headed straight for the Mexican border, less than an hour away. Just north of the line, she'd found a fenced lot where she parked her truck—she'd heard about the perils of driving in Mexico—and then proceeded on foot through a tall, cumbersome turnstile to the other side. Her subsequent visits to Tijuana had been rare, always piggybacking on one of her more frequent trips to the Quail gardens. But today, she'd spun right by the site's arched entrance and continued on due south.

Now, among the *Avenida*'s stalls, she spotted the familiar medicinal herb stand about fifty yards away. She hurried toward it, passing the auto detail shop ("Cash only! Cheap!") that abutted Dr. Marco Ortega *Dentista*'s bare office; the huge clay pots bunched on the sidewalk like impossible-to-carry terracotta balloons; and a pair of *burro-cebras*—live donkeys painted black and white to look like zebras. Later in the day when the tourists emerged, they'd pose beside the *burro-cebras* while a skinny teenager snapped Polaroids, sombreros and serapes provided at no extra cost.

A little breathless, Claire arrived at the medicinal plants. She nodded to the wizened vendor, who nodded in reply. The last time she was here, he'd sold her some *yerbanis*—"Mexican marigold," as it was known stateside. When drunk as a tea, the yellow petals had great calming powers, the old man had informed her, for jangled nerves, the common cold, and even for *resacas*—"hangovers." He knew all this and more. His grandmother, a healer from the mountains of Nayarit, had taught him well when he was a boy.

From her past visits to the plant stand, Claire had learned much about the curative powers of plants. A poultice of indigo leaves applied to the forehead would take away a child's headache; mashed prickly poppy seeds mixed with water and drunk three times a day soothed stomach pains. For the dreaded *susto*, in which the soul departs the body after a sudden fright, a simple tea infused with orange blossoms could ease the malady's powerful effects. In the most serious cases, when the fear turned into horror—*espanto*—a healer could be summoned to perform a sweeping ceremony with branches of basil, purple sage, or rue.

Claire stared at the medicinal plants in the bins: twisted roots of grey, brown, or black; leaves lobed and saw-toothed—rough, smooth, dull, or shiny; and seed pods, stems, and blossoms of every hue. As she took in their bounty, she felt a familiar sense of wonder rise. For every ailment, it seemed, plants possessed a cure.

But today she sought their darker powers, something she'd not done before. Moles were ruining her Valley client's garden and she needed a toxic herb to drive them away. Planted in the proper spots, caper spurge would do the trick, repelling the blind burrowers rather than poisoning them. The herb wasn't sold stateside—too dangerous, probably—and though it was said to be rampant in the wild, she'd never come across any.

"*Topo de plantas spurge,*" she said, regretting her words as soon as she spoke them. Ingested, the plant was deadly, every part of it. Suppose a bird or pet ate some? Or, worse, a curious child? Her muscles tensed, then softened. What were her options? she asked herself, as she inspected the blue-green leaves and bulbous brown seed clusters on the plant the vendor held up. In a garden, plants and moles couldn't coexist. At least she wasn't using chemicals or a deadly gas to get rid of the creatures. Lost in her thoughts, she reached for the caper spurge; she was startled when the vendor yanked the plant away from her.

You must be careful, señora, " he said, pointedly wrapping it in layers of old newspaper which he wound round and round with twine. "*Cuidado,*" he repeated and passed the packet to Claire.

She took the bundle of spurge from the vendor, sensing its potency through the newspaper. She wanted to ask him more about the plant and about the properties of other poisonous plants as well. But she mustn't linger. She was due at Jake's in a few hours; her *first* visit to his house. She was spending the weekend there. Mandy would arrive on Sunday.

Claire's heart beat faster. Though she'd found out about

Jake's daughter only a week ago, Claire felt as though she'd been waiting to meet the little girl for a long time. Perhaps since the day she'd met Jake. Or even before that.

As she was about to leave the stall, her eyes drifted back to the vendor's display: plants with the power to heal or harm lay side by side in plastic bins. Despite the midday sun, she felt a sudden chill and quickly backed away, clutching the packet of caper spurge and half-running as she retraced her steps.

When she reached the *burro-cebras*, she spotted the arrow that pointed to the border. She was hurrying toward the sign when a splash of colors on a side street caught her eye. She stopped and turned to see a lone stall with dozens of piñatas—frogs, pigs, and grinning skeletons; chickens, Santas, and clowns—all jouncing from a cord strung high above the sidewalk. Claire smiled. She'd get one of them for Mandy. A piñata would be a perfect gift. At Christmas or for her birthday party, the little girl could stuff it with candies. In the meantime, it would decorate her room.

Claire approached the stall, squinting as she looked up at the figures bobbing bright as beach balls against the August sun. It was a nearly monochromatic cat, though, that drew her—a darkish creature with black and gray crepe-paper stripes and a jaunty crook in the tip of its tail. Claire bought it on the spot.

It was only after she'd re-crossed the border and was driving home that she began to feel uneasy about her purchase. Had she picked the wrong animal? Should she have chosen a pig or a turtle or a donkey instead? The cat was perched on the seat beside her. She turned her head to look at it, taking in its distinctive markings—dark stripes, white bib and paws, a slight bend in its tail—and her discomfort grew. This cat was special. Familiar, too. Her breath caught. Frisky. The piñata looked just like Sarah's cat. Her eyes now back on the road, Claire pictured the piñata dangling from a rope strung between two trees while a blindfolded child flailed at it with a stick. What if Sarah were watching from the sidelines? When the other child's stick slammed into its target, Sarah would see the cat's striped body split open. Her eyes would grow round. Her face would blanch then crumple, and, as small candies rained on the green lawn, her tears would begin to flow. Claire reached over and touched the piñata's rough crepe-paper surface and imagined Sarah's fingers running through Frisky's luxuriant fur. She glanced at the piñata again and pressed her lips together. She could never give this cat to Mandy.

The clock on the dashboard read twenty past four. Claire pressed down on the accelerator. Jake was expecting her at six. She'd have to meet Mandy empty-handed. Next week she'd buy the girl another present, something soft and cuddly—a stuffed animal, maybe even a cat—one that was white or ginger-colored, though. She'd have a sense of Mandy by then and would know just what to get her. In the meantime, she decided, she wouldn't mention this trip to Jake. Without the piñata, there was no need to tell him anything about how she'd spent her day. She rolled down the window and let the outside air blow across her face.

As she turned off Santa Monica Boulevard and onto Sawtelle, her thoughts wandered back to Tijuana. Over the years, the Mexican town had come to feel like her secret garden, the one she'd read about when she was small. But though she was acquainted with its outskirts—the part most tourists went to—she'd never strayed far from the turnstile. She could have ventured deeper, visiting the large herbal healing centers she knew existed further on, but for some reason she didn't. Just knowing they were there, waiting for her, was enough for now. Someday, when the time was right, she'd get to know them. When the time was right, and she was ready.

She turned onto her street, parking at the curb, and started up the path to her cottage, but stumbled on a rock, dropping the piñata. As she stooped to pick it up, the image of the white cabinet with its stacked drawers rose in her mind. Something about it was different. The cabinet seemed taller. She counted the drawers—*one, two, three*—and drew a sharp breath. Instead of three drawers, now there were four. She continued toward the house, gripping the piñata's looped handle. Four drawers. Gardens, Sarah, Jake, and now the new one—Mandy.

The realization that plants could kill seemed new as well, though of course she'd long known it.

Chapter 5: Mandy

On her way to Jake's kitchen, Claire paused outside the door to Mandy's room. The coffee cups and wine glasses on the tray she carried slid forward. All weekend long, the door had been closed. Claire stared at the door's blank surface and tried yet again to imagine what lay on the other side. The round knob pulled at her eyes. She'd fingered it several times since she'd first arrived. Once she even turned it but immediately let go. She was following Jake's lead. He hadn't gone into his daughter's room at all. Why was that? Claire wondered.

She had looked for traces of the little girl elsewhere in the house—a doll or game or hair bow she might have left around—but found none. Although the rooms were pleasantly cluttered—newspapers and stacks of magazines; a stray hammer, a blackened light bulb, a saucer full of thumbtacks, paper clips, and rubber bands; and, open and face-down, books about Hannibal, the Colosseum, the Second Punic War

(Rome had always fascinated Jake, he'd told her)—he'd put away every remnant of his daughter's life. She cast a final glance at the door's knob. No need to turn it now, even if she weren't holding the tray. In less than an hour, she'd be meeting Mandy in person.

She continued down the hall, elbowing open the swing door to the kitchen when she reached it. The dishes clattered as she set them on the counter. The hard sounds startled her. Since the beginning of the weekend, the only sounds she'd heard had been soft—the sliding sounds of their bodies, the rustling of the sheets.

"Just stick everything in the dishwasher," Jake's voice boomed from the bedroom. Their bedroom. For the past two days, they'd hardly been anywhere else. "She'll be here by noon. We can do a load after lunch."

As she rinsed the dishes before loading them into the machine, Claire's thoughts were churning. Since Jake's initial revelation, she'd learned nothing more about Mandy, not even the color of her hair. He had no pictures of his daughter. (Didn't need any, he'd explained. He had *her*.) What he *did* say, what he seemed eager to point out, was that he was a competent parent and Mandy's mother was not. As the divorce ground along, Rita wanted nothing to do with her daughter. Jake could keep the child all year round, she had told him. Just before the decree became final, however, Rita's father intervened. The grandfather, himself divorced and re-married, was fond of Mandy and wanted to be able to see the child from time to time. He insisted that Rita, who was living with her father and stepmother rent free, retain her visitation rights. Blackmail, Jake called it, his voice bitter. Since Rita had never lived on her own and had no desire to do so, she complied. How ugly divorce is, Claire thought. Hard on everybody, but hardest on children, though Jake seemed oddly unconcerned about its effect on his daughter. "Mandy doesn't need a mother," he said, to Claire's astonishment. "She has *me*."

The tap water was scalding Claire's knuckles as she rinsed the tray. She set it on the counter to drain and turned off the spigot. How did Rita feel about Jake's possessiveness? Claire wondered. And how would *she*? The questions whined around her, but she swatted them away.

The clock ticked above the sink. It was almost noon. Jake had been restless all morning, tightening light bulbs in lamps and ceiling fixtures, fiddling with screws in cupboard doors, and leveling and releveling the refrigerator. Was it Mandy he was afraid wouldn't measure up? Or was it Claire? The faucet was dripping. She turned it hard to the right.

Jake came up behind her. "The bedroom's more or less presentable," he said, his breath warm on her neck. "I don't know whether to wash the sheets or frame them."

Claire blushed. Her heart was beating inside her ears. She and Jake were both wound tight. He moved his hand across her pelvis. She glanced at the clock and wondered what time Mandy went to bed, then leaned back, wanting to burrow into Jake's body. But as she moved, he stepped away, and she had to catch herself to keep from falling.

"There's the car," he said, his hand cupped behind his ear. She hardly recognized his voice, taut and suddenly devoid of overtones. With long strides, he headed toward the front door. He went out and down the steps. Claire sat alone on the sofa, staring into the rectangle of light.

Then, there she was, coming through the doorway, a solid, rosy child in black vinyl boots that matched the dark glossy curls cascading to her shoulders. She wore large magenta-rimmed sunglasses in which Claire saw herself reflected—dwarfed and doubled in their twin, dark lenses. Jake's arm stretched across Mandy's shoulders like a bar.

They marched toward the sofa, the little girl matching her steps to her father's, halting a few inches from Claire's knees. Mandy pushed her sunglasses up above her forehead, her face expressionless. Beneath her bubble-gum-colored blouse, tied in a knot above her jeans, her bare midriff filled Claire's field of sight. Mandy's navel stared at Claire. Claire stared back, scrutinizing its dark center. She heard the child breathe a long raspy breath and looked up at her face just in time to see it shift into a dazzling smile.

"Hello," Claire said. The smile seemed strapped to Mandy's face, concealing everything in a bright mask of light.

"Are you my daddy's girlfriend?" Mandy asked, still smiling. Her voice was high and breathy.

"Well," Claire said, taken aback by the question and wondering what to reply, "I'm a girl—a woman—and I'm your daddy's friend. So I guess that makes me his girl friend."

She must have blinked, for the next thing she knew, the smile was gone.

"No, no, no," the child said, shaking the shiny black curls. "Are you a *real* girlfriend, the kind that stays over-night?"

While Mandy waited for an answer, Claire tried to settle on the color of her eyes. One moment they seemed green, the next, violet. She stared into the black mirrors at their centers. They reflected everything in the room except Claire.

"I'm afraid I can't spend *this* night," she said brightly, as if the child had invited her. "I have to be at work early."

"But Claire..." Jake began.

"Claire!" Mandy exclaimed, drowning him out and pointing at Claire. "Claire, Claire? Where's Claire? Claire, Claire? She's over there!" The smile was back, and her index finger was touching Claire's nose. "I made a rhyme!" she said, looking up at Jake. "Daddy, I made a rhyme!" She pulled on Claire's arm and dragged her to her feet. "Come on, Claire, Claire, Over There," she said, tugging harder. "I'm going to show you my room!"

She clamped her hand around Claire's wrist and pulled her down the hall.

"You gals have fun," Jake called, as Mandy flung open her bedroom door. "I'll rustle us up some lunch."

Claire wanted to pause at the threshold to take in the room—her mind was spinning, she wanted to slow it down—but the child drew her inside, kicking the door closed behind them with the heel of her boot. She led Claire straight toward a white wicker vanity covered with shiny bottles and gleaming tubes, plopped herself down on the small cushioned bench in front of the mirror, and motioned Claire to sit beside her. Silently, they studied one another in the glass. Claire's wispy, no-particular-color hair and inconspicuous eyes contrasted with Mandy's physical intensity: her bright cheeks and full lips; her lustrous curls and dark, wide-set eyes ringed by luxuriant lashes. Still looking in the mirror, Mandy reached for a tube of lip-gloss, cherry-flavored, judging by the smell.

"How come you don't wear make-up?" she asked, smearing the gloss around her mouth.

"I don't know, Claire said, as the child blotted her lips with a smacking sound. "I can't be bothered, I guess." She watched Mandy dunk her middle finger in a jar of eye shadow and rub blue powder flecked with glitter on her eyelids and under the lower lashes. Who had given her all this stuff? she wondered, and hoped it wasn't Jake.

"You really should wear make-up," Mandy said, picking up a short, black-tipped pencil sharpened to a thin point. "It would bring out your eyes."

She leaned forward and, with small flicking motions of the pencil, pushed the arch of her eyebrows up toward her hairline. Claire studied her mirrored self—nose, mouth, ears, eyes—none of them distinctive. But in an unobtrusive way, they all went together.

"Well, you've certainly brought out *your* eyes, Mandy," she said.

The pencil stopped mid-stroke. Their eyes met in the glass, Mandy's deep brown near their centers shading to green and purple at the rim, her own a light blue. The child seemed about to speak but instead returned to the pencil, extending the tip of the eyebrow downward now, digging into the skin, only millimeters from her eye.

Almost afraid to breathe, lest the child's hand slip, Claire slid off the bench. Quietly, she moved around the room, examining it wall by wall as if she were in a museum. On the wall adjoining the one with the mirror and vanity, Mandy's bed, covered by a lumpy quilt with a Strawberry

Shortcake motif, jutted into the room. At its foot was a pink plastic toy chest filled with dolls and plush animals, their heads, arms, and legs sticking out higgledy-piggledy.

On the third wall, the wall with the door, bookshelves held ragged pyramids of games (Candyland, Chutes and Ladders) and dog-eared paperbacks (*Pippi Longstocking*, *The Little Mermaid*, and *Winnie the Pooh)*. To Claire, it seemed a typical little girl's room, predominantly pink and cluttered with books, games and toys.

She turned toward the fourth wall—the one opposite the girl's bed—and saw that it was bare but for the sole piece of furniture, a tall, plain, pine dresser that faced the foot of the bed. The top of the dresser was anything but bare. A large, elaborately framed photograph dominated the surface. In front of the picture, an array of objects had been placed in rows, ranked according to height. Nearest the photograph, held upright in lumps of Play-Doh, were a gold candle, a toothbrush, a peacock feather, and an American flag. Next came a rhinestone-studded lipstick, a vial of perfume, and trial-sized bottles of Jergens lotion and Breck shampoo. In the row farthest from the picture were a silver comb, a miniature red-satin chocolate box shaped like a heart, a seashell, and a white porcelain cat.

Claire glanced around the room. The meticulous arrangement of items on the dresser seemed at odds with the casual disorder everywhere else. Her gaze returned to the dresser top. Stranger than the precise order of the rows was the placement of the framed picture. Rather than facing the opposite wall—the one with Mandy's bed—it had been turned sideways to face the wall with the vanity and bench. Why was that? Claire wondered.

She examined the photograph more closely. Enclosed in a glittering oval frame composed of bits of mirrors was a tense, small-boned woman wearing a long-sleeved white blouse that looked like silk and a single strand of pearls. It was Rita, though she looked too young to be the mother of an eight-year-old. The dark eyes—slightly flattened spheres, wide-set with thick lashes—were like Mandy's. The mother's skin was paler, though, and stretched so tightly across her cheekbones, it seemed about to tear. Her lips, thinner than her daughter's, curved into a smile, but her eyes seemed cold as the glass mosaic framing her face.

"That's my mom." Mandy's voice needled the back of Claire's head.

"She's pretty," Claire said, not looking around.

"She's *beautiful*," Mandy replied. From the depths of the vanity mirror behind her, Claire felt the child's eyes.

"You look like your mom," she said, thinking Mandy was much prettier.

The little girl was silent, apparently mollified. Claire

turned her attention back to the items in front of the photograph. The tiny objects, so carefully placed, reminded her of headstones. She bent closer and saw that an aisle running from the center of the photograph down the length of the dresser top bisected the neat rows in a wide swath. At the end of the aisle, propped upright precariously on a makeshift cardboard easel, was a small mirror, the kind that fits in a purse. A pearl necklace, doll-sized, was tucked underneath the mirror.

"Don't touch that," Mandy said sharply. "It'll fall."

As Claire straightened, out of the corner of her eye, she caught sight of Mandy's arm disappearing into the back of the vanity's middle drawer. She watched the child pull out a small shiny object and slip it into her pocket.

Claire moved to the opposite side of the dresser and stationed herself once more behind the photograph. From here she could see Mandy's face in the vanity's glass. The little girl was making spit-curls. With fierce concentration, she licked her thumb and forefinger, pinched a lock of hair, sculpted it into a *C*, and pasted it, glistening with saliva, onto her forehead. Although Claire's face reflected in the vanity mirror was plainly visible to Mandy, their eyes didn't meet.

Claire looked back at the photograph. On impulse, she stooped behind it and followed Rita's line of sight. In the little mirror at the bottom of the aisle, Rita had an unimpeded view of herself and of each of the articles on the dresser top—even the tiny necklace tucked under the easel. Claire gripped the edge of the dresser. As Rita gazed at her own reflection and her favorite artifacts day after day, she was cut off from her child as absolutely as any pharaoh sealed in his tomb.

Once again the tiny necklace caught Claire's eye. "Is this your doll's?" she asked, pointing to the necklace and raising her eyes to the vanity glass where Mandy was shaping another spit-curl.

Mandy let go of the strand of hair. "Not anymore," she said, looking down. "I gave it to my mom." A flush rose from her chest and spread across her face.

"But your mom already has a necklace," Claire said, puzzled. "The one she's wearing in the picture. It looks just the same."

Mandy hunched her shoulders and lowered her head, as if to bury it in her chest. "That necklace got broke," she whispered, almost inaudibly.

"But she's wearing it," Claire persisted. "Look, Mandy, here"—she picked up the picture and tapped the glass —"here, you can see it around her neck."

"That's not her now," Mandy mumbled. "That's her before I was born." She spoke as if these were two distinct people, one of whom no longer existed.

Claire let out a breath she hadn't realized she'd been holding. No wonder Rita seemed so young. The photograph had been taken more than nine years earlier.

"That necklace"—Mandy gave the word three syllables—"got broke when I was a baby. I was playing with it. I wasn't being careful." Her voice stumbled. She breathed in spasms. "I made her c-c-c-cry."

Cry over a broken necklace? Claire looked back at the artifacts—Mandy's offerings to her mother—and at the smiling woman surveying herself from the glittering picture frame. She set the picture down, grimacing slightly, walked over to the vanity and put her hands on Mandy's shoulders. The little girl's back was rigid with guilt and grief. Claire drew her closer.

"I'm sure it wasn't your fault, honey," she said, rocking the child gently from side to side.

Mandy didn't speak, but her shoulders relaxed under Claire's fingers. She slid off the bench and spiraled into Claire's outstretched arms. With the unfinished curl forgotten, they headed slowly toward the door. As they passed the dresser, Claire glanced once more at the picture, at those unforgiving eyes.

In the hall, Mandy ducked away from Claire and ran into the kitchen where Jake was preparing lunch: tuna sandwiches, carrot sticks, and grapes. He'd already set out three place mats; two on the near side of the formica table, and another opposite them. He was standing beside the refrigerator, pouring Mandy's milk into a tumbler.

"Daddy," the little girl said, planting herself beside Jake and holding out her hand, palm down. "Look at my new ring." She shook her curls and looked up at him through her dark lashes. A mound of green glass the diameter of a dime glittered from her fourth finger. Claire remembered the child's hands when she was putting on makeup. There hadn't been any jewelry on them then.

Mandy fluttered her hand. The glass caught the light. "My mom gave it to me—to remember her by. It's an emerald. I'm not supposed to take it off. Not ever. Not even when I have my bath."

"It'll melt," Jake said, his mouth barely opening.

"No it won't, Daddy." Mandy shut one eye and squinted at the ring. "Real emeralds never melt."

Jake stepped to the table. The tumbler clattered and milk splashed over the rim as he set it down beside the single place mat. "Well, your sandwich *will* melt if you don't get over here," he said.

But Mandy had already reached for the milk and was sliding it back across the table, leaving a smeary wake.

"I want to sit by you, Daddy." The smile. "Claire can sit over there." Another smile—holding it this time. "She'll have more room."

Jake glanced at Claire. "You don't mind?" he asked, his eyes anxious.

Of course she didn't, did she? After all, it was Mandy's first day home.

"Claire, Claire? Where's Claire?" the child chanted, pointing across the table.

"Claire, Claire? She's over *there*!"

A Real Daughter

Lynne McKelvey

FALL 1978

Lynne McKelvey

Chapter 6: Off to School

"Here, Mommy."

Sarah burst into the kitchen, clutching a pink hairbrush and a barrette shaped like a butterfly. Claire tore a length of wax paper off the roll, wrapped the triangle of bread, cheese, and tomato she'd just made, and set the sandwich in Sarah's new tin lunchbox. As she gazed at her daughter, the lump she'd felt in her throat all morning seemed bigger and harder. The navy dress Sarah was wearing made her hair seem even more luminous, her skin fairer, and her eyes a deeper blue than usual. She'd grown over the summer; her hemline was now well above her knees.

Sarah handed her mother the brush and barrette and sat down, first stooping to pat Frisky, asleep under the table.

"Big day, Punkin," Claire said, struggling to get the words past the lump. She leaned over the back of the chair, kissed the top of her daughter's head, and felt the warmth radiating from the child's scalp. "You going to be all right?"

she asked, and instantly regretted her words. Today of all days should be about helping her daughter feel strong.

Sarah tipped her head back and looked up at her mother, eyes unblinking. "Of course, Mommy," she said, her voice as steady as her eyes. A beat. "You going to be all right?"

Claire stared at her child's upside-down face. Was Sarah mocking her? Claire's mouth tightened, then relaxed. What if she was? Weren't mothers supposed to be both glad and sad on their child's first day of school?

"Of course I will," she said, and felt the lump melt a little. "We'll both be fine." She gave Sarah another hug and began running the brush through her hair. "Ninety-nine, ninety-eight, ninety-seven..." Claire chanted. It was a game she'd devised when Sarah was younger to help her sit still. She was old enough to brush her own hair now, but on special occasions, like today, she let her mother do it. Claire loved the rhythm of the strokes, the small tugs of her child's head, the barely audible hiss of the bristles as they slid through the child's silky hair. "Ninety-one," she said, and dropped the brush on the kitchen table. "Hardly any tangles this morning, Punkin. You must have slept like a statue."

"No, Mommy, I already brushed it so we'd be done sooner."

Claire felt a fresh jab of sorrow and joy. "Sounds like

you can't wait to go to school," she said. She lifted the lock of hair that had fallen over Sarah's face and clipped it back with the barrette. "Time to meet the bus," she said, hoping her daughter wouldn't detect the tremor in her voice.

She was about to snap the lunchbox closed when she noticed the cookie tin on the counter. Usually, sweets were for after dinner. But today was a special day. She removed a cookie, wrapped it in wax paper, and slipped it in beside the sandwich. Sarah ran her tongue around her lips and smiled a conspiratorial smile. Claire grabbed the lunchbox, took her daughter's hand, and started for the door.

"Wait, Mommy," Sarah said, dragging Claire back into the kitchen. "I have to say good-bye to Frisky." She wriggled out of her mother's grasp, crawled under the table, and burrowed her face into the cat's fur.

"Time to go, Sarah," Claire said, trying to sound firm, though in fact, she was considering keeping her daughter home for the day. Just one more day. What was the harm? But Sarah had already scrambled to her feet and was pulling her mother toward the door.

"Hurry, Mommy," she said, taking her lunchbox from Claire. "I might miss the bus." She let go of her mother and raced outside.

"Wait, Sarah," Claire called. She tried to run after her daughter, but her feet felt heavy. "Wait," she cried, contorting

her body and lifting one foot then the other as if she were walking on stilts. Right foot, left foot, right foot, left—slogging through mud, out the door, which she left open. Right, left, right, left—into the sunlight, the bright sky, the clear, crisp air. Right, left—hopping, stumbling down the steps, then onto the sidewalk. Right, left—sinking into layers of multicolored leaves. Around the corner—faster now that the pavement was clear—to the bus stop, where the bus—huge, yellow, impregnable—was already leaving, its doors sealed tight. As it pulled away from the curb, red lights flashing, Claire stared at the windows—so many of them, all in a row, all of them black and impenetrable. Perhaps they were made of one-way glass. Hadn't she read of some that were? She waved and waved as the bus grew smaller, then waved some more. Just in case.

Chapter 7: Breasts

Claire parked her truck in front of Jake's flat-roofed tract house, finger-combed her hair, and checked her reflection in the rearview mirror. Since Mandy's arrival, Claire had gotten in the habit of coming over for dinner on Wednesdays after work. She slid from the cab to the ground, headed up the cement path, and climbed the three steps to the slab front porch. Mandy, decked out in a pink princess costume with a satin bodice and rhinestone spaghetti straps, greeted her at the door. The little girl's lips, cheeks, and eyelids were caked with makeup. A red and purple boa was draped around her neck. On her frequent visits to Jake's house over the past weeks, Claire had seen Mandy in this costume before. But tonight something seemed different. She scanned the child's face and tried to figure out what it could be. Eye shadow? Penciled eyebrow? Lip gloss? All were liberally applied, but no more than usual when the little girl played dress-up.

Claire lowered her gaze to the pink bodice. Her mouth

opened in surprise. Straining against the shiny satin, precisely where the tips of the boa ended, were two round swellings. Mandy had breasts. Claire stared at them, amazed. How could this be? She was sure they hadn't been there before. Had Jake noticed? Through the open doorway, she could hear him rattling pots in the kitchen. She must tell him right away. She moved to go inside, but Mandy blocked the way. As Claire tried to push past her, the little girl's breasts brushed her thighs. Claire recoiled and backed down the steps. By the time she reached the ground, her eyes were almost level with Mandy's. The child drew herself to her full height. She seemed taller than Claire. She spread her arms wide. The tips of the boa quivered as she sucked in air.

"Greetings," she said, bowing low.

Staring in frozen fascination, Claire watched the breasts tilt forward. As the little girl leaned over, the ends of the boa swung out from her body, and the top edge of the shiny bodice gaped away from her bare chest. Scarcely breathing, Claire peered down the opening. There, fastened to the fabric with tiny gold safety pins, were two pink socks, each rolled into a tight ball.

"You may enter our house," the child intoned, as Claire stood speechless.

After dinner, as they ticked off Mandy's nightly rituals—bath, teeth, bedtime story, glass of water, goodnight kiss—Claire waited for Jake to say something—anything—about his daughter's "breasts." But throughout the evening, he continued to act as though nothing was amiss. Had he even noticed them? Alone in the kitchen while he made his final good nights to Mandy, Claire wondered how she herself had been fooled.

"Well, that's done," Jake boomed, brushing his hands together as he shouldered through the swinging door. Claire started, rattling the plates she'd just removed from the dishwasher. "She's out for the night." He paused to nuzzle the back of Claire's neck, reaching to open the refrigerator door at the same time. As she loaded the still-warm plates onto the cupboard shelves, cold air chilled the back of her legs. The refrigerator's motor started to hum. As if on cue, Jake began to whistle "You Are My Sunshine."

Claire closed the cupboard door with the heel of her hand and turned around. Still whistling, Jake set out sandwich fixings for Mandy's lunch the next day. He seemed oblivious to Claire. With mounting impatience, she watched him spoon mayonnaise onto bread, slap slices of baloney and cheese on top, cut the sandwich in two, and encase it in Saran Wrap. When he'd finally finished and put everything away, she gave a loud cough and caught his eye. Surely now they would discuss his child. Claire kept her gaze steady and waited for him to begin. Instead, to her astonishment, he winked. Before she knew it, he'd grabbed a sponge and was wiping down the kitchen table, whistling all the while.

"*You make me hap-PEE...*"

Her face felt hot. She never liked the song. And he was off key. Lips compressed, she pulled the plastic basket, bristling with utensils, out of the dishwasher and set it on the counter. Usually she liked sorting the silverware—knives, forks, spoons—each into its own compartment in the drawer. Usually she made sure all the knife blades were parallel, handles pointing forward, and the forks and spoons nested precisely inside one another. But tonight, she mixed the teaspoons in with the soupspoons and let the knives mingle with the forks.

"*You'll never know, dearrrr, how much I love yooooo...*"

Leaving the utensils in disarray, she slammed the drawer shut, scrambling its contents still more, and turned to face Jake.

"*Oh please don't take my sunshine...*"

With each bar of the hateful song, it was becoming clearer that *he* wasn't going to mention his daughter's behavior. It was up to her. She took a breath and tried to choose her words carefully.

"That was quite a show Mandy put on tonight, don't you think?" She strove for a light tone—at least one that sounded neutral. After all, Jake himself was probably wondering what to do. He must be upset, maybe too upset even to think about the problem, let alone address it. Quite possibly he was waiting for Claire to help him out.

He continued to swipe the sponge across the table, easing bits of food off the edge and into his cupped hand.

"That Mandy," he said fondly, shaking his head. "She does love to play dress-up."

The air in the room weighed on Claire's shoulders. Why didn't he look at *her* instead of beaming at the sponge?

"It was a bit more than that tonight, though, don't you think?" she said, her mouth barely opening.

Jake paused, mid-swipe.

"What do you mean?" he said, straightening and meeting her gaze.

Mean? Could he really not know? Was she going to have to spell it out? She waited, but his face remained blank.

"Why those, those ridiculous...*breasts*, of course!" The word ricocheted around the room.

Jake's brow furrowed. For a moment, he stared straight ahead, not at Claire, but through her, his eyes glinting behind his glasses.

His forehead smoothed.

"Oh, *that*," he said, his face relaxing into a grin. "She's a little card, all right, that one. Loves to pretend she's all grown up."

Claire felt his familiar rumbling laugh unrolling like a wave.

"And you think that's okay?" She raised her voice to make herself heard over the laugh. "It's really okay for a child barely eight-years-old to be stuffing rolled-up socks in the top of her dress and parading around?"

Jake stopped laughing. He looked at Claire with a puzzled expression.

"What's the harm?" he asked, shrugging. He picked up the sponge and resumed wiping down the table. His strokes were broad and sure.

Claire opened her mouth and closed it again. *What's the harm?* Put that way, she had no reply.

Chapter 8: The Violinist and the Hatbox

As she drove along the Pacific Coast Highway to meet her new client—a violinist who'd won contests in Edinburgh, Ravenna, and Berlin—boundaries blurred. In the early morning fog, even the articulated cliffs outside the passenger side of the truck were indistinct, their rich red-browns blanched, their vertical ridges flattened, their furrows filled with fog. Beneath the wheels, the pavement had no edge. It merged with the gray sand, which melted invisibly into the gray, horizonless ocean. Usually, Claire liked driving in fog. Its gauzy layers moistened plants and kept the past at bay. Sitting tall in the truck's sealed cab, she could look out at the blurry world and feel herself defined. Today, though, the fog had crept inside the cab. She sensed it all around her, an invisible invader, attaching itself to her bare skin, fusing her fingers, mitten-like, as they held the steering wheel, dissolving the features on her face, sucking her out willy-nilly through the closed windows to the concealed universe outside.

She checked the windows—they were rolled up tight—and turned on the heat. The fan's white noise mingled with the masking fog, damping the swish of passing cars and the steady thud of the more distant waves. She gripped the wheel with clenched hands and stared straight ahead.

That night Jake and Mandy were coming for dinner. A first. Usually, Claire went to their place or they went out. She hadn't spent the night, though, not since Mandy arrived. In spite of Jake's entreaties, she'd leave his house around midnight, climb into her truck, and join the stream of red taillights heading north on the 405. Claire hoped this particular evening would go well. There wasn't much in her cottage to interest an eight-year-old. Except for the hatbox with Sarah's clothes, Claire had brought nothing from her old life when she moved to L.A. Jake's house was crammed with furnishings and his projects—tools, books, and lesson plans—and now that Mandy was back—crayoned pictures, Barbie dolls, and half-completed board games. If Claire moved in with them as Jake was begging her to do, would there be a place for *her*?

Inside the truck's cab it was now sweltering. She turned off the heater, but left the windows rolled up. She could hear sounds beyond the glass. The fog had gotten denser. Ocean, sand, cliffs, road, and cars, even those right beside her whooshing down the long ramp that connected Wilshire Boulevard with the Coast Highway, were uniformly gray. As she inched forward, she stared into the miasma, hoping to glimpse the bulky shape of the car or truck or van she was following before she drove into it. But in fact, she was driving blind.

A small orange disk materialized in front of the windshield. Like a ghostly sun, it hung in the mists for a moment before its color shifted to red. Claire braked hard, almost colliding with the SUV that emerged ahead of her. While the cars on her right roared down the ramp, she waited for the light to run its course—heart pounding, eyes desiccated from the heat and staring.

The light turned green and the SUV crept forward. Claire followed closely, keeping its taillights in sight. When at last she saw Santa Monica Canyon gaping through the cliffs, she peeled off the highway and headed inland. As she followed the road's steep ascent to Sunset Boulevard, the fog thinned. Her grip loosened on the steering wheel. She rolled the windows down. Cool salt air bathed her eyes and cleansed her lungs. She savored the ocean's strong, unmistakable smell and felt reclaimed.

She pressed the accelerator. Large recent houses—imitations of larger and much older homes in Europe, Massachusetts, and the antebellum South—swept by. Despite their different facades, they seemed indistinguishable. Their gardens too seemed oddly interchangeable. Both houses and gardens were immaculately groomed. Neither belonged.

When she reached Sunset Boulevard, the fog vanished. Fuchsias and tuberous begonias gave way to gardenias and oleanders—as if the miles-long, asphalt umbilical cord that linked the center of Los Angeles with the ocean had been placed there on purpose to mark the boundaries of the marine and thermal zones.

Pleased that her client had picked the warmer side of Sunset, Claire crossed the boulevard and plunged into a world of color and light. She found the house—a small, thirties-style Mediterranean bungalow not far from a cluster of shops and cafes—and parked her truck. A Bermuda grass lawn splotched with brown patches and dandelions sloped up from the street. A ragged colonnade of cypress trees all but obscured the front of the house. As she made her way up the driveway, noting the festoons of spider webs that draped the trees, she heard a violin.

The music stopped abruptly when she reached the front porch and, before she could ring the bell, a tall, large-boned woman, her own age or a little older, opened the door. She was wearing a crimson tunic over a black turtleneck and loose jeans. A bow dangled from her right thumb and index finger. In the crook of her other arm, she cradled a violin.

"Hello," she said, holding out the hand with the bow. She had a wide, welcoming smile. "I'm Althea. You must be Claire." Her hair, dark and springy, fit her head like a jaunty cap. Her black eyes shone. Their color didn't change in the light. "Come in, come in!"

Claire entered a modest-sized living room with a beam ceiling and Indian rugs. The walls were bright with Mexican folk art. At the far end of the room was a grand piano, its lid covered with skewed stacks of music and an open violin case with a red plush lining. She thought about the featureless rooms in her own cottage and felt a twinge of envy. She imagined her living room the way it might have looked had she added a lamp here, an artifact there, a rug with a rhythmic design: bright and warm and welcoming. Would Sarah still have come to her, she wondered, if the house weren't so bare?-

She asked about the violin.

"It's a Guarneri," Althea said, rolling the *r*s. Next to the instrument, her hands appeared huge, like a man's carrying a child. It had been made in Cremona in the 1730s, she told Claire. A wealthy patron had presented it to her when she was in her teens.

"Wow," said Claire, running her eyes over the instrument. "Aren't you afraid of thieves?"

"They'd do well to be afraid of me," Althea replied with a short laugh. She paused, her eyes narrowing. "In Sicily, once, when I was on tour, a street kid snatched my violin while I was waiting for a bus. Scrawny little guy. Couldn't have been more than ten years old." She pressed her lips together and stared straight ahead. "I ran after him, grabbed him by the scruff of the neck—pure reflex—and twisted his arm a good one hundred and eighty degrees."

Claire winced. Who *was* this woman? she wondered. A minute earlier, she'd have sworn Althea wouldn't hurt a fly.

"He flailed and yelped but I held on until he finally let go of the case." Her face softened as she glanced at the instrument in the bend of her arm. "I wasn't through with him, though." She looked up, eyes flashing. "I wanted to make sure he remembered what he'd done." She weighted the words. "He fell over like a bowling pin when I knocked him down." A smile flickered on her face. "I didn't say a word to him. Just glared at him lying on the cobblestones. Kept my boot on his chest." She sounded proud.

"Was he okay?" Claire was almost afraid to ask.

"Hmm?" Althea was squinting down her bow now, one eye closed.

"The little boy," Claire half-whispered.

"Oh, *him*." She loosened the horsehairs and shrugged.

"Probably didn't break anything," she said, as she secured the bow under the clamps inside the case, but he must have had some pretty colorful bruises for a good long time—plus a really sore arm." She paused and gave another laugh. "Lucky for him he didn't hurt my violin." She held the instrument in front of her perpendicular to the floor, her thumb and index finger ringing its slender neck. As it swung to and fro, its yellowed varnish caught the light. "You have to protect the thing you love most," she said, her face and voice serene. She laid the violin in its velvet case, lowered the lid, and snapped the brass locks closed.

"Tea time!" she caroled, pivoting toward the kitchen.

Claire blinked. She was still wondering how a woman so tender toward a wooden box could have been so violent with a child.

"I always have a cuppa, 'round about now," Althea continued. "Picked up the habit when I studied in London. Tea's one of life's true pleasures, don't you think?" She hugged herself, smiling, eyes shut tight, as she said this.

Claire followed her long, loping strides into the kitchen where Althea filled a bulbous kettle that matched her red tunic and set it on the stove. While she fished in the cupboards, Claire cleared away the cobwebs of the story she'd just heard and seated herself at the table next to a window that looked out on a small enclosed area filled with debris. Entangled in the thigh-high weeds were remnants of a canvas awning, a roll of rusted wire, broken bricks, and a child's brown Wonder Horse with a plate-sized hole in its plastic flank. A regular junkyard, Claire decided. But she noted the northern exposure and imagined the shade-loving Ramona monkey flower and yerba buena that would flourish there.

"Welcome to my Museum of Found Objects," Althea said, following Claire's gaze. Her laugh started low and rippled up the scale. She set down two mugs and an assortment of tea bags and sat across from Claire, elbows on the table, fingers locked under her chin. Claire kept staring out the window. She felt an urge to go home to her own museum, the one in the hatbox, her museum of Sarah. The moment passed, and she shifted her attention back to Althea.

They talked about the new garden.

"I've wanted one for years—a house with a garden. Mostly, I wanted the garden." Althea laughed again, blushing slightly, as if confiding a delicious secret. She looked at her hands, palms up now, cupped in front of her. "I grew up in a row house in East Baltimore," she said, flexing her fingers. They were broad and muscular, seemingly better suited to wringing laundry than playing the violin. On her left hand, the fingertips had calluses as thick as mushroom caps. "My family never even owned a potted plant," she said.

A tone emerged from the kettle—a pure reedy note tunneling through the cloud of steam. Althea sprang to her feet and curved her hand behind her ear. After a moment, a second higher note sounded, forming a chord with the first. Her mouth widened into a smile. "That's a real Hohner harmonica," she said. Her face was luminous. "A cellist pal gave it to me." She lifted the kettle and poured the singing water into the mugs.

As Claire watched her stir in milk and sugar, she was surprised to notice that Althea was not beautiful in any traditional way. Her features were slightly irregular, her mouth and nose perhaps too prominent. Yet there was something commanding in her demeanor. Claire imagined her standing behind the footlights, wearing a long, beaded dress—black or silver or red. As Althea's fingers hammered the violin's neck and she drew the bow across the strings, her large hands would be visible as a dancer's. To her audience, unseen beyond the footlights, she'd look like a queen.

"I love giving concerts," she said, as if following Claire's thoughts. "The spotlights make me focus on the music." She took a swallow of tea and wiped her mouth with the back of her hand. "I mean, *really* focus." She paused, staring into the middle distance. "Some nights the music I play seems to be coming straight from the composer's brain." She exhaled the words then shook her head briskly. "When I'm practicing at home, though," she continued, her black eyes locked with Claire's, "I don't want spotlights." She shook her head from side to side for emphasis. "I want to look up in the middle of a scale or a passage and see my garden outside the window. I want it to surprise me, to be a little different every day. I want it to change."

"As if *it* were on the stage?"

Althea nodded, her smile radiant. She set down her cup and hugged herself again. "I want it to have hummingbirds and fat, striped bees."

As Claire drove back to her cottage, she felt aglow. "Native plants," Althea had told her. "Or at least nothing that couldn't grow here on its own." No roses, no ponds, which some of her clients insisted upon. "I don't want an English garden or a New Orleans courtyard," she'd said.

Already, Claire could picture the front of the house with a wide wooden porch and a pergola strung with native wisteria replacing those preposterous cypress trees. She'd flatten the top of the slope and use drought-tolerant sageleaf rockrose and maybe some pink joey that would back away from the house in tiers and screen it from the street. Near the sidewalk she'd plant trees, a couple of eucalyptus, perhaps—they'd be as high as the pergola within a few years—and an acacia that would attract the hummingbirds Althea had imagined. On grey spring mornings, its yellow blossoms would shine like tiny suns.

She reached the Coast Highway, turned south, and accelerated. The fog had dissipated completely. To the west, sailboats crept across the horizon and whitecaps trembled on glittering blue waves. She rolled down the window and started to sing:

This old man, he played one,
He played knick-knack on my thumb,
With a knick-knack paddywhack
Give a dog a bone,
This old man came rolling home.

It was a song she sang to Sarah when she was teething. Claire would set the baby on her knee and bounce her up and down. The child would laugh until she got the hiccups. Claire remembered feeling her tiny rib cage jerk, the gargling sound of her laugh, and the bright spittle on her chin.

In Sarah's nursery, sunlight shone through the branches of the pear tree outside her window. In the spring just before she was born, its white blossoms had shimmered; its leaves glowed red and yellow in the autumn when she died. The rocker where Claire nursed Sarah had belonged to her grandmother, as had the rag rugs on the rough pine floor. On the walls, Claire had hung prints of Babar: riding up the Paris elevator, being fitted for his new green suit, sailing off with Celeste in a balloon.

She thought of Althea's house, already bright with me-

mentos even though she'd just moved in. On the kitchen wall, there was a poster of a young woman alone in a flooded living room. She was sitting in a wing-back chair holding a china cup and saucer, sipping tea. The water was lapping over her ankles. Household objects bobbed all about her, but the woman was smiling an impish smile. She looked like Althea. She was having fun.

Claire gripped the wheel, her throat hard with envy.

As she approached her own front door, her cottage seemed smaller and drabber than she remembered. The paint on the trim was peeling and the once white shingles had become a dingy gray. She turned the key reluctantly, wishing she had somewhere—anywhere else—to go. Inside, her footsteps echoed unpleasantly off the bare walls. The living room seemed hollow, eviscerated. Even her drawing-board on the workbench seemed alien—a mere geometric object rather than the wellspring of her new life.

She stood motionless in the center of the room and listened. Except for the regular whoosh of her breath, there were no sounds anywhere. She closed her eyes and absorbed the silence. Finally, she heard the familiar drumbeat. *Da-da-duh. Da-da-duh. Da-da-duh*—muffled at first, but getting louder, as if a procession was passing by. *Da-da-duh. Da-da-duh.* With slow, solemn steps, she joined the beat. She marched forward—through the living room, into the bedroom, toward the closet, where she stopped and reached for the box on the shelf above the hanging clothes, her knees flexing under its weight. She set the box on the bed and studied it while she waited for the drumming to fade. Tall and cylindrical, it looked like a drum itself; in fact, it had been her grandmother's hatbox. Black ribbons laddered up its parchment sides, meeting in a bow at the center of the lid. *Da-da-duh. Da-da-duh.* The thudding was nearly inaudible now. *Da-da...* she sat down beside the box and pulled the ends of the ribbon. The bow dissolved and the ribbon fell away. She lifted the lid.

She began with the infant-ghost nightgown, with its trailing skirt and the drawstring sewn into the hem. She held it up in front of her, shaking out the wrinkles, and laid it flat, arms outstretched, on the bed. Then the booties, the cap, the crocheted sweater; the square book with real buttons, zippers, buckles, and shoelaces sewn to its cloth pages. The bed was nearly covered with items now, but there were more. She reached deep into the box and drew out the blue corduroy overalls and yellow tee shirt Sarah wore the day she died. Claire tucked the shirt inside the overalls and laid the outfit lengthwise on her thighs. The nap on the knees was worn and shiny. With the flat of her hand, she smoothed the fabric. Once more, she plunged her arm into the box, her nails scrabbling down the sides, and fished out a flannel bear no bigger than her palm. Cotton oozed from its tiny seams; its ears were chewed to a colorless pulp. She held the bear under her nose and sought out the faint metallic smell of saliva. As she breathed in, she could sense Sarah's warm weight in her lap. The baby's knuckle-less hands shot up toward the bear. As she tried to wrest it from her mother, her satin-soled feet flailed beneath Claire's chin.

The hatbox was not yet empty. There remained the white blanket with strawberries and Sarah's birth date embroidered on the binding in red thread. Soft and fluffy, it filled half the box when there were no clothes on top pressing it down. Claire left it there. She always did. She'd almost gotten rid of the blanket that chilly day she'd left Vermont, the day the sky was white and the trees were black. She could have weighted it with stones and drowned it in the middle of the half-frozen lake; or burned it to ashes on the shore. In the end, though, she'd folded it precisely, like a flag, and laid it in the box, where it remained untouched.

Under the blanket, on the very bottom, was a manila envelope containing photographs—a half dozen or so, none in color. Claire's brother Roger had taken them. Roger was a pediatrician, Sarah's pediatrician. When Sarah died, he closed his office and shut himself inside it. For two weeks, he'd barely eaten or slept. "There must have been something I missed," he kept saying as he pored over Sarah's charts. "I'm a pediatrician, for Christ's sake!"

There was something, of course. But Claire didn't tell him what it was. For six months, three days, and fourteen hours, Sarah had thrived. Then she was gone. Claire didn't blame her brother. Not in her head. How could she, knowing what she knew? In her heart, though, it was another matter. She let the envelope lie. She rarely looked at the pictures anyway. She didn't need to look at them. She'd always have Sarah—the real Sarah, the Sarah who danced through time.

Lynne McKelvey

Chapter 9: Moving In

Claire shifted the drawing board balanced on her hip and surveyed the table in the middle of Jake's dining room. Attendance rosters, textbooks, student handouts, hole-punchers, and felt-tipped markers all but obscured the table's surface. Today was moving day. Jake had already weeded out the bedroom closet and assigned her one of the nightstands. She still needed a place to work, though.

"Why don't we share this table?" she proposed. "We could each take an end."

Jake shook his head. "Won't hear of it," he said. "You can have it all. I'll use the table in the living room. You need the space."

Claire began to protest, but he'd already scooped up an armload of books and lesson plans and was heading through the doorway. She set her drawing board down in the space he'd cleared. Jake was right. He preferred reading and grading papers in the big brown recliner by the front door anyway. The sturdy table across from the recliner, used only for playing games with Mandy, would be perfect for his textbooks and papers. As Claire mentally arranged her own plant encyclopedias, sketchpads, and pencils next to the drawing board, she gave a sigh of pleasure and relief. She'd not only have a large table for her own work, she'd have a whole room.

She was searching for a socket where she could plug in her work lamp when she heard a high, sharp cry. She rushed to the living room and saw Mandy, her face contorted almost beyond recognition, clawing at her father's shirt. Like an animal, digging—a badger, Claire thought, remembering the thick lashes ringing the girl's eyes.

"No, Daddy, *nooooo,*" the child wailed. "This is our *special* table. We need it for our games."

Jake shot Claire a nervous smile. His eyes darted back to his daughter. "It's okay, Mandy," he said, stroking her shiny hair. "We can use another table for games. The kitchen table, let's use *that*. It's much bigger, and there'll be more light." He sounded hearty, but also pleading.

Mandy only howled louder. "No, no, *no,*" she bawled, her face puckered and red. "*Claire* can use another table. This one's *our* table. Our *special* table. Don't take away *our* table. Please, Daddy, *please, please, please.*" The child's shoulders shook. Mucus bubbled from her nose. An image of herself, alone in her cottage, pencil in hand, bent over her sketch-book, flashed through Claire's mind. She could almost feel the heat from the swing-arm lamp clamped to the table pooling on the left side of her neck, hear the tungsten wires humming as she tried to decide exactly where the swath of salvias in front of Althea's house would leave off and the meadow garden would begin. She glanced at Mandy beseeching her father, then at Jake beseeching *her*. Was this the way it would be from now on? The thought was dismaying. It wasn't too late, though, even now. Her lease on the cottage wouldn't expire until the end of the month. She could still move back. Mandy's wails grew shriller, Jake's demeanor more imploring. Father and daughter, Claire felt pressed between them. Again, she tried to imagine herself back in her own living room seated on the four-legged stool in front of her desk. Instead, she saw a pair of eyes staring out from a glittering frame. As she remembered Rita regarding herself in the small mirror propped behind the rows of artifacts on Mandy's dresser, Claire looked at the little girl's tear-stained face. Poor thing. She'd never really had a mother. Jake was all she had. To Mandy, Claire was an interloper. The child must be scared to death she'd lose her daddy. For now, she needed extra reassurance. She'd come around in time. "It's okay," Claire said gently. "You guys keep the game table. I'll have plenty of room." Jake dropped his arms and exhaled audibly. Mandy's sobs ebbed. She wiped her sleeve across her nose and threw her arms around her father's legs, grasping them in a steel embrace. Jake patted his daughter on the back and mouthed "Thank you" to Claire over Mandy's head.

Claire stared back at him, expressionless. What would have happened if she *had* held him to his offer? Mandy would hate her—at least temporarily—but what about Jake? He was stroking his daughter's dark curls now, smiling serenely. The child's left cheek was pressed against his body, just above his belt buckle, her face turned toward Claire. All traces of her tears had vanished. Her one visible eye—dark and ringed—was fixed on Claire. It didn't blink.

After dinner, Claire stretched out on the sofa in Jake's living room and let the Metro section of the *L.A. Times* slide off her lap to the floor. The early evening light was too dim to read by anyway. Through the closed kitchen door, she heard shrill laughter. Jake and Mandy were baking brownies to celebrate Claire's moving in. It was supposed to be a surprise.

"Mandy, leave the oven shut." Jake's baritone startled Claire. "Mandy, no! Don't open it! Not yet. It's too soon!"

Scuffling sounds.

"Daddy! Dad*dee*! Put me down!" Half laugh, half cry.

He teased her a lot, but Mandy didn't seem to mind.

"I'll put *you* in there, if you don't watch out. Baked Mandy. Yum, yum, yum." The oven door slammed, and their voices dropped to whispers.

Silence settled over Claire. I'm here now, she told herself. Did that mean she was "home?" The word teetered in her mind. Despite the years she'd lived in the cottage, she'd never thought of it as home.

When she'd moved from Vermont in the middle of winter, she'd left tulips buried in the garden there. She couldn't remember what colors they would bloom—red or yellow, purple or white. But she remembered the bulbs distinctly. She pictured them as they'd been, six inches deep in the frozen soil, lodged among the stones: hard, scaly, and brown.

She felt exhausted suddenly and closed her eyes. Somewhere a clock was ticking. Tick-*tock*, tick-*tock*, tick-*tock*—in little hiccupy clicks. Odd, she hadn't heard it before. Tick-*tock*, tick-*tock*, tick-*tock*. And then:

"Now, Daddy? Are they ready now"?

"Almost, Sweetie. Here, you set out the plates."

"I want to sit by you, Daddy. Can I sit by you? Please, please, please?" Successive, thuds of Mandy jumping up and down.

Jake cleared his throat and mumbled something, but Claire couldn't make out his reply.

In the plaster ceiling above her head was a barely visible crack that ran the entire length of her body. She imagined a blade emerging through the crack, descending on her, splitting her precisely in two. She clutched her arms, hugging the halves of herself together. She drew up her knees, pulled them to her chest, and rolled over on her side. She pictured herself folded this way inside her mother and Sarah folded inside her. Claire's own mother had died six months after Sarah; Claire had scarcely noticed at the time. Now, she pictured the three of them nested within one another like hollow Russian dolls.

In Jake's bed that night, their bed now, Claire was still contracting with aftershocks of pleasure, when she heard— thought she heard—a soft thump and brushing sound in the hall. She stared up at the ceiling illuminated by the bedside lamp. They'd left Mandy's door open. Usually, she wanted it shut tight. The dark felt warm and furry, she claimed, like her teddy bear. But tonight, the night Claire moved in, the child insisted her door be left ajar. "In case Claire needs me," she said.

Had Mandy heard her untrammeled cries? Had she wondered—perhaps hoped—something terrible was happening to Claire? She imagined the little girl rolling out of bed and tiptoeing down the unlit corridor. She pictured her standing right outside the door now, her toes touching the ruler of light that lay along the sill. If she *were* there, she might be wondering whether to turn the knob.

Claire imagined Mandy bending to the keyhole. The

metal plate beneath the doorknob would feel cold against her chin. She'd position herself as if settling into the oculist's chair. The door was only a few feet from the side of the bed, the keyhole the same height as the mattress. She could be looking through it, now, Claire thought. If she were there. Watching.

With her eyes still on the ceiling, Claire imagined what the little girl would be seeing. The keyhole made a perfect circular frame around Claire's spread legs and naked torso. Mandy wouldn't see her arms, which were flung back toward the top of the bed. The sight of Jake's head between her thighs would make the child gasp. Since the frame would block out the rest of his body, she'd think she was seeing an enormous *mons veneris*—though she wouldn't know those words. Her heart would leap into her eye sockets. Perhaps she'd shift her gaze or blink. As her heart hammered inside her skull, she'd realize that what she was seeing was not one mound but two, that the larger mound must be the back of her father's head. Though the hairs on the mounds blended, now she'd note that they were different, that Claire's, in fact, were the more luxuriant. This would surprise Mandy. She'd have supposed that Claire's hairs...there...would be colorless and wispy like her eyelashes. Instead, she'd see they were thick and glossy—a rich chestnut shade, like the hair on Mandy's own head. Claire imagined herself throwing the door open and hissing, "Go back to bed," so she didn't wake Jake. Heart pounding, the child would scurry back to her room, closing the door behind her.

Claire didn't pull up the sheet.

She lay still as marble now, aware only of the gentle friction of Jake's beard inside her thighs whenever either of them breathed. Then slowly, deliberately, she turned her head sideways toward the keyhole. Unblinking, she stared at Mandy's imaginary eye and envisioned a wire strung between their pupils, hers and Mandy's.

She felt the lamp on the night-stand shining down on her. Without shifting her gaze, she opened her legs wider, letting in the light. She felt it sculpting the planes of her body, hollowing out the curve above her hips, modeling the low mounds of her breasts, articulating her nipples, which were still raised. She saw herself as Mandy would have seen her, within the round frame.

Like an artist adjusting a model, she arched her back and rotated her torso until it was at a forty-five degree angle to the keyhole. As she moved, she felt the light undulate over her body. The skin on her abdomen was stretched taut. Her breasts, which had spread like pools while she'd been lying on her back, now hung side by side. They were luminous and round. Almost imperceptibly, she began to contract and release her thighs. She felt Jake stir between them. Still watching the keyhole, she continued her invisible motions, adding a slight pelvic thrust. Hidden under his hair, Jake nuzzled her thighs. His lower body began to rock. Claire felt the mattress dip as he shifted his weight to his arms, raised himself, and sat back on his heels.

Now, only Claire would be visible in the keyhole's round frame. As he knelt above her at the bottom of the bed, out of sight, she knew his eyes were on her, licking her with their tongues. She felt her body open, felt it begin to flow. She groped for the nightstand, aware as she did so of the way the light quivered over her breasts when she moved. She could hear Jake's breath slide rhythmically in and out of his lungs.

Her fingers found the lamp. Languorously, they slid down the metal stem, then circled twice around the base. Jake's breathing quickened. Claire felt him coil. With a dancer's deliberate grace, she rotated her head and torso toward him in a single, slow movement. Just before he sprang, she pressed the switch.

Lynne McKelvey

Chapter 10: The Garden and the Game

As she strained to lift the tub of red-tipped leucadendron for Althea's garden, Claire's leather work gloves slipped on the tub's plastic sides. Though only a five-gallon container, it felt like ten. Her fingers ached from holding on.

"I take that, Señora," said a velvet voice behind her. Grateful, Claire stepped back onto the path while Tomás, her helper, lifted it barehanded. As he clasped the tub and bore it away, she noted his missing finger, the middle one on his left hand, and grimaced as she tried to unlock her own fingers. She watched him glide toward the last unfilled hole, skating over the curds of loam. He was an inch shorter than Claire. From the back, he looked like a young boy; in fact, he had grown sons with children of their own. Beneath his umber neck his shoulders sloped like drooping wings. How could anyone so slight be so strong? They'd been working together ever since her first garden had won the city's Water Conservation Prize and new clients started to call. He taught her

Spanish. She taught him about plants. But the exchange wasn't equal. Most of what she'd learned about gardens Tomás seemed to have been born knowing.

She watched him rap the side of the tub smartly and slide the root ball out, loosening its tangled shoots near the base with his damaged hand. The stump of the missing finger, white and perfectly smooth, was shaped like a tombstone. Claire wondered what he felt when the bare roots rubbed against it. He squatted beside the planting hole. Gauging its dimensions, he centered the bush exactly, lowering it with both his hands. There was something priestly about the gesture. Instead of using a trowel as most gardeners would, he scooped in the backfill with his hands, cupping them together to make a bowl. Through the gap above the missing finger, soil fell in a fine, steady rain.

When the planting hole was packed nearly to the rim, she passed him the hose. While water percolated down inside the hole, he shaped a mound around the perimeter, forming a basin. After probing the wet soil for air pockets, he added more backfill, distributing it evenly around the base of the new plant, careful not to let even a single particle of dirt clog the tiny pores on the silver leaves.

"Is okay, Señora Claire," he said, when the basin was filled with water. "Is finished."

"*Padrisimo*!" Claire said, turning off the spigot and

smiling at the exuberance of the word. As she reeled in the hose, she watched Tomás. He knelt over the new plant and pressed the hand with the missing finger into the soft surrounding soil. It was a ritual act—blessing, signature, or both. He did it—with his left hand always—whenever they installed a plant. He removed his hand. The impression was clear: a palm, three fingers, and a thumb stamped into soil still glossy enough to reflect the sky. He rocked back on his heels, then pulled himself upright in a swift, single movement. For an instant, he stood motionless beside the shrub, rooted in the moment. Then he grinned and brushed his hands together. "*Hecho,*" he and Claire said in unison, she standing on the hard path, he on the fresh soil, high-fiving one another against an invisible wall of air.

They sat on the redwood steps that led to a new front deck, sipping Cokes from Claire's cooler. It was already late afternoon. The installation had taken longer than Claire expected. She was drenched in sweat; her head, back, even her legs felt sticky and wet. The mercury had been rising ever since early morning, topping off in the nineties. She must remind Althea to give the plants an extra watering.

She surveyed the day's work. Each plant was exactly where she wanted it to be, where she'd drawn it on her plans. But a new garden was not yet a garden. There was something almost ridiculous about the way it looked now. The eucalyptus saplings were spindly and only half Tomás' height. The manzanitas, whose silvery leaves and soft pink flowers would one day screen the houses and the hard gray surface of the street, were barely visible above the flat-topped berm. Individually, the plants looked a bit forlorn. There were gaping holes between them. They didn't yet connect. But she'd done her part, and they'd do theirs.

A year from now—two years, three…She tried to picture the garden. But of course she couldn't. You never knew how new plants would grow. One spring the pride of Madeira would dazzle passers-by with purple blossoms thrusting skyward; the next year it would barely bloom. But then in February, the acacia, whose flowers seemed almost drab the rest of the year, would illuminate the garden with a thousand tiny suns. What was it Althea had said? She never knew how her music would sound until she played it. That was like the uncertainty of a new garden. And *that* was like Claire's new life with Jake and Mandy.

After dinner that night, Jake proposed a game of Hearts. Seated at the square table in the living room, Claire picked up her cards and spread them into a fan. Seven diamonds, four spades, and six clubs. She'd never played Hearts before. But Mandy had. She played when she was in Riverside with her mother and grandfather. It was their favorite game.

"We don't play Hearts here," Mandy told Claire while

they were setting up folding chairs around the square table in the living room. "Here…usually"—she glowered at Claire —"usually, it's just my daddy and me." In the lamplight, the rims of her irises shifted from violet to green.

"You need three players for Hearts," Jake explained. "With two, you always know who has the queen of spades— that's the card you want to unload, like the Old Maid. "With three"—he paused to stroke his daughter's cheek—"you can keep the other players guessing."

Claire studied her hand and led the six of diamonds. Jake followed with the nine, and Mandy took the trick with the jack. She led a low heart, Claire laid down a club, and Jake played the ace of hearts.

"Nyanny, nyanny, Daddy lost a poi-int. He got my hear-art." Mandy bounced up and down in her chair. Hearts counted against you—though much less than the queen of spades.

"Two points," Jake said, frowning at his cards. He led the seven of hearts, but Mandy underplayed him. Once again he was forced to take the trick.

As they continued, Claire stifled a yawn. By the time she'd left Pacific Palisades, the sun was setting and she'd been up since daybreak. Now it was her lead. They were down to three cards apiece. No sign yet of the queen of spades. She laid down her five of clubs, Jake followed with the seven, and Mandy took the trick with the nine. While Mandy sucked a strand of hair and studied her two remaining cards, Claire tried to recall how far east the summer coastal zone extended. Was Althea's garden far enough inland for red bauhinia?

Mandy looked up. Her eyes darted from Jake to Claire, then squeezed shut, their thick lashes pulsing. She opened her eyes to a squint, pulled out one of her remaining cards, and dropped it on the table. The ten of hearts. Claire played the eight of spades. Jake tapped his cards. "Eeny, meeny, miny, moe," he recited. A little smile flickered on his lips. "Eeeny meeny..." He set down the queen of spades, holding the edges between his thumb and middle finger.

Mandy jerked back as if she's been slapped. "Daddy," she shrieked, "you did that on purpose. You gave me the mean queen. You gave me her on purpose." She swept all the cards off the table, pushed over her chair, and ran weeping out of the room.

Claire looked at Jake across the bare table. To her amazement, he was laughing. His shoulders shook; his beard jiggled up and down. Mandy's door slammed. They could hear her sobbing inside her room. Claire half rose, wanting to go to her, wanting to draw the little girl up onto her lap and comfort her. But Mandy wanted Jake. She always did.

"Well?" Claire said, sitting down and looking pointedly

at him.

"I know." Jake reached under his glasses to wipe the corners of his eyes. He was no longer laughing. "I'll go to her." He rose quickly but moved toward Claire. "She'll be all right," he said, his voice reverberating through his beard. "She's gotta learn she can't always win. Even Pompey the Great got his comeuppance once from King Sertorius." He smiled then noted Claire's blank expression. "Sorry," he said, lowering his eyes. "Just riding my hobby horse. It's a silly comparison." He put his arm around Claire's shoulders and leaned down to kiss her, simultaneously righting the over-turned chair with his free hand. He was like that, she thought—always doing two things at once. "You're a saint to put up with us," he murmured in her ear and giving her a squeeze before he strode away. She heard him in the hall, opening, then softly closing, Mandy's door.

Claire leaned against the back of her chair. How could she be a saint when she felt exasperated with Mandy so much of the time? And, for that matter, with Jake? His teasing bordered on cruelty, it seemed to Claire. At the same time, the child was manipulative and Jake hardly ever even tried to rein her in. Would he be different with his daughter if her mother were around? Jake took over their baby's care right from the start. Rita didn't want to touch her, he had said. How had Rita felt in those early weeks? Claire wondered. Perhaps his calm competence made Rita feel left out, made it harder for her to love her child. For the first time, Claire felt a twinge of sympathy for the brittle-looking woman in the glittering frame.

She looked at the spilled cards on the carpet. Except for the queen of spades, they'd all landed face down, in a serpentine line. The intricate red and white Bicycle pattern looked like scales. She picked up the queen of spades and held it in front of her, her thumbs covering the lower half of the card. The queen's pale face seemed almost lost in the elaborate orange, red, and blue swirls of her headdress and gown. She didn't look mean. Her head was turned to the right, and she gazed outward with a slightly troubled expression, as if she'd just said goodbye to someone who might not return. Her left hand was raised, palm forward, as if she'd been waving and had forgotten to lower her arm. In her other hand, she held a single red rose. When Claire laid the card on the table, the queen's double, which had been hidden behind Claire's thumbs, was suddenly revealed, upside down. The two queens stared in opposite directions. Their parallel gazes could never meet. Under their ornate, shared gown, they were joined.

A Real Daughter

Lynne McKelvey

WINTER 1978-1979

Lynne McKelvey

Chapter 11: Christmas Tree

Late afternoon. Under a gray, luminous sky, the two figures climbed the snowy hillside speckled with trees—daughter ahead, mother behind—their boots crunching the thin crust of ice.

"Here's one, Mommy," the child said, her words wreathing in the cold air. She wrapped her arms around a young Fraser fir, her red mittens momentarily decorating its blue-green branches. "Mommy, look. It's just as tall as me."

Claire set the handsaw she was carrying on the snow and circled the tree. It was a symmetrical, shapely little tree, its foliage dense and fragrant.

"Ummm," she said, taking a branch tip, and holding it to her nose. "Smells like Christmas."

Sarah giggled, took a little skip, slipped, caught herself, and laughed some more.

"Can we get it Mommy? Can this one be ours?" she asked, tugging on her mother's parka.

Claire pursed her lips, arms akimbo, pretending to look stern. Sarah planted herself in front of her mother, mirroring Claire. Together, they held their breaths, their cheeks ballooning with choked-back laughter as each tried to stare the other down.

"Oh, I suppose so," Claire said. Her puckered mouth broadened into a smile. She tweaked Sarah's cold nose and picked up the saw. "Want to make the first cut?" she asked, offering the saw to her daughter.

Sarah stared at the serrated metal edges and backed away. She clasped her hands behind her and looked at the ground.

Claire set the saw upright in the snow. "What's the matter, Punkin? You getting cold?" She knelt in front of her daughter and tucked some stray hairs that had fallen onto the child's face back under the hood of her parka, tightening the drawstrings.

Sarah shook her head. Her eyes darted from the saw to the fir tree and back again. She looked at her mother, eyes clouded, forehead creased. "Won't it hurt the tree, Mommy?" she whispered, her head beside her mother's ear. "Won't the tree die?"

Claire put her arms around the little girl and held her close. "Plants can't feel pain," she said, rubbing circles on Sarah's back. "They're not like people."

For a moment, the child seemed persuaded. Then her body stiffened. She looked at Claire, blue eyes flashing. "But plants do die, Mommy," she said, her voice fierce. "I know they die."

Claire stared at her daughter. She felt helpless. She should have gotten a living tree this year—one with a root ball, one that could be transplanted. It was too late for that now. She could never dig a hole in the frozen ground.

"This tree won't die, Punkin," Claire said, using her most soothing tone. "Not for a long time. Not 'til way past Christmas." She rose and kissed the top of the child's head. "After Christmas, when its needles and branches are brittle and brown, we'll turn the tree into mulch and spread it around in the garden. When spring comes, we'll look at the flowers and know that our little Christmas tree helped make them grow beautiful and strong."

Sarah's forehead smoothed. Her eyes seemed calm now, though they were less bright. She pulled the saw out of the snow. "Here Mommy," she said in a small voice, holding the saw at arm's length and handing it to Claire. "You cut it down."

It was getting dark by the time they reached the car, parked on a high ridge overlooking a town and farmlands. Claire brushed away the snow the tree had gathered as they dragged it down the hillside. With a stout cord, she bound the tree to the roof of the car, cutting the cord with the handsaw and tying the ends in a square knot.

"We'll put it in water as soon as we get home," she told her daughter. Sarah nodded, but didn't reply. She hadn't said a word while they were making their way down the hill. Claire hoped she wasn't still fretting about the tree.

Night descended, yet the sky, as if gathering light from the white earth, seemed even more luminous than before. Snow began to fall, gently at first, then faster, harder. Not speaking, mother and daughter stood side by side at the edge of the ridge, arms clasping one another's waists. Through the swirling flakes, they watched the lights come on below, filling the dark valley like stars. Somewhere—from no particular direction—unaccompanied voices began to sing:

Oh little town of Bethlehem, how still we see thee lie;

Above thy deep and dreamless sleep, the silent stars go by.

Chapter 12: Here Comes the Bride

Getting married was Mandy's idea. When she asked her father if he was going to marry Claire, he'd laughed and hugged them both, one with each arm. "We'll have to ask Claire," he said, beaming down at his daughter. He must have felt Claire stiffen. "*I'll* have to ask her," he added quickly. "Later," he said, clearing his throat and looking away.

At breakfast the next morning, Mandy gave a shriek when she heard the news. She sprang from her chair. "Claire's getting married. Claire's gonna be a bri-ide," she sing-songed, skipping around the room.

But when she learned that the wedding would take place in the courthouse and that Claire planned to wear an ordinary dress, her face fell. "No long dress? No veil? No train? "You won't be a *real* bride," she said, staring at the floor. Her eyes slid sideways. "My mom was a *real* bride when *she* married my daddy." She paused to watch this bit of news sink in. "There's a picture of her in Grandpa's room." A beat. "Right next to his bed," she added, drawing out the syllables.

Claire looked at her and tried to think of a reply. Mandy was standing stock still, her face a mask. Her small hands had fisted and her pressed lips were white. The child's stillness was unnerving, like a crouched animal's, Claire thought, and wondered what feelings could be roiling inside her. Anger? Disappointment? Fear?

Mandy raised her shoulders and took a deep, raspy breath. "What's the point of getting married, if you're not going to be a *real* bride?" flinging the words at Claire. But as the edges of her eyes shifted from yellow-green to a deep violet, Claire saw they were bright with tears. She glanced at Jake. He was thumbing the Builder's Emporium insert in the *L.A. Times,* oblivious of his daughter's outburst. The night before, Claire remembered, Mandy had decked out her Barbie doll in wedding regalia. To an eight-year-old, trappings mattered.

"Mandy," she said, kneeling and placing her hands lightly on the little girl's shoulders. The child's chin was buried in her chest. "Let's you and me go shopping. Just the two of us."

Mandy raised her head, wary of the bait.

"Look," Claire continued, "I've already been a bride. And your daddy's been a groom." Jake looked up from the insert and made a guttural sound, as if he were about to say something, but changed his mind. "But I'll bet *you've* never been a bridesmaid."

Mandy shook her head, eyes fixed on the floor.

"Well," Claire said, massaging the child's shoulders gently, "if you're going to be a bridesmaid, you'll need a very special dress."

Why was Jake staring at her now? Claire wondered. Didn't he want his daughter to have a new dress?

Mandy looked up. Her eyes flew open, then narrowed as they met Claire's. "A long white dress?" she asked, half pleading, half demanding.

Claire nodded and smiled. She tried to catch Jake's attention, wanting to share the moment. But he was looking at the newspaper again. Not reading it, though. His eyes didn't move a bit.

"One that goes all the way down to the floor? " Mandy asked.

Claire nodded again.

"And will it spin way out when I twirl? And can I have real flowers on my head like a crown?"

Claire watched Mandy's face light up, unmasked and radiating pure joy. She put her arms around the child and hugged her hard, burying her face in Mandy's luxuriant dark hair. Maybe they were going to be all right, she and Jake and

Mandy. Perhaps, in time, this little girl would come to feel like a real daughter.

When Claire looked up, Jake was staring at her again. At her or through her? Claire couldn't tell. When she tried to engage his eyes, they looked back at her blankly, as if he didn't recognize her.

It was only hours later, after she'd slipped into bed beside her soon-to-be-husband, that Claire realized her mistake. The day had spun by in a flurry of shopping with Mandy. As a special treat after they'd bought the dress, Claire suggested that, instead of going straight home, they have lunch in the department store's tea room. Almost too excited to eat, Mandy had gawked at the linen napkins, tinkling glasses of iced tea with lemon slices straddling the frosted rims, and finger sandwiches. "Would you make my lunchbox sandwiches like these?" she'd begged, "without the crusts?" Claire, smiling, had promised that on special occasions she would.

Once they were home, Mandy had insisted on putting on a fashion show for Jake. He'd admired the new dress, but said little to Claire. Right after dinner, he hurried off to Santa Monica to pick up a part he needed to fix the vacuum cleaner. That night it was Claire who put Mandy to bed, indulging her with a bubble bath and reading an extra chapter from *Dorothy and the Wizard of Oz*.

"Don't forget to tell my Daddy to come kiss me good-night," Mandy had said, when Claire was about to turn out the light.

"Sure thing," Claire replied.

As she bent down to kiss Mandy on the forehead, the little girl flung her arms around Claire's neck. "I'm glad you and my daddy are getting married," she said, pulling Claire down and hugging her tight.

Claire had paused for a moment and reviewed the day. No doubt it was the new dress that pleased Mandy so. But wasn't the little girl also signaling she was glad Claire was planning to stick around? "Me, too," she said, and kissed the child on the lips, something she'd not done before.

Jake was propped up on pillows reading a magazine with a picture of Hadrian's Wall, looking high and impregnable, on the front cover when Claire slid across the bed and curled up next to him. What with the shopping spree and Jake's errand after dinner, they'd been apart much of the day. It felt good to reconnect. When she touched his shoulder, though, he stiffened and moved, almost imperceptibly, toward his edge of the bed.

There was clearly something wrong. But what? Jake wasn't usually a moody man. On the contrary. At times, especially where Mandy was concerned, Claire almost wished he were more outspoken. Was it something *she'd* done? Something about the dress? He'd seemed as delighted with it as Mandy herself when the little girl had modeled it for him.

He closed the magazine, laid it on the nightstand with his glasses on top, and gazed at the ceiling. His hands were clasped on his chest, and his elbows protruded—angled, sharp.

"Why didn't you tell me you'd been married before?" he asked. His voice was so low that for a moment Claire wondered if she'd only imagined what he'd said.

"Married?" she croaked, ducking under his elbow and hiding her eyes in the sheets while her mind tore through the day.

"Married," he repeated. "This morning," his voice strong now, and impatient, for once. "You said you'd been a bride before."

And your daddy's been a groom. Her words arrowed back to her.

She'd let her guard down. It was only for an instant, but long enough. The cabinet. The separate drawers. How could she have been so careless? Now the rest of the secret must come out, mustn't it? She could try and deny her words, say he was mistaken. But Mandy was right there. *She'd* remember what Claire had said.

Claire felt his silence arm-wrestling her own; but his was strong, hers collapsing. Better to tell him the truth, some truth, about the marriage, at any rate, and quickly.

"Oh that," she said, clearing her throat. "It happened so long ago and was so brief, I guess it didn't seem important." The words formed themselves so easily. Almost as if she were speaking the truth. As if? They *were* the truth, she realized with a shock. All these years she'd hardly given a thought to her first marriage. It was Sarah, not Scott, who mattered, not only after her daughter's death but from the moment she'd been born. Her child had emerged like a wondrous statue from a dull block of marble. Once she appeared, the stone she'd sprung from seemed irrelevant.

Jake rolled over on his side and faced Claire, his teeth raking his lower lip. She braced herself for more questions. But none came. "I don't like secrets," was all he said.

She looked up and met his gaze. His eyes were the same brown they'd always been—steady, uncurious, and not unkind. Her secret—the part that really mattered, anyway—was still safe.

Lynne McKelvey

Chapter 13: The Honeymoon

For their wedding night, Jake had reserved a room at a funky little inn north of Santa Barbara. Mandy was supposed to go to her mother's for the weekend. But when they returned from their courthouse wedding, Mandy's grandfather called. Rita might be coming down with the flu, he told Jake. It was best that Mandy not visit her mother.

"Vintage Rita," Jake said, grimacing, as he hung up the phone. "She used to stay in bed for a week if she thought she was getting a cold."

Claire felt breathless with disappointment. She hadn't gone away with anyone since Sarah died. Mandy's eyes grew wide when Jake told her she wouldn't be going to Riverside. "I'm not going to my mom's?" she said, her cheeks vermilion. She ran her tongue around her lips. "Oh wow," she said, and raced out the door and headed toward her room.

A few minutes later, there was a rustling sound in the hall and the tap tapping of leather soles. Mandy swirled through the living room door. She had on the long white organdy dress, the garland of yellow roses, somewhat wilted now, and the patent leather shoes she'd worn earlier to the courthouse. She'd added makeup and earrings. Looped over one arm was her purple overnight case with Barbie's picture on the lid.

"OK, everybody," she said, flashing her smile. "I'm all packed. Let's go!"

As Claire watched her pirouette around the room, the overnight case orbiting about her turning body like a purple satellite, she wondered what was going through the child's head. Surely Mandy understood that she wasn't going to her mother's after all. Jake had been quite clear when he told her. Perhaps she didn't want to accept the change of plans. After all, the little girl must have been counting on seeing her mother and showing off her new dress.

Claire approached the child, dodging the whirling bag. "Mandy," she said, catching the child's free hand and holding it firmly. "Your mom may be coming down with the flu. She doesn't want you to get sick." As Mandy strained to escape her grasp, Claire glanced at Jake. He was the one who ought to be handling this. Instead, he was smiling his fond smile. Claire fought back her annoyance. "So you won't be able to go to Riverside," she said, striving to sound both sympathetic and definitive, "not this weekend."

"I *know* that," Mandy replied, breaking away from Claire's hold. "My *daddy* just told me." She articulated each syllable, as if she were speaking to a foreigner. "He told me all about the new plan, didn't you Daddy." She looped the purple bag high on her arm, grasped Jake's belt with both her hands, and, backbending as she held on, swung from side to side. As she looked up at him through her long lashes, her hair swayed just above the floor like a glossy pendulum.

"Yes, well..." Jake cleared his throat and continued to beam.

Claire stared at the child. The dress, the overnight case—they didn't make sense. Mandy was swinging harder now. The purple bag slammed into Claire's ribs.

"Here, let me have that suitcase," Claire said. "You won't need it today." As she reached out to take it, Mandy let go of Jake and snatched the case away.

"I will *too* need it, won't I, Daddy." The arm with the suitcase swished. "I have my p.j.'s in it. I'll need my p.j.'s for our honeymoon." She looked up at Claire with badger eyes.

"Mandy," Claire said, trying not to laugh. "Honey-moons aren't for bridesmaids. They're for the bride and groom." She tried to catch Jake's eye to share the joke, but he was gazing at his daughter. His expression had become more serious. Above his beard, his teeth raked his lower lip.

"We'll do something special *here*," Claire hurried on,

after a silence, "a trip to the zoo, maybe, or..." She racked her brain for an alternative. Why had she mentioned the zoo? She hated seeing caged animals. And why wasn't Jake helping her out? Mandy was *his* daughter.

"That's not *fair*," Mandy said, her eyes points of fire. "I want to stay in the hotel. I want to go with my daddy."

Jake's scraggly eyebrows lifted. A slow smile spread across his face. "We *could* all go, Claire. We've paid for the room. I doubt they'll refund our money. We could get a rollaway for Mandy. Would you mind?" The furrowed brow. The pleading look.

Claire pictured the tiny board and batten cottage on a windswept hill overlooking the sea. The winter rains were late this year. The grass would be a pale shimmering yellow with occasional eruptions of dark green where live oaks grew. Along the front of the cottage, there'd be a rickety verandah, sagging with the weight of bougainvillea, and a rusty porch swing where she and Jake could sit, the sides of their bodies touching. With the balls of their feet, they would push themselves back and forth in unison while the sun dipped slowly below the horizon. Inside their room, the light would be soft. The turned-back sheet would smell of salt and sunlight.

We could all go, Claire. Would you mind?

Foam was filling Jake's living room, crowding out the

molecules of air. Claire felt it envelop her body, covering her eyes, mouth, nose, and ears. Jake and Mandy's stares bored through it. A reply. They were waiting for her to reply. The foam dissipated. Father and daughter came into focus. Mandy was leaning back against Jake, jaw thrust forward, arms crossed over her chest like a tiny Roman senator. Jake was rubbing his daughter's arms just below the shoulders, his eyes hopeful.

Later, Claire wondered whether things would have turned out differently if she'd said no. At the time, though, she'd felt she had no choice. As their eyes drilled into her, she decided she was being childish making so much of a honeymoon. Maybe it would be good for the three of them to go away, she'd told herself, to get away from all the ghosts, to begin their life as a family.

At the lodge, Mandy insisted on wearing her long white bridesmaid's dress to dinner and, as usual, Jake let her. The only child among adults in Levis and flannel shirts, she looked ridiculous in the rustic dining room. But everyone said she looked cute. "My daddy and Claire and me are on our honeymoon," she told the other guests. People were skeptical, but they laughed and patted the top of Mandy's head.

In bed that night, to Claire's amazement, Jake approached her with a bridegroom's ardor. The anger that had been simmering inside her all day boiled over. But they couldn't quarrel now. Mandy's cot was only a few feet from the side of their bed. Claire could feel the child's breath blowing on her cheek—stoking her fury. Even in sleep, the child held her hostage.

For the first time Claire could remember, she turned away from Jake. He stroked her hair, kissed the back of her neck, then fell asleep while she stared into the night.

A Real Daughter

Lynne McKelvey

SPRING 1979

Lynne McKelvey

Chapter 14: The Voice from the Past

"Airclay?" Warm and familiar, her brother's voice flowed through the phone, addressing her with the nickname he'd used when they were children. "How're you doing, kiddo?"

Though she'd been dodging Roger's calls for years, recently, on an impulse, Claire had written him about her marriage. She'd kept it brief, a few lines on a postcard: *Guess what? I've married a history teacher. He has a daughter. She's eight.* Claire hadn't added that Mandy lived with them—only later realizing that Roger likely assumed she didn't.

"Claire?" Her fingers dug into the handset. She could feel his eyes on her from three thousand miles away. "Hey, are you still there?"

Claire mumbled that his call had caught her by surprise and braced for an onslaught of personal questions—about her health, her state of mind, her new marriage. Why had she written that letter? She didn't want Roger in her life now or ever, bringing up the past and watching her with his knowing blue eyes.

But all his questions were about her gardens. What kinds of plants did she grow? What did she think of drip irrigation? How did she manage pests and disease? As she described the care and feeding of gazanias, it occurred to her that Roger would have made a first-rate gardener. He loved tending things. In that way, they were alike.

She told him about Althea's garden—the berm she'd used to screen the street, the native grasses she'd selected, the salvia and the shade-loving yerba buena. Roger whistled appreciatively. "Guess you're not in Kansas anymore, Airclay."

In spite of her misgivings about the call, Claire felt a flush of pleasure. For as long as she could remember, she'd looked up to her brother. Now, he was looking up to her.

"Speaking of Kansas, Claire, I have a meeting this week in Las Vegas. I could pop over to see you while I'm there."

He kept talking, but his words had lost their borders. They merged like raindrops and streamed toward her, gathering momentum. Now and then a phrase would crystallize above the water's roar. "Hotel reservations…see your gardens…meet that husband of yours."

"So, how 'bout it, Claire? I could fly over on Saturday afternoon. Take all of us out to dinner, head back the next day."

She clutched the receiver. For years her brother had let her be. She thought they had a pact, unspoken though it was. When she first moved to Los Angeles, he phoned her constantly. She'd put him off, though, never returning his messages until, finally, he'd stopped calling and settled for a card at Christmas and on her birthday. How reckless she'd been to write him. No one knew her as well as her brother. When they were children, he used to meet her when she came home from school. He'd watch her step off the bus, his round blue eyes protruding slightly, as they did when he paid close attention. By the time her feet touched the sidewalk, he'd know just how she was feeling, how her day had gone.

After Sarah died, Roger had combed through the baby's medical records, peering at his own scrawls, holding the sheets of paper to the light, turning them this way and that to scrutinize the ink scratches as if they held some hidden meaning, as if by staring hard enough he could crack their code. He'd pelted Claire with questions. How high had Sarah's fever spiked the last time she'd been sick? 100? 101? 102? He'd barked out the numbers, insisting Claire respond, as if he were a lawyer and Claire a hostile witness. Had Sarah ever had a rash Claire hadn't mentioned? What about after her immunizations? Polio? Measles? DPT? Any reactions to these? What about Sarah's breathing? Had it ever sounded raspy? During the day? What about at night? In quick succession, he asked the questions, his round eyes unblinking. But she couldn't answer. Sarah was dead. His questions were irrelevant and Claire never dared to ask her own.

Now his silence weighed on her, pressing down on her head, compacting her spine.

"Claire?"

She tried to clear her throat, but the muscles wouldn't flex. She remembered a photo of Roger when he was six, sitting in a rocking chair cradling her. "As if you were an eggshell," her mother used to say. "There wasn't anyone who held you that way—not your dad, not the nurses in the delivery room, not even me."

"Saturday? Did you say *this* Saturday, Roger?" Claire managed, finally. Her voice sounded high, like a cartoon character's.

"Or Sunday. I could come on Sunday. Take the Red Eye back."

She ran her tongue over her dry lips, snagging the tip on dead skin.

"This weekend?" Her voice rose higher. The silence grew. She remembered a fall she'd taken roller skating one summer day when she was a child. She'd lain face skywards on the sidewalk, holding her injured leg above the ground. In the instant before pain engulfed her, she'd felt oddly peaceful. The pavement was warm, almost comforting. The street was deserted. The world seemed to have stopped. As she watched the blood bloom on her knee—a beautiful red against the blue sky—the silence seemed absolute. Except for the whir of her skate wheels, which, to her astonishment, continued to spin.

"What bad luck," she said into the phone and made a little clicking sound with her tongue. "This weekend, we're going out of town."

Lynne McKelvey

Chapter 15: The Visitor

On the steep road connecting Pacific Palisades to the coast highway, Claire took her place in the long line of cars waiting to turn left. Her blouse was soaked. She'd stopped by Althea's house to check on the new pride of Madeira she'd planted and replace the ones that had died. Althea was out of town. The scheduled soloist for the Tucson Symphony had broken his wrist and she'd been asked to substitute. As Claire watered the plants, the hose had slipped through her fingers, dousing her while it thrashed on the ground.

The light at the bottom of the hill had just turned red. A full minute would pass before it turned green again. She didn't mind. Chautauqua Boulevard and the Pacific Coast Highway was one of the most scenic intersections in Los Angeles. The ocean lay before her, a brilliant blue today, patterned with whitecaps and the occasional bobbing sail. The air was unusually clear. If she squinted, she could make out Catalina Island—a treasure trove of native plants—with

Mount Orizaba looming above it. Someday, she meant to visit the island.

Home again, she parked her truck in the driveway behind Jake's Mustang. She was heading for the back entrance to the house when she caught sight of a cream-colored, trumpet-shaped flower blooming next to the hedge. She'd never noticed it before. She stopped abruptly, observing the sturdy stalk beneath the flower and the toothed leaves. It was *Datura stramonium* all right—jimsonweed—a toxic native if there ever was one, though by now it had spread throughout the world. She'd ask Jake to dig it up or remove it herself sometime soon. Not that it posed much danger here. Cattle got sick if they grazed on it. Every so often, tuned-out hippies miscalculated how little *Datura* it took to get high and ended up in the hospital. Or worse.

The back door was ajar. As Claire scraped the mud off her shoes, she heard Jake's voice on the kitchen phone: "No, Roger, no. We'll all be here…no, no plans for the week-end…it must be a misunderstanding. We haven't gone any-where in months. Claire's up to her ears in her latest project. She probably told you about it. Some concert violinist's gar-den in Pacific Palisades. Matter of fact, she's over there right now."

Claire froze. She wanted to rush inside and snatch the phone away from Jake, but her legs wouldn't move. Why had her brother called? To check up on her story? *Roger?* He'd never do that. Not on purpose. But he'd found out she'd lied to him all the same.

"Las Vegas?" Jake was saying. "That's practically next door. Say, why don't you pop over? Come right now, if you like. There are flights every half hour. You could surprise Claire."

A plane buzzed overhead, drowning out what he said next. Claire stared at the pavement, the engine droning in her ears, and noticed a zigzag crack no wider than a penciled line running directly under her feet. The noise above her faded and was gone.

"Sure you don't want me to pick you up?" she heard Jake say, as she continued to stare at the crack. "See you around five, then."

Claire backed away from the door and lurched toward the driveway, covering her face with her hands. If only she'd gotten home in time to take Roger's call. Five minutes earlier, ten at the most. She could have explained to her brother why she and Jake hadn't left for the weekend yet—compounding her lie, but no matter—tell him they were just about to leave. Something—anything—so he wouldn't come here with his inquiring eyes, wouldn't hunt her down and ask the question, the one question he hadn't yet asked her about Sarah's last night.

She leaned against the truck, hugging her ribcage. And Jake? The sun-hot metal steamed through her wet blouse as she felt her anger rise. What right had *he* to invite Roger? He should have consulted her first. She seized the side of the truck bed and tried to shake it. Her knuckles banged into the metal, and she gave a yelp of pain.

She let go of the side rail. She would not allow Jake to interrogate her—confront her with her lie. No. *She'd* go on the offensive. Tell him her relations with her brother were *her* business. Jake had acted unilaterally, as if Claire didn't even exist. It was a betrayal, that's what it was. Jake had betrayed her. She tossed back the hair that had fallen across her face and retraced her steps to the house, propelled by anger.

Jake was at the sink, his back to her as she came through the kitchen door. He was humming something peppy from the Beach Boys.

"Hi Love," he called, as the screen door slammed behind her. He didn't sound accusatory. The sleeves of his denim work shirt were rolled up. He was marinating steaks in a shallow pan.

"Everything okay up there on the hill?" he asked. He shook the purple marinade off his hands, rinsed them under the faucet, and turned around.

"Guess what," he said, before she could reply." Your brother's in town—or, will be in town." His eyes shone behind his glasses. "He's flying here from Las Vegas. I invited him to come for dinner." He tucked in his chin; his beard spread over his chest hairs like a shaggy necklace. He looked at Claire and beamed.

Claire studied his expression. It was open and guile-less—all pleasure, no blame. Her anger drained away, her diatribe remained unspoken. Jake meant well. He thought she'd be pleased to see her brother. He had no way of know-ing she didn't want to see Roger—not here, not anywhere. She wished she'd told her husband that much, at least. She could have done so safely. He'd respect her feelings. Jake wasn't an inquisitive man. He probably wouldn't even have asked her *why*. And if she'd told him that much—that she didn't want to see her brother again—and nothing more? Chances were, he would have kept Roger away.

"He called just to leave a message." Jake paused and glanced at her oddly. "For some reason, he thought we'd be out of town." Claire held her breath, but exhaled when he continued. "Anyway, he'll be here at five." He clapped his hand over his mouth. "Oops, I think it's supposed to be a sur-prise."

A kind man, Claire told herself, as he returned to the steaks. Generous too. She missed her anger, though. At least it had taken away her fear. She shivered under her wet clothes. As she breathed in the mingling smells of garlic, red wine, and oregano, her gorge rose.

"Looks like you're fixing a real feast for tonight," she said, trying to sound hearty. "Roger loves red meat. Or, at least, he used to..." her voice trailed off. It had been six years since she'd seen her brother. Perhaps he'd changed since Sarah's death.

She looked at her watch. It was nearly three.

"I better take a shower and get into some dry clothes," she said, and started toward the hallway. "Need any help?" She hoped he'd say no. She needed time to prepare herself, though, of course, that was impossible.

"It's all under control," Jake said. "We're a little low on coals, but I can wing it. Mandy's going to help me make a boysenberry pie. Why don't you just take it easy? I don't want your brother thinking we're not taking good care of you. Didn't you tell me he's a doctor?" Claire froze, blinked, and hurried out of the room.

The sun was low in the sky when Claire coasted her pickup truck into the driveway for the second time that day. She could hear their laughter even before she opened the cab door—Jake's resonant bass, Roger's staccato, just the way she remembered it. Would he still look the same she wondered? Short and compact with probing blue eyes?

She reached for the bag of charcoal she'd picked up at Safeway—her excuse to get out of the house, if only for a few minutes, before Roger arrived—and slid it across the seat. Jake had insisted that he didn't need more coals, but she'd dashed off anyway. Let Jake greet her brother. After all, he'd invited him.

She closed the cab door quietly, not latching it. Smoke from the Weber Kettle was already curling above the hedge. She paused at the opening in the hedge and took in the scene. Jake was telling a "kids will say the darnedest things" anecdote about his history class and poking at the fire. The boom of his voice muffled the hammering inside her chest. Winter pale even in the rich glow of the late afternoon light, Roger was in an aluminum lawn chair, leaning forward. His right hand steadied the frosted can on his knee. His mouth twitched, ready to laugh. Claire shifted the bag of coals, holding it perpendicular in front of her like a shield.

Roger must have sensed her presence. His head turned slowly, gravitating toward her. He stared at her over his shoulder for a long moment, his eyes as blue and round and bright as she remembered. He stood up slowly. They faced one another in silence, neither moving, each waiting to see what the other would do.

He raised one heel, but lowered it again. The beer can made a crackling noise as he flexed its cold skin. In the late-day light, his knuckles were iridescent. "Hello, Claire," he said. His words sounded muffled, as if he'd wrapped them in a thick wool scarf.

"What took you so long?" Jake's voice burred in her ear. "Fire's ready. Everyone's hungry." His beard grazed her cheek. "I'll take these," he said, scooping up the coals with his free arm. He set the bag down by the barbeque and brushed his hands together with a slapping sound. "Time to get this show on the road!" he boomed, leaving Claire naked at the edge of the lawn.

"Lord, but it's good to see you." Roger was up on the balls of his feet, shifting his weight from right to left. His eyes bulged as they swept over her, not missing a thing. A beat and he swooped toward her, his eyes fixed on her, his arms spread wide.

In a moment, he'd surrounded her—smelling faintly of plane cabins and conference rooms. It was a familiar embrace. Roger didn't have to stoop when he hugged her, and Claire didn't have to crane her head. She and her brother were about the same height. Her chin had always rested so comfortably on his shoulder and her cheek had nestled into his neck as if they belonged there. But tonight she found no fit.

When he pulled away at last, he kept his hands on her shoulders, pinning her in place. "Just look at you," he said, grinning. What was he seeing? Claire wanted to know. He was shaking his head from side to side. "Just look," he repeated—there was that examining word again—his smile spreading easily across his face. He hugged her once more, holding onto her as if he'd never let go, swaying the two of them as if they were one.

Finally, he released her but didn't move away. Instead, he kept looking at her. Behind her, from his vantage point by the barbecue, she knew Jake was also watching her. She could feel his eyes glued to the middle of her back.

Now it was her turn to say something. They were waiting, both Roger and Jake. She hadn't uttered a syllable since she'd arrived. Words whirled in her head. She tried to grab hold of a few of them, but they were spinning too fast, eluding her like rings on a merry-go-round. *How are you, Roger? How's Alice? How're the kids?* Was that the sort of thing she used to say? Wouldn't it sound stilted? As if she and her brother didn't know each other through and through. As if Roger hadn't been a central fixture in her life—before Sarah was conceived, after she was born, the night she died.

Their eyes—husband's, brother's—held her as if in a vise. They were waiting for her to speak, to greet Roger, at least. Surely she could manage something. *How was the flight? Was it hot in Las Vegas?* If only they'd take their eyes off her, she could say that. But as her silence lengthened, they stared even harder, compressing her body between their gazes, ironing the air out of her lungs.

A rustling behind her. Abruptly, the eyes released her.

"Hi Roger," said a thin breathy voice.

"Why hello there." Roger smiled over Claire's head, while Jake coughed softly. "You must be Mandy."

Mandy! Claire had almost forgotten about her. Where had she been? Usually she rushed to answer the front door the moment someone rang.

"Oh my." Roger made a clicking sound with his tongue and folded his arms across his chest. "That's a really special dress. Did you make it yourself?" His words blew across Claire's scalp, lifting the hairs.

"It's your surprise," Mandy said, her voice coy.

Claire spun around, wondering what the child had been up to. At first she saw nothing but a bright shimmer. Gradually, the form of the little girl emerged. She'd dressed herself from head to foot in aluminum foil. Long metallic strips attached to a cord that she'd tied around her waist hung to her knees. A series of silver necklaces shingled down her chest. Crinkled bracelets adorned her ankles, wrists, and arms. Circling her head was a serrated silver crown.

Framed by the doorway, Mandy posed for a moment on the kitchen stoop, then stepped onto the grass, her aluminum skirt rattling as she moved. She walked to the center of the lawn, swishing her hips. She pivoted and bowed—to her father, first, then to Roger, who had joined Jake beside the barbecue.

Claire felt her face redden. Why had the child decked herself out this way? She thought of Roger's two daughters. Though she hadn't seen them since they were toddlers, Claire couldn't imagine either of *them* parading around like this in front of company. She tried to telegraph her disapproval to Roger, raising her eyebrows and pursing her lips. This show Mandy was putting on, it was none of Claire's doing, she wanted him to know. She thought back to the child greeting her in the pink princess dress, socks stuffed in the bodice; to the rustic lodge where the three of them had "honeymooned" and the little girl, wearing her long white bridesmaid's gown, had insisted upon mingling with the denim-clad guests. This child wasn't like other children—not his, not hers.

She couldn't catch her brother's eye, though. He was watching Mandy. To Claire's amazement, he was grinning.

"Can you twirl?" he asked, making circles with his index finger. Mandy nodded and started to spin, slowly at first, then more and more quickly.

As the child turned, she reflected the sun's last rays. One by one, her necklaces loosened and dropped to the grass. Now foil strips were falling off Mandy's belt, spiraling down like bright leaves. Still she swirled, her body rosy in the sunset, bare now except for her underpants, her glossy hair sweeping through the lingering light like a comet's tail.

She staggered to a halt. "Oh wow, am I dizzy," she

gasped, and dropped to the ground. As she lay panting on the grass, arms outstretched, face to the sky, her silver sheddings seemed to emanate from her like rays. She lifted her head and plopped it down. "I can't get up," she giggled. Her breath came in hard, short bursts. "That was so *fun!*"

Jake beamed at his daughter, spread-eagle on the grass. But Roger was looking at Claire. A smile played on his lips, as if he were inviting his sister to smile with him. But all Claire saw were his eyes, blue and penetrating—drilling into her memory vault, riddling its casing with twin beams of light.-

"Daddy! Claire! Oh, wow! Look at the sky! The clouds! The colors! Can you see them? All pink and orange and gold!"

There was a crackling sound and Claire watched herself, as if from a distance, seem to catch fire.

"Spectacular," she heard her brother say.

And then she was running, running down a dark hallway, her breasts heavy with milk, her nightgown aflame.

"Where are you going?" she heard Jake call.

And Roger's "Airclay, are you alright?"

As she ran, her body seemed to be melting—flesh, cartilage, bones, all disintegrating in the flames. She ran faster. The blazing soles of her bare feet no longer gripped the rough pine planks beneath them. Still she willed herself to run, racing against the flames even as they consumed her, racing, running, knowing even as she ran, she'd never get there in time.

Bang. Bang. Bang.

Hammer blows…somewhere.

Bang. Bang.

Behind her. Behind her head.

"Claire!"

She opened her eyes and saw the porcelain toilet bowl and the white side of the tub.

"Dinner's ready, Claire!"

What was she doing here, curled up like a sow bug on the bathroom floor?

Bang. Bang. Mandy's knuckles were rapping on the other side of the door.

"Daddy says, 'Hurry! The steaks are getting cold!'"

The tiles pressed into Claire's ribcage. She liked the way they felt—cold and hard and reassuring.

"Claire?"

The knocking stopped.

Claire stared at the bathtub and imagined it full of water. Eventually someone—who?—would pull the plug. Slowly, almost imperceptibly, the water would sink down the smooth sides, its still surface hiding the commotion around the drain. Only when the tub was almost empty would the swirling become visible, the rings of water spinning clockwise with the motion of the planet before spiraling out of sight.

The doorknob jiggled.

"What are you *doing*?" Mandy asked. "Everyone's wondering."

Claire uncurled her body.

"Nothing," she said, rolling over on her back.

"I'm starving."

The underside of the washbasin floated above Claire. She hooked her fingers over its porcelain lip.

"I'll be right there," she said, hoisting herself up.

"Hurry, Claire. I'm starving."

"Then go! Go now! Go eat!"

Claire steadied herself on the basin and gazed into the mirror. There were smudges under her eyes. Her face was pale. A lock of hair was stuck to her cheek.

"My daddy says we have to wait for *you*."

Claire tried to run her fingers through her hair. How had it gotten so matted? She reached for her brush.

"I told you, I'll be right there," she said, watching her mirror-self grimace as she pulled the bristles through the tangles.

"Cold steak is gross."

"I'm coming, I'm coming." Claire slapped her cheeks,

left then right, to give them color.

"Go. Tell them. Tell them I'm on my way."

Moments later, as she shuffled down the hall, she heard the dining room erupt with laughter—Jake's cannon boom, Roger's rat-a-tat, and Mandy's shriek.

The sounds stopped when she entered the room. Silently, their three heads turned toward her. Jake sat at the head of the table, Roger on his right, with Mandy, now clad in jeans and a tee shirt, sitting in her brother's lap. His smooth chin grazed the top of the child's head.

He peered at his sister. "You okay?" he asked, his forehead creasing.

Through the doorway, the kitchen windows were black. Claire wondered how long she'd lain on the bathroom floor and what they'd talked about while she was gone.

There was a hole in the evening, round and deep and dark as a well. She crept to the edge of it and peered in.

Nothing.

"I'm fine," she said, fastening her gaze on Roger's upper lip—anywhere but on his eyes. She hoped her *fine* sounded confident and not defiant. At least she'd spoken. His eyes were still on her, though, waiting for more.

"You sure?" he asked.

Claire ducked into the chair at the foot of the table. "I'm fine," she repeated, fixing her eyes on the platter of steaks.

They looked cold and unappetizing.

Mandy lunged across the table, reaching for the place-mat that had been set there, and slid it in between Roger's and Jake's mats.

"I want to stay here," she said, tipping her head back and looking up at Roger through her lashes.

"Well," Jake began.

"I'd be honored," Roger said, grinning down at the little girl on his knees.

"Okay, then," said Jake, passing the steak platter to Roger. "Help yourself."

The table appeared asymmetrical now, with a swath of bare wood running the length of one side and three of the four placemats clustered at the far end of the other.

For a while, the room was quiet except for the tap of utensils on china, the gurgle of liquids being poured, and murmurs of "have some…" and "please pass…"

Claire stared at the food heaped on her plate. Would she be able to eat any of it?

"That do it for you, sweetie?" she heard Roger say.

She looked up. He was cutting Mandy's steak into neat, small squares. The girl nodded, picked up her fork, and dug in.

Claire felt calmer. It was touching to see her brother tending to Mandy—the way he once looked out for her. She peeked at her watch. His plane would be leaving in a couple of hours. Maybe she'd get through this evening after all. Lucky for her that Mandy had glommed on to him. The little girl would make sure Claire and Roger weren't alone. He'd have no chance to ask her why she'd left Vermont so suddenly, why she'd never written or called, why she'd avoided him all these years. Questions she'd never dared to answer fully, even to herself.

"Everything all right, Claire?" Though his voice was gentle, she looked away. She could feel his eyes, relentless, probing, always wanting to know.

"I've *told* you, I'm *fine*, "she said, no longer caring if she sounded annoyed.

"You're not eating very much."

She pushed a lettuce leaf around her plate. "I had a late lunch," she said.

"You seem...far away," he persisted. She heard the longing in his voice. It was his sister he'd come to see, to be with. Roger. Her brother. Her best and oldest friend.

"Claire's not far away," Mandy said, pummeling Roger's chest with her elbows. "She's right here, isn't she Daddy?"

Jake guffawed and Mandy flashed her smile.

"Far away?" Claire said, her voice faint and raspy.

Roger nodded. He seemed to be pleading with her to

say more.

Their six eyes were fastened on her now. She clung to the edge of the table and cleared her throat. "I was just thinking," she said.

Roger leaned forward eagerly, but Claire trailed off.

Now was the time to say something ordinary: *It's nice to have you here*, she could tell her brother. A mere handful of words and Roger would smile his wide, kind smile. He'd reach down to Claire's end of the table and squeeze her hand. Then, maybe, they'd all start talking at once, talking and laughing the way they used to talk and laugh long ago in Vermont when everyone got together for birthdays or holiday dinners or for no reason at all. Maybe tonight, she and Jake and Mandy and Roger would talk and laugh like that.

Claire glanced around the dining room, past their stares. In the soft light spilling from the overhead lamp, she saw the books that were usually strewn across the table—Jake's and her own—now stacked on the sideboard. She saw the solitary roller skate turned turtle in the corner of the room and Mandy's fuzzy jacket with pink and purple pompoms slung over an empty chair. A placid family scene with, as far as Roger could see, Claire at the heart of it.

She looked at the food heaped on her plate and listened to each of them breathe—Mandy, quick and shallow; Jake, loud; Roger, nearly inaudible, as if he were pressing his stethoscope to a child's chest. They were all waiting for Claire to speak.

"I was thinking," she said more forcefully. "I was thinking…about the shore, about going there in the summer when we were kids, and how we used to dig holes in the sand."

"Big, deep holes. I remember!" Roger let go of Mandy and made eager measuring gestures with his hands.

Claire saw herself in her red-checked sun-suit, splayed on the sand beside her brother, her chin resting on the edge of the hole they'd just dug. She reached her gritty fingers deep into its damp depths and listened to the fine dry particles of sand hiss as they cascaded over the rim. The hot sand under her stomach burned through her sun-suit, then cooled and blended with her own body temperature. A breeze ruffled her damp, sticky hair, and she would feel herself one with the sun, the sea, and the sand.

"And you said 'Forever. We can dig forever.'"

"*I* said that?" Roger clasped Mandy again and began bouncing her on his knees.

"'Forever,'" Claire repeated. "That's what you said."

"I don't remember."

"I didn't believe you." Claire looked at her brother and shook her head. "'What's on the other side?' I'd ask you over and over. I felt I *had* to know."

"And I said, 'China,' I suppose," Roger murmured, and

blew on Mandy's hair. The little girl squirmed and giggled. "I don't remember," he said.

"You said, 'There is no other side.' I remember very clearly." Claire gazed into the middle distance, silent for a moment, then continued. "'There is no other side,' you told me. I've never forgotten. 'You just dig and dig and dig.' That's what you said."

Roger looked at Claire, his eyes soft, now, his mouth slightly open, willing her to go on.

She couldn't.

"Roger, more pie?" Boysenberry filling quivered on the spatula Jake held over Roger's plate.

"Thanks, but no thanks. I better get going, or I'll miss my flight."

"Sure you can't stay the night?"

Mandy twisted on Roger's lap. "Don't go! *Please* don't go!" she said, pounding his chest with the sides of her fists.

Jake beamed. "Guess Mandy likes having an uncle," he said.

"Fine with me, cuz I sure like having a niece."

Uncle? Niece?

"We'll put you up on the sofa," Jake boomed.

"We'll make you pancakes for breakfast." Mandy sang, sidesaddle now on Roger's lap. She wrapped her arms around his neck and arced backwards. "With *real* maple syrup," she added, looking up at him through her lashes and swishing her long hair across his knees.

From the other end of the table, Claire watched them in silence.

"Real maple syrup? Wow!" Roger said, unlocking Mandy's arms. "Afraid I have to go, sweetie." He eased her off his lap. "Maybe another time."

"But I want you to stay *this* time," Mandy said, stamping her foot. "I want you to stay *here*. *Now*."

Roger laughed. "Tell you what, sugarplum," he said, bending down and cupping his hands around her chin. "Maybe your whole family"—his eyes swept over Mandy and Jake and lingered on Claire—"maybe all of *you* could come to Vermont and see where real maple sugar comes from."

Vermont? Go back to Vermont? Claire felt the cold mist rising.

Mandy's eyes widened. "Vermont? Really?" Her voice skittered up the scale. "We could go *there*?"

Roger raised an eyebrow and gave Mandy an "anything's possible" shrug.

Layer upon layer, the mist wound around Claire.

"And I could see the pond and the tree house and ride Katie's pony and meet Henry and Jessica and Nate?" Mandy said, jumping up and down.

Roger turned to his sister. "How 'bout it, Airclay?" he said, smiling, his head tilted to the side and his expression hopeful. "Next summer. After school's out and all your gardens are dormant. You and Jake and Mandy"—his smile broadened and he made an expansive gesture—"all three of you could come for a visit."

The mist was encasing Claire, eradicating everything except a pair of eyes—blue eyes hurtling toward her through the mist. Familiar eyes, but they weren't her brother's. Whose eyes were they, then? Just before they slammed into the empty sockets beneath her forehead, she recognized them. They were her own.

For a moment the world went blank. Then she peered into the mist again.

It was because of the mist, she'd killed her infant daughter.

Because of the mist of sleepless nights and too-long, too-bright Technicolor days, she'd lowered the child, light as dawn, into the iron rib-cage of her bed.

The sheet was damp.

Because of the mist, the tired, lazy mist, she covered over the damp sheet with a blanket— the cloud-soft blanket her grandmother's stiff, arthritic fingers had managed to embroider with strawberries.

She'd laid the child face down—the right way, all the

books said so. No one, not even her doctor brother, ever told her otherwise.

Because of the mist, she herself had succumbed to a too long, too deep sleep, her breasts drained, her soul at peace.

When she awoke, the late-night birds were singing. The mist had melted away.

Full and heavy and hard, her breasts bounced under her flannel nightgown as she ran barefoot to fetch her little daughter, down the dark and silent hall, her bursting breasts demanding the child's urgent lips. Right away.

Her daughter lay on the blanket. Face down and still. As she dream-screamed the child's name, the birds stopped singing and her milk turned to blood.

Gently, she lifted the baby's still-warm head—weighing more now than before—and whisked away the blanket, like a magician removing a tablecloth. She stashed the blanket in the closet, on the highest shelf, out of sight.

Only the moon looked in through the window with its all-seeing eye.

"Impossible," Claire said and met her brother's gaze straight on. She could never go back. What Roger knew or guessed, or could know, if she told him, no longer mattered. In any case, he'd say she wasn't to blame. And perhaps she wasn't. But the eyes—her own eyes, she knew that now— told her differently. Her daughter had died. Claire might have saved her, and for that, the blue eyes of her mind would gaze into the mist, forever beholding.

Chapter 16: The Birthday Party

Claire threw herself into planning Mandy's birthday party. Jake was busy grading midterms, so Claire was in full charge. Secretly, she was glad. It felt good to have Mandy all to herself. It would be fun. And it was…at first.

Mandy had been wild with excitement. They spent an hour at the variety store picking out the invitations. At night Mandy slept with the packets of balloons under her pillow—"to keep them safe," she told Claire. They conferred constantly—about the guest list, the games, prizes, ice cream flavors, and decorations for the cake. On more than one occasion, they bolted their dinners and dashed out to Newberry's, just the two of them, in search of heart-shaped pencil sharpeners, rainbow stickers, or purple yarn. The "us" felt good—to both of them, Claire suspected.

But as the day approached and still no package from Rita arrived, Mandy grew more and more distant, barely greeting Claire when she came home from school and shuffled, head bowed, down the hall and into her room. They'd chosen a Saturday for the party, but her real birthday was the Monday before. Mandy had been sure her mother's present would arrive by then. "That's my mom's specialest day," she'd said, "the day I was born."

At school that Monday her classmates sang "Happy Birthday," and her teacher excused Mandy from all her homework. But still there was nothing in the mail. "It'll probably come the day of the party," Claire had told the child, trying to sound upbeat.

"Why don't you call Rita?" she'd asked Jake, after Mandy was in bed. He was in the dining room, marking papers with a felt-tip pen. "Maybe her gift got lost in the mail."

"That's her problem," he'd said, and returned to his work.

"But she's so unhappy," Claire persisted. "She's suffering, Jake. She hardly ate a thing tonight."

Jake's fingers tightened on the pen.

"What is it you want me to do, Claire?" he said, tilting his head back to meet her gaze. "Lie to her about her mother?" His mouth stretched wide, revealing all his teeth. Usually his lips covered them, even when he smiled. As she stared at his teeth that night and tried to think of a reply, she remembered the plaster of Paris jaw she used to play with in her father's dental office when she was a child. She'd click the two halves together like castanets. Jake's teeth didn't look anything like the ones in that model—straight and gleaming and long. Jake's were irregular, had a weathered appearance, and were small.

He shoved away the paper he was grading and rested his right ankle on his left thigh.

"Look," he said, tipping the chair back with his grounded foot, "Rita is what she is. I can't change her." His voice was resonant. "Mandy's got to face facts. The sooner she gets over her mother the better." He said this in a teacherly way, as if he were explaining some basic principle to one of his students. "Anyhow," he added, "she doesn't need Rita. She's got me." He rocked the chair legs back to the floor. "Us," he amended, after a beat.

Claire felt her face redden, but remained silent. Suppose Sarah had lived and she and Scott had divorced. Would Claire have felt like Jake? Surely not, she told herself. A child needed both parents. She knew that with her mind, but did she really believe it?

"Get over her," she'd repeated aloud while she cleared away the breakfast dishes the next morning. *Get over her?* What an odd expression, as if a mother were a bad habit or a cold. She'd set the frying pan to soak and wondered whether Jake really loved his daughter as much as he thought he did. *Get over her!* She turned on the faucet, harder than she meant to, splashing water onto the counter. For a brief moment Claire considered calling Rita. She'd never called her before. They'd never even spoken. The birthday party could be her excuse, she thought, going so far as to take the receiver off the red wall phone. She could tell Rita the date of the party—*that* would jog her memory—then ask her if she'd like to come.

What if she did come? Claire tried to picture Rita arriving at the front door. Would she look the way she did in the photograph, with a shiny dark bob, white silk blouse, and pearls? Suppose Jake wouldn't let her in? Abruptly an image of the three of them—Mandy, Jake, and Rita—arose in her mind, lined up in front of her, their forefingers pointing at her. Lost in the mental image, the receiver slid through her hand and clattered to the floor.

"I found it!" A shrill voice shattered Claire's reverie. Under the canopy of pink and purple balloons, she saw a girl dive to the carpet, copper braids flying, and clamp her hand over a blue speck. Someone with a paper bag and another girl holding a list skidded to a stop and tumbled to the ground beside her.

"Let's see, Becky. Let's see!" they squealed, foreheads knocking, noses inches from the floor. Breathing noisily, they stared at the girl's cupped hand, oblivious to the other children churning above them. Claire watched as the red-headed child's hand rotated sideways, revealing a dot of blue fuzz. The girl with the list pinched the fuzz between her thumb and forefinger and dropped it into the other child's paper bag. She drew a line through an item on her list. "A paper clip, a rubber band, a ballpoint pen that doesn't work," she read, sounding out some of the words.

"Mandy's room. Let's look in Mandy's room," one of the girls suggested. They scrambled to their feet and spun out the door.

As their voices faded, Claire closed her eyes and savored the lull. All afternoon she'd felt as if she too were spinning. The party was supposed to have been outside. But this morning, after months of drought, a Pineapple Express had rolled in from the Pacific. They'd had to move everything—cake, games, scavenger hunt, presents—indoors. Now, as she listened to the water drumming on the roof, images of the seedling yarrow and gazania in Althea's garden flickered in her mind. She pictured their tiny leaves being pounded into the ground, their fragile roots exposed.

"Owwie, owwwie, ow!"

Her eyes flew open and she rushed into the hall. In the middle of a ring of children, Mandy was hopping up and down, her back toward Claire. She was holding her hand up, looking at it as if it were a mirror.

"I cut myself!" she howled, now leaping from foot to

foot. A small red bead quivered on the whorls of her thumb. It was only a pinprick. Why was she making such a fuss? When she'd fallen off her bike and skinned both knees, she'd hardly even cried.

"I'm bleeeeeeding!" she wailed, while the children around her stared at her thumb, wide-eyed. "Owwie, owwie, owwwww."

"Yuck. Blood," said one of the girls, wrinkling her nose, but not looking away.

"You need a Band-Aid," another declared, a stolid blond child with many siblings. "Get your mom!"

Mandy halted her dance. "She's not my mom."

The girl bent over the wound, ignoring Mandy's icy stare. "You're gonna get germs," she said matter-of-factly. "Your thumb's gonna fill with pus. It'll turn green." She gave a knowing nod. "Mrs. Wethers," she called, catching sight of Claire. "C'mere." She patted Mandy's shoulder. "Your mom's coming," she soothed.

"She's not my mom," Mandy said, jerking away. "My mom lives in Riverside. She wears real pearls."

"Mandy's cut her thumb, Mrs. Wethers. She needs a Band-Aid," the child continued, sounding cool and professional.

"She's *not my mom*," Mandy shouted, breaking through the ring of children and running down the hall.

Claire followed her into her room.

"Mandy?"

The child's back stiffened.

"How's your finger?"

Silence.

"Can I have a look?"

She walked around the bed to face the little girl. Mandy crossed her arms, jamming her fists into her armpits, and turned her face away. Claire knelt, feeling oddly like a petitioner. "Let's have a look," she said.

Mandy's head twisted further. The cords in her neck bulged. Despite the carpet, the cement floor felt cold and hard under Claire's knees. She thought of Sarah's birthdays, the ones she'd celebrated in her mind. Would they really have turned out the way she'd imagined them, luminous pearls in a long, long strand?

"Mandy!" The child's silence was getting to her. What was the matter with the girl anyway? Claire had knocked herself out for this party. All of Mandy's friends had come. In spite of the rain, everything had gone well and exactly as they'd planned.

Claire's knees hurt. She shifted her weight to ease the pressure. Where was Jake? she wondered. Parents would be arriving soon to pick up their kids.

"Please, Mandy. Please tell me what's wrong." She felt

ridiculous kneeling on the floor, pleading with a nine-year-old. Mandy herself probably didn't know why she was upset. Best just to let her be. Claire started to rise.

"*You* took it." Mandy's head was still turned. As she spoke, all Claire could see of her face was the corner of her mouth.

She sat back on her heels. At least the child had spoken.

"Took what?" Claire asked.

"You know," Mandy said, still looking away.

What she was talking about? With the rain and general confusion, Claire had hardly seen the little girl all afternoon.

"You know," Mandy repeated. Claire watched a blue artery pulse on the side of her neck. Her own neck ached from looking upwards, beseeching. The doorbell rang. Would Jake get it? Why wouldn't Mandy look at her? "You took my present," the girl said.

"Your present?" Claire lurched to her knees. "I haven't gone near your presents. They're stacked on the dining-room table. You haven't even unwrapped them all!"

Mandy turned toward Claire, finally, her head pivoting slowly. "Not *those* presents." Her lip curled slightly. She paused, her eyes slits of light. "My *present*. My *mom's* present. You took it. I know you did."

A dozen rebuttals flashed through Claire's mind, all of them useless. Nothing would dissuade the child from the accusation. Claire knew it. She could tell by Mandy's eyes. She sank down again. Maybe Jake could...no, that would be worse. He'd only laugh and sweep Mandy into his arms. Claire imagined the child's triumphant gaze as he bore her away. She looked down at the floor and felt Mandy's stare, her ancient eyes.

Chapter 17: The Near Miss

Claire brought the knife down on the chopping block, severing the celery stalks from their root. She sliced them into finger-length segments and turned around. On the chair nearest the refrigerator, a little girl, clutching a fat yellow crayon, knelt at the kitchen table, her head bent over a sheet of paper. Her fair hair, tenting her face, brushed the paper with a whispering sound.

"Punkin, you'll have to move now," Claire said. "I need to get into the fridge."

"Just a minute, Mommy. I'm making the sun." The girl's brow creased. Her new front tooth—the first permanent one—bit into her lower lip.

Claire watched the child complete a wobbly circle in the upper right corner of the paper. "Hang on tight," Claire said, grabbing the back of the chair. "You're going for a ri-ide." She whirled the chair around the table, skidding it to a stop on the opposite side, while the girl squealed with glee.

Still kneeling, she reached for her picture and the box of crayons and slid them across the table.

"What'cha drawing?" Claire asked, taking a jar of peanut butter out of the refrigerator and returning to the sink.

"I told you, Mommy, the sun."

"Just the sun?"

"A big, big sun...to shine on Frisky."

Claire's hand tightened around the jar. Frisky, Sarah's half-grown cat had been killed—run over by a car—a few weeks before. Sarah had found it lying in the street right in front of the house when she'd come home from school. For days, the child had been inconsolable. "I want Frisky. Mommy, I want her back," she had wept. "Mommy, Mommy, Mommy, I want her so much. Mommy, make her come back. Please, Mommy, please. Make Frisky come back."

Never had Claire felt so helpless. She'd lined a shoebox with velvet, and they'd buried the animal under a red oak tree. "The tree will grow taller and be more beautiful now, because Frisky's nearby," she'd told her daughter. But Sarah had put her fingers in her ears and kept on weeping.

"How about we get another cat," Claire proposed. "A cute little kitten. How about we go right now and pick one out?"

Sarah had fixed her mother with a long hard look "That kitten wouldn't be the same," she said, her blue eyes steely.

"That new kitten would never ever be Frisky."

Finally, Claire had given up. Sarah's tears subsided. Claire thought she'd forgotten about the cat.

Now, as she watched her daughter pick out black, grey, and red crayons from the box, her stomach knotted. When Sarah found Frisky, the cat was lying on its side, head tipped back, throat exposed, rivulets of blood running out the corners of its mouth and disappearing into its soft, dark stripes of fur. The cat must have been directly under the tires, for its body was flat. Ants were crawling into its anus and flies tiptoed across its lidless eyes. When Sarah screamed, Claire had rushed outside and herded her into the house. But she was too late. The child had already taken in the gruesome sight. Most likely, she'd been staring at the cat for some time before she was even able to scream.

"How about a snack?" Claire said, hoping to distract Sarah from drawing. She pressed peanut butter into the trough of one of the celery sticks, spreading it evenly, the way her own mother used to when Claire was small. "Canoes" her mother had called them.

"Not now, Mommy," Sarah said. "I'm drawing Frisky."

Claire sighed. Of late, her daughter had been showing an independent streak. Since Frisky died, it seemed to be getting more pronounced. She turned back to the celery sticks, filling them precisely, one by one. She remembered coming

163

home from school when she was little. Her mother would be in her flowered housedress, her nut-brown hair short and permed. An hour later, her brother would lope through the door, slapping a baseball into his man-sized mitt. He'd tousle Claire's hair, then gulp down a quart of milk straight from the carton. Their mother would admonish him, but Claire and Roger both knew she didn't really mind.

The front door opened. Claire's heart began to pound. Mandy was back from school.

"Who's that Mommy?" Sarah asked. "Who just opened the front door?"

"No one." Claire said, gripping the celery stick she'd just filled. Her eyes darted around the kitchen. She must hide Sarah at once. But, where?

"It is too someone," Sarah said, pummeling the table with her fist. "Someone just came through that door."

"No one you know, honey." Claire could barely hear herself above her thudding heart.

The door banged closed.

"Is that a child, Mommy?" Sarah asked. Her eyes were fixed on Claire. They seemed bluer than they used to be. "I want to meet that child. I want us to play."

Claire crushed the celery stick, smearing peanut butter on her fingers. She wiped them on her jeans and scanned the room again. The cupboards under the sink were big enough to hide a child, if only Sarah would stay put. She never would, though. Not in her present mood.

"You must go now, Sarah," Claire said. Her voice was brusque, but her throat felt hard. Never before had she asked Sarah to leave. She turned to take hold of the child, to march her out the back door. Sarah's chair was just where it had been, pushed close to the table and slightly askew. But the chair was empty. Claire circled the room—peering into the low cupboards, the broom closet, under the table—anywhere a child might hide. Sarah had disappeared.

Claire felt lightheaded. She steadied herself on the back of the vacant chair and stared at the formica table top. The crayons were gone, but the sheet of paper was still there. She held it at arms' length, bracing herself against the refrigerator. There, against a backdrop of blue sky and a brilliant yellow sun, stood Frisky. The cat's striped tail was high and proud, its paws firmly planted on the ground, and its body, covered with luxuriant black and gray fur, perfectly intact. Huge and foreshortened, its head—complete with eyes, ears, whiskers, and a pink nose—was turned ninety degrees so that it faced outwards. The cat looked straight at Claire.

Footsteps clomped in the hall. Claire stood on tiptoe, slapped the picture face-down on top of the refrigerator, and turned around just as Mandy burst into the kitchen.

"Where's my daddy," she demanded, flinging her metal

lunch box on the table. Her entrances still astonished Claire. The child exploded into a room, abolishing its space. Backed against the refrigerator door, Claire felt flat as a shadow, as though Mandy had appropriated one of her dimensions.

"He's not home," she said, and offered the child a celery stick. Mandy made a face and slunk off to her room.

Claire glanced at the top of the refrigerator, but stayed her hand.

She turned her back on the drawing. She still saw it, though, bobbing right in front of her like a mote in her eye. The cat seemed to be taunting her now. Stupid beast with its ridiculous grin. She wanted to tear up the paper.

She closed her eyes and massaged her forehead, slowing her breathing as she smoothed the skin. When she opened her eyes again, she stared at the celery canoes. They lay every which way on the white plate, filled to their gunwales with peanut butter. She cleared a space with the side of her hand and arranged them symmetrically so that they all radiated out from an imaginary center like spokes on a wheel. She imagined them pulling away from the hub, each moving in its own path. On and on they'd travel, moving further from each other and from their invisible center.

She covered the plate with Saran Wrap and carried it to the refrigerator. As she opened the door, Mandy's school calendar, scotch-taped to the front, blurred past her, accompanied by a chilly blast of air. She set the plate on the bottom shelf, reaching under the plastic to grab one of the celery sticks before she closed the door. She didn't need to look at the calendar; she already knew exactly what date school let out for the summer. Mandy would be leaving for Riverside that same afternoon.

She moved over to the table and pulled out a chair—the same chair Sarah had been sitting in, the one that was slightly askew. Mandy would be away the whole summer—eight, nine, almost ten weeks. Claire bit into the celery stick, savoring the succession of tastes and textures—the crisp stalk, the dense rich filling, and the satisfying sound of the crunch.

She wanted Mandy gone.

Lynne McKelvey

SUMMER 1979

Lynne McKelvey

Chapter 18: The Departure

Claire stooped to pick up the purple-inked papers Mandy had dropped as she raced out the front door—her round overnight case banging against her thigh, her smile strapped to her face—and put them back in the new green folder labeled *Mandy's School Work, June, 1979*. For a moment, she considered running after the child—following her out to the big car with its engine thrumming—and handing her the folder, but she changed her mind. Mandy knew what she was doing. It had been Claire's idea she take the papers to Riverside. "I bet your mom would like to see your school work," Claire had said. "I bet she'll be amazed to see how much you've learned." Mandy had looked at the folder and scowled. "We don't talk about school when I'm with my mom," she muttered. What *do* you talk about, Claire had wanted to ask, but didn't.

Now, Claire stood at the living room window and

watched the shiny black Buick pull away from the curb. Mandy was in the back, her mother in the passenger seat, her grandfather at the wheel. Shirley, his second wife—whom he married after Rita's mother had divorced him—never joined them. "Shirley's too busy," Mandy had told Claire, matter-of-factly. "She has to visit her *real* grandchildren. She has lots and lots of *real* grandchildren." She held up her hand, palm to the ceiling, and curled her fingers one by one. "Lots and lots," she repeated, when her fingers had made a fist. "They take up all her time."

Rita didn't drive. "Doesn't drive, doesn't work, doesn't screw," Jake liked to say. His knuckles bulged when he talked about his ex-wife. Claire strained for a glimpse of Rita through the Buick's tinted glass. In all this time, she'd never actually seen the woman. Rita didn't get out of the car, not even to greet Mandy with a hug. Especially not that. She'd never liked to touch her daughter, not even when Mandy was a baby, Jake said. After the child was born, Jake took over pretty much completely.

The car glided down the street, bearing the three of them away. As Claire watched it grow smaller, she felt inexplicably sad. It reminded her of a hearse. She wondered who would be in the coffin. Her mother? Sarah? Or was it Mandy?

Her eyes stung with tears. She turned away from the

window and found Jake standing behind her. Blindly, she stumbled toward him, grabbed his bare arms, and slid her fingers down them as if they were poles. She seized his hands, running her thumbs over the calluses, then pulled them behind her, cupping them under her buttocks. His shirt was open. She moved her mouth across his chest, tasting its heat and its resilient hairs. She pressed harder on the backs of his hands, indenting his body with her own.

She awoke in the late afternoon. Jake was still asleep, sprawled beside her, his mouth slightly open. Sunlight shining through the trees outside made shifting patterns on the walls. They hadn't lowered the shades. The off-shore breeze blew through the open window, rippling over her thighs, etching Jake's passion in a cool, definite design.

She lay still and listened to him sleep. The door beside the bed was wide open. Scattered along the length of the hall were articles of their clothing—sandals, a tee shirt, a belt, a bra—like the bright pebbles the children dropped in the forest so they could find their way home. She kept staring though the open doorway. As she stared, the walls melted away. In their place, she saw the sky, blue and unbounded.

Lynne McKelvey

Chapter 19: The Phone Call

All across the city, buildings rippled in the midday heat. Traffic was light; even on the freeways, cars and drivers seemed lethargic. The neighborhood was deserted. Perhaps everyone was away, or maybe it was just too hot to go outside.

Claire was sitting at the dining-room table, the drawings for Althea's new kitchen garden spread out before her. Jake's ancient history textbook bulged beneath the *Carmel Sur* manzanita bed. She'd have more space working in Mandy's room while the child was gone, but Claire liked it better here. The light was dimmer but more constant. She liked seeing Jake's books and papers piled together with her own, liked the way they touched.

From the driveway, she heard the shrill whine of his circular saw. He was building two cabinets, one for Claire's outsized reference books and the other for Mandy's Barbies. The dimensions were the same. She pictured him out in the broiling sun, teeth clenched, sweat rolling off his forehead and seeping into his beard. She imagined his broad hands guiding a 1x6 through the jagged wheel. He liked working in the heat. He said you weren't really working if you didn't sweat.

A fly buzzing above her head echoed the saw. She leaned back and listened to the antiphony of fly and saw. Closing her eyes, she heard a third tone, the high-pitched music of a dentist's drill. It was her father's. On hot summer days when she was bored at home, her mother would send her down the street to his office with a "very important message." She'd run barefoot beneath the canopy of maples, scarcely feeling the whirlybird seed pods through her thick calluses. She'd race up his clapboard building's worn wooden steps, taking them two at a time, and tear through the doorway to the front desk. Flushed and panting, she'd tilt her head and listen. If she heard the sound of the drill above her own loud breathing, she knew she'd have to wait to see him. She didn't mind, though. The receptionist gave her Lifesavers—she saved Claire all the lime ones from her rainbow rolls. Claire would suck each candy until she couldn't tell where the sweet rim ended and the hole began. She'd read *Jack and Jill*s and feel her tongue turn green.

From the kitchen, the telephone rang, shattering her memories. She rose and was about to answer it when Jake stomped in through the back door, his glasses smeared and his denim work shirt dark with sweat. He grabbed the handset off the wall and said *hello*. "It's Mandy," he mouthed to Claire, his knuckles white against the red receiver. "Hang on a minute," he muttered into the phone.

He dropped the receiver, took one giant step to the sink, and turned the cold-water faucet hard to the right. He let the water run, testing its temperature with his wrist. Behind him, the phone handset bobbed on its coiled cord. He ducked his head into the basin and gulped straight from the tap. He turned off the faucet, shook the water from his beard, and wiped his sleeve across his mouth. Claire looked at him expectantly. His eyes flashed behind his glasses, but they didn't meet her gaze. The cord hung from the phone, stretched by the weight of the handset into an undulating red line. Jake squared his shoulders and turned away. Staring straight ahead, he marched past Claire, out the kitchen door, and down the hall toward their bedroom.

Claire could hear Mandy's short, shallow breaths just above the baseboard.

She imagined the child in the blistering inland heat with her grandfather, her mother, and Shirley, her grandfather's second wife. Their house was the same one Rita had grown up in. Her room was preserved just as it had been when she left for college. Jake had described it to Claire in minute detail, his jaws clenched. Rita's old *Nancy Drew*s were arranged in order on the shelves, starting with *The Secret of the Old Clock.* She still slept in her white canopy bed with her stuffed animals spread symmetrically on the pillows. Mandy slept on a futon in the living room. She wasn't allowed in her mother's room.

Claire looked at the dangling receiver. Maybe *she* should talk to Mandy. But what would she say? That her father was coming?

She picked up the phone.

"Hello, Mandy," Jake said in Claire's ear. She started, almost dropping the receiver. How odd he sounded—metallic and distant. Why was he using the bedroom phone? Did he want his conversation to be private? Not likely. Jake wasn't a secretive man. Quite the contrary. When Mandy was with him—*especially* when Mandy was with him—he liked Claire to be around. He liked her to witness how well he cared for his daughter. He wanted her to understand why the child belonged with him. Claire imagined Jake sitting on the edge of their bed, his strong, stubby fingers crushing the receiver. He hadn't gone all the way down the hall to the bedroom in order to be alone with his daughter. He'd been buying time. He needed to tamp down his fury—at Rita for depriving him of his daughter, at himself for not preventing her, and—though he might not admit it—at Mandy for daring to love her mother.

178

"Hi, Daddy," Mandy drawled, just as Claire was about to hang up. She hesitated a moment, then pressed the handset to her ear. "I got here. Grandpa thought you'd want to know." The words were uninflected, rehearsed.

Jake cleared his throat. "Yes, uh, well…" Claire waited for him to go on; to ask his daughter how she was, talk about the weather, tell her a joke. She felt the seconds ticking by, encircling the little girl like an embroidery hoop, pulling her taut in all directions. Claire willed Jake to say something, *anything*. She wanted to put the handset back on the phone, but the click on the other end would sound deafening to those still on the line.

A series of scraping sounds entered her ear—Mandy sucking air. "Mom's got a new perm. Her hair's feathered in back now. It's short for summer." Rat-a-tat-tat. No pause between sentences, not even to take a breath. "Mom's got a new bikini. It's black with sparkles. It's got under-wire cups. She wears it around the house all the time. She says there's no point wearing lots of clothes when it's so hot." Rat-a-tat-tat. Rat-a-tat-tat. "We're going out to dinner." Speeding up, now. "Shirley says it's too hot to cook. It's Shirley's birthday. Not her real birthday. Her real birthday was last Tuesday. Her real grandchildren made a party. Shirley said there was lots of hoopla. Mom didn't go. She was getting her period. She said she felt yucky. Grandpa stayed home to keep Mom company.

Grandpa's taking us to Knott's Berry Farm." Faster, faster, as if any pause would devour her. "Shirley wants to take her real grandchildren. Grandpa isn't sure they'll all fit in the car. Mom told him to forget it. She said one child was all she could handle. Mom's getting a cat, an adult cat. She's getting it after I leave. Mom says adult cats don't get along with children. She says…"

Claire let go of the receiver, buffering it with her hand so it wouldn't bang against the wall. The frantic staccato continued, but she couldn't hear the words. She thought of the picture in the glittering frame, Rita's cold eyes, Mandy's tears over the broken necklace. Despite Jake's refusal to rein in his daughter, his excessive fondness, his fierce sense of ownership, he was right, mainly: Mandy *was* better off with him. Was she also better off with Claire? The question hung.

And then,

"Who's that?" a small voice said behind her.

Claire froze. Not here. Not now. In slow motion, she turned around, eyes shut tight and holding her breath as if she were under water. Still not breathing, she opened her eyes. Sarah was wearing jeans rolled up to her knees. She was barefoot. Her hair was pulled back in a ponytail held in place with a rubber band. What was she doing here?

"Shhh." Claire hissed, motioning the child away from the receiver.

"Who's that talking on the phone?"

Claire frowned. She didn't like ponytails. Not on Sarah. She liked her daughter's hair flowing freely, draped on her shoulders, framing her face in light.

"Shhhh," she repeated, spitting out the sound.

"Who is it, Mommy?" Sarah's eyes were fixed on the red receiver dangling just above the floor. With her hair pulled back, her features seemed almost severe. Her voice was stronger than it used to be. It sounded older.

Sweat beaded Claire's forehead. Why hadn't she hung up when she had the chance? Her eyes swept the room, looking for something—anything—to distract her daughter. The cupboards were shut tight, the formica table and countertops bare.

The red receiver stood out against the white wall—like a bull's eye, Claire thought.

"No one," she said, realizing her folly even as she spoke the words.

"It is too *someone," Sarah shot back. "Someone's talking inside that phone." She cocked her head. "It sounds like a kid!"*

Claire stared at the phone. As Mandy chattered on, it seemed to pulse with life.

"No one you know, " Claire said, her voice faint.

Sarah faced her mother, arms akimbo.

"But I want to know that person. I want her to come over. I want us to play." Her ponytail bounced as she made her points. Her *to come over? How did Sarah know it was a little girl's voice?* Claire grabbed her daughter's arm just as she lunged toward the phone. She'd never seen Sarah like this. Red-faced. Defiant. It was Mandy's fault. Even on the telephone, she could cast a spell.

Sarah struggled to pull free, but Claire had no choice. The girls must never meet. This she knew. On this, everything depended. She dragged her daughter across the kitchen, past the throbbing phone, through the screen door, and into the blinding sun outside.

It had been two weeks since Jake had sprayed the lawn with Deep Green Vigaro 16-2-5, but the metallic smell still lingered. She let go of Sarah's arm and flexed her fingers, which were numb. As soon as the blood began to flow in them, she would remove that horrid rubber band. She would run her fingers through her child's hair, smoothing out the tangles, inhaling its fragrance, stroking its shine. She would put her arms around her daughter and kiss the top of her head, which would be warm from the sun. They would breathe as one.

Chapter 20: In the Bathtub

Jake wasn't there when Claire got back from a day of digging up Bermuda grass in Althea's garden. "Gone to Builder's Emporium," the note said. "Sink stopped up" (frowning Happy Face). "Dinner under control" (smiling Happy Face). "Love you."

Instead of showering in their small bathroom as she usually did, Claire went into the bathroom Mandy used and filled the tub. A dry sponge shaped like a fish, soap crayons, and a bottle of No More Tears shampoo were perched on the rim. On the porcelain wall, she glimpsed the faint outlines of a drawing. She couldn't make it out, though. The sun's late rays slanting through the window were blinding her. She looked away and peeled off her filthy clothes, tossing them into the hamper. Slowly, she lowered herself into the tub, pillowed her head on the porcelain, and closed her eyes. For a while, the sun's orange afterimages careened across her retinas; eventually, they subsided. She lay motionless, letting the hot, clear water drain away her stiffness and fatigue.

The memory of the old cast-iron tub with griffin claws, where night after night she and Sarah had bathed together, emerged. Sarah would squirm and crow even before Claire turned on the faucet. While the water roared downward, Claire unwrapped her like a present. As they lay belly to belly in the warm water, the baby scrabbled up Claire's torso, pummeling her breasts and collar bones with padded knees, pausing now and then to run her tiny fingers over the corrugations of her mother's teeth. With demon eyes, she'd lunged for Claire's nose, rasping with joy as she tried to twist the tip a hundred and eighty degrees. She'd grab a chunk of Claire's hair in her fist. Swinging the bell rope with a triumphant cock-a-doodle-do, she'd summon the world. The universe swirled around them in clouds of steam as they lay together at its bright center, Sarah's flesh firm and resilient on her own.

Tears dammed behind Claire's closed eyes. She clenched her lids together, but the pressure grew. It ripped the skin seams apart. Hot tears spilled out, saturating her cheeks, seeping into her nose, stopping up the airways. Her throat was swollen shut. She felt pinned, fathoms deep, to the sandy bottom of the sea. She could neither swallow nor breathe. She strained to hear a sound—the whir of a car, the rustle of a leaf, a reassuring thump inside her chest. The silence was frightening.

The sound that broke it, a loud wind howling inside her ears, terrified her more. With gale force, it blew its way through brine-filled passages, tunneling down her throat, entering the cavity of her chest. Her lungs inflated to bursting, suddenly and completely, as if she'd just been born. She breathed out and felt the gush of tears. Her shoulders shook—first in small spasms, but soon convulsively. With each exhale her lungs bellowed forth tears. As she breathed and wept, her whole body shuddered. She'd never cried this way before. Not that moonlit midnight when she'd awakened with bursting breasts and run dry-mouthed into the silent nursery. Not that chilly afternoon, a lifetime later, when they'd centered the box so precisely within the dark margins of the hole, shifting it a little to the left, a little to the right, before lowering it—as if the position of the box could possibly matter. Nor months afterwards, when she found Scott's note: "I'm leaving. I'm sorry. I have to move on."

As she lay in the tub, Claire cried and cried and kept on crying. With each breath she took, more tears poured out. Then, as suddenly as she'd begun to cry, she stopped. She opened her swollen lids and saw the plastic bottle: *No More Tears*. She laughed a hiccupy laugh and said out loud, "All right." She reached forward, tore a piece of toilet paper off the roll on the wall, and blew her nose—long and loud and hard—then lobbed the soggy wad toward the wastebasket. It landed inside—a direct hit. "All *right!*" she said again, this time without a hiccup, and sat up in the tub.

The sun had moved beyond the window. Now she could see the picture Mandy had drawn on the porcelain—two stick figures with huge heads and wide smiles: a man with a beard and glasses and a girl with a triangle skirt and masses of curls. They were wearing crowns and holding hands. At the lower edge of the wall, there was a third figure—a boy, Claire thought at first, since it had no skirt. This figure was much smaller than the other two and wore no crown. But now she noticed a few wispy strands of hair hanging almost shoulder length and realized the small figure must be her. It had no eyes or nose on its face, only a slotted mouth. Its arms hung rigidly next to the stick body, as if they'd been tied there.

She stared at the picture. Mandy must have drawn it right before she left for Riverside.

Claire grabbed the sponge, dunked it, and wrung it out so hard it started to tear. As she held it poised in front of the picture, her hand wavered. Which of the three figures should she obliterate? Jake or Mandy or herself?

Claire dropped the sponge. It hit the water with a splat. She slid forward on the bottom of the tub and rifled through the crayons, picking out the one with the boldest color and the sharpest point. She braced herself on the porcelain rim and extended the little girl's legs until the figure was almost as tall as the man. She retrieved the sponge and rubbed out the figure's myriad curls, taking pains not to erase any part of the round head or the crown. In place of the curls, she drew in strong vertical strands of hair. She paused to survey her handiwork. With the figure's new height, its skirt now seemed exceptionally short, hardly more than a breechcloth. Claire let it be and turned to the small plain figure on the periphery. She dabbed eyes and a nose on its face and added long, springy hair. She hesitated a moment, then drew a triangular skirt the same size as the woman's; it came down below the small figure's knees. Finally, she widened the mouth, curving its edges into a pleasant smile, and added a tiny crown.

She set the crayon down and slid back from the wall, nodding as she studied what she'd done. The original picture was still recognizable, but it had been transformed. With its new features, its skirt, and crown, the small figure at the edge now harmonized better with the other two. Still, something about the design bothered her. She hugged her knees and studied it some more. The distance between the two larger figures and the smaller one was too great. They didn't seem to belong in the same picture. She picked up the sponge and was about to wipe away the small figure when she pulled back her hand. She couldn't erase any of the figures. All three must remain. She stared at the gap, feeling stymied.

With no specific plan, she took up a crayon and found herself drawing a circle in the middle of the empty place. She had no idea why she was doing this, but immediately afterwards she began adding on lines—first a horizontal, then a series of verticals. Though her strokes were strong and sure, she still didn't know what she was drawing. Her hand moved autonomously. When she finally set the crayon down, she stared at the new drawing on the wall. There, crawling vigorously in the space between the two large figures and the smaller one, was a baby.

Chapter 21: Baking Bread

The dough had been rising for nearly two hours. It had doubled in size, a warm pale mound brimming above the bowl like a giant mushroom cap. The kitchen was hot—redolent of yeast and the memory of her mother in the summertime wiping the back of a flour-dusted hand across her moist forehead. "Bread weather," her mother used to say.

Claire balled her hands and plunged them into the warm dough. The mushroom collapsed with a sigh. The dough lay heavy and dormant at the bottom of the bowl. She folded it over—already it was getting cold—and flopped it onto a wooden board. As she began her rhythmic rowing movements—the heels of her hands weighing into the viscous mixture, her shoulders circling with each stroke, her body rocking back and forth as if to music—she felt implicit life.

When she'd married Scott, she used to make bread every week—dark, sturdy loaves with molasses or sorghum and steel cut oats, or stone ground wheat, or rye. She made all their bread back then, in that brief parenthesis before Sarah died.

Already the dough was changing—becoming silky and resilient, now, and warm as skin. Making bread was like planting a garden. You had to pay attention. You had to wait. In Vermont, while the yeast was working in the dough, she'd listen to the cicadas trilling in the grass or curl up in the wicker chair on the screen porch and read and read. Making bread slowed you down. You had to synchronize yourself with its rising times, its resting times, the rhythms of its life.

The front door snapped open. Jake was home from teaching summer school. "Hi Love," he called.

Claire's heart turned over when he called her that.

He came up behind her and buckled his hands across her stomach. "Mmmm. Smells like a bakery in here." As he spoke, his warm breath blew a part in her hair. "How'd I get so lucky?" He nuzzled the back of her neck then unclasped his hands. "Got a meeting at the District office," he said, turning to go. "Back about five. Love you." As he sailed out the door, Claire reached up and smoothed her hair.

She formed the dough into a ball, pinched it in half, and mounded two loaves. These she placed in metal pans and covered each of them with a wrung-dry cloth. She glanced at the clock: 2:45. She set the oven to 350 degrees and left the loaves to rise. She'd done her part. Now it was up to the yeast. She pictured the loaves in another hour. Plump and airy, they'd be ready to slide into the oven. Her mouth watered. It had been a long time since she'd felt this hungry.

She scraped out the mixing bowl and set it to soak. Already the oven had raised the temperature of the room. Her face was beaded with sweat. She ran cold water into a tumbler. As she lifted the glass to her lips, she felt a gush between her legs. She sputtered and dropped the glass into the bowl full of water. There was no time to protect her clothing. The blood was coming out too fast. Now it was trickling down her calves and dripping onto the floor. She stared at the red spots on the gray linoleum. She hadn't menstruated in years. After Sarah died and her milk dried up, her monthly cycles never returned. All this time, her uterus had clung to its lining, memorializing her dead daughter.

She stepped back and studied the bright dabs. Some had scalloped edges, some were spiked like stars. More blood dripped out between her legs, making new splotches. She took another step and jumped up and down in place, watching fresh spots appear beneath her. She moved around the kitchen—to the sink, to the stove, the refrigerator—jumping then pausing just long enough at each station to deposit new flecks of blood. Soon the whole drab surface was speckled with red. She backed into a corner, walking on her heels so as not to smudge the drops. The linoleum was transformed, as when, after long awaited rain, the chuparosa pushes aside the slippery shale and its crimson blossoms illuminate the hard desert floor.

Chapter 22: The Getaway

In the passenger seat of Jake's Mustang, Claire spread the map out on her lap, humming Brahms. Cars, trucks, and roadside signs rushed by, fusing with each other, with the parched hills, and the seamless, no-color sky. She and Jake were heading for Idyllwild, a small resort town in the San Jacinto mountains, a couple of hours east of L.A. Nowhere far, they'd decided that morning. Nowhere fancy. Just a place they'd never been. Jake's summer school session had ended, and most of Claire's clients were out of town. Their gardens were going dormant, the plants exhausted after months of exuberant growth.

They'd decided to go away on impulse. These days, without a child around, they did everything on impulse—hiked a canyon, caught a midnight movie, waited in the moon-shadows of the Santa Monica Pier for the grunion to run. The night before, they'd driven to West Hollywood to see an actors' equity play. They'd missed the curtain, so they drove on to the Hollywood Bowl instead. As they climbed the steep path to the benches at the top of the hill, hugging a couple of blankets and a bottle of wine, Jake related odd facts he'd collected about the Romans' theaters. "Back then, you'd have *had* to sit way up here in the nosebleed section," he'd said, as he guided her into a half-empty row near the summit. "The Roman men were afraid their womenfolk would run off with an actor if they sat too close to the stage. "Though in *your* case"—his eyes skimmed over the tiered heads and shoulders and came to rest on the musicians who were tuning their instruments at the bottom—"in your case"—he looked at Claire with a mischievous smile—"it'd probably be one of the cellists." He took her hand and raised it to his lips. Under silent stars, they sat close together, breathing in the pungent resins of eucalyptus and sumac, the sweet night smell of jasmine. All around them, the vast city lay hushed and invisible while Brahms' Third Symphony radiated from the blue shell far below. Claire fell asleep, drifting off to the strains of the slow movement, her head in Jake's lap.

Still humming—it was a theme from the Allegro—she glanced at the map now, then bent to look more closely. The state highway they were on ran just north of Riverside. She gripped the edges of the map. Was Jake planning to see Mandy? The car's thick windows suddenly seemed porous. The loud outside air scraped against her cheek. Was Mandy going to join them? Why hadn't he said anything to Claire? The memory of the child in her long white bridesmaid's dress sashaying around the lodge when they were on their honeymoon rose up in Claire's mind. She sat up straight, back rigid, and pressed her shoulders into the seatbelt. She wouldn't make the same mistake again. His daughter or his wife; this time Jake would have to choose.

She turned toward him, primed for a confrontation. He was staring at the road, his back curving into the contours of the seat, his hands easy on the wheel. He looked calm and ordinary, a little tired and, perhaps, a little bored with driving. Her body loosened. She rested her head on the back of the seat. He wasn't going to stop to see his daughter. Whatever made her think he might? He hadn't called Mandy all summer. Since she'd left for her mother's, he'd hardly even said her name.

Claire remembered the grunion run she and Jake had seen at the pier a few nights before. At the peak of an especially high tide, the adult fish flung themselves on shore to spawn, transforming the drab sand into a silver carpet. The mating drama lasted less than a minute—time enough for a female, excavating with her tail, to drill herself into the damp sand up to her pectoral fins and deposit her eggs; and for a male, or several males at once, to curl around her exposed head, releasing sperm. Their goal accomplished, the adult grunion caught the next wave back, leaving their offspring to their fates, to the mercy of wind, tides, and predators. An hour after the run began, the beach was dull and bare once more.

Was Jake leaving Mandy to her fate, Claire wondered, when the little girl went off to Riverside? The only time he spoke to his daughter all summer was after she'd arrived and *she* had called *him*. Claire tried to recall what she'd overheard of Mandy's monologue. Other than throat clearing and an occasional grunt, Jake had hardly made a sound. The child had gone on about her mother's new haircut and under-wire bikini. Why was Rita running around in a bikini in her father's home, and how did her father's new wife, Shirley, feel about *that*? Claire could only wonder. There was also something about a new cat on the horizon. Mostly, though, Claire remembered how Mandy sounded —the way her words poured out: non-stop, high-pitched, in a rapid-fire staccato. Poor little girl. Under the bravado, she was probably scared to death. Scared that any day now Rita might replace her daughter with a cat. Scared too that while she was gone, Jake might replace *her* with Claire. As the weeks dragged on and no call or letter came from her father, how else would a nine-year-old interpret his silence?

Claire watched Jake stifle a yawn. His eyes were a bit bloodshot from staring into the light. Without looking away from the road, he reached for her hand. "Penny for your thoughts," he said, his thick fingers stroking hers. "Though these days, maybe it's a quarter." He laughed, squeezed her hand, and looked more alert.

"We could see Mandy." The words tumbled out as if of their own accord. Had Claire really just said that? Jake turned to look at her, his brow furrowed.

"Mandy?" He sounded mystified.

"Yes, *Mandy*," Claire said, suddenly wanting very much to see the little girl, to hear what she'd been doing, to see how much she'd grown, to give her a hug. "We could take her out for 31 Flavors." She imagined Mandy's smile—her real smile, not the fake one—as she dug into her favorite: mint chip with sprinkles on top. *And remind her that her father hasn't forgotten her completely*, Claire added silently.

"Mandy?" Jake repeated, his frown deepening. He let go of Claire's hand and gripped the wheel.

"Why not?" Claire asked. Besides seeing Mandy, Claire could meet her mother. Maybe Rita wasn't the monster she seemed. Maybe, if Claire helped break the ice, Rita and Jake could begin to tolerate each other, at least, for their daughter's sake.

"We're going right by Riverside." Claire tapped the map. "We could surprise her. You could call ahead."

She trailed off. Jake was staring at the car in front of

them, a navy Oldsmobile with a wobbly path. It was traveling a little under the speed limit a couple hundred yards down the road. Jake's knuckles bulged on the steering wheel. He was sucking air.

"What's wrong?" she asked, hoping he wasn't getting sick. She was looking forward to this getaway. It would be their real honeymoon.

He floored the accelerator but didn't reply. The car lurched forward. The long strip of highway between their car and the Oldsmobile ahead vanished, as if someone had just cut a taut gray ribbon. She gripped the seat, crumpling the edges of the map spread across her lap. What was wrong with Jake? He never drove recklessly before.

He braked—just in time—pitching Claire against the seatbelt. The other driver, an older man with a plaid beret, blinked his intent to move onto the shoulder, and his gray-haired passengers turned their heads and glared at Jake.

Claire buried her fingers in the folds of her denim skirt. Though the road ahead was reassuringly empty, images of a violent coupling, with crumpled metal and windshields shattering into translucent webs, careened through her mind. As the images receded, she felt, rather than heard, guttural sounds beside her. Jake's mouth was moving. Shaping words, she realized, at last.

"What?" she asked, startled to find her own voice audible. "What did you say?"

"I said, 'Mandy is with Rita now.'" He assigned each word an equal weight.

Such an ordinary sentence. One she'd heard from him before. She groped for the lever on the floor beside her and reclined her seat. She could no longer see the road, the cars, or rushing buildings. All she saw was the dashboard and, above it, a thin band of sky. *Mandy is with Rita now.* Jake's words echoed off the upholstered ceiling. Claire thought she understood them—finally. He hated his former wife for depriving him of his daughter—hated her so much he refused to see her—even if that meant not seeing his child. There was more, though, and it was darker. Jake couldn't bear to think of Mandy existing anywhere without *him.*

The car was almost silent now. No longer porous, the glass panes sealed out the wind's roar. The only sound was the engine's hum. Depleted, Claire closed her eyes. The map slid off her lap, landing on the floor mat with an almost inaudible rattle. Just before she slipped from consciousness, a thought arrowed toward her. She'd never shared Sarah with anyone either, not even with Scott. She'd clung to her little daughter lest she lose her; she'd lost her all the same.

Lynne McKelvey

Chapter 23: New Life

Claire sat on the edge of her bed drawing rapid circles with her foot and felt the weight of the hatbox on her knees. She listened for the familiar thudding of the drums. She always waited until the procession had passed by before she untied the ribbon. Today, though, all she heard was the beating of her heart. *Her* heart only? She closed her eyes and strained to listen. The beat seemed to be tripping over itself. Was she hearing a second beat—the new one, still faint but growing stronger every day?

Claire had wondered for weeks if she was pregnant. She hadn't said anything to Jake. She'd held off, she told herself, because she wanted to be sure. But that was only partly true. She wanted to keep this new life—a boy, she knew it would be a boy—to herself. She wanted time to sort things out.

The hatbox pressed down hard on her thighs—there would be a mark if she looked—but still no drums. What happened? In the past, the procession always came. She closed her eyes and tried to focus on what was inside the box. Instead of the corduroy overalls or the little ghost nightgown with the drawstring hem, she saw a tiny sea creature—some kind of crustacean—darting in and out of a coral reef. She willed the image away and listened again for the approaching drums. Silence. No heartbeats. Not even her own.

She opened her eyes and slid the hatbox off her lap and onto the bed, its black bow still intact. Summer was almost over. Mandy would be back in a few days. Was Claire sorry or glad? The time alone with Jake and her gardens was just what she'd longed for. Yet as the weeks slipped by, she found herself increasingly wondering—worrying—about the little girl. Mandy was cooped up in the house in Riverside with her grandfather, though he seemed benevolent enough; with Shirley, his new and less benevolent wife who gushed about her "real" grandchildren; and with Rita, who spent much of each day, so far as Claire could tell, sequestered in her childhood room. Rita, who couldn't bear to touch her own daughter.

Claire needed to tell Jake about her pregnancy soon, certainly before Mandy arrived. He'd be pleased, she supposed. On more than one occasion, he'd said he wished Mandy had a sibling. Still, Claire wondered if that was true. Could a second child ever measure up to the first? The question hovered, then melted away. Jake would be fine, she decided. But what about Mandy? She'd had her father to herself most of her life, until Claire arrived. That had been hard on the little girl—on both of them, Claire thought, her jaw tensing. Now Mandy would also have to share her father with a sibling. Together, Jake and Claire would figure out how and when to tell the child the news. Best to get her settled in school first, Claire decided. Wait until Claire's belly began to round. Wait until Mandy could feel the undulations when she pressed her hand against it. Wait until this new baby was an undeniable fact. There was plenty of time.

They hadn't heard from Mandy since her call when she first arrived in Riverside at the beginning of the summer. Jake hadn't phoned, much less tried to see his daughter. He rarely mentioned her name. He'd built her a lath arbor, though, working furiously for a solid week in the hot sun. He'd set the arbor in the center of his new lawn, surrounding it with floribunda, and placed a small stone bench underneath. "We can all sit here when she comes back," he said, beaming at his handiwork. "When she comes back and we're a family again." Claire had looked at the bench, wedged between the two legs of the archway. In reality, it was only big enough for one adult and a child. Claire didn't mind. She didn't want to sit in the middle of his water-guzzling lawn, alone or with Mandy. Still, Jake might at least have thought to include her when he came up with his design.

She rose, carried the hatbox to the closet, and hoisted it

high above her head, shoving it far back on the top shelf where neither Jake nor Mandy would find it.

Chapter 24: She's Back

"She's here," Jake boomed from the living room. "They just parked the car." From Mandy's room, where she was tidying up, Claire could hear his pent-up energy. His voice got deeper when he was on edge, but it lost some of its timbre. "They're not coming in." *Relief.* "They never do." *A dig at Rita, who couldn't wait to be rid of her daughter.* "Mandy's coming up the walk now." *Triumph.*

Claire swiped the dust cloth over the windowsill, gave the Strawberry Shortcake quilt a final shake, and propped the little girl's favorite teddy bear on the pillow. Jake had barely mentioned his daughter for months, so it jarred Claire now to hear him keep repeating her name. He'd begun a couple of days ago. Once he started, he couldn't seem to stop. It was Mandy this and Mandy that, over and over. He'd find any excuse: "Gonna stock up on peanut butter for Mandy's lunch," "Gotta patch that bad tire on Mandy's bike," "Wonder how long it'll take Mandy to notice the new arbor?" as if he'd just been released from a vow. Claire was glad he'd broken his silence. It had been a cloud, a small cloud, over an otherwise idyllic summer. Still, as she listened to him repeat the name until it almost became an incantation, she wondered what it had cost him not to say it all these months, to excise Mandy, or try to, from his mind.

The image of Sarah, still and silent in the crib, flashed before her without warning. No time for her daughter now, Claire thought, pushing the image away and wondering, for a fleeting second as she did so, what *that* was costing *her.*

She hurried off to the living room, arriving just as Mandy burst through the front door.

"Hi Daddy," she said, in her high, breathy voice. She looked at Jake from under her lashes and swished her purple suitcase to and fro. She was wearing a new Disneyland tee shirt with Minnie Mouse in a polka-dotted hair bow on the front. She seemed different. Taller, of course, but it was more than that. She seemed more defined.

"Hi Claire," she said, her voice dropping half an octave. Her round, lash-rimmed eyes slid between her father and stepmother, as if she were watching a tennis match. When the ball stopped mid-air, she fixed her gaze behind it. "Here I am!" she said, spreading her arms out wide. Despite her confident stance, her eyes were wary.

Jake grabbed her under her shoulders and began to

whirl her around and around. As her legs flew out, one of her leather sandals sailed off, smacking Claire in the belly. Instinctively, Claire clapped her hands over her blouse. Locked in their spinning embrace, Jake and Mandy didn't notice.

Claire sidled along the wall—flinching with each rotation—and thought about the summer she and Jake had spent without Mandy. The child had just returned but, already, those halcyon weeks seemed distant as a dream.

As she watched Mandy's legs fly by, Claire's anger welled. Narrow eyed, she counted their rotations. *Five, six, seven...*she squeezed her lips together and felt pressure build behind them. She couldn't recapture the summer idyll, not with Mandy around. But that didn't mean she was powerless. *Nine, ten, eleven...*

"Daddy, you're hurting me," the girl shrieked. "Daddy, stop! You're making me dizzy! Put me down!" she yelled.

Claire let the feet—one bare, one shod—complete another orbit before saying, "Put her down." Her voice was low, but its effect was immediate.

On the ground again, Mandy giggled and staggered around, rolling her eyes. Arms akimbo, Jake watched her, beaming.

"I'm going to have a baby," Claire said, astonished by the baldness of her declaration. She could almost see the words hanging in the air.

"A baby!" Mandy screeched, even before she'd regained her balance. "Claire!" she screamed, her eyes fastened on Claire's belly.

Jake stood frozen, for once oblivious of his daughter. What was he thinking? Claire wondered. She was sure he welcomed the news, but she should have told him earlier, by last night at the latest, the way she'd planned. She had tried to find the moment, to frame the announcement, but the words never came.

She scrutinized his face for signs of fear or anger. There were none. Instead, his eyes were unusually bright and his throat muscles worked beneath his beard, causing it to wobble. His smile started slowly, but kept expanding until it seemed to encompass his beard, his cheekbones, his entire being. She was glad that Mandy was here to see the way his smile spread. He's absorbing the news, Claire thought—*my* news—and felt her power ripple through the room.

He walked toward her, arms outstretched like a blind man's, then stopped.

"Are you *sure*?" he asked, his arms dipping.

Claire nodded and felt her color rise. She *wasn't* positive. She hadn't seen a doctor yet. Didn't need to, she'd told herself. After all, hadn't she been a mother before? Wouldn't a mother just know?

Now Jake was rushing forward and it was *her* turn to be

swept into his arms.

"Wonderful," he said in a husky voice, as he clamped her to his chest. "*You* are wonderful," he murmured, swaying the two of them from side to side.

As Claire laid her cheek on his chest, she caught sight of Mandy. The little girl's eyes were downcast; her shoulders drooped; her purple suitcase lay forgotten on the floor. She looks bereft, Claire thought, wishing again she hadn't sprung the news so suddenly.

"Such perfect timing," Jake was saying.

The words needled. *Perfect timing*? What was he talking about? Her timing was terrible. She understood that now. Why didn't he? She should have told *him* first—privately. Together they could have planned how and when to tell Mandy.

"Perfect," Jake repeated, emphatically.

Claire backed away. Was he being sarcastic—the way he was about Rita? She watched him remove his glasses and wipe the corners of his eyes. He paused to look at her, the glasses dangling from his thumb and index finger. His eyes were a velvet brown. For several moments, they lingered on her, drinking her in as if nothing and no one else existed. Then, they pivoted toward his daughter. He slipped on his glasses, scooting them up the bridge of his nose, coughed, and cleared his throat.

"Claire's going to have a baby," he said, beaming as he stepped toward Mandy.

The little girl stared at the floor and shuffled her feet.

Jake knelt and placed his hands on her sagging shoulders. "That means *you* are going to have a little brother or sister," he said, shaking her gently.

Her eyes stayed on the floor. Her shoulders stiffened.

"Hey Mandy, *look* at me," he said, shaking her a little harder. "You're gonna *love* being a big sister."

No response.

"Won't she?" he asked, glancing at Claire for corroboration.

Claire opened her mouth to speak. Nothing came out. Her thoughts were going every which way. Try as she would, she couldn't harness them. But Jake had already returned to his daughter.

"You'll be old enough to hold and feed and burp the baby," he told her. The *b*'s came out in puffs. "You'll *love* that." He smiled broadly and chucked Mandy under the chin. "You'll even be old enough to change its diapers," he winked at Claire, "only if you want to, though," he added quickly, feeling his daughter recoil. "It'll be just like having your own live doll."

Clare couldn't see the child's face, but her body was rigid. Had Mandy ever seen an infant? Or even owned a doll, a real doll, not one that looked like Barbie?

She watched Mandy take a breath, eyes still lowered. It was a long, deep breath that filled her chest and bloated her cheeks. She held it—until her face turned crimson, until Claire thought she'd burst or faint. Then, in a sudden gust, she let out all the air and looked up, shoulders squared. There was the smile—the strapped-on smile, the same smile Claire had seen the day she first met Mandy.

Lynne McKelvey

Chapter 25: Swap

Jake had made spaghetti and garlic bread to celebrate Mandy's homecoming. There'd been no chance for Claire and him to talk; Mandy was always around. The day kept going, unrolling like an endless spool. Would night never come? Claire had lost all sense of time.

As the three of them gathered around the kitchen table, Jake set a heaping plate in front of Claire. She was starving. She couldn't remember ever being this hungry. As she devoured the spaghetti, slurping the slippery strands into her mouth, Jake beamed approvingly.

"Eat," he said, adding extra chunks of avocado to the salad on her plate. He sat across from her, Mandy by his side.

Claire crammed the salad into her mouth then tore off the middle section from the loaf of garlic bread. She ate and ate but still felt hungry—a clear sign of pregnancy, wasn't it?—though she couldn't remember being particularly hungry when she was carrying Sarah.

"Eat," Jake said, leaning forward. He watched her eagerly, his chin propped on his hands.

"Eat," said Mandy, mimicking his pose.

They nodded approvingly as Claire gobbled more food. Still famished, she reached for the heel of the loaf. Mandy's arm darted out. Her fingers closed over Claire's. As the girl tightened her grip, the brittle crust cracked and butter from the soft white center oozed onto Claire's palm. Still Mandy hung on, their fused hands moving back and forth across an invisible line.

Mandy let go without warning, and Claire's hand snapped back, clutching the crust.

"Take it," the child said. "Take the bread. You can have it. You and your baby." She smiled a smile Claire hadn't seen before—a long, thin smile that covered her teeth like a seam.

"Take it," Jake rumbled amiably. "She wants you to." He put his arm around his daughter.

Claire unclenched her fingers and stared at the slick lump in her hand. It was riddled with crumbs and dense as clay.

"Eat," Jake said, smiling approval.

"Eat," said Mandy, her ringed eyes large and bright.

To Claire's surprise, Mandy headed for her room right after dinner. She smiled her new thin smile and glided by the sofa, not looking at the two adults sitting there. Midway down the hall, she stopped and shut the door behind her so quietly it barely clicked.

Claire turned to Jake.

"I shouldn't have told her like that," she began.

"Like what?" Jake asked. His forehead creased as he rewound the day.

"You know, so suddenly. Out of the blue. Practically the moment she came home." Claire paused, looked down, and pinched the fabric on the cushion. "I should have told you first," she said in a low voice, "before she got back. We could have told her together. Not even right away, but maybe in a month or two, when I'm further along and she's settled in school."

"It's such wonderful news." Jake said quietly, when she'd finished. "I'm glad she knows *now*." He looked at Claire, searching her face. "I don't like secrets," he said, and leaned over and kissed her on the lips.

The calm finality of his words disconcerted Claire, more than if he'd been upset. She wanted to point out to him that children often worry they'll be displaced by a new sibling. For Mandy, given her cold mother, her parents' acrid divorce, and a new stepmother, this fear could fester. Once the baby was born—unless they were constantly vigilant—Mandy might even…she looked at Jake smiling his fond smile, his eyes flat and steady, his capable hands resting on his knees, and knew her words would pass right through him. Much as Jake loved his daughter, in many ways they were strangers.

Now black with night, the windowpanes looked inward, mirroring Jake and Claire sitting slightly apart on the sofa, hands folded in their laps staring at their reflections. Except for the hiss of sprinklers on the front lawns and the occasional rustle of a car in the street, all was quiet. Claire's thoughts—the thoughts she hadn't spoken—still hovered in the air, inchoate motes darting this way and that and drifting steadily down.

A loud thump from Mandy's room, followed by several thuds, broke the silence. Claire half rose, but Jake's arm barred her. "Leave her be," he said quietly, sliding closer to Claire. He brushed back a strand of hair from her face and kissed her lightly on the forehead. "She's just settling in." He lifted Claire's legs into his lap and began to massage her feet. His hands worked steadily, rhythmically, kneading the muscles, the metatarsal bones, the thin, taut skin.

Through the wall on the other side of the hall, the noises continued but Jake didn't seem to notice them. As the minutes passed, Claire settled back and wondered vaguely what he was thinking about. She felt too relaxed to ask him. Maybe Mandy's changed, she told herself as Jake rubbed her instep. The little girl had never left them alone for this long before. Maybe she was becoming more independent. That augured well for the year ahead. If so, Jake was right, though not in the way he intended. Claire's timing *was* good. Now she was nine, Mandy wouldn't need her daddy the way she had before. He'd have more time for his wife and their new baby.

In the hallway, a door opened and shut. There was a scraping sound, as if a large heavy object were being dragged somewhere. Then all was silent. More than an hour had elapsed, Claire guessed, too lazy to look at her watch. After dinner, usually, all three of them rushed around cleaning up the kitchen, drawing Mandy's bath, getting her ready for bed. But tonight there was no hurry. School didn't start for another week. Claire had no gardens that needed her immediate attention. Her eyelids drooped. While Jake thumbed the hollows beside her anklebones, she pictured Mandy engrossed in a book or playing with her Barbies. The child was growing up, all right. Claire felt full and warm, like an animal in its den.

"Gotta run to Builder's Emporium, I'm outta *Dap*." Jake's low voice reverberated off the walls of her cave. "They close at nine." He gave her feet a final squeeze and lifted her legs off his lap.

"You asleep, Claire?"

"Mmmmm," she mumbled, opening her eyes with an effort.

"I won't be long," he said, kissing her belly. "Why don't you turn in?" He dug in his pocket for his keys.

"Why don't you take Mandy?" she asked as he started for the door. "She hasn't seen you all summer." It would be good for Jake and Mandy to spend some time alone now. "You could stop at 31 Flavors on the way back."

She stifled a yawn and struggled to her feet. "I'll get her. You go start the car."

Mandy's door was open, and her lights were off. Claire peered into the dark room, wondering if the little girl was asleep. But the bed was smooth and flat. When Claire turned on the light, her fingers stayed on the switch. The room was unrecognizable. Instead of the Strawberry Shortcake quilt, Jake and Claire's queen-sized chenille spread covered the bed, its fringed edges pooling on the floor. The toy chest was gone. Four dents in the carpet were the only sign it had ever been there. Mandy's clown lamp with its bulbous red nose had also disappeared. In its place was Claire's bedside lamp; beside it, the book she'd been reading lay open, face down, just as she'd left it. In the bedroom she shared with Jake.

Still in the doorway, Claire looked around the room. Smudged rectangles outlined where Mandy's pictures used to hang. The shiny bottles and tubes that had covered the wicker vanity were gone. Claire's bathrobe was draped across the padded bench. She stepped through the doorway, her shadow lengthening as she entered the room. She already knew what she'd find in the closet: all of Mandy's clothes had been replaced by Claire's. One by one, she looked in the dresser drawers and saw her own sweaters and tee shirts, bras and panties, hastily folded, but orderly.

When she raised her head, her eyes met Rita's eyes, smiling icily from the glittering frame. Repelled, Claire stepped away, backing into the end of Mandy's bed. Unable to shift her gaze, she stared at the photograph and wondered why Mandy had left it behind. The footboard dug into her calves as she studied the picture and the artifacts ranked in front of it. Everything was there—the gold candle, the tiny heart-shaped box, the porcelain cat, and the miniature pearl necklace. All were in their proper places, with the purse-sized mirror perched on its makeshift easel at the edge of the dresser, silvered side out. Still, something about the display looked different. She scanned the objects once more, then sat down on the end of bed. Instantly, the small objects disappeared, sunk below her newly raised horizon. Now, only the photograph remained in her line of sight. Claire's eyes locked with Rita's, and she realized what had changed. Where once the picture was turned sideways on the dresser top so that Mandy couldn't see her mother from the bed—or, more likely, so Rita couldn't look at *her*—now it faced the bed dead on. Claire stared at the photograph and shivered. Without the ranks of appeasing gifts in view, Rita's eyes seemed even colder. They followed Claire when she turned her head. When she closed her own eyes, they monitored each breath.

Jake honked the horn, startling Claire. A second honk. She hurried to the window, raised the sash, and poked out her head. "Come here," she called to him, her voice low, but the words unmistakable. "You need to come in here right now." She ran into the hall, not waiting for his reply, but stopped short at the closed door to their bedroom. Below her, yellow light seeped from under the door and onto the hall carpet. As she flung the door open, she heard the jingle of Jake's keys, approaching. In front of her, in their bed, she saw Mandy. The little girl was tucked under the Shortcake quilt, wearing a candy-striped nightgown and surrounded by Barbies. Propped up on pillows, she lay on Claire's side of the bed. Claire stood in the doorway and stared into the room. Jake came up behind her. The tip of his beard grazed the top of her head. Mandy looked at them both appraisingly, then flashed her smile, stretching it wide.

Jake sucked in his breath.

"Amanda Wethers," he bellowed above Claire's head. "What in God's name have you been up to?"

Claire moved aside and retreated into the hall. Jake seemed huge, his shoulders filling the doorway, blocking out light from the clown lamp on the bedside table. He leaned into the door jamb, one-on-one with his daughter. The front of his body was lit, the back was dark, like the two sides of the moon. Claire couldn't see his face, though she saw Mandy's clearly. The child's smile was as wide as ever, but it had lost its give.

Jake scanned the tilting pictures on the walls, the thicket of tiny bottles on the dresser, the toy chest angling out from the footboard of the bed. He looked at his daughter and shook his head—sharp, definite movements from left to right. Mandy burrowed herself back into the pillows. Her eyelids flickered. Jake's head was still, but his shoulders started to jiggle—loose, rubbery movements, up and down. Mandy stared at her father, at his bouncing shoulders. Her eyes opened wide, and her jaw went slack. She clapped her hand over her mouth and peered out above her fingertips at Claire. A high staccato laugh erupted behind the fan. Jake, guffawing, joined in. Claire felt a fist in her throat. Father and daughter laughed out loud, treble and bass. Still laughing, Jake lunged toward the bed, scooped up Mandy, draping her over his arms, and held her in front of him like a trophy. Her black curls, perpendicular to her body, swung to and fro. She turned her head in Claire's direction. Their eyes locked.

"You monkey," Jake said, nuzzling her. "You little, little monkey." He sounded affectionate and something more: he sounded proud. "Bet you're all tuckered out." He dipped his head and looked at her. "Bet you're too tuckered out to go to Baskin Robbins."

The fanned fingers fluttered, and the child's bare feet beat the air, but her gaze never left her stepmother's face. The fist in Claire's throat flexed to the point she could barely breathe.

"Hurry up kiddo. You gotta get dressed." Jake set Mandy on her feet and ruffled her hair.

"But this room," Claire said. "All of this…"

"Oh, we'll deal with it later," Jake said, running his fingers through Mandy's hair. He lifted the thick, glossy strands on the top of her head and combed them back into a peak. "We'll deal with everything just as soon as we get back. Right Mandy?" He leaned away and inspected his handy work, then patted the mound of hair. When it was flat and smooth again, he gave the child's bottom a light, propelling whack. As she scurried toward the bureau, Claire stared at Jake, but she hardly saw him. He was fading before her eyes like the messages she and her brother used to write each other with disappearing ink.

Mandy hadn't faded, though. As she dashed around the room—opening drawers, the closet door, grabbing jeans, a tee shirt, a pair of shoes—a spotlight seemed to follow her. Just as she reached for one of the tiny bottles of cologne she'd placed on Claire's bureau, Claire found herself inside the circle of light, her fingers clamped around Mandy's wrists.

"What are you doing?" she heard herself shout. Mandy flinched. "You're not going out," Claire yelled. "No. Not until you've put *everything* back." She tightened her grip, feeling huge as she loomed over the child. "This is *not* your room. You are *never* to come in here, not without permission." Mandy's arteries throbbed beneath Claire's fingers. She felt the fragility of the little girl's bones. "Do you hear me, Mandy? Do you understand?"

Mandy studied Claire's face with a new expression; respectful, even awed. Cheeks flaming, she looked at the floor and nodded. Jake cleared his throat, and the child's head whipped around to face him. "Better listen up," he said in his deepest baritone. And winked.

Mandy looked at Claire again, the girl's eyes now bold, their expression cunning. "But I'm giving you *my* room, Claire," she said, in a velvet voice. "It's my *present*"—ducking her head with a smile and a blush and tucking in her chin—"for you and your baby." She tugged at the manacles around her wrists—a small, reminding tug, as if Claire must have forgotten she was still holding Mandy prisoner.

Claire let go and watched the little girl float toward her father. Silently, in slow-motion, the two of them bounded and bent in tandem, taking down pictures, opening and emptying out drawers. The pink quilt billowed, light as a parachute, when they lifted it from the bed. They wafted around the bedroom and across the hall to Mandy's room then back again, like moon-walkers, weightless but focused on their tasks. Claire marveled at their buoyancy. Her own body felt heavy and dense.

Once they'd left—laughing, flushed, racing one another to the car—Claire wandered through the house. Everything was back the way it was before, but nothing seemed familiar. In the master bedroom, Claire hardly recognized her sweaters piled in the bottom drawer, her jacket hanging on a closet hook, the book face down on the table next to her side of the bed. She ran her hand over the white chenille spread, fingering the nubby ridges as if they were Braille.

Was it only this morning that Mandy had been in Riverside and she and Jake were lying here? She clutched the fabric and remembered how he'd played with Mandy's hair. In her mind, she saw him clearly, framed by the doorway, limned against the darkness of the hall. As he'd ruffled the glossy strands, he'd seemed oblivious to everything else—to Claire and even to Mandy. Claire squeezed the spread until her knuckles turned white then let go, leaving a puckered mound on the surface of the bed.

A Real Daughter

FALL 1979

Lynne McKelvey

Chapter 26: Tide-Pooling

They teetered barefoot on the wrinkled rocks that lined the shore, mother and child, hand in hand. The newest wave foamed toward them. It swirled around their legs, ringing their ankles with salt and sand, then hissed its retreat. The offshore wind ruffled the woman's hair, the child's longer, brighter hair, and brought color to their cheeks before heading, heavy with brine, toward the open water. Far down the beach, in silhouette, a dog romped with its master.

The child dropped her mother's hand and crouched beside a shallow, just-filled pool. "Look Mommy," she said, pointing to a purple mound in the pool, "Is that a baby porcupine?"

Claire squatted beside her daughter and studied the creature. It was globular with spines. "Well, it sure has enough stickers to be one," she said, touching its back gingerly. "I think it's a sea urchin, though. Usually they're submerged..."—she caught the child's blank expression—"you know, completely under water all the time like fish," she explained. "But when the tide's low, like now, they're stuck on land."

Sarah curled her body over her folded knees and laid her cheek against the ground. She squinted at the urchin. "Does it have legs, Mommy?" she asked. "Can it walk? Can it swim?"

"Not really, Punkin." Claire's fingers glided through her daughter's hair streaming over the black rocks. "Mostly it just stays put."

"But how does it eat? Where's its mouth?"

"Underneath it, Punkin, in the middle of its body. We'd have to pick the urchin up and turn it over to see." Sarah made a face. "Not a good idea, I agree," Claire said with a laugh.

The little girl sat up and looked at the bare terrain surrounding the tide pool. "But what does it eat, Mommy?" she asked, her brow creasing. "There's nothing here."

The rocks had dented the child's cheek. Claire brushed away the clinging grains of sand.

"It has to wait for the tide to come in and then wait some more for its dinner, things like plants or small animals, to float by. Its spines can trap stuff like algae or small crabs and wave them toward its mouth."

"Poor thing," Sarah said, looking at the sea urchin. "It

must hate being stuck in one place all the time, just waiting and waiting." She wagged her head from left to right. "I bet it gets hungry."

"I bet you're right," Claire said, smiling at her daughter. "But really, it doesn't have a choice. If it lived in deep water, other animals, predators, would eat it. If it lived on land, it would starve. Living between the land and water is the only way it can survive."

A volley of barks rang out. Sarah's head spun toward the sound. "Look Mommy," she shouted. "There's a dog chasing a Frisbee." She scrambled to her feet. "Oooo, look at him run!"

Claire followed Sarah's gaze. The man and dog she'd seen earlier were right below them on the sand now. The man was lunging forward, one arm outstretched, face to the sky, while the dog, large with a dun-colored coat, tore down the beach, its four legs a blur. Suddenly the dog's body arced high above the ground, attaining what seemed like an impossible height for its bulky frame. Airborne, it caught the spinning disk, landed without a stutter, gave a celebratory toss of its head, and, trophy held high, trotted toward its master.

"Good catch, Buddy," the man said, holding up two thumbs. "C'mere, boy, and we'll do it again."

The dog stopped, sat, and cocked its head.

"C'mon, boy," the man urged. "Let's see you do it

again." He pursed his lips and whistled.

The dog shook his head.

Sarah giggled.

Claire rose to her feet, smiled at her daughter, and took the child's hand. "Which way now, Punkin?" she asked. "Up toward the cliffs? Down to the water?"

Sarah didn't reply. Her eyes were fixed on the dog.

"If we go higher," Claire persisted, "we can look for periwinkle snails. They live where only the spray can reach them."

Still no response.

"Or," Claire continued, pumping enthusiasm into her voice and giving Sarah's hand a squeeze, "we could try to find a sea star or an anemone nearer the low tide mark."

Silence. Had Sarah even heard her?

The dog stood up and pointed toward its master.

"C'mon, Buddy" the man cajoled. "C'mere, boy. It'll be fun."

For a moment the animal stood perfectly still. Abruptly, it feinted toward the man, wheeled around, and galloped off in the opposite direction, its pace barely slowing as it plunged into the churning water. Frisbee aloft, it breasted the waves, swimming toward Japan.

Sarah jumped up and down, hooting with laughter.

As if aware of its audience, the dog switched course and

surfed the waves back to the shore. Once on land, it streaked toward Sarah and Claire—ignoring its master's calls and whistles—then scrambled up and over the rocks and skidded to a stop in front of Sarah. Panting noisily, it laid the Frisbee at the little girl's feet.

Sarah wiggled her hand free of her mother's grip and clapped.

The dog raised its head and sidled closer to the child. It shook itself, long and hard, soaking both mother and daughter. Sarah doubled over with laughter. The dog gave a final shake and sat down, its head cocked, its pink tongue lolling out between its teeth.

Sarah's eyes shone. Before Claire could stop her, she'd reached her hand out and begun petting the dog behind its ears. "It's okay, Mommy," she said, sensing Claire's alarm. "This dog and me are friends."

She stroked the dog's sodden back for several moments, making little crooning sounds, then picked up the Frisbee. The dog sprang to attention, its body quivering from nose to tail. Although she threw with all her might, the Frisbee barely cleared the rocks before it dropped, rim first, into the sand.

The dog ambled over, sniffed the disk, and seemed about to walk away but changed its mind. After much maneuvering, it managed to nose and paw the Frisbee into its mouth. It looked toward Sarah, then toward the man, who stood with his arms folded over his chest. He seemed to have given up calling. Once more, the dog looked from man to child and back again while they awaited its decision. Then, with the Frisbee firm between its jaws and head held high, the dog trotted toward the man at a sure and steady pace.

While Sarah watched their reunion, Claire climbed higher on the rocks. She looked out to sea. Although it was nearly noon, tatters of the night's mist still hung in the sky. The sun was white behind the scrim. Sky and sea were neither blue nor gray, but a nameless shade in between. Claire searched for the horizon, but stare as she might, she could not find the single, definite line she sought, the blade that would make the separation absolute.

Chapter 27: Boxes

"Claire," Mandy called from the bedroom doorway, "have you seen my Barbie's gold crown?"

Claire was in the closet, organizing boxes on the top shelf. From her vantage point on the stepstool, all she could see of Mandy were her denim bell-bottoms and her white sneakers shifting impatiently in the doorway. "Come on in," she said, the hanging clothes muffling her voice. These days, Mandy waited to be invited.

"I've looked and looked for it," said Mandy, lunging over the threshold and rushing past the many boxes that covered the bed. She stood panting at the base of the stool, her salmon-colored tee shirt pale beneath the brightness of her cheeks. "How can my Barbie be prom queen without her gold crown?" she demanded, face tilted up toward Claire, arms akimbo. "How *can* she?" Her voice had an urgent edge.

Claire slid a heavy brown carton off the shelf, backed gingerly down the steps, and set it on the crowded bed.

Mandy stared at the array of boxes. "What are you doing?" she asked.

"Spring cleaning," Claire replied, and wondered if she had vacuumed up the crown.

"What's in all these boxes?"

"Stuff."

"What kind of stuff?" Mandy edged closer to the bed.

"Books, papers, kitchen stuff from my cottage."

Mandy studied the cartons, lips pursed, the crown now forgotten.

"What's in this one?" Her finger arrowed to the hatbox, parchment colored and banded with black grosgrain ribbon.

"Don't touch that." Claire grabbed the hatbox and hoisted it out of the child's reach.

"Why not?" Mandy's eyes rolled upwards.

Claire tightened her grip and tried to think of a reply.

"Why not?" Mandy said again, standing on tiptoe and clawing the air below the box like an animal digging the ground.

Claire gazed at the little girl's raised arms. Her own arms ached from holding the box so high. It seemed heavier than she remembered, as if it contained not just the things she'd packed that snowy afternoon she'd left Vermont, but the things she'd left behind: the tiny white shoes Sarah had never grown into, the wooden beads she'd never learned to thread, the velvet Christmas dress she'd never worn. The box dug into Claire's palms. She shifted the weight.

"You just can't," she said, staggering up the stepladder and shoving the hatbox onto the closet shelf. "C'mon," she said, clapping her hand on Mandy's shoulder and steering the child out of the room. "I think I remember where I saw Barbie's crown."

She closed the door, and the boxes vanished.

Chapter 28: The Tar Pits

"Hey, Daddy. Look over there—elephants!" Mandy said, pointing to a cluster of animals with trunks and tusks on the other side of the lake. She tugged on her father. "Let's go check 'em out."

They were spending the afternoon at the La Brea Tar Pits, the ancient body of water in the center of Los Angles, repository of a million bones from animals trapped during the Ice Age. All around the lake were couples, many with children that scampered and screamed.

Couples. Claire repeated the word silently. She and Jake were one of those couples now, a couple with a child. And another on the way, she reminded herself, running her finger across her belly, which had not yet begun to swell.

She stared into the water. It reeked of asphalt and had a rainbow sheen. Dry leaves stuck to its viscous surface, unmoved by any breeze. Methane boiled up from below, forming opalescent domes. Mirrored in the dark water, the city's ubiquitous palm trees, their skinny, cross-hatched trunks topped with shaggy fronds, thrust downward, sweeping the lake's invisible floor. Ridiculous-looking, thirsty trees, Claire thought, squinting as she looked up at the actual palms clustered along the shore. They offered neither edible fruit nor shade, yet generation after generation, the city kept planting them.

"Good idea," Jake said, beaming at his daughter. "Only those aren't elephants, Mandy. They're mastodons. Replicas of mastodons," he corrected, clearing his throat. "Real mastodons died out fifteen thousand years ago." He smiled into his beard and squeezed Claire's hand.

While Mandy skipped on ahead, he slipped his arm around Claire's waist and steered her down the path that curved around the lake toward the mastodons. As Claire moved, the hem of her new dress—a light cotton print with a gathered skirt and a bodice that showed off her still slim torso—brushed her bare legs. Jake's fingers slid over the curve of her hip, and she felt a current of pleasure. She breathed in and found herself savoring the acrid air.

The mastodons were life-size replicas, large, but not gigantic. There were three of them, two adults—the parents, most likely—and a baby. One of the adults, the father, Claire supposed, was half immersed in the lake, mired in the tarry bottom, not far from the shore. With its one free foot, it pawed the water's surface. Its head was thrown back; its trunk, fisted at the tip and raised, was framed by the long parentheses of its tusks; its mouth was wide open, as if in a roar. Watching the struggling animal were the other mastodons; the mother, surely, with its four feet planted firmly on dry land and the baby, contained between the guard-rails of the mother's tusks. The baby's small trunk stretched straight out, reaching toward its hapless parent.

Despite the warm sun, Claire shivered. "Poor little thing," she said. "Do you suppose it knows that's its father?" She gestured toward the animal trapped in the lake.

"Probably," Jake said. "If mastodons were anything like elephants, they'd have had close family ties." He paused, looked at Claire, and smiled. "By the way," he said, pushing back a strand of hair from her forehead, "It's the mother that's stuck. The father's taking care of the baby."

Claire studied the two animals safe on shore. Beside her, she heard Mandy suck in air, but Claire kept her eyes on the mastodons. Jake must be mistaken, she decided. The adult was so close to its baby, so protective. That mastodon had to be the baby's mother.

"Says so on the sign," Jake rumbled. Claire didn't argue. Jake was usually right about his facts.

She shifted her gaze to the mastodon in the lake and felt a familiar horror well. *The still form in the crib.* Though she could scarcely breathe, she couldn't look away from the trapped animal. That mother mastodon knew she was about to die. Her hunger pangs would grow acute. Attracted by her thrashings and cries, predators would descend, even as she starved; saber-tooth cats lunging from the shore, huge birds swooping from the sky. They'd devour her alive. The mother knew all this. And she knew she was losing her child.

A small figure blurred by Claire, grazing her elbow and interrupting her reverie. She watched Mandy race to the shore. The girl entered the lake and began to slog, ankle deep in the oily muck, toward the mother mastodon.

"Mandy!" Jake bellowed, bolting after his daughter. He leaned over the inky water, his legs braced on land, grabbed the girl under the armpits, then dragged her—red faced, lips sealed and white, cheeks ballooning, body flat and heavy as a board—onto the muddy bank.

"What in God's name were you doing?" he shouted. He pulled her upright, keeping his grip on her shoulders. She was still holding her breath and seemed unwilling to stand. "What's the matter with you?" he said, shaking her hard. Mandy stared at his glasses, fiery as they reflected the afternoon sun. "This is a *tar* pit, for Christ's sake. Did you think you were at the beach?" The girl blinked hard but didn't reply.

Claire looked at the two of them, the looming man and

the rigid child, and felt her stomach clench. How could he be so harsh? Couldn't he see how upset his daughter was? Claire considered intervening. But what could she say or do? She'd only make things worse. Whenever Mandy saw Claire, the girl's first thought, still, was "she's not my mom."

Mandy exhaled without warning, her cheeks collapsing with a whoosh. All at once the child looked old, weary and hollowed out. She wiggled free of her father's grasp. Her eyes travelled back and forth between the mastodon in the water and the two mastodons on land.

"He could have helped her," she said, barely opening her mouth and looking at her tar-spattered shoes.

"No way," Jake said emphatically, almost before her words were out. "He'd have got *himself* stuck. *Then* who'd take care of the baby?" It was his "gotcha" tone. His mouth expanded in a victor's smile.

"He could have helped her," Mandy repeated, hands balled, toe kicking the wet grass.

"What rot," Jake said, the corners of his mouth drawing together. "These animals don't even exist anymore." He tapped the father mastodon's metal leg. "They aren't even real."

The little girl lifted her head and took a deep breath but didn't hold it.

"He could have tried," she said, looking straight at her

father, through his glasses, which no longer reflected the sun, and right into his eyes. "Even if he hated her, he could have tried."

Jake made a guttural noise. "That's enough, Mandy," he said, his voice tight. "Time to leave." He grabbed her wrist and pulled her toward the park exit. His strides were long and brisk. The child stumbled to keep up. "C'mon. Claire," he called over his shoulder, almost as an afterthought.

Claire followed slowly. The distance between them increased.

He doesn't get it, she thought, pausing beside the baby mastodon and its imploring trunk. Doesn't get that Mandy is a child in mourning, a child in mourning for her mother. The fact that Rita really never was a mother only made Mandy's grief more desperate, made her sadder, angrier, more frightened and alone.

"Claire. Claire. Claire."

Side by side at the top of the path, Jake and Mandy were gesturing and calling her name in unison.

Claire waved back. She resumed her journey, but just before she took the first step, she glanced down at her skirt and drew a sharp breath. Above the rippling hemline, was a black smear, broad as a thumb.

Chapter 29: The Discovery

Claire turned into the driveway and parked the truck. Jake's Mustang was gone. He and Mandy must be off running errands. She'd have the house to herself. She could use some rest and solitude. She'd spent the day bent-backed, pulling weeds and sweeping walkways in Althea's garden. The garden was a year old now and Althea was throwing a party to celebrate. Claire would be the guest of honor. In spite of her aching back, Claire smiled. She'd never had a client more delighted with a garden.

Claire slid to the ground and closed the cab door. As she was entering the back yard, her pant leg caught on a straggly plant. Its white trumpet flowers were gone, but the smooth, undulating leaves, dark green on top and light green underneath, the sturdy stem, and the spiny seed pods that now replaced the flowers were unmistakable. The jimsonweed was thigh high. She ought to have dug it up long ago. For a moment, she hesitated. Her spade was in the truck bed, only an arm's length away. But she'd done enough digging for one day. She headed for the kitchen door, with a long, loping stride.

A few minutes later, freshly showered and wearing clean jeans and tee shirt, she stood on tiptoe inside the bedroom closet and eased the hatbox off the shelf. She hadn't opened it in months, not since before Mandy left for the summer. Usually Claire sat on the edge of the bed, the box unopened in her lap, and waited for the drumbeats to sound. But today for some reason, she was in a hurry. She found herself tugging at the black ribbons and prying off the round cover even before she'd set the box down on the bed. Usually she removed one item at a time, feeling its texture with her fingers, with her lips, holding it to her nostrils and inhaling its fragrance before putting it back in the box. But today she poured out the entire contents of the box, even the white blanket and the manila envelope at the very bottom, and spread them over the bed. For the first time in seven years, the hatbox was completely empty. She could see everything it contained. Almost everything, she corrected herself. She picked up the bulging envelope, threaded the splayed brass prongs through the eyelet on the flap and removed the photographs inside. Roger had taken them. Claire never took any herself. How could a daughter be captured in a moment of time?

She set the pictures face down on top of the manila envelope without looking at them, then cleared a space and seated herself on the bed. She placed her hands on her belly, probing the flesh with her fingers, but felt no movements, no bulges, nothing. Perhaps it was still too early. She started to count the weeks since her period—there'd been only the one—but stopped abruptly. How could she think about the shrimp-like creature growing inside her when all around her were the relics of Sarah's life? Was she forgetting her dead daughter? Would Sarah still come to her once the new baby was born? Claire wondered, and for a moment couldn't breathe. She picked up the tiny undershirt that fastened at the side and rubbed it against her cheek. She closed her eyes and softly began to hum.

Lullaby, and good night,
Wi-ith roses be dight.

In a corner of her mind, she thought she heard a door open then close. But she kept on humming, louder now to drive the sounds away.

Wi-ith lilies be decked,
O'er ba-a-by's sweet...

The air stirred. There was a raspy breath, and a shadow moved across her sealed lids.

Her eyes flew open.

"Mandy," she gasped. The little girl stood in front of

her, a few inches from Claire's knees, her eyes devouring the objects on the bed. "You're supposed to *knock* before you come in," Claire said, and cursed herself for not shutting the bedroom door. "Where's your father?" She strained to hear Jake's footsteps, but the rest of the house was silent. He must have seen Claire's parked truck and dropped his daughter off before going on to run more errands, she decided, and wondered how to get the little girl out of the room.

"Clothes!" Mandy shrieked, her voice skidding up the scale. She lunged toward the bed, where Claire sat paralyzed and voiceless. "Clothes for your baby!" She pounced on the tiny pink sweater Claire's grandmother had knit.

"Mandy, wait," Claire said, grabbing the little girl's hands and pinning them down with her own. "These clothes aren't for the baby...not for *this* baby." She placed Mandy's hands on her abdomen. The child's gaze darted between the items on the bed and Claire's belly then halted on her face. "They belong to...another baby I had...once." Claire heard herself say, as if speaking from the depths of a well.

"*Another* baby?" Mandy stared at her, round eyed.

"Her name was Sarah," Claire said, looking down. "She died." Claire set the words side by side, balancing them precisely, as if in a scale's shallow pans, and braced for a torrent of questions.

To her surprise, Mandy merely nodded. "Oh," she said,

as if Claire had told her some small fact.

Claire took the sweater, smoothed it, and laid it on the bed out of Mandy's reach. But the little girl wasn't paying attention. She was watching Claire instead.

"What did Sarah look like?" she asked. "Was she pretty? Did she look like me?"

For a moment, their eyes locked. Then Mandy's gaze slid toward the pile of photos on top of the envelope. Her hand shot out and curled over them. With her free hand, she shoved aside the clothes and plopped herself down on the edge of the bed, squeezing in next to Claire.

"I'll take those," Claire said, her voice steely. She reached for the pictures, which Mandy relinquished without protest, and placed them in her lap. To her surprise, Claire found she too was curious to see them. She hadn't looked at them for years. Besides, noting Mandy's rapt expression, at this point, did she really have a choice? Mandy would hunt them down, no matter where Claire hid them.

She turned over the first picture. In it Sarah was nursing, her wide eyes fixed on Claire's, kneading her mother's breast with her tiny nails. Claire glanced at Mandy. The girl's face was inscrutable. Had she ever seen a baby nurse? Claire wondered. Rita had bottle fed her, of course, the bottle propped, most likely, when Jake wasn't around. Claire turned over the second picture, this one of Sarah and Claire asleep on a wide bed. Claire's arm curved around the baby's body, following its contour like a frame. In the third picture, Claire held Sarah high above her head. The baby was swimming in the air and laughing. Mandy shifted on the bed and began to draw jerky circles with her foot. In the next picture, Sarah was sitting in her mother's lap, Claire's body making a cave around her. The baby's face was puckered, her cheeks shiny with tears.

Mandy jabbed her heel into the side of the mattress.

"Sarah was a spoiled baby," she said, and jumped off the bed. "You hugged her too much."

She stomped toward the door.

"No wonder she died," she said, looking at Claire over her shoulder before she disappeared down the hall.

Chapter 30: The Serenade

Claire buttoned her jeans, newly ironed and a bit tight, and slipped a white peasant blouse over her head. The blouse, embroidered with leaves and flowers, was frillier than what she was used to; but Althea's party was a festive occasion. Claire felt anything but festive. She felt taut, like a bowstring someone was drawing back and back. But, who, exactly, was the archer? Where was the arrow headed? She closed her eyes and breathed in, hoping for answers.

Almost twenty-four hours had passed since Mandy learned about Sarah. Claire had been sure the girl would tell her father right away. Mandy loved to feel important. Even if she didn't understand everything about Claire's secret—how could she?—she understood its power. *Her* power now.

Claire had imagined the child sidling over to Jake, cheeks aglow. "Daddy," she'd say, puffing herself up, "Did you know Claire already had a baby?" While Mandy waited for her words to sink in, she'd parse Jake's expression, hoping he'd look surprised. "That baby's name was Sarah," she'd continue, her mouth stretched wide, framing her white teeth when she said the name. "Sarah died," mouth downward now, but eyes exulting. "Claire has a box with pictures and her dead baby's clothes in it. C'mon, Daddy," she'd say merrily, shaking her curls and taking Jake's wrist. "I'll show you where it is." And she'd give a little skip—Claire winced at the image—as if they were going off to Baskin Robbins.

But Mandy hadn't told her father. Why not? Claire wondered. Perhaps the girl believed she was taunting her stepmother, causing Claire, suspended in Mandy's new power, to twist and turn as she waited to be cut down. But the child had miscalculated. Now that Mandy knew her secret, it hardly mattered who else found out. This should have freed Claire, but it didn't.

For seven years, she'd had Sarah to herself. Here in California, far from her native Vermont, she'd dreamed about her daughter. She'd loved her, mourned her, watched her grow. Now, Mandy owned a part of Sarah. Never again would Sarah belong to Claire and Claire alone.

"Ready?" Claire started as Jake's voice boomed from the kitchen. She'd almost forgotten about the party. "Can't be late. You're the guest of honor!"

Claire mumbled something noncommittal and grabbed her hairbrush off the dresser. The Santa Ana winds had blown in from the desert overnight and the air was bone dry. Her hair stood on end as she brushed it, crackling with static electricity.

She set the brush down and patted the flyaway hairs. As she turned to go, she recalled the cabinet with the stacked drawers she'd once believed in: gardens, Sarah, Jake, and Mandy. She'd meant to keep them separated. Now, all but the garden drawer were off their runners, their contents scattered, mixed and mingled on the floor. She pictured the lone drawer in the cavity of the tall cabinet. There wasn't much point in keeping it there. Still, the thought of removing it made her sad.

Three abreast, they made their way up Althea's driveway, Claire in the middle, Jake on her left side, and Mandy—in a cotton-candy colored skirt and tee shirt—on the right. Claire paused for a moment to look at the garden. It still had a coltish appearance: the young trees seemed wobbly, and the wisteria at the base of the pergola's posts had barely begun its long climb to the roof. Between clumps of plants were patches of bare soil. But the rockrose and pink joey were filling in, Claire noted, and above the purple salvia, she caught the shimmer of a hummingbird's wings.

A dozen or so guests, casually dressed and clinking long-stemmed glasses, had spread themselves out on the tiered redwood steps that ran the length of the house. On the top step, in a saffron tunic and flowing, chocolate-colored pants, Althea stood like a queen, presiding over guests and garden. She spotted Claire at once, and ran to greet her.

"Isn't it exciting?" she exclaimed, hugging Claire and gesturing to the garden, while Mandy, squinting into the sun, gazed up at her. "Sometimes I sit out here, close my eyes, and just breathe. I never realized how delicious plain old earth can *smell.* I can't *wait* to see what it'll be like once the trees begin to grow." Without letting go of Claire, she held her free hand out to Jake. "Isn't she *wonderful?*" she said, hugging Claire tighter. Jake cleared his throat. But before he could say a word, Althea, in a single, swift movement, had dropped to her knees. "You must be Mandy," she said, taking the child's small hands in her own large ones and stroking them with her strong thumbs. For a moment, Mandy looked uncertain, her dark-ringed eyes frightened and thrilled, as if a giant mythical bird in bright plumage had just swooped down from the sky. "I see you like pink," Althea said, still massaging the girl's hands as she ran her eyes over Mandy's outfit. She gave the child a conspiratorial smile. "Me too," she stage whispered. Mandy tucked in her chin and beamed. "I have a special fizzy drink just for you," Althea said in her regular voice. "It matches your skirt. Wanna give it a try?" Mandy nodded, never taking her eyes off Althea as the woman stood, rising to a great height. Spellbound, the little girl followed her into the garden. "You guys come too," Althea called over her shoulder. "There's plenty of bubbly for grownups. None of it pink, though." Her laugh rippled into the afternoon.

An hour later, Althea again stood at the top of the steps, this time tapping her champagne glass with a fork. Now low in the sky, the sun bathed the garden, plants and bare patches alike, with a golden, unifying light. In a year, Claire reflected, the bald spots would vanish and all the plants would connect, no matter the time of day.

She closed her eyes and imagined the garden at midnight, its shapes vague or invisible, their textures and colors gone. Sounds unheard by day would lace the darkness, the chameleon calls of the mockingbird and the *hoo-hooty-hoo-hoo* of the great-horned owl. The scents of the plants would emerge—lavender, sage, and lemon verbena—stepping forth like actors from the wings. One by one they'd present themselves, their odors distinct at first but merging as night went on, bound together by the sharp salt smell of the sea.

She breathed in the smells surrounding her, those she could already detect and the ones awaiting her. She inhaled more deeply. She wanted to preserve these smells, bottle them up and take them with her. She remembered her grandmother lifting the lid of her marble jar on a long winter evening and breathing in the scent of the bouquet she'd carried more than fifty years before when she was a bride.

The ding of Althea's champagne glass broke Claire's reverie.

"I want to thank all of you for coming here to celebrate my garden's first birthday," Althea was saying.

Someone gave a cheer. Another person yelled, "right on!"

"You're all invited to come again next year," Althea continued, "when my garden turns two."

Everyone clapped. Several people stood up and were making motions to leave when Althea again struck her glass. "Before you go, though," she said, with a mischievous smile, "come on into the living room. I have a surprise."

Another round of applause, and the guests trooped inside.

As Claire turned to follow them, she noticed a stream of water jetting from the *hippocrepis* bed at the northwest corner of the house. Darn. The pressure regulator must be leaking. Tomás was off in Tijuana for his niece's *quinceañera*. Claire would have to drop by in the morning and fix it herself.

She took a last look around the garden, mounted the stairs, and stepped inside. Now that the huge cypresses no longer blocked the windows and French door, light streamed into the living room, reflecting off the bright Mexican folk art on the walls and pooling on the polished floor. Althea's

Guarneri lay on the grand piano beside its plush-lined case. Claire felt a little thrill. Perhaps she was going to play something.

Althea ushered Claire to a wing-backed chair near the middle of the room opposite the curve of the piano. The other guests seated themselves on the sofa or folding chairs, whatever was available. Jake perched on an ottoman, Mandy sat cross-legged in front of him on the floor. Her dark eyes were fixed on Althea, as though she feared this magical being might disappear if she shifted her gaze, even for an instant.

Althea picked up her violin, checked the pitch of the open strings, and gave a little bow. The guests murmured, then grew silent. "For Claire," she said smiling, her eyes serious.

As she nestled the violin between her chin and collarbone, she seemed to be looking inside herself, even though her eyes were on Claire. She was gathering herself, the way a runner does at the start of a race. She closed her eyes for a moment, lids quivering, then took a breath and began to draw her bow across the strings.

"Twinkle Twinkle Little Star." Claire recognized the tune immediately. The simple melody entered her like a shaft, and for a moment she thought she was going to cry. Her grandmother sang the song to her mother, who sang it to her. In the sunlit nursery, she sang it to Sarah, rocking her daughter in her arms, feeling the warm, solid weight of her child.

The image of Althea stomping on the Sicilian boy's chest rose unbidden, then was gone.

The tune started again but this time with little turns and embellishments and then again with rapid runs and scales. Althea swayed with the music. Her fingers blurred on the neck of the violin. Each variation was longer and more complicated than the last, and soon the original melody was unrecognizable, though Claire knew it was there, powering the torrent of notes that poured into the room. Faster and faster, how could anyone's fingers move so swiftly? How did she know where to press them on the strings? How could a small wooden box bring forth so much sound?

Claire thought of her own box: tall, cylindrical, and tied with black ribbons. It too contained music of a sort.

Althea's body kept moving, accompanying her fingers like a tall tree bending while the wind rushes through its leaves. The music built and its pace quickened. Her forehead was beaded with sweat. Her lips were parted. She was breathing hard. She paused, her bow hovering for an instant over the strings. Then she began a series of chords and arpeggios that started low but hurled themselves upwards to the very highest register of the violin. When they reached their summit, the music suddenly stopped, its recent notes suspended in the middle of the room. Claire leaned forward expectantly, knowing the piece wasn't over, but wondering what could possibly follow such a display. Once more, Althea gathered herself, drawing inward, but in a different way. Her eyes met Claire's, not seeing her. She played the theme again, the same unadorned melody she'd played at the start of the piece. But it sounded different now. Perhaps she was playing it in another key.

Up above the world so high
Like a diamond in the sky…

As the melody came to an end, Claire saw herself looking at the pear tree outside the nursery window, Sarah asleep in her arms. On the tree's sagging branches, green and glossy leaves hovered like hands around the ripening fruit.

Lynne McKelvey

Chapter 31: Strike

"Get the pressure regulator fixed?" said a disembodied voice from under the car as Claire walked up the driveway, her shirt dripping wet. The Mustang's front end was jacked up and a pair of denim-clad legs stuck out from under the bumper. Jake's voice sounded low and loose. He was focused on the oil change. It was the kind of task he relished, a practical problem he could solve. She approached the legs. Clearly, Mandy still hadn't told him about Sarah. Why not? Claire wondered. Could it be that Sarah's life and death meant nothing to Mandy after all? The thought was unsettling.

"Get it fixed?" Jake repeated, while the sound of metal scraped the pavement under the car.

"Eventually," Claire said, addressing his legs. "It got me first, though. I'm soaked. But, it's a good thing I went over there today. By Monday, the place would've been a swamp."

"Mmmm," said Jake. His legs shimmied further under the car.

"Where's Mandy?" Claire asked, surprised she wasn't hanging around her father.

"Dunno," Jake mumbled. "She was here a while ago, handing me tools and such. Guess she got bored and went inside."

A grunt, followed by a clank and a growled, "goddamnit."

"What happened?"

"Dropped the plug in the oil pan."

A blue-gloved hand emerged from the side of the car and groped for a filthy rag that lay crumpled on the ground.

"Say," Jake said, the glove and rag retreating, "as long as I'm doing this, why don't I change your oil too, now, before the engine's cold? Mandy can help me, if she's at loose ends."

"I'll send her out," Claire said, smiling as she pivoted toward the house. She was glad her husband had a way with tools. Taking the truck in for servicing was one of her least favorite chores.

"Thanks," she said, looking back over her shoulder. "Love," she added a moment later and strode away.

She kicked off her muddy sneakers, leaving them on the back stoop, and padded into the kitchen in her socks. The house seemed oddly quiet for the middle of the day. Claire could hear her own breathing and even the clock ticking. A lime-green plastic basket full of Mandy's laundry, clean and folded, rested on the formica table top. She touched the clothes—they were still warm—and scooped up the basket, her arms barely able to surround it, then elbowed her way through the swinging door into the hall. She had to hand it to Jake. He took total care of his little daughter. Maybe he was right. Maybe Mandy didn't need a mother. She had him.

The child's door was shut and no sound emerged from her room. Was Mandy even there? Claire felt for the knob, invisible below the bulging laundry basket. She turned the knob, kneed the door open, and froze. She stared straight ahead, her leg stuck midstride, raised and rigid, while her hands compressed the basket's flimsy sides, and the clean warm clothes oozed through its interstices.

The hatbox was open and empty on Mandy's bed, its contents scattered helter-skelter, the grosgrain ribbon leaking to the floor. A pair of utility scissors lay beside the box; sharp, silver, and splayed. Mandy sat on the bench in front of the vanity mirror, her back to Claire. Sarah's pink sweater was stretched over her head, its tiny sleeves, pulled long and taut, knotted under her chin. The white blanket, a large hole cut out of its center, was draped poncho-style over Mandy's shoulders. The strawberries embroidered on the satin binding emerged from under her glossy black hair, meeting in a *V* in the middle of her back. Twin blue bracelets lopped off from the corduroy legs of Sarah's overalls dangled from her wrists. Thumbs jammed in her ears, fingers flapping up and down, tongue sticking out, Mandy was focused on her reflection.

Her badger eyes met Claire's in the mirror and her hands stilled. Without lowering her arms, she ran the tip of her tongue across her lips, then looked down. Her eyes slid sideways. Claire followed her gaze. In shards and slivers, the photographs lay strewn on the floor, an eye and a nose here, an ear there, two dimpled knees, and part of a hand. They'd been dismembered with care.

Claire looked into the mirror again but saw neither herself nor Mandy reflected. Instead, there was Althea, smiling slightly and drawing her bow across her violin, her boot pressing into the street urchin's chest. Their eyes met and exchanged smiles. Claire listened to the music coming from the glass. Though unfamiliar, it sounded strong and sweet.

"Your Daddy needs you to help him change the oil," Claire heard herself say. "Better run along now."

She did not see Mandy's eyes grow rounder; did not see the girl turn to stare up at her, mouth open, then closed; did not see her gauge the distance from the wicker bench to the hall. Mandy whipped off the blanket, the bonnet, the bracelets and flung them all on the bed. But Claire did not see her do these things. Nor did she see the girl race across the room and out the door. Claire stood motionless, holding the lime-green basket and looking deep into the mirror. She was listening. Listening to the strange, sweet music. Listening hard.

Mandy clung to her father for the rest of the day, chattering nonstop and averting her eyes whenever she passed Claire. After dinner, Claire excused herself. "Got work to do," she said, and headed to the dining room where she clamped a fresh grid-sheet on her drawing board, picked up a No. 2 pencil, and sat down at the table. While she pretended to work, Jake did the dishes and put Mandy to bed. Just before he closed the door, Claire heard Mandy remind him to sign a permission slip. Something about a class trip to McDonalds, a reward for perfect attendance. To Claire's relief, he turned in early.

It wasn't until the house was completely still that Claire felt her belly harden. The intensity of that first contraction took her breath away. A second followed. She reached under her blouse and massaged the flesh, breathing in pants, but the clenched hand inside her belly wouldn't let go. Finally, the muscles softened. She knew they'd contract again. Again and again until—tonight, tomorrow, perhaps not until many days from now—they'd expel the contents of the sac and leave Claire empty. She waited for a third contraction. It didn't come. Or if it did, she didn't notice. Her head was filled with the music she'd heard Althea play from the mirror earlier that day. But now the chords were harsh. Open-stringed. The melody was raw and scraping, unmitigated by vibrato.

It was past midnight when Claire set the pencil down beside the blank paper. The music still played in her head. She slipped into bed beside Jake, lifting the covers just high enough to slide beneath them, and aligned her body precisely along the edge of the mattress.

The music stopped. She fell asleep.

Chapter 32: Counterstrike

Gray light was seeping through the slats in the Venetian blinds when Claire awoke. Her mind was clear. She felt refreshed. For a few moments, she stared up at the cottage cheese ceiling, breathing shallow, deliberate breaths she synchronized with Jake's so as not to wake him. Then, in the partial darkness, she dressed quickly. She pulled on a full denim skirt and a short-sleeved blouse and eased the hatbox off the closet shelf. After Mandy fled the day before, Claire had slipped the cut-up photographs back into the manila envelope, which she placed in the bottom of the box and covered with the mutilated clothes. She stacked the intact items on top then tied on the lid. She'd wondered briefly where to put the box. In the end, she put it back where it had been before, but closer to the front edge of the shelf.

Now, bearing the box, she glided noiselessly from the room, down the hall, and into the kitchen where she pocketed the utility scissors she'd re-hung on the hook beside the stove, then proceeded out the back door. She paused on the stoop and breathed in the crisp, early morning air. Goose-bumps pebbled her arms as she passed through the break in the hedge and toward the driveway. Quietly, she opened the passenger side of the truck and set the hatbox on the floor. Although the streetlights seemed to fade as day dawned, the windows in the look-alike houses were still dark.

She headed back, rubbing her cold arms, and halted by the tall plant growing next to the hedge. Though the white flowers that once blared from its toothed leaves were gone, the jimsonweed had shot up. The soft green seedpods, nesting in the angles of the stems and large as her thumb, had become hard and brown, their spines sharp. As the sky whitened, Claire bent to inspect the pods. Most had already burst open, exposing their four chambers abounding in tiny black seeds.

She reached into her pocket for the scissors, spread the leaves apart with her free hand, and snipped off a pod, careful not to let the spines prick her skin. She cut off a second pod and, holding her skirt in front of her like a basket, dropped both pods inside the folds and waddled back to the kitchen. Standing on tiptoe, she eased the prickly pods onto the countertop, then brushed off her skirt and washed her hands with soap.

The light was growing stronger. Down the street, a car

door slammed, and an engine coughed to life. Within her walls, though, there was only silence. Claire tilted her head toward the hall and strained her ears, making sure Mandy and Jake were still asleep. They both hated getting up in the morning. An early riser herself, Claire had often made Mandy's lunch on school days and left for her gardens before Jake and Mandy woke and shuffled, bleary-eyed and half dressed, into the kitchen. She didn't have to check the clock now. She could tell by the light she still had time. Time, but none to spare.

With quick, deft movements, she assembled a loaf of whole wheat bread, a large jar of chunky peanut butter, and a smaller jar of strawberry jam on the countertop, placing them between the paddle-shaped cutting board and the metal lunchbox with black and white Dalmatians on its lid. She slipped her hand under the orange cellophane that wrapped the bread, pulled out two slices from the middle of the loaf, the freshest part, and set them side-by-side on the cutting board. As she smeared peanut butter evenly over the slices, she noted the hard bits of nuts already embedded in the spread. What luck that Mandy preferred chunky peanut butter to the creamy kind.

Next, Claire rummaged in the catchall drawer under the counter for a pair of poultry tweezers and some tongs. She lifted one of the seedpods with the tongs, noting how the sharp quills crumbled between the metal arms. With her free hand, she picked up the tweezers and carefully, surgically, removed a single jimson seed from its pod chamber and dropped it near the corner of one of the slices of bread. The seed was about the same size and hardness as the peanut bits. She removed another seed, then another, spacing the seeds evenly in rows until the viscous tan surface was flecked with black. She repeated the process with the other slice then smeared a second layer of peanut butter over each piece of bread, wiping the knife before she dipped it back into the jar.

By now the sun had risen above the horizon, its rays bouncing off the stucco of the house next door. The peanut butter gleamed in the early light. The jimson seeds were invisible.

Moving more quickly, she opened the strawberry jam and spooned it onto the bread, spreading quivering red dollops evenly with the knife. She licked off her fingers, folded the two bread slices in toward each other as if she were closing a book, and trimmed off the crusts. She cut the sandwich diagonally then cut each triangle in half, forming four equilateral sandwiches that were bite-sized and crustless, like the ones they'd had in the tearoom the day they'd shopped for Mandy's bridesmaid dress. She slipped the sandwiches into a plastic Baggie.

She removed the matching thermos from the metal

lunchbox, sniffed to make sure the container was clean, and filled it with fresh, cold milk. Then she placed the thermos, the sandwich bag, a paper napkin, and a small red apple inside the lunchbox. As she was about to close the lid, she removed the apple and polished it on her skirt, then put it back again. She snapped the lunchbox closed and set it upright on the counter, pocketing the extra seedpod. She grabbed her purse off the countertop and left the house.

Chapter 33: The Border Crossing

The *Flecha de Oro* hissed to a halt. "*San Ysidro y la frontera,*" the bus driver sang out over the loudspeaker. "*Fin de la línea,*" he rhymed.

End of the line. It sounded almost jaunty in Spanish.

Even before the bus doors whooshed open, rumpled passengers spilled into the aisle, jostling one another as they wrested their possessions—stained backpacks, rope-bound cartons, and bulging mesh bags—from the overhead racks. Claire stayed in her seat, waiting for the aisle to clear, the hatbox balanced on her knees. She checked the pocket of her denim skirt and felt the sharp pricks of the *Datura* pod.

Finding the *Flecha de Oro* had been a piece of luck. She'd planned to take the noon Greyhound from L.A. to the border, but it was sold out. Fridays were always busy, the ticket agent told her. The next bus wouldn't leave 'til four. Darkness would be falling by the time she crossed into Tijuana. The *farmacias* there would be closing, if they weren't already closed. Navigating her way through the city at night would be difficult, maybe even dangerous. As she'd weighed her options at the ticket counter, the round box she was holding had grown heavier, the line behind her longer. The agent drummed his fingers on the desk. Her choices were clear: either check into one of the sleazy hotels near the bus station and leave in the morning or leave later today and arrive in Tijuana after dark. Both had their risks. What if she changed her mind?

It was then she'd felt a tap on her shoulder. "Excuse me Miss," she heard a low voice say.

She turned, saw a small, dark-skinned man with sloping shoulders, and froze. Tomás. What was *he* doing here? Wasn't he supposed to be at his niece's *quinceañera*?

"Excuse me," the man repeated, looking at her politely, but without recognition. "If you hurry, there's another bus to the border, *La Flecha d'Oro*, the Golden Arrow. He leaves in…" As the man raised his left arm to look at his watch, she'd exhaled; all his fingers were intact. "In five minutes, Miss. Through that doorway. Over there."

She'd raced in the direction he was pointing, clutching the hatbox, her shoulder bag thumping against her hip. Within minutes, she'd swapped a crisp twenty-dollar bill for a flimsy paper ticket. No receipt. No record. Not a trace of her ever having been here.

As she surged onto the bus with the other passengers, she'd felt exhilarated. She chose a window seat near the rear and sat down. So far, everything had gone off without a hitch. Leaving the pickup truck in the long-term lot at L.A.'s Union Station was brilliant. No one would think to look for it there. Even if they did, they'd assume she'd gone off somewhere on a train. As she settled back in her seat, she imagined the police, weeks from now, riffling through the hundreds, perhaps thousands, of train tickets that had been sold that day. She'd almost laughed out loud.

As the bus bobbed down the 5 Freeway, heading south, she closed her eyes, hugging the hatbox and remembering how she'd parked the truck in the middle of the lot where it was least likely to be noticed and, balancing the box on her thigh, locked the cab doors. She walked right past the grand tiled entry to the train station, where people were milling. Arms encircling the box, she'd made her way the mile or so to the city's downtown bus depot, inhaling the pungent smells of Chinatown as she slipped behind the pagodas. She'd threaded her way between the souvenir stalls and mariachi bands that jammed Olvera Street, dipped into the long cool shadow cast by City Hall, and skirted the pawn shops, cardboard shelters, hand-lettered signs—"*Homeless, Plese Help*," "*Jesus Saves*," "*Rev. 9:13*"—and curled up bodies in the doorways of Skid Row along the way.

On the bus, while billboards, subdivisions, marshlands, oil refineries, and shopping centers blurred by outside the windows, she'd stroked the grosgrain ribbon on the hatbox, feeling the tiny ridges. From time to time, she touched the prickly pod inside her pocket, making sure it was still there. As she listened to the lilting words of the strangers all around her, she felt as though she'd already crossed the frontier.

When she stepped onto the pavement, the sunlight blinded her. Her eyes adjusted, and she saw a tangle of pedestrian bridges, dim underpasses choked with cars, and covered walkways ascending from the street in a zigzag pattern, blocking out whatever lay behind them and obliterating even the sky. Over the din of traffic, she heard the loud chatter of jackhammers.

She shifted the hatbox and inhaled the fumes of idling engines and cooking oil that had been heated and reheated many times. Her gorge rose and she clung to the box. The nausea passed, and she found herself stumbling forward behind a gray-haired woman who was balancing a microwave oven on her head. Claire joined the long procession walking single file in tight formation up a sloping covered passageway that angled ever higher.

The passage narrowed. Their shoulders rubbed against the smudged wall. Up ahead was the point of the *V* where they would double back to continue their journey across the highway. No signs. Not even an arrow marked the way.

As they rounded the bend, they found themselves going downhill, as if they'd just crossed the fulcrum of a giant see-saw. Below them lay the Interstate, clogged with vans and trucks and cars, all heading north. Beside the highway rose a tall chain-link fence with long strands of barbed wire topping it like guitar strings. Down, down the line of people marched, zigging this way, zagging that, until, without warning, they spilled out onto the pavement.

The crowd dissipated. Claire looked for the woman with the microwave, but she had disappeared. A cavernous discount store, a Bank of America with opaque windows, and a cluster of hotdog stands lined the broad sidewalk in front of her. Somewhere behind the buildings, blocked from view, lay the Pacific, blue and empty, curving invisibly toward a faint horizon.

After the press of bodies on the pedestrian bridge, the sidewalk seemed strangely unpopulated: a couple of college kids in cutoffs, a stooped man in paint-spattered overalls, and a quick-stepping woman whose long black braid swung like a pendulum across the middle of her back. She was heading north. As Claire watched her get smaller, she admired the woman's purposeful stride.

Claire turned to look back at the bridge. People streamed off it onto the sidewalk, all of them going the same direction. None of them looked back. She shifted her gaze to the fence and noted the barbs perched on its wires like tiny blackbirds. Far away, along the fence, she could barely make out the woman with the braid. Claire closed her eyes for a moment, wished the woman well, and headed south.

A smudged sign reading *Tijuana* pointed to a narrow walkway that doglegged to the left. Squat stucco buildings, once pastel but now bleached colorless by the sun, lined the path. Metal grills with flaking paint covered the windows. Doors with signs above them—*Cambio, Tourist Information, Real Estate Offerings*—gaped open.

At the end of the path was a tall turnstile with thick iron bars that meshed like fingers. *Límite de Los Estados Unidos Mexicanos/Boundary of the United States of America.* In the past, she'd always had an easy passage to the other side, hardly given it a second thought. Today, her heart was pounding, her chest about to burst. She'd been a visitor before. Now she was a fugitive and here to stay. Her eyes darted back to the doorways. Suppose an official emerged? She had no passport, no papers, no plausible destination, no reason at all—certainly not one she dared give—for crossing the border. Her hatbox would be seized and she arrested. She imagined herself an armless statue, wrists manacled behind her back, and hugged the hatbox harder. As she gauged the distance to the turnstile, the jackhammers, which had been mute, resumed their racket.

Fifty yards to go, but it might as well have been five hundred. She longed for shadows, but the relentless sun illuminated every corner of the walkway. Fifty yards. She must keep moving. She remembered the woman with the braid and willed herself forward. Though the walkway was deserted, she could feel eyes peering out at her from the dim recesses of the buildings. She heard no voices. The hammers and her thundering heartbeat drowned all other sounds.

Dry-mouthed, she entered the turnstile, balancing the hatbox on her hip. She leaned into the iron bars and followed their slow spin. One lumbering dance step and the opening appeared. For an instant she paused to gape at the plaza widening before her. It seemed oddly empty, but at the far end, green and yellow taxis were revving their engines. *2 km. al Centro*, a sign in front of her read. Quickly, joyfully, she stepped outside.

As she moved away, the turnstile's metal bars slammed into the hatbox, gouging a hole in its side. Horrified, Claire watched Sarah's tiny shoes and bibs and shirts and bonnets—all that Mandy had not desecrated—tumble out, as if from a piñata, to the filthy pavement below. Before she could stoop to pick them up, a crowd had materialized, as if on command. Where had everyone come from? The plaza had seemed deserted a moment before. Old and young, women and men, they snatched up the clothes. But instead of running off with them as Claire expected, they shook them out, picked off clinging bits of dirt, patted and smoothed them. Talking all at once, loudly and unintelligibly, they swarmed around her, waving the little garments in front of her face. Did they want money? She'd give them what she had. But would it be enough?

As she reached for the wallet zipped inside her shoulder bag, an ancient woman no taller than a ten-year-old child took hold of the hatbox. Her front teeth were black and one of her eyes was shut. She wore a striped *rebozo*. Her skinny fingers, bent and twisted, gripped the box with surprising strength. Claire tried to back away, but she'd forgotten about the turnstile, and she found herself trapped in its iron embrace.

The crowd pressed forward, sealing off the opening, blocking Claire's view of the plaza and the taxis. The clothes fluttered against her face. All the while, the old woman hung on to the hatbox, tugging at it insistently and making little crooning sounds. If one of them didn't let go soon, the box would be torn to pieces and anything still left inside would spill to the ground. Claire imagined the people lunging at the remaining items, the damaged clothes. The crowd would trample them in a frenzy. They'd finish the job Mandy had begun, ripping everything to shreds.

"*Dámela, señora,*" the old woman said, pulling at the box. She sounded neither pitiable nor demanding, but strangely maternal. Claire held on for another moment then let go. The old woman flashed a toothless smile that seemed more approving than triumphant, turned, and, holding the torn box in front of her solemnly as if she were carrying a statue in a religious procession, walked into the crowd. "*Andele, andele,*" she said, flailing her elbows right and left.

The people made way.

When she reached a clear space, the woman knelt down. She balanced the box on her knee with one hand and unwound her long *rebozo* with the other, spreading it on the ground like a runner on a banquet table. Carefully, she lifted the box and placed it in the center of the cloth.

The crowd fell silent, all eyes on the hatbox. Was she going to divvy up the spoils? Claire's heart thudded in her ears as she watched the woman untie the ribbons, her stiff, misshapen fingers surprisingly adroit, and lift the lid. One by one she removed the remaining items. If she noticed the corduroy pant legs unraveling where Mandy had hacked off their hems or the jagged opening in the center of the white blanket, she didn't show it. She laid all the articles, whole and defiled alike, gently, almost reverently on the *rebozo*. Finally, she took out the manila envelope and set it unopened beside the other items. She picked up the box and rotated it to the gash on the side. Squinting with her good eye, she pressed the jagged edges back together. The hole was no longer visible, but when she probed where it had been, the flap reopened.

The woman sat back on her heels. Under the bright embroidery on her cotton blouse, her thin chest heaved.

"*Necesito 'scotch,'*" she said, in a clear reedy voice.

She needed a scotch?

"*Lo tengo!*" a girl in a school uniform called out, digging into her backpack and producing a roll of Scotch tape.

Necks craned in unison, following the woman's bent fingers this way and that as she patched the tear.

She needed some strong paper, she said. *Papeles fuertes*, the *fuertes* whistling between her teeth.

A murmur rippled through the crowd, and someone handed the old woman a couple of paper bags. She creased them deftly, fashioning an inner lining she then inserted into the box. As the onlookers nodded approvingly, she placed the manila envelope at the bottom of the box. One by one, people stepped forward and set the items they'd been holding on the rebozo. Head bowed, the woman folded the clothes and put them back in the box on top of the envelope. She replaced the lid, tied the black ribbons into a firm bow, and, with a slight grimace, rose stiffly to her feet.

"*Está bien,*" she said, nodding to Claire as she gave her the hatbox.

For a second time, Claire reached for her purse, but the woman pulled her hand away. "*No te preocupes,*" she said, stroking Claire's palm with her calloused fingers. Don't worry about it. "*Necesitas todas para tu bebé.*" Claire would need everything for her baby.

Claire felt tears well up and tried to speak, but her throat had clamped closed.

"*No te preocupes,*" the woman repeated quietly. "*Mira, qué tan fuerte es, tu caja.*" She rapped the box with her knuckles to show its strength and smiled. "*No te preocupes,*" she soothed. She took Claire's arm and propelled her forward a few steps toward the center of the plaza, then let go.

In the blink of an eye, or so it seemed, the old woman and everyone else around Claire had slipped away, dissolving almost as suddenly as they'd first appeared into the fumes and noise and sprawl of the city. For a moment, Claire wondered if she'd been dreaming. But the taxi drivers beeping their horns, poking their heads out their windows, and shouting in Spanish and English—"Mees, Mees, I take you to hotel!" "*Venga, señora!*" "Cheap prices. *Precios baratos!*"—seemed real enough. And the box she hugged felt solid.

And the box she'd left behind? The small metal one, with black and white puppies on the lid? Mandy would have carried it off to school by now, swinging it gaily at her side as she chattered with her friends. Perhaps there still was time…

For an instant, Claire glanced back at the turnstile. It offered no return.

She slid between the bumpers, avoiding eye contact with the imploring drivers, skirted a roundabout choked with cars, and followed arrows pointing to *Avenida Juarez*. "*2 km. al Centro*" the sign by the turnstile had said. A manageable walk, even with the cumbersome hatbox. The driver might remember her if she took a cab.

The *Avenida* was broad and tree-lined. On either side were glass and steel banks and office buildings guarded by soldiers in camouflage, rifles at the ready. Cars and taxis hurtled by, weaving in and out of blue and white buses in unmarked lanes. Claire settled into a comfortable stride and felt the hatbox bounce against her belly every time she took a step. Her arms were throbbing from the weight. She traced the edges of the tape that sealed the tear and for a moment wondered why she'd brought the box with her. But what else could she have done with it?

The street narrowed. Motorcycles with side-cars, public minivans bulging with passengers, and pedal carts heaped high with pottery, metal cookware, bananas, and bolts of colored cloth scraped the curb, horns blaring, bells tingling, drivers shouting. Her stomach rumbled. The box blocked her view of her watch, but she guessed it was well past noon. Mandy would have had her lunch. She'd have eaten the whole sandwich. She was a hungry child. Despite the potency of the seeds and the number of them she'd swallowed—many times the lethal dose—it would be a while before she felt their effects. As much as an hour might go by until she began acting goofy: laughing raucously, talking loudly to the air, complaining of thirst. At first, her teacher would think she was just being disruptive. More time would pass before anyone thought to send her to the school nurse. By then her face, already naturally rosy, would have become a bright and unalleviated red. Her pupils would have all but eclipsed the irises, reducing them to thin rims. And what school nurse, or even doctor, hours later in the emergency room, would suspect the cause of these symptoms in a nine-year-old? In any case, by then it would be too late.

The sheen of white satin caught Claire's eye. Turning, she saw a tall blond bride with parted lips and frozen eyes staring out from a storefront window. Her white lace veil was tossed back over her plastic hair; in her arms she carried a faded silk bouquet. To the left of the bride was a slightly smaller figure, also in white satin, with a flowered tiara on her head and heart-shaped pillows for *quinceañeras* strewn in front of her. On the bride's right was a large array of white and purple funeral wreaths made from hundreds of satin bows. Beside these lay an assortment of smaller wreaths composed of tiny pink-silk roses. For children, Claire realized with a jolt, and hurried on.

Inside the *Centro Botánico: El Remedio*, around the corner a few doors down, the air felt pleasantly cool. Like a lath house, Claire thought, as her eyes adjusted to the soft filtered light that seemed to have no source. *Plantas y Medicinales Naturales* read the sign that hung above the door. On the shelves lining the walls, everything glowed: the rows of flimsy boxes with elaborate floral designs, the dark bottles rising like sentinels, the clear-glass Mason jars with handwritten labels. Even the dusky skin and embroidered robe of the Virgin of Guadalupe on the yellow banner hanging in an alcove emitted a mysterious light.

The herb and natural remedies shop was empty except for a teen-aged boy on a ladder restocking shelves, an older woman in a blue smock bent over a ledger book, and a young woman with bright red lipstick and long shiny earrings perched on a high stool beside the cash register. She was swinging one leg and flipping through the pages of a romance comic book.

No one seemed to notice Claire's entrance, although a bell had announced her with a ding. She scanned the ranks of jars and bottles and boxes. There were hundreds, if not thousands, of items on the shelves. All were neatly arranged, but there were no signs grouping them or stating what they were for. She closed her eyes, swaying slightly as she breathed in the faintly musty smells and the silence.

"*Le ayuda, señora*?" May I help you?

Claire blinked. The young woman stood in front of her, red lips curved into an expectant smile. Claire felt her throat constrict. The woman was hardly more than a girl, only a couple of years past her own *quinceañera*, Claire guessed. How could Claire tell *her* what she'd come to buy? But perhaps she didn't even need to buy it. Eventually, all on its own her body would rid her of the creature growing inside her. Hadn't it already begun the process? Furtively, she touched her belly, hiding her hand behind the box. The flesh was soft and pliant. She hadn't felt any contractions since the night before. No matter. The expulsion had its own timetable. But it might not be the same as hers. Should she take the chance?

"*Quiere algo*?" the young woman said, while Claire debated whether to stay or leave. *Centro Botánico* had every kind of remedy, "*todos*," the woman assured her with an expansive wave of her arm.

"*Todos*?" Claire echoed.

"Well, almost everything," the woman replied, laughing. Her cheeks dimpled, and she looked even younger than she had before.

Claire looked down at the hatbox. The old woman at the turnstile had tied a neat bow precisely in the center of the lid. Beneath the bow, the flat ribbons set out in four directions before they dropped over the edge and out of sight.

"I—I have a friend," Claire began then paused. She adjusted the hatbox over her belly and felt her face redden. "A friend who is pregnant," she continued in Spanish, her eyes glued to the center of the bow. *Embarazada.* What a curious word for "pregnant." Yet somehow it seemed just right.

As she slogged on, she felt cold beads congealing on her forehead. "This friend is very unhappy, *es muy infeliz*," she said. *"Ella quiere abortar a su bebé."*

The phrase took Claire's breath away. She wants to abort her baby. She'd never uttered it aloud before, not even in English. Not even to herself. The image arose of a shrimp-shaped body with a huge head, a relentless heartbeat, and a looped black cord conjoining the creature with herself. She had no doubt now. She must rid herself of the abomination. Her womb belonged to Sarah. Selfishly, thoughtlessly, Claire had desecrated the space. Now she must pay the price.

And the price for what she'd done to Mandy? Images of the little girl—sobbing over her mother's broken necklace, pirouetting in front of the department store's mirrors as she tried on bridesmaid's dresses, giggling in Roger's lap the night he came to dinner, and waiting, stoop-shouldered and hollow-eyed, for her mother's birthday present to arrive—rose unbidden. Claire tried to will them away, but couldn't.

She looked at the young woman across from her through the scrim of memories. The woman's dimples had vanished, and her red lips barely curved. Would she upbraid Claire? Call the police? What if she didn't even *have* the herbs Claire sought? What would Claire do then? She imagined herself wandering the streets of Tijuana as night fell, listening to the hollow clang of the shops' steel doors slam shut one by one.

The corners of the young woman's mouth drew together, and faint lines creased her brow. As the silence lengthened, Claire felt her body chill.

"*Pues, quiere la señora un té?*" the woman said, at last.

Un té? She was offering Claire a cup of tea? Had the few words she'd uttered misfired so completely?

"*Un té?*" Claire said aloud, glancing at the doorway and mapping her escape. The weight of the hatbox was becoming unbearable. She felt as though her arms would break.

"*Sí, señora,*" the woman said in a calm voice, "*para el aborto.*" Which did Claire prefer—the woman paused for an instant—for her "friend": herbs to make a tea, *una infusión,* or pills her friend could swallow? The *Centro Botánico* had both. She sounded as neutral as a waitress asking a customer whether she preferred her coffee black or with cream.

Claire felt giddy with relief.

"*Permítanme,*" the woman said, taking the box out of

Claire's arms and setting it down on the counter. "*No se preocupe,*" she added, catching Claire's worried glance. "*No pasa nada.*" She smiled and patted the box.

She led Claire to the back of the shop where the older woman sat making entries in the ledger book. The pills, the young woman explained, worked gradually. They needed to be taken over a period of days. The herbs varied, but one in particular—she indicated a tall column of blue and gold boxes piled almost to the ceiling—would start to take effect almost immediately, provided the leaves were steeped in very hot water for at least thirty minutes. "Isn't that right, mamá," she called to the older woman.

"*Sí, sí, mi amor,*" the mother answered, smiling, but not raising her eyes from the ledgers. "She knows everything, this child."

"Only because you've taught me so well," the young woman replied, walking over to her mother and giving her a hug.

The tea would taste a little bitter, she explained, but it was *seguro*, surefire. The *señora* could have complete confidence. Moreover, she added, besides its intended effect, the infusion would contribute to the *señora's* overall good health.

Claire nodded, reached into her skirt pocket, and felt the pod.

As she headed for the *Avenida Niños Héroes* where

she'd been told the Number 3 buses plied regularly between downtown and the beach, Claire wondered whether the hatbox could sustain the weight of her new purchases. Its lid was now piled high with plastic bags containing a wide-mouthed thermos, a mug, a long-handled spoon, and a white bed sheet. Unable to see the pavement, she stepped off an invisible curb and stumbled, barely catching the bags before they slid off the hatbox. Stupid not to have brought these items with her from L.A. She'd spent over an hour going from store to store to find them here. The sun was already low in the sky. It could take another hour to get to the city beach.

She craned her neck around the packages and saw a knot of people climbing onto a bus half a block away. She started to run for the bus, but stopped, fearing the thermos might drop and its glass lining shatter if she tripped. What would she do then?

The bus pulled out, belching black smoke, late-comers hanging off the doors. Already, a new line, including large clumps of school children in blue and white uniforms, had begun to form. If she took the next bus, she'd almost surely have to stand. She leaned back against the spiked iron fence that bordered the sidewalk. Her arms throbbed; her shoulder muscles had frozen; her fingers were numb.

She looked for a bench near the bus stop, but saw none.

There was a pink and white stone church with tall square towers across the street. Perhaps she could sit in one of its pews for a while. Too risky getting there, she decided, after watching the trucks and cabs and cars she'd have to dodge whiz by in an unending flow.

The metal fence posts were digging into her back. She stepped away and noticed that behind the barricade there was a hillside covered with dry grass and scruffy Bristol pine, the first native plants she'd seen since she crossed the border. A young woman pushing a stroller ambled by and turned into a gateway marked "*Jardin de Niños*" a few yards further on. Impulsively, Claire followed her down a steep path, past a dry fountain with cracks in the basin, to a small playground with rusty swings, a sandbox, and a faded plastic slide.

As the woman with the stroller joined the handful of women who ringed the playground, rocking their infants while keeping an eye on the toddlers and older children in the center, Claire noticed a wooden bench on the other side of the path, behind an unkempt hedge and beneath a large jacaranda tree. She made her way to the bench and sat down, sliding the bundles off her lap. She closed her eyes and breathed in. The air smelled only faintly of traffic fumes. The women's musical chatter and the children's gleeful cries damped the city sounds. Time stopped, and she felt her fingers tingling back to life.

She awoke with a start. Dry-mouthed, she counted her packages. All were there. She sank back, weak with relief. The playground was much noisier now. The swings squealed, and children shrieked as they chased each other up and down the slides. The benches edging the playground were filled with mothers sitting side by side. The newcomers had walked right by her while she slept.

She yawned, stretched, and rotated her shoulders. Her muscles unlocked, and she turned toward the packages. After a moment's thought, she consolidated the items, wrapping the thermos carefully in the white bed sheet and slipping one bag inside another for extra strength. She rose quickly, clutching the now bulging single plastic bag. Only the hatbox remained. She leaned over and fingered the frayed ends of the bow. Should she untie it one more time?

"*Mami, mami!*" a high voice called from the playground.

"*Qué quieres, mi amor?*" a lower voice replied.

Claire let go the ribbon and stood up, leaving the box on the bench. Sarah didn't need these clothes anymore. She'd outgrown them.

With a last glance at the hatbox, Claire stepped onto the path and ascended swiftly to the street. She didn't look back.

Lynne McKelvey

Chapter 34: The Cave

The damp rock lining the shallow cave surrounded her, trapping the smells of wind and salt and beached seaweed that blew through the opening. The light faded, the wind quickened, masking all sounds but the periodic whoosh of the waves. Under her thin blouse, Claire felt the chill.

She reached beside her for the thermos, filled to the brim with boiling water. For a picnic, she told the manager at the cantina near the bus stop. He looked at her curiously but pressed the spigot on his coffee machine without comment. Now, as she loosened the plastic cup and set the thermos down on the white sheet she'd spread over the sandy floor, she wondered if he'd remember her. What if he did? They'd never identify her when they found her—tomorrow or the next day or the next—a nondescript *gringa* in a denim skirt, a striped blouse, and no-particular-color hair. As for the fetus, the red jellyfish long since expelled between her thighs, the gulls would devour it, if the tide didn't carry it away.

Night fell. The cave's jagged rim melted into the darkness; the ocean and the sloping shore met invisibly. On the dark sand in front of the cave, a bar of light was blinking. Where was it coming from? she wondered. On, off, on, off, like the opening and closing of a hand. She turned sideways to avoid the light. The blinking continued at the rim of her gaze. She shut her eyes to block it out.

By now, she thought, Mandy was lying motionless on the gurney, for surely by now it was over. Her eyelids sealed, color absent from her face. Her lips were slightly parted. No more smiles—real or false. Beautiful teeth, strong and straight and white. The dark curls draped over her shoulders still danced with light.

Had she suffered long? Claire wondered, and felt the rocks forming the cave wall shift. She hoped the child entered the coma quickly, before the ambulance was called and Jake arrived. Before squirrels began flying from the ceiling and snakes coiled about her body. Before insects crawled into her dry mouth and down her dry throat and birds by the hundreds began pecking at her flesh.

Claire's eyes sprang open and she gasped for air, not remembering, for a moment, where she was. The light blinked on, reminding her. She reached into her pocket, found the pod, and withdrew an empty hand. The pod's turn would come.

She groped for the herbs from the *Centro Botánico*. The box felt so light she feared it was empty, but she quickly found the sealed bag inside. She wanted to crumble some of the leaves, feel their dry texture before she immersed them in the hot water. Would there be remnants of stems and burrs among them? she wondered. But she dared not waste any part of the plant. She opened the bag and waved it under her nose. The herb's sweet smell, almost cloying in its intensity, surprised her. But soon the scent mingled with the sharp sea air and the dank smells of the cave. The drink, the girl in the shop told her, would taste bitter.

She anchored the thermos between her legs, and, with the tall spoon, began transferring the leaves to the thermos, her free hand shielding them, like small flames, from the wind. When the bag was empty, she stirred the brew.

The air grew colder. Her teeth chattered. She pulled the sheet up around her shoulders. Had the leaves steeped long enough? She'd thrown her watch away, along with her wallet and car keys, in a dumpster near the park. No matter. The brew was already stronger than it needed to be, ready for her any time.

At the edge of her vision, the light kept flashing. To keep it out, she cupped her hand beside her eye and stared into the moonless night. Far away, a dog barked once then was silent. Now, everything was still. Even the waves stopped breaking. She heard them hiss as they receded farther and farther, gathering themselves for their next assault on the shore.

"How deep can we dig?" she had asked her brother long ago on another shore.

"Forever. We can dig forever."

"But what's on the other side?"

"There is no other side."

She kept asking. But his answer didn't change.

The sound of the waves, nearer and louder than before, crashed through her reverie. The tide was coming in. Time was running out.

Would Sarah come to her once more? Claire stared at the invisible ocean and tried to imagine her daughter, a point of light at first, bobbing like a lamp on a distant masthead, but becoming ever larger, ever brighter as she sped across the dark waters toward her mother.

Instead, she saw Mandy, seated at her vanity, face fisted, tongue sticking out, fingers flapping beside her ears. The pink sweater was tied over the child's head, its small sleeves knotted under her chin. The white blanket, its center cut away, was draped over her torso. The mutilated photographs lay scattered on the floor.

There was the hat box, open and empty on Mandy's bed. There it was again, on a wintry day in a different room long ago. There, *she* was, Claire, filling the box for the very first time. There she was, sifting through the box's contents, deceiving herself—again and again and again—pretending that by seeing, touching, smelling those lifeless bits of cloth and paper she could resurrect her dead daughter.

"You loved her too much," Mandy said.

She had been right.

Claire lowered her hand to her lap. The blinking resumed: on, off, on, off. Though the rhythm was steady, the light seemed paler than before. Her heart beat faster. Dawn was near. She must be quick. Soon she would be visible. Someone—an early fisherman, perhaps—might discover her before she was ready.

She unscrewed the thermos cup and placed it, hands trembling, on the sheet. She pulled the jimsonweed pod out of her pocket and rolled it on her palm, letting the spines etch a small circle of pain. With her little finger, she scraped the seeds into the thermos and emptied the pod's four chambers. She stirred the brew, mixing the ingredients thoroughly with the tall spoon.

Dar a luz. Give to the light.

A beautiful phrase for giving birth.

For naught.

She poured some of the liquid from the thermos into the cup, filling it to the brim. As she raised the cup to her lips, the bar of light blinked on. She jerked backwards, spilling some of the tea. There, illuminated in the center of the lit space, stood a dapper brown bird with a spotted white breast, wiry legs, an orange bill, and a long tail. The creature teetered in place for a moment then, with its head lowered and a bobbing gait, disappeared into the darkness.

Claire set the cup on the sheet. The sudden appearance of the bird was unsettling. Even more unnerving was the blinking rectangle—on, off, on, off—its rhythm now stamped on her retinas. Where was the source of the light? she wondered, and suddenly had to know.

She dipped her finger in the cup. Should she first drink the brew? The liquid was already lukewarm. Better to wait, she decided. She wanted to be clear headed when she ventured outside. In any case, she'd be back soon.

She tried to stand but couldn't; she'd been immobilized too long. She stretched out her legs, flexed her feet, and rolled her shoulders, gradually regaining sensation, then rose and waddled out of the cave, stooping to clear the entrance. As she stood tall on the sand, the offshore wind slapped at her cheeks, restoring their color.

She stepped into the bar of light, so faint now she could barely discern it, and turned around. Suspended in the black void behind the cave, she saw a large wooden sign framed with flashing white lights. "Kentuky Fried Chiken" the sign read. Crudely painted below the words was a smiling white-haired man with spectacles, a luxuriant white mustache, and a goatee. Man and words appeared and disappeared as the lights flashed on, flashed off. Nothing else was visible: no headlights, no lit windows, no billboards.

Claire stood rooted and stared at the sign. The lights blinked off, the lights blinked on. Like code, she thought, and felt her blood stir. On, off, on, off. Her heart began to pound.

*White-haired colonel...Kentucky Fried Chicken...golden arches...McDonalds...*McDonalds!

She broke into a sweat, hot or cold or both at once, she couldn't tell. The attendance award. Lunch at McDonalds. That permission slip. Wasn't it for today?

In her mind, she pictured the kitchen countertop, Mandy's lunchbox still there, right where Claire left it—a day, a night, a lifetime ago. She imagined Mandy, hands unencumbered, arms swinging freely, walking to school. She saw her perched on a yellow stool, giggling with her classmates as they tucked into hamburgers and fries.

A wave broke over Claire's calves, churning around her ankles, tugging her backwards toward the sea. She resisted its pull.

The sky was growing lighter. The air felt moist. A fog was rolling in, blearing the flashing sign. Below the sign, the cliff emerged, a dark, featureless mass hulking against the starless sky. Claire peered into the cave and made out the ghostly outlines of the cup and thermos. She searched for the narrow path that led steeply up from the base of the cliff to the main road. She couldn't detect it, though she knew just where to look.

Untinted, dawn arrived: beach, cave, cliffs, and boundless sky revealed in varying shades of gray. Could she get back in time? Today was Saturday. Would the lunchbox stay put until she returned?

She pressed her hands into her belly and marveled at its softness, its resilience. In all this time, she'd hadn't had a single contraction. Not one.

Dar a luz?

Hardly.

Inhabit this new gray world?

Perhaps.

A Real Daughter

Lynne McKelvey

Acknowledgements

Thanks to Jim Krusoe, my extraordinary teacher who saw what was hidden in plain sight; Cristina Garcia for her luminous spirit, her daring, her example; Mary Morrissey, ever insightful, ever kind; the indefatigable Amin Ahmed and the amazing writers in his master class.

Special thanks to Elizabeth Bogner, whose editorial acumen helped me hone the manuscript, word by word, line by line, always with joy; Suzanne Richardson for her thoughtful reading and incisive comments; Eric Wilson, writer, critic, stalwart friend; Hilary Reyl, who has been generous beyond reason; and to my late aunt, Margaret Ringnalda, who always believed in me.

Thanks also to Barry Campion, whose real gardens inspired Claire's; to Jackie Flor for helping me plant my imaginary gardens; and to bird-whisperer Lila Eisberg for knowing who'd be out and about in them at night.

Finally, thanks to my wonderful partner, David Luria, who listens, lifts, and gives me the space.

Lynne McKelvey

About the Author

At age fourteen, Lynne McKelvey won Seventeen magazine's short story contest. Then—after earning degrees in English at Harvard and UC Santa Barbara and founding a singles club for people with advanced degrees—she veered off into academia, returning only recently to writing fiction. A native Southern Californian, she now divides her time between Pacific Palisades and Washington DC, where she dotes on her four grandsons.

Author website at www.arealdaughter.com

Lynne McKelvey

If you enjoyed *A Real Daughter*, consider these other fine books from
Savant Books and Publications:

Essay, Essay, Essay by Yasuo Kobachi
Aloha from Coffee Island by Walter Miyanari
Footprints, Smiles and Little White Lies by Daniel S. Janik
The Illustrated Middle Earth by Daniel S. Janik
Last and Final Harvest by Daniel S. Janik
A Whale's Tale by Daniel S. Janik
Tropic of California by R. Page Kaufman
Tropic of California (the companion music CD) by R. Page Kaufman
The Village Curtain by Tony Tame
Dare to Love in Oz by William Maltese
The Interzone by Tatsuyuki Kobayashi
Today I Am a Man by Larry Rodness
The Bahrain Conspiracy by Bentley Gates
Called Home by Gloria Schumann
Kanaka Blues by Mike Farris
First Breath edited by Z. M. Oliver
Poor Rich by Jean Blasiar
The Jumper Chronicles by W. C. Peever
William Maltese's Flicker by William Maltese
My Unborn Child by Orest Stocco
Last Song of the Whales by Four Arrows
Perilous Panacea by Ronald Klueh
Falling but Fulfilled by Zachary M. Oliver
Mythical Voyage by Robin Ymer
Hello, Norma Jean by Sue Dolleris
Richer by Jean Blasiar
Manifest Intent by Mike Farris
Charlie No Face by David B. Seaburn
Number One Bestseller by Brian Morley
My Two Wives and Three Husbands by S. Stanley Gordon
In Dire Straits by Jim Currie
Wretched Land by Mila Komarnisky
Chan Kim by Ilan Herman
Who's Killing All the Lawyers? by A. G. Hayes
Ammon's Horn by G. Amati
Wavelengths edited by Zachary M. Oliver
Almost Paradise by Laurie Hanan
Communion by Jean Blasiar and Jonathan Marcantoni
The Oil Man by Leon Puissegur

A Real Daughter

Random Views of Asia from the Mid-Pacific by William E. Sharp
The Isla Vista Crucible by Reilly Ridgell
Blood Money by Scott Mastro
In the Himalayan Nights by Anoop Chandola
On My Behalf by Helen Doan
Traveler's Rest by Jonathan Marcantoni
Keys in the River by Tendai Mwanaka
Chimney Bluffs by David B. Seaburn
The Loons by Sue Dolleris
Light Surfer by David Allan Williams
The Judas List by A. G. Hayes
Path of the Templar—Book 2 of The Jumper Chronicles by W. C. Peever
The Desperate Cycle by Tony Tame
Shutterbug by Buz Sawyer
Blessed are the Peacekeepers by Tom Donnelly and Mike Munger
The Bellwether Messages edited by D. S. Janik
The Turtle Dances by Daniel S. Janik
The Lazarus Conspiracies by Richard Rose
Purple Haze by George B. Hudson
Imminent Danger by A. G. Hayes
Lullaby Moon (CD) by Malia Elliott of Leon & Malia
Volutions edited by Suzanne Langford
In the Eyes of the Son by Hans Brinckmann
The Hanging of Dr. Hanson by Bentley Gates
Flight of Destiny by Francis Powell
Elaine of Corbenic by Tima Z. Newman
Ballerina Birdies by Marina Yamamoto
More More Time by David B. Seabird
Crazy Like Me by Erin Lee
Cleopatra Unconquered by Helen R. Davis
Valedictory by Daniel Scott
The Chemical Factor by A. G. Hayes
Quantum Death by A. G. Hayes and Raymond Gaynor
Big Heaven by Charlotte Hebert
Captain Riddle's Treasure by GV Rama Rao
All Things Await by Seth Clabough
Tsunami Libido by Cate Burns
Finding Kate by A. G. Hayes
The Adventures of Purple Head, Buddha Monkey and Sticky Feet by Erik and Forest Bracht
In the Shadows of My Mind by Andrew Massie
The Gumshoe by Richard Rose

Lynne McKelvey

In Search of Somatic Therapy by Setsuko Tsuchiya
Cereus by Z. Roux
The Solar Triangle by A. G. Hayes

Coming Soon:
StoryTeller by Nicholas Bylotus
Bo Henry at Three Forks by Daniel D. Bradford

Savant Books and Publications
http://www.savantbooksandpublications.com

A Real Daughter

And from our imprint, Aignos Publishing:

The Dark Side of Sunshine by Paul Guzzo
Happy that it's Not True by Carlos Aleman
Cazadores de Libros Perdidos by German William Cabasssa Barber [Spanish]
The Desert and the City by Derek Bickerton
The Overnight Family Man by Paul Guzzo
There is No Cholera in Zimbabwe by Zachary M. Oliver
John Doe by Buz Sawyers
The Piano Tuner's Wife by Jean Yamasaki Toyama
Nuno by Carlos Aleman
An Aura of Greatness by Brendan P. Burns
Polonio Pass by Doc Krinberg
Iwana by Alvaro Leiva
University and King by Jeffrey Ryan Long
The Surreal Adventures of Dr. Mingus by Jesus Richard Felix Rodriguez
Letters by Buz Sawyers
In the Heart of the Country by Derek Bickerton
El Camino De Regreso by Maricruz Acuna [Spanish]
Diego in Two Places by Carlos Aleman
Deep Slumber of Dogs by Doc Krinberg
Prepositions by Jean Yamasaki Toyama
Saddam's Parrot by Jim Currie
Beneath Them by Natalie Roers
Chang the Magic Cat by A. G. Hayes

Coming Soon:
Island Wildlife: Exiles, Expats and Exotic Others by Robert Friedman
The Winter Spider by Doc Krinberg
Illegal by E. M. Duesel

Aignos Publishing | an imprint of Savant Books and Publications
http://www.aignospublishing.com

Made in the USA
Middletown, DE
06 July 2020

11007792R00176

The Awakening
of Zen

Dr. Daisetz Teitaro Suzuki in London, 1954

The Awakening
of Zen

DAISETZ TEITARO SUZUKI

Edited by Christmas Humphreys

1980
Prajñā Press • Boulder
IN ASSOCIATION WITH
The Buddhist Society • London

Prajñā Press
Great Eastern Book Company
P.O. Box 271
Boulder, Colorado 80306

IN ASSOCIATION WITH

The Buddhist Society
58 Eccleston Square
London, SW1 V1PH

LIBRARY OF CONGRESS CATALOGING IN PUBLICATION DATA

Suzuki, Daisetz Teitaro, 1870–1966.
    The awakening of Zen.
    1. Zen Buddhism—Addresses, essays, lectures.
I. Humphreys, Christmas, 1901–   II. Title.
BQ9266.S94   1980   294.3'927   79-17444
ISBN 0-87773-715-0

Printed in the United States of America

Contents

FOREWORD

In the course of his very long life Dr. D. T. Suzuki wrote and lectured enormously on the subject of Zen Buddhism. His works total some fifty books in Japanese and English, a wide variety of articles and essays for numerous publications and lectures, formal and informal, which were taken down and transcribed.

When, in 1946, I returned from a visit to Japan, where I had been able to spend much time with him, I was appointed his agent for works published in Europe. I arranged with Rider and Co. to publish and republish them as they appeared, and for many years kept them in print, in some cases with American editions and foreign translations.

But I soon possessed material for a further volume of lectures and articles from various sources, and published them through Rider and Co. as *Studies in Zen* (1955). Years later I had sufficient material to rescue from oblivion a further selection which the Buddhist Society published as *The Field of Zen* (1969), and this was followed in 1971 by *What is Zen*, containing two articles acquired by Mr. Lunsford Yandell and a reprint of *The Essence of Buddhism*, being the two lectures to the Emperor of Japan, first published in 1946.

Articles and lectures continued to be added to my files. I noted the series of posthumous essays published in the last few years in *The Eastern Buddhist*, and am happy to learn that they will, before long, be published in volume form, but many more have appeared in journals such as the Buddhist Society's *The Middle Way*, and these would be lost to the general public unless collected in book form. Hence the present volume, containing items extremely varied in nature.

In Dr. Suzuki's writings in English there seem to be at least four types of style and purpose. The first is scholarship, in which he adds to the world's knowledge of the history of Ch'an (in Japanese, Zen) Buddhism, and the meaning of the recorded sayings of Masters which constitute its scriptures. Then there are those occasions where he is transmitting, if the term has meaning, the "Zen" of the Rinzai School, and its methods of achieving this state of consciousness for those with minds capable of receiving it at a high intellectual level. Thirdly, there are articles and lectures pitched in a lower key, to help those of humbler capacity to gain at least some idea of "what it's all about." Finally, there are comparisons of Zen with other fields of enquiry, as with Jung's psychology. All are represented in this voume, but it is not for the Editor to suggest into what category any one item should be placed.

The author himself had clearly achieved a very highly developed intuition, which is the level of consciousness on which Zen "functions," and he would speak, impromptu if need be, to a meeting large or small from that level, choosing his words according to the needs and ability of his audience. Hence, as many have found, although one may read numerous books and articles in which he tried to convey the spirit of Zen to a Western audience, there may be in one more talk or lecture that sudden spark from mind to mind which lights up the reader's ignorance, as nothing has before. Sooner or later the last word of transmission from this profoundly illumined mind should be recovered and preserved. Here at least is further material. While planning the volume I had the good fortune to meet again Mr. Samuel Bercholz of Shambhala Publications, Inc. of the United States of America, and he at once suggested joint publication with the Buddhist Society, an offer gladly accepted.

Little difficulty arises in the matter of copyright, especially when all the material came into being at least twenty years ago. I have done what I can to obtain permission to reprint articles from magazines but find that several have ceased to exist. As for the talks, many were given at or under the auspices of the Buddhist Society, or on occasions where it has proved impossible to trace the organizer of the meeting at which they were given. I apologize to those, if any, to whom I seem to have been discourteous.

The material in this volume covers a wide field, from that of Mahāyāna Buddhism generally to the Zen school of Buddhism in particular; from Japanese art and culture to the first translation into English of a sermon from the "Sayings of Rinzai"; from formal lectures to informal talks to an enraptured audience at the Buddhist Society; from Zen Buddhism and its relation to Western psychology to the famous lecture at the Queen's Hall in London in 1936 on "The Supreme Spiritual Ideal," which none of us present will forget.

An adequate biography of this famous and deeply spiritual man has yet to be written, but as most of the material in this volume appeared on visits to Europe I have added part of the report on the Centenary of his birth as celebrated at the Buddhist Society in London in October 1970.

Dr. D. T. Suzuki

(October 18, 1870–1970)

The Lecture Hall was crowded on October 21st last to commemo-
rate the Centenary of the birth of Dr. D. T. Suzuki whom the
President, in the Chair, described in terms of spiritual grandeur as the
greatest man he had met. He reminded the audience of this great
scholar-sage's life, from his birth in Kanazawa of a long line of
doctors, through his early education to the time when, abandoning
his university career to sit at the feet, first of Kosen Imagita Roshi and
then Soyen Shaku Roshi in Engakuji, Kamakura, he broke through
the veils of thought, and achieved his enlightenment.

Mr. Humphreys read from the chapter in *The Field of Zen* in which
Dr. Suzuki gives his own description of this, the greatest event in his
long and fruitful life. He agreed to help Dr. Paul Carus in Chicago in
his Buddhist writings, and knew that the time was short to achieve his
"break-through." His master had given him the koan "Mu," and the
winter *sesshin* of December 1896 might be his last chance. As he
wrote in "Early Memories," "I must have put all my spiritual strength
into that sesshin. Up till then I had always been conscious that Mu
was in my mind. But so long as I was conscious of Mu it meant that
somehow I was separate from Mu, and that is not a true *samādhi*. But
about the fifth day I ceased to be conscious of Mu. I was one with Mu,
identified with Mu, so that there was no longer the separateness
implied by being conscious of Mu. This is the real state of *Samādhi*.

"But this *Samādhi* alone is not enough. You must come out of that
state, be awakened from it, and that awakening is *Prajñā*. That
moment of coming out of *Samādhi,* and seeing it for what it is, *that* is
satori. When I came out of that state of *Samādhi* I said, 'I see. This is
it.'"

The next day his master approved his *satori,* and he concludes, "I remember that night as I walked back from the monastery seeing the trees in the moonlight. They looked transparent, and I was transparent too."

It must have been at this time, said Mr. Humphreys, that his master gave him his Buddhist name of Daisetz, "great humility."

Thereafter the speaker told of his long sojourn in the U.S.A. and of his first visit to England in 1912, when he took part in the work of the original Buddhist Society of Great Britain and Ireland. In 1921, back in Japan, he founded *The Eastern Buddhist* and remained its Editor for the next thirty years. In 1927 London received the first series of his *Essays in Zen Buddhism,* which opened the eyes of English Buddhists to the range and glory of the Mahāyāna and in particular to the direct school of Rinzai Zen. Further volumes followed, and in 1938 Dr. Suzuki wrote a foreword to his wife's book *Mahāyāna Buddhism* which she kindly wrote for the Society. Meanwhile, for his famous two volumes on the Laṅkāvatāra Sūtra and Commentary upon it he was given an Hon. D. Litt. by Otani University, Kyoto. In later life he was more fully honored with membership of the Japanese Academy and the Cultural Medal presented to him by the Emperor.

But Mr. Humphreys was mainly concerned with Dr. Suzuki's connection with the Society, the first occasion being in 1936 when he came to Europe for a lecture tour, and to attend the London meeting of the World Congress of Faiths. The speaker described his memorable speech at the Queen's Hall on the set subject of the Supreme Spiritual Ideal. It seemed that Dr. Suzuki had to be woken up to give his contribution, but then, brushing aside the given theme, which he said he did not understand, he spoke of his "little thatched house" in Japan, and thus brought the vast audience down to the realities of Zen which are to be found in matters here and now rather than in abstract phrases.

When he paid his first visit to the Society, on 20th July 1936, he proved himself, said the speaker, a real Zen master. Quoting from Alan Watts's recollection of that memorable evening, which tallied with his own diary, he said,

"A member of the audience asked him, 'Dr. Suzuki, when you use the word reality, are you referring to the relative reality of the physical world or to the absolute reality of the transcendental world?'

He closed his eyes and went into that characteristic attitude which some of us called 'doing a Suzuki,' for no one could tell whether he was in deep meditation or fast asleep. After about a minute's silence he opened his eyes and said, 'Yes.'"

Dr. Suzuki spent the war in seclusion, writing in English and Japanese, suspect for his Western sympathies. "In 1946," said Mr. Humphreys, "I went to Japan for some seven months as a lawyer concerned in the International Trials. I spent my days in my office, and my evenings and weekends working for Japanese Buddhism. I was not troubled by this dichotomy—nor were the Japanese. I found Dr. Suzuki in his 'little thatched house' in Kamakura and he was delighted indeed to renew his contact with the West. I took down in long-hand his translation of the two lectures which he gave to the Emperor on Japanese Buddhism, which we published in London as *The Essence of Buddhism,* and took possession of the commentary on the Sutra of Hui Neng which we published in London as *The Zen Doctrine of No-Mind.* I noted the profound respect in which he was held in all monasteries, although of course he was not a monk, much less a great Abbot. He was busy founding the Matsugoaka Library with his own books and those of the late Mrs. Suzuki. He taught me in one remark what Zen is not, and gave a hint of what it is. We were discussing Buddhism as pantheism. 'I see what you mean,' I said, 'all is God but there is no God.' 'No,' he said, after the usual moment's thought. 'It would be better to say, "All is God and there is no God."' You must work that one out," said Mr. Humphreys to his puzzled audience, "for yourselves."

The speaker then described how Dr. Suzuki made him his London agent and how, with the help of Rider and Co., some eight volumes of the Collected Works in English were rapidly published.

"In 1953," said Mr. Humphreys, "he came to London again, this time with Miss Mihoko Okamura, his lovely and charming secretary-companion who gave her life to the old gentleman—he was already eighty-three—for the next twelve years." Quoting from a report in *The Middle Way* of Dr. Suzuki's attendance at the Annual General Meeting he read, "We noted he was one of the few who could lift the audience for the time being beyond the limitation of concept, and enable them to share what was to him a living and immediate experience."

"He came again in 1954, but his longest stay was in 1958, and we made the most of him. He arrived in time for Wesak, with a full program of lectures and visits already planned. We claimed every moment of his spare time, and although then eighty-eight he gave us lectures, attended classes, and meetings at members' homes, and we took him sight-seeing. He possessed the most dreadful old umbrella, but finally allowed us to substitute a new one, and to place the old one, as it is here tonight, on the mantelpiece for meetings of what was immediately called 'The Brolly Club.' His sense of humor was so deep-grained that somehow a large part of our time with him was taken up with laughter. Writing on his bed in the Rembrandt Hotel he gave us six most beautiful specimens of his handwriting.

"But all things have an end, and in time we had to say good-bye. Even at the airport he was helping me to understand a point made on the previous evening, on the relation of the unconscious to *satori,* and as he demonstrated what he meant with a diagram on the back of an envelope, for the moment I understood. Then he went away.

"I continued a long correspondence with him, and he was most generous in help on the precise meaning of Japanese terms in my *Popular Dictionary of Buddhism.* He promised to bequeath us one half of the royalties I collected on some of the books we published in London, but in 1965 most generously gave us there and then one half of the sum already collected, some £1,800.

"A year later he was taken ill, just before, at the age of 95, leaving for a summer holiday on which he proposed to read proofs, finish a book and write an Introduction to another. He died on 12th July 1966. As was written by Sohaku Kobori Roshi in the Memorial issue of *The Eastern Buddhist:*

On the afternoon of 14th July, his body became a wreath of white smoke in the crematorium in Kita Kamakura. The smoke vanished into the cool breeze blowing from the sea. Where did he go? Look, here he is. He will never die—the vow he made! His great will, which communicated the incommunicable, and shared it with all human beings, will not vanish forever. The wheel of this vow, which had gone throughout his 95 years, must be driven further and further, generation after generation, as long as human beings exist on the earth.

"He was," continued Mr. Humphreys, "a Zen man, a man of Zen. Of Westerners I only knew R. H. Blyth and Father Thomas Merton who seemed to speak with even comparable authority. His appeal was that of Bodhidharma, Hui Neng, Huang Po and Rinzai himself, to direct enlightenment, where the Wisdom of *Prajñā* is merged in ceaseless action in the service of mankind. He was in the direct line of the great masters, and spoke and wrote from their awareness. He lived in the Wisdom with a truly divine compassion for all living things.

"In fifty years of work in the field of Buddhism I have known great men and women of many nationalities. I have met and studied with great Theras of the Theravada, great Lamas of Tibet, great Roshis of Japan, but all in all I have met none with the sheer spiritual grandeur of Daisetz Teitaro Suzuki."

The Chairman then called on Dr. Carmen Blacker, Reader in Japanese in Cambridge University, who had worked with Miss Okamura to obtain from Dr. Suzuki the material which now appears under "Early Memories" in *The Field of Zen*. Dr. Blacker gave a most vivid description of personal visits to Dr. Suzuki and his secretary companion, Miss Mihoko Okamura. She asked him if he would give an account of his first contacts with Zen, and she wrote down his description, as he gave it, in his little house on the hillside, looking across the valley to the roofs of the Engakuji Monastery.

Dr. Suzuki described visits to Zen masters, and the harsh, tough treatment he had endured. She was struck by the mind which had responded to the koan training, and his treatment had not been resented. Time and again he said "This was not cruel—this was kind treatment." Dr. Blacker said this method of training had produced great self-control and depth of wisdom-compassion, and we were not likely to meet another like him.

As a final contribution Mr. Humphreys then read a collated series of extracts from the Memorial Volume of *The Eastern Buddhist,* each bringing out some quality in Dr. Suzuki which the writer wished to emphasize. He closed with a memorable extract from the contribution of Father Thomas Merton.

Speaking for myself, I can venture to say that in Dr. Suzuki, Buddhism finally became for me completely comprehensible, whereas before it had been a very mysterious and confusing jumble of words, images, doctrines, legends, rituals, buildings, and so forth. It seemed to me that the great and baffling cultural luxuriance which has clothed the various forms of Buddhism in different parts of Asia is the beautiful garment thrown over something quite simple. The greatest religions are all, in fact, very simple. They all retain very important essential differences, no doubt, but in their inner reality they all end up with the simplest and most baffling thing of all: direct confrontation with Absolute Being, Absolute Love, Absolute Mercy or Absolute Void, by an immediate and fully awakened engagement in the living of everyday life. In Christianity the confrontation is theological and affective, through word and love. In Zen it is metaphysical and intellectual through insight and emptiness. Yet Christianity too has its tradition of apophatic contemplation or knowledge in "unknowing," while the last words I remember Dr. Suzuki saying (before the usual good-byes) was "*The most important thing is Love!*" I must say that as a Christian I was profoundly moved. Truly *Prajñā* and *Karuṇā* are one.

Closing the meeting Mr. Humphreys said: "May I close with an apt quotation from Chuang-Tzu, whom Dr. Suzuki regarded as the greatest philosopher of China. 'The master came because it was his time to be born; he went because it was his time to die. For those who accept the phenomenon of birth and death in this sense, lamentation and sorrow have no place.' Nevertheless, we shall remember, bearing in mind this sound advice, 'Seek not to follow in the footsteps of the Ancient Ones. Seek what they sought.' Peace be with him."

The audience sat for a while until the deep notes of the bronze gong had slowly died away.

The Development of Mahāyāna Buddhism

This article was written for the Buddhist Review, the journal of the newly formed Buddhist Society in Great Britain and Ireland, in 1909. Concerning the use of the term Hīnayāna, meaning smaller vehicle (of liberation) as distinct from the Mahāyāna, large vehicle, Dr. Suzuki refers to the "historical odium" of the former term but retains it for convenience. I have done the same throughout and the article appears as first published.—ED.

European Buddhist scholars are accustomed to divide Buddhism into two, Northern and Southern. They understand by Southern Buddhism that which mostly prevails in Ceylon, Burma, and Siam, while Northern Buddhism is represented by Tibetan Lamaism, as well as by that in China, Korea, and Japan. This geographical division, however, does not seem to be quite correct or justifiable, for we know that the Buddhism of Tibet is as different from the Buddhism of Japan, as it is from that of Ceylon or Burma, not only in some of its teachings but principally in its practical aspect. Take, for instance, the Chinese or Japanese Zen Sect (Ch'an in Chinese and Dhyāna in Sanskrit), or the Sect of the Pure Land, and compare it with Tibetan Buddhism as it is known today, and it will be found that the difference between the two is wider perhaps than that between the so-called Southern Buddhism, and one of the Japanese or Chinese Buddhist sects, known as Risshu (Li in Chinese and Vinaya in Sanskrit).

It is probably better to divide Buddhism into the Buddhism of Arhats and that of Bodhisattvas, understanding by the former, that Buddhism whose ideal attainment is Arhatship, and by the Buddhism of Bodhisattvas, that system of Buddhist teaching, which makes the conception of Bodhisattvahood its most prominent feature. Or we can retain the old way of classifying the followers of Buddhism into the

1

Mahāsāṅghika and the Sthavira, or even invent a new method of division, and call the one progressionists and the other conservatives.

Taking all in all, however, it seems that the distinction of Mahāyāna and Hīnayāna Buddhism is preferable to all the rest, as far as our present knowledge of the development of Buddhism is concerned. Of course, this distinction recalls an historical odium, which it is best for modern scholars to avoid. Neglecting this latter objection, the term Mahāyāna is comprehensive and definite enough to include all those schools of Buddhism, in which the ideal of Bodhisattvahood is upheld in preference to the attainment of Arhatship, and whose geographical distribution covers not only the Northern parts of India but extends eastward. Let us therefore use the term Mahāyāna in this article more for the sake of practical convenience than anything else, until the time arrives when Buddhism is thoroughly studied in all its diverse aspects, historical, dogmatic, ritualistic, etc.

The object of the present article is to expound briefly, what in our opinion constitutes the essential characteristics of the Mahāyāna Buddhism, in contradistinction to the Hīnayāna Buddhism.

If one wishes to sum up Mahāyānism in one word, it can be said that it is essentially speculative. Buddhism generally teaches three forms of discipline: moral, contemplative, and intellectual; and of these the last seems to have been particularly emphasized by the Mahāyānists, while moral discipline has become the chief feature of Southern Buddhism, so called—in fact, to such an extent, that most Western students of Buddhism, whose principal source of information is the Pāli Tipitaka, are apt to take Buddhism as neither more nor less than a sort of ethical culture society, which therefore must not be called a religious system in the same sense of Christianity. While the Buddha apparently taught a well-balanced practice of *Śīla, Dhyāna,* and *Prajñā,* his followers became one-sided, as is generally the case with all religious teachings, and emphasized one point at the expense of others. Mahāyānism in one sense can be said to have gone too far in its speculative flight, almost to the point of forgetting its ethical code, the *Vinaya,* while the Hīnayāna adherents are apt to bring upon themselves the criticism of too much conservatism, and a refusal to adapt themselves to their ever-changing environment. Whether these criticisms be well-founded or not, a practical reformer of Buddhism today, would do well to endeavour to restore the equilibrium between the three forms of discipline, and thus carry out more perfectly the original spirit of its founder.

This one-sided development of the two forms of Buddhism can also be seen in their respective histories. In Ceylon, there has been practically but one sect ever since its introduction. The Singhalese Buddhists have one code of morality, the *Vinaya,* which is recorded in detail in their scriptures, and which, being so explicit in its enunciation that even the unlearned could comprehend it readily, does not allow any very widely divergent interpretations. Accordingly, there were few chances of dissent. The *Vinaya* as it is practiced today in Ceylon has not changed perhaps, even in its details, since the day of its first promulgation in that island. In this respect, we can say that Hīnayāna Buddhism faithfully preserves the practical form of Buddhist moral culture as it developed during the time that elapsed between the decease of the Buddha and the despatch of the Aśoka missionaries to Ceylon. We emphasize this latter point, for it is quite reasonable to suppose, as is justified by the records in our possession, that Buddhism began to change, among the Buddha's variously-endowed disciples, soon after his time.

History, however, records quite a different state of affairs among the Mahāyānists. Into how many schools did it divide itself, and how vehemently did each school contend for its own doctrines against the others? While the Hīnayānists evidently kept quiet, the Mahāyānists treated their fellow-believers in a way which was not in perfect accord with their professed liberalism. In fact, it was through their self-conceit, that they came to designate themselves as Mahāyāna Buddhists, followers of the Great Vehicle of Salvation, to the disparagement of their somewhat conservative brothers in the faith. This spirit of self-exaltation was exhibited, not only against those in a sense the more orthodox ethical adherents of Buddhism, but also among themselves, as is seen in the policy of the famous founder of the Nichiren or Puṇḍarīka Sect in Japan. His denunciation of the other Buddhist sects then existing in his country was so strong and vehement and almost abusive that the authorities of the time thought it expedient quietly to get rid of him, though we must add that his prosecution was not entirely for religious reasons.

This struggle and conflict, however, was in accord with the somewhat one-sided development of Mahāyānism in the direction of speculative philosophy. Intellect is always inclined to dissent, to quarrel, to become self-conceited, and the rise of the ten or twelve sects of Japanese Buddhism was the inevitable result of the Mahāyāna movement in general. Of course, they have not forgotten phases of Buddhism other than intellectual, for the practice of *dhyāna* is still in evidence—indeed, there is one sect in Japan and China bearing the very name, and exercising much influence especially among the educated classes, but the fact remains that the Mahāyāna Buddhism is a development of one side—the intellectual, speculative, philosophical side—of Buddhism, while Hīnayānism preserves its ethical ideals. To realize the perfect form of Buddhism, the threefold treasure, triratna, must be equally developed: the Buddha, the Dharma, and the Sangha must stand side by side, imbued with the same spirit as when they were first established, whatever outward transformation they may have undergone. If Hīnayānism is said to preserve the Sangha in its perfect form, Mahāyānism may be considered to have fully developed the religio-philosophical significance of Buddhism, while both schools claim the Buddha as their common founder. The problem that faces faithful Buddhists at present is how best to effect a complete reconciliation of the moral discipline of Hīnayānism with the speculations of Mahā-yānism.

Now in order to see how Mahāyānism has developed speculation as compared with Hīnayānism, we will first discuss the doctrine of *Anāt-man,* or "non-ego." This is considered to be one of the most important and characteristic features of Buddhism, and justly so, for both the Hīnayāna and the Mahāyāna uphold this as essential. The Hīnayāna school, however, seems to have remained almost too faithful, as it were, to the doctrine—it has not gone beyond its negative statement, it has not carried out its logical consequence to its utmost limits; while Mahāyānism has not only extended the theory from its subjective significance to the objective world, but has also boldly developed the positive conclusion implied in it. We do not mean that the Hīnayāna has none of the tendencies shown by the Mahāyāna; in fact, the former seems to contain everything Mahāyānistic in its germinal form, if we may use the term. What most conspicuously distinguishes the Mahā-yāna school in this connection is that it makes most explicit, manifest, unequivocal, and fearless assertions on the religio-philosophical questions which deeply concern the human heart.

In the case of the non-ego theory, the Mahāyānists assert that there is no *ātman* or ego-soul not only in its subjective aspect but in its objective application. That is to say, they deny with the Hīnayāna followers

that there is such a thing as the ego-substance behind our consciousness, as a concrete, simple, ultimate, and independent unit; but they go
still further and declare that this objective world too has no *ātman,* no
ego, no God, no personal creator, no *Īsvara,* working and enjoying his
absolute transcendence behind this eternal concatenation of cause and
effect. This is technically known as the double negation of the subjective and the objective world, and for this reason the Mahāyāna
school has often been called, though unjustifiably and quite incorrectly,
nihilism or *śūnyavādin.*

It may be interesting to quote a Western Buddhist scholar's opinion
of Buddhism as typical of a prejudiced and uncritical judge. Eitel, a
noted student of Chinese Buddhism, thus speaks of the Buddhist
doctrine of Nirvāṇa in his "Three Lectures on Buddhism," delivered in
Union Church, Hong Kong, 1870–1871. "Nirvāṇa is to them (Buddhists) a state of which nothing can be said, to which no attributes can
be given; it is altogether an abstract, devoid alike of all positive and all
negative qualities. What shall we say of such empty, useless speculations, such sickly, dead words, whose fruitless sophistry offers to that
natural yearning of the human heart after an eternal rest, nothing better
than a philosophical myth? It is but natural that a religion which started
with moral and intellectual bankruptcy should end in moral and intellectual suicide." (Page 21, col. 2)

As a matter of fact, the Mahāyānists do not regard negation as the
ultimate goal of their speculations; for with them negation is but a road
to reach a higher form of affirmation, and they are aware of the fact
that the human mind lives in affirmation, and not in negation. Any
critic of Mahāyāna philosophy, who has sufficient sympathetic insight
to penetrate deep enough into its heart, would readily find that behind
the series of negations offered by the Mahāyāna thinkers there is really
the assertion of a higher truth, which, owing to the limitations of the
human mind, cannot be represented by any other means than negation.
It is not on account of sophistry or mere abstraction, that Buddhists
sometimes appear to delight in a negative state of truth. They are most
earnestly religious, they know that the deepest religious truth cannot be
presented in a stereotyped philosophical formula. Only those who are
timidly shortsighted, stop at the negation and refuse to go beyond, and
if they thus misjudge the signification of Mahāyāna Buddhism, the
fault is on their own side.

What is then that positive something offered by Mahāyāna scholars as the logical conclusion of the theory of non-ego? It is generally designated as *Tattva* or Suchness. This is a philosophical term, and when its religious import is emphasized, it is called *Dharmakāya.* The term, *Dharmakāya,* is very difficult to define. Essence-Body, Being-Body, Being-System does not exactly express all the ideas contained in it. Dharma is a very comprehensive term in Buddhist philosophy, and in this case it means essence, being, law, and doctrine. In short let us understand *Dharmakāya* here as the source, the ultimate reality, from which is derived the reason of existence, morality, and religion. In this conception of Suchness, or *Dharmakāya,* Mahāyānists find the highest possible affirmation reached after a series of negations, and unifying all forms of contradiction, psychological, ethical, and ontological. Aśvaghoṣa, one of the greatest of the early Indian Buddhist philosophers, says in his *Awakening of Faith in the Mahāyāna,*[1] "Suchness is neither that which is existent, nor that which is non-existent; it is neither that which is at once existent and non-existent, nor that which is not at once existent and non-existent; it is neither that which is one, nor that which is many; neither that which is at once one and many, nor that which is not at once one and many. . . . It is altogether beyond the conception of the human intellect, and the best way of designating it seems to be to call it Suchness."

Nāgārjuna, the founder of the Mādhyamika school of Buddhism in India, who was equally great as Aśvaghoṣa, declares in his *Treatise on the Mean,* "No birth, no death, no persistence, no oneness, no many-ness, no coming, no departing: . . . this is the doctrine of the Mean." Again, "To think, 'it is,' is eternalism: to think 'it is not,' is nihilism. To be and not to be, the wise cling to neither."

All these statements have been construed as nihilistic and leading the mind nowhere but to absolute emptiness. But, as we have said before, such critics entirely ignore the fact that the human understanding, owing to its constitutional shortcomings, often finds it most expedient and indeed most logical to state a truth in the form of a negation, as really expressing a higher form of affirmation, and comprehended only through a process of intuition. The Mahāyāna thinkers have denied with their conservative fellow-believers the existence of a concrete ego-soul;

[1]Translated by the author from the Chinese, 1900.

they have refused to accept the doctrine of a personal God; they are further reluctant to assert anything dogmatically; and the ultimate logical consequence of all these necessarily negative statements could not be anything else than the conception of Suchness. Beyond this, one enters upon mysticism—philosophy must bow her head modestly at this gate of Suchness, and let religion proceed by herself into an unknown wilderness, or "Wülde, or "Abgrund," as the German mystics are fond of designating this realm of "Eternal Yes," or that which is the same thing, of "Eternal No." At this point, therefore, Mahāyānism becomes mysticism. Intellectually, it has gone as far as it could. *Vidyā* must give way to *dhyāna* or *Prajñā,* that is, intellect to intuition, which is after all the ultimate goal of all religious discipline. Mysticism is the life of religion; without it religion loses the reason of its existence—all its warm vitality is gone, all its inexpressible charms vanish, and there remains nothing but the crumbling bones and the cold ashes of death. We said before that Mahāyānism was highly speculative, but it must now be added that it is most deeply and thoroughly religious.

It is apparent that with the conception of Suchness, Mahāyāna speculations have reached their culminating point, and upon this stands the grand religious edifice of Mahāyāna Buddhism. Superficially, Mahāyānism seems very different from Hīnayānism; but when its development is traced along the lines indicated above, one will readily comprehend that in spite of the disparity which exists between the two yānas of Buddhism, the one is no more than a continuity of the other, which started intellectually and ends in speculative mysticism.

When the conception of Suchness is established, the reason of Mahāyānism becomes evident. Buddhism is no more an agnostic system than a system of atheistic ethics. For in Suchness or *Dharmakāya* it finds the reason of existence, the true reality, the norm of morality, the source of love and goodness, the fountain head of righteousness, absolute intelligence, and the starting point of karma—for Suchness, according to the Mahāyāna thinkers, is not a mere state of being, but it is energy, intelligence, and love. But as Suchness begins to take these attributes upon itself, it ceases to be transcendental Suchness; it is now conditioned Suchness. So long as it remained absolutely transcendental, allowing neither negation nor affirmation, it was beyond the ken of the human understanding, and could not very well become the object of our religious consciousness. But there was the awakening of a will in

Suchness, and with this awakening we have conditional and self-limiting Suchness in place of the absolutely unknowable. (As to the why and how of this process, we have to confess a profound and eternal ignorance.) It is in this transformation, so to speak, of Suchness that the Mahāyāna system recognizes the religious significance of *Dharmakāya.*

The *Dharmakāya* is now conceived by the human heart as love and wisdom, and its eternal prayer is heard to be the deliverance of the ignorant from their self-created evil karma which haunts them as an eternal curse. The process of deliverance is to awaken in the mind of the ignorant the *Samyaksambodhi,* or most perfect wisdom, which is the reflection of the *Dharmakāya* in sentient beings. This wisdom, this *Bodhi,* is generally found asleep in the benighted, who are in a spiritual slumber induced by the narcotic influence of evil karma, which has been and is being committed by them, because of their non-realization of the presence in themselves of the *Dharmakāya.* Deliverance or enlightenment, therefore, consists of making every sentient being open his mental eye to this fact. It is not his ego-soul that makes him think, feel, desire, or aspire, but the *Dharmakāya* itself in the form of *Bodhicitta* or "wisdom-heart" which constitutes his ethical and religious being. Abandon the thought of egoism, and return to the universal source of love and wisdom, and we are released from the bond of evil karma, we are enlightened as to the reason of existence, we are Buddhas.

In trying to make a sentient being realize the presence in himself of the *Bodhicitta,* the *Dharmakāya* can be said to be working for its own awakening. Here is involved a great philosophical and religious problem. In the beginning, the *Dharmakāya* negated itself by its own affirmation, and it is now working to release itself from the negation, through which this world of particulars was created. This is, as it seems to our limited intellect, an eternal process of Suchness, from affirmation to negation, and from negation to affirmation. To this mystery of mysteries, however, we fail to apply our rules of syllogism, we have simply to state the truth, apparently contradictory, that our religious consciousness finds in this mystery something unspeakably fascinating and indeed the justification of her own eternal yearning.

At any rate, as a consequence of the conception of Suchness or *Dharmakāya* as eternal motherhood, as the source of infinite love, the doctrine of karma had to modify, as it were, its irrefragable severity. Here we observe another phase of differentiation as effected by the Mahāyānists from the doctrine commonly held by their ethical, monastic brethren; we do not maintain that the doctrine of karma is denied by Mahāyāna thinkers, far from it. They adhere to the doctrine as firmly as the Hīnayāna philosophers; they have taken away only its crushing effects upon the sinful, who are always too timid, too weak-hearted to bear the curse of all their former evil deeds. In other words, the Mahāyāna Buddhists offer a doctrine complementary to that of karma, in order to give a more satisfying and more human solution to our inmost religious needs. The Mahāyāna doctrine of *Pariṇāmanā,* therefore, must go side by side with that of karma; for through this harmonious co-working of the two, the true spirit of Buddhism will be more effectively realized. In this phase of development, Mahāyāna Buddhism must be said to be profoundly religious.

The doctrine of *Pariṇāmanā* is essentially that of vicarious sacrifice. Apparently it contradicts the continuity of karmaic activity; but in Mahāyāna Buddhism, it must be remembered, karma is conceived more in its cosmic aspect than individualistically, and it is therefore possible to reconcile the two notions, karma and *Pariṇāmanā.* We will try to make this point clear.

First, what does *Pariṇāmanā* mean? It comes from the root *nam,* to which is prefixed the particle *pari,* and we take the term as meaning "to bend toward," "to deliver," "to transfer," or "to renounce," for which the Chinese Buddhists use *hui shang,* meaning "to turn in the direction of." The doctrine of *Pariṇāmanā,* then, is to turn one's merit over to another, to renounce oneself for another, to sacrifice one's interests for the benefit of others, to atone for the evil karma of others by one's own good deeds, or to substitute oneself for another, who ought properly speaking to suffer his own karma. To use Christian terminology, the doctrine of *Pariṇāmanā* is in some respects identical with the doctrine of vicarious sacrifice; but it must be remembered that while vicarious sacrifice in Christianity means the death of Christ on the cross for the sin of mankind, the Mahāyānists do not confine the principle to a solitary historical incident. Christianity is built upon the history of a person, whatever its intrinsic authenticity, and not directly upon intellectual necessity and the facts of religious consciousness. Therefore, it is unable to uphold the universal application of the principal of vicarious sacrifice, and cannot appreciate the importance of the principle of karma. Herein lies the strength of Christianity, the strength of concreteness and objectivity, as compared with Mahāyāna Buddhism; but herein lies also its weakness—at least so it seems to Buddhist thinkers. A religion built upon history naturally appeals more vividly to our imagination, but the foundation does not seem so firm, as that of one which derives its sanction directly from the human heart.

The Mahāyāna notion of *Pariṇāmanā* is based upon the following truths: The universe is a grand spiritual system composed of moral beings, who are so many fragmentary reflexes of the *Dharmakāya*. The system is so closely knitted together that when any part of it or any unit composing it is affected in any way, good or bad, all the other parts or units are drawn into the general commotion which follows, and share the common fate. This subtle spiritual system, of which all sentient beings are its parts or units, is like a vast ocean in which the eternal moonlight of *Dharmakāya* is reflected. Even a faint wavelet which is noticed in one part of the water is sure to spread, sooner or later, according to the resistance of the molecules, over its entire surface, and thus finally disturb the serenity of the lunar image in it. Likewise, at every deed, good or evil, committed by any of the sentient units of this spiritual organization, the *Dharmakāya* rejoices or is grieved. When it is grieved, it wills to counteract the evil with goodness; when it rejoices, it knows that so far the cause of goodness has been advanced. Individual karma, therefore, is not really individual, it is most intimately connected with the whole, and is not an isolated phenomenon originating from the individual and returning to the same agent. In fact, it is no mere abstraction to say that the lifting of my arm or the moving of my leg is not an accidental, indifferent act, but is directly related to the ultimate cause of the universe. This assertion applies with an immeasurably greater emphasis to an act which has a moral bearing. "If," we can ask ourselves, "in our spiritual plan of existence things are so intimately related to one another, why could we not make the merit of our own deeds compensate or destroy the effect of an evil karma created by an ignorant mind? Why could we not suffer for the sake of others, and lighten, even to a small degree, the burden of evil karma under which weak and ignorant ones are groaning, though they have nobody but themselves to blame for their own wretchedness?" These questions were answered by Mahāyāna thinkers, affirmatively. They said, "It is possible for us to dedicate our own good karma to the cause of universal goodness, and to suppress or crush or to make quite inefficacious the evil karma perpetrated by the ignorant. It is possible for us to substitute ourselves for others and to bear the burden in their behalf, thus saving them from their self-created curse." The result of this conviction is the doctrine of *Pariṇāmanā*.

In this, therefore, it is seen that quite in accordance with the cosmic conception of *Dharmakāya*, Mahāyāna philosophers emphasize the universal or supra-individual significance of karma more than its solitary, individual character. In the Hīnayāna system, the conception of karma is individualistic pure and simple, there is no escape whatever from the consequence of one's evil or good deeds, for it follows one even after death which is merely another form of birth. The Mahāyāna Buddhists believe in this as far as the law of karmaic causation is concerned, but they go one step further and assert that karma has also its cosmic or supra-individual aspect which must be taken into consideration when we want to realize fully the meaning of our spiritual existence. Though a man had to reap what he had sown, and there were no possible escape from the consequence of his evil deeds, the Mahāyānists would say, a Bodhisattva wishes from his fullness of heart to turn over to the general welfare of his community whatever merit he can have from his acts of goodness, and to bear upon himself whatever burden of evil is going to befall his ignorant, self-destroying fellow-beings. The good he does is not necessarily for his own interest; the evil he avoids is not always for his own benefit; whatever deed he performs, he does not forget its universal character; above all, he desires to be of service in any capacity to the whole spiritual community of which he is a unit.

In point of fact, therefore, the doctrine of *Pariṇāmanā* is more than that of vicarious sacrifice. It is that, in so far as a Bodhisattva wishes to bear the burden of evil for the real offenders, and to save them from sufferings, but when he works to add to the "general stock of goodness," and to nourish the "root of merit" in this world, he is doing more than merely substituting, he is doing something positive. *Pariṇāmanā* is vicarious sacrifice, self-renunciation, the transference of merit, the promotion of universal goodness, the annihilation of "me" and "thee," the recognition of the oneness of all things, and the complete satisfaction of our inmost religious yearnings.

The doctrine of karma is terrible; the doctrine of *Pariṇāmanā* is humane: karma is the law of nature, inflexible and irreconcilable; *Pariṇāmanā* is the heart of a religious being, filled with tears: the one is rigidly masculine and knows no mercy whatever; the other is most tenderly feminine, always ready to weep and help: the one is justice incarnate; the other is absolute love: the one is the god of thunder and lightning, who crushes everything that dares to resist him; the other is a gentle spring shower, warm, soft, and relaxing, and helping all life to grow: we bow before the one in awe and reverence; we embrace the other as if finding again the lost mother: we must have the one to be responsible for our own thoughts, feelings, aspirations, and deeds; but we cannot let the other go, as we need love, tolerance, humaneness, and kindheartedness. Mahāyāna Buddhism can thus be said to have a singularly softening effect on the conception of karma. Karma cannot be denied, it is the law; but the human heart is tender and loving, it cannot remain calm and unconcerned at the sight of suffering, in whatever way this might have been brought about. It knows that all things ultimately come from the one source; when others suffer I suffer too; why then should not self-renunciation somehow moderate the austerity of karma? This is the position taken by Mahāyāna Buddhists in regard to the doctrine of karma.

With the moderation, as it were, of karmaic theory, another change took place in the system of Mahāyāna Buddhism concerning the notion of an ideal man, that is, as to what constitutes the true ideal Buddhist, or what kind of being he must be, who really embodies all the noble thoughts and enlightened sentiments of Mahāyāna Buddhism. Arhatship was not quite satifactory in this respect, and ceased to be the goal of religious discipline for the followers of the Mahāyāna. They considered the Arhat as one not fully realizing all the inmost aspirations of the religious consciousness, for he was a Buddhist who sought only his own deliverance from the whirlpool of birth and death, in which all beings are struggling and being drowned. So long as karma was looked upon in its individualistic aspect, Arhatship was quite the right thing for the Buddhists to aspire after; but karma could be interpreted in another and wider sense, which made the doctrine of *Pariṇāmanā* possible, and Mahāyānists thought that this was more in accord with the deepest yearnings of a religious being, who wants to save not only himself but the entire world as well. Therefore, the speculative Buddhists came to establish the ideal of Bodhisattvahood in place of Arhatship; and for this reason Mahāyānism is often designated as Bodhisattvayāna, in contradistinction to Śrāvakayāna and Pratyekabuddhayāna.

The development of the ideal of Bodhisattvahood was quite natural with Mahāyāna Buddhists. Grant that the followers of the Hīnayāna more faithfully adhered to the moral, monastic, and disciplinary life of primitive Buddhism, while the Mahāyānists were bent on the unfolding of the religio-philosophical significance of the teachings of Buddha, and it will be seen that the further they go, the wider is their separation from each other. To the moralists, such a bold flight of imagination, as that conceived by the Mahāyānists, was a very difficult thing to realize; moral responsibility implies a strict observance of the law of karma; what one has done cannot be undone; good or bad, one has to suffer the karmaic consequence. Nobody can interfere with it; Arhatship alone, therefore, could be made the goal of those self-disciplining moralists. With the Mahāyānists, however, it was different. They came to look at the import of our moral action more from the point of view of its cosmic relations, or from that of the most intimate interdependence that obtains among all sentient beings, in their moral, intellectual, and spiritual activities. With this change of point of view, they could not but come to the realization of the doctrine of *Pariṇāmanā*.

There are not two Buddhisms; the Mahāyāna and the Hīnayāna are one, and the spirit of the founder of Buddhism prevails on both. Each has developed in its own way, according to the difference of environment in which each has thrived and grown—understanding by environment all those various factors of life that make up the peculiarities of an individual or a nation. The lack of communication has hitherto prevented the bringing together of Buddhists, and they have therefore not yet arrived at a complete understanding of one another. The time is ripening now when each will fully realize and candidly admit its own shortcomings and advantages, and earnestly desire to cooperate with others to bring about a perfect assimilation of all Buddhist thoughts and practices into one uniform system, and thus contribute to the promotion of peace and goodwill towards all beings, regardless of their racial and national differences.

The Message of Bodhidharma

FOUNDER OF ZEN BUDDHISM

The history of Zen Buddhism starts with Bodhidharma, popularly known as Daruma in Japan and Tamo in China, who came to China late in the fifth century. But the significance of Daruma was not fully recognized until the time of Yeno (Hui-neng in Chinese) when a dispute arose between him and his opponent, Junshu (Shen hsiu). They were both disciples of Gunin (Hung-ien, died 675) and each claimed to transmit the orthodox line of the Zen teaching traceable to the First Patriarch, Bodhidharma. This being the case, we can say that the value and signification of Zen Buddhism as distinct from all the other schools of Buddhism so far developed in China was not manifestly appreciated by its followers until late in the seventh century.

What is then the teaching of Daruma? Three characteristic features of it may be pointed out as distinguishable from other Buddhist schools. As Daruma's teaching, which later came to be known as Zen Buddhism, belongs to the practical wing of the Mahāyāna it does not attempt to offer any novel method of philosophizing on the truth of Buddhism. Daruma was no logician. He simply wanted to live the truth. Whatever he taught, therefore, consisted in presenting a method considered by him to be most effective in the attainment of the final goal of the Buddhist life. The characteristic features of his teaching are thus inevitably all related to the Buddhist discipline.

(1) The first thing needed for the discipline then was to know definitely what the objective of the Buddhist life was. Without full knowledge of this, the yogin would be like a blind man running wild. Daruma pointed out that the objective was to see into the nature of one's own being, and this he designated *shin* or *kokoro* (or *hsin* in Chinese). *Shin* or *hsin* corresponds to the Sanskrit *citta* but fre-

quently to *hridaya*. When it is translated as "mind," it is too intellectual; "heart" is too emotional; while "soul" suggests something concrete—it is so strongly associated with an ego-substance. Provisionally I shall make Mind with a capital "M" perform the office of *shin* or *hsin*. Now Daruma wants us to see into this Mind. For it is only when this is perceived or grasped that we attain the end which is the "peaceful settling of the mind" called *anjin (an-hsin)*.

Daruma's interview with Eka (Hui-k'e) is significant in this respect. He did not talk about realizing Nirvāṇa, or attaining emancipation; nor did he discourse on the doctrine of non-ego, that is *anatta*. When Eka told his master how troubled he was in his mind, the latter at once demanded that he produce this troubled mind before him so that he could calm it for its owner. For this was Daruma's patented method, which had not yet been resorted to by any of his predecessors.

When Eka complained about his mind being in trouble, he used the term "mind" in its conventional meaning, which, however, indicated also that his thought followed the conventional line of reasoning. That is to say, he cherished an unconscious belief in the reality of an entity known as mind or *shin,* and this belief further involved a dualistic interpretation of existence leading to the conceptual reconstruction of experience. As long as such a belief was entertained, one could never realize the end of the Buddhist discipline. Daruma, therefore, wished to liberate Eka from the bondage of the idea of a mind. Liberation was a "pacific settlement" of it, which was at the same time the seeing into the inner nature of one's own being, the Mind.

Eka must have spent many years in this search for a mind, with which he was supposed to be endowed, philosophically or logically as well as conventionally. Finally, it must have dawned upon him that there was after all no such entity as to be known as mind. But this recognition failed to ease his mind, because it still lacked a final "stamping"; it did not break out in his consciousness as a final experience. He appeared again before Daruma and gave an answer to the master's former demand for a mind: "I seek for the mind but it is not attainable." Daruma now exclaimed, "I have your mind peacefully settled!"

Eka now had a real experience; this authoritative "stamping" on the part of the master broke the intellectual barrier and made Eka go beyond the mere formulation of his insight as the unattainability of a mind. Without Daruma's absolute confirmation, Eka did not know yet where to have his "mind" fixed. A fixing was no-fixing, and therefore the fixing, to use the *Prajñā* dialectic. In other words, Eka found his "mind" where it was not to be found, and thus his "mind" came to be finally peacefully settled. This is Daruma's doctrine of Mind.

(2) Did Daruma teach us any definite form of meditation? Zen means *dhyāna,* i.e. meditation. Being the First Patriarch of Zen in China, Daruma naturally advocates meditation. But his is the one specifically known as *Hekkwan (pi-kuan),* literally "wall-gazing." He has never defined the term and it is difficult to know exactly what kind of meditation it was. This much we can say, that as long as it was differentiated from the traditional method and claimed to be Mahāyānistic, it was not mere tranquilization, nor was it a form of contemplation. It was to follow the idea referred to in the *Vimalakīrti:* "When a mind is controlled so as to be steadily fixed on one subject, such a one will accomplish anything." This means "to keep mind as self-concentrated as a rigidly standing cliff, with nothing harassing its imperturbability." For thereby one can enter the Path *(tao).*

Daruma's *Hekkwan,* therefore, means "concentration," fixing attention steadily on one subject. But there must have been something more in it. The *Hekkwan* was the method of finding out the "abode of all thoughts," in other words, of having an insight into the nature of Mind. The method is always defined and controlled by the object. When the object is to experience what is immovable in the movable without stopping its movement, the self-concentration means a state of utmost activity, and not at all mere quietude or passivity. The *Hekkwan* then in connection with its object begins to have a definite signification of its own.

In fact "wall-gazing" is not at all appropriate to explain the *Hekkwan.* "To stand rigidly like a cliff" does not mean the bodily posture assumed by the Zen practicer when he sits cross-legged with his backbone straight. "Being like a cliff or wall" refers to an inner state of mind in which all disturbing and entangling chains of ideas are cut asunder. The mind has no hankerings now; there is in it no looking around, no reaching out, no turning aside, no picturing of anything; it is like a solid rock or a block of wood; there is neither life nor death in it, neither memory nor intellection. Although a mind is spoken of according to the conventional parlance, here there is really no "mind," the mind is no-mind, *shin* is *mushin, hsin* is *wu-hsin, citta* is *acitta*. This is the *Hekkwan* meditation.

But if we imagine this to be the final state of the exercise, we are greatly in the wrong, for we have not yet entered into the Path *(tao)*. The necessary orientation has been achieved, but the thing itself is far beyond. When we stop here, Zen loses its life. There must be a turning here, a waking-up, a new sense of awareness reached, the breaking of the deadlock, so to speak. All the intellectual attempts hitherto made to seek out the abode of all thoughts and desires could not come to this; all forms of contemplation, all the exercises of tranquilization hitherto advocated by the Indian and the Chinese predecessors of Daruma could not achieve this. Why? Because the objects they erected severally for their discipline were altogether amiss and had no inherent power of creation in them.

(3) What may be called the ethical teaching of Daruma's Zen Buddhism is the doctrine of *Mukudoku* (*wu-kung-te* in Chinese) which means "no merit." This is the answer given by Daruma to his Imperial inquirer as to the amount of merit to be accumulated by building temples, making offerings to the Buddha, providing shelters for monks and nuns, etc. According to the First Patriarch, deeds performed with any idea of merit accruing from them have no moral value whatever. Unless you act in accord with the "Dharma," which is by nature pure, beyond good and bad, you cannot be said to be a Zen follower.

According to Daruma, there is no antithesis in the Dharma of good and evil, of detachment and attachment, of "self" and "other." In Daruma's discourse on "the Twofold Entrance" he describes the life of a wise man in the following terms:

As there is in the essence of the Dharma no desire to possess, a wise man is ever ready to practice charity with his body, life and property, and he never begrudges—he never knows what an ill grace means. As he has a perfect understanding of the threefold nature of Emptiness *(śūnyatā)*, he is above partiality and attachment. Only because of his will to cleanse all beings of their stains, he comes among them as one of them, but he is not attached to form. This is the self-benefiting phase of his life. He, however, knows also how to benefit others and again how to glorify the truth of Enlightenment. As with the virtue of Charity, so with the other five virtues: Morality, Humility, Indefatigability, Meditation, and Intuition. That a wise man practices the six virtues of perfection is to get rid of confused thoughts, and yet there is no consciousness on his part that he is engaged in any meritorious deeds—which means to be in accord with the Dharma.

This concept of meritless deeds is one of the most difficult to understand—much more to practice. When this is thoroughly mastered the Zen discipline is said to have been mastered. The first intellectual approach to it is to realize that things of this world are characterized by polarity as they are always to be interpreted in reference to a subject which perceives and values them. We can never escape this polar opposition between subject and object. There is no absolute objective world from which a subject is excluded, nor is there any self-existing subject that has no objective world in any sense standing against it. But unless we escape this fundamental dualism we can never be at ease with ourselves. For dualism means finitude and limitation. This state of things is described by Mahāyānists as "attainable." An attainable mind is a finite one, and all worries, fears, and tribulations we go through are the machination of a finite mind. When this is transcended we plunge into the Unattainable, and thereby peace of mind is gained. The Unattainable is Mind.

This approach, being intellectual, is no more than a conceptual reconstruction of reality. To make it a living fact with blood and nerves, the Unattainable must become attainable, that is, must be experienced, for *anjin* (that is, peaceful settling of the mind) will then for the first time become possible.

In a recently recovered Tung-huang manuscript, which for various reasons I take to be discourses given by Daruma, the author is strongly against mere understanding according to words. The Dharma, according to him, is not a topic for discourse; the Dharma whose other name is Mind is not a subject of memory, nor of knowledge. When pressed for a positive statement, Daruma gave no reply, remaining silent. Is this not also a kind of meritless deed?

According to a Buddhist historian of the T'ang dynasty (618–907 A.D.) the coming of Daruma in China caused a great stir among the Buddhist scholars as well as among ordinary Buddhists, because of his most emphatically antagonistic attitude towards the latter. The scholars prior to him encouraged the study of Buddhist literature in the forms of *sūtras* and *śāstras;* and as the result there was a great deal of philosophical systematization of the dogmas and creeds. On the practical disciplinary side, the Buddhists were seriously engaged in meditation exercises, the main object of which was a kind of training in tranquilization. Daruma opposed this, too; for his *dhyāna* practice had the very high object of attaining to the nature of the Mind itself—and this not by means of learning and scholarship, nor by means of moral deeds, but by means of *Prajñā,* transcendental wisdom. To open up a new field in the Buddhist life was the mission of Daruma.

When Zen came to be firmly established after Yeno (Hui-neng) there grew among his followers a question regarding the coming of Daruma to China. The question was asked not for information, but for self-illumination. By this I mean that the question concerns one's own inner life, not necessarily anybody else's coming and going. While apparently Daruma is the subject, in reality he has nothing to do with it, and therefore in all the answers gathered below we notice no personal references whatever to Daruma himself.

In order to see what development characteristic of Zen Buddhism the teaching of Daruma made after the sixth patriarch, Yeno (Hui-neng), in China, I quote some of the responses made to the question cited above, in which the reader may recognize the working of the Mind variously given expression to:

UMMON YEN: Do you wish to know the Patriarch (Daruma)? So saying he took up his staff, and pointing at the congregation continued: The Patriarch is seen jumping over your heads. Do you wish to know where his eyes are? Look ahead and do not stumble?

KISU SEN: How did people fare before the coming of Daruma to China? Clean povery was fully enjoyed. How after his coming? Filthy wealth is the cause of many worries.

KEITOKU SEI: How were things before Daruma's coming to China? Six times six are thirty-six. How after his coming? Nine times nine are eighty-one.

GYOKU-SEN REN: How were things before Daruma's coming to China? Clouds envelop the mountain peaks. How after his coming? Rains fall on the Hsiao and the Hsiang.

HOUN HON: How as the world before Daruma's coming to China? The clouds dispersing, the three islets loom out clear. How after his coming? The rain passing, the flowers in hundreds are freshened up. What difference is there between before and after his coming? The boatman cleaving the light morning fog goes up the stream, while in the evening he comes down with the sail unfurled over the vapory waves.

To the question, "What is the meaning of Daruma's coming from the West?" the following answers are given by various masters:

RYUGE: This is the question hardest to crack.

RYOZAN KWAN: Don't make a random talk.

FUSUI GAN: Each time one thinks of it one's heart breaks.

SHOSHU: A happy event does not go out of the gate while a bad rumor travels a thousand miles.

DOSAN: I will tell you when the river Do begins to flow upward.

In Zen there is no uniform answer, as far as its apparent meaning is concerned, even to one and the same question, and the spirit is absolutely free in the choice of material when it wants to express itself.

Zen Buddhism

"Zen" is an abbreviation of *Zazen,* which is Japanese; the Chinese original is *Ch'an* which is the translation of the Sanskrit term *Dhyāna*; in Pāli it is *Jhāna.* Chinese scholars do not like to use the original Sanskrit terms; they prefer every Sanskrit term to be translated into Chinese. When they find the Chinese equivalent of the original Sanskrit, then they try to blend the Chinese with the Sanskrit; a kind of hybrid is created in that way. To the Chinese mind these hybrid terms are very expressive and long usage has established words in that hybrid terminology as technical terms.

Now the terms *Ch'an* and *Za-zen* have been dropped and "Zen" alone is used. That means *Jhāna,* which, in its original sense, means "meditation"—not exactly meditation as used in the West, although something very similar to it. So *Jhāna* we may take to mean meditation, contemplation, tranquilization or concentration; such terms nearly express the original meaning of *Jhāna,* but not exactly. But the way in which Zen Buddhism uses the term "Zen" is quite different from its original meaning. This has to be emphasized at the outset.

Zen developed in China in the eighth century. It is traditionally ascribed to Bodhidharma, known as Tamo in China and Daruma in Japan. Bodhidharma came to China from India in the sixth century but what he taught was not exactly what came to be known as Zen. Zen really developed about 150 or 200 years after Bodhidharma came.

The real founder of Zen in China is known as Hui Neng, Wei Lang, or Yeno. What distinguished Hui Neng from his predecessors and from the rest of the Chinese Buddhist teachers is this, which really constitutes the essence of Zen teaching:

Enlightenment is an experience which Buddha had and through which he was able to teach Buddhism. Buddhism really means "the Doctrine of Enlightenment." *Prajñā* is used quite frequently as synonymous with enlightenment.

21

In China, previous to Yeno, it had been thought that this enlightenment could be attained only after one had practiced *Jhāna*, and attained proficiency in meditation. Yeno maintained that *Prajñā* and *Jhāna* should go together; neither alone would do. These two are considered most essential in the study of Buddhism.

There are three forms of discipline in the observance of Buddhism: (1) moral precepts, i.e., non-stealing, etc.; (2) *Jhāna* or Zen; and (3) *Prajñā*. Leaving aside the first, let us begin with Zen or *Jhāna* and *Prajñā*. Yeno said that *Jhāna* is *Prajñā* and *Prajñā* is *Jhāna*. Those two are not to be separated; one does not begin with *Jhāna* and then obtain *Prajñā*. Where there is *Prajñā* there is *Jhāna*, and *vice versa*. When one is attained the other comes with it; no separation between them is possible. This was his original teaching.

So when we say "Zen Buddhism," this "Zen" is used in a somewhat different sense from the ordinary one. Usually "Zen" is meditation, concentration or contemplation, but in Zen Buddhism "Zen" is used not in that sense but as synonymous with *Prajñā*. To understand Zen Buddhism, therefore, it is necessary to know that *Dhyāna* is not something different from *Prajñā* and that *Prajñā* is not something obtained after Zen is obtained. When we practice *Jhāna*, that is the very moment that *Prajñā* unfolds itself. This was the original teaching of Yeno and it was the beginning of Zen Buddhism.

One day a Chinese Government Officer who was also a poet and a painter called on the immediate disciple of Yeno and asked: "What is this one way; what is the teaching of your school which denies the distinction between "Zen" and "*Prajñā*"? The disciple of Yeno replied: "Zen is where you are talking; you ask a question and Zen is there. It is not that one comes before the other; they are simultaneous. When you talk to me there is Zen; there is *Prajñā*; they are not different."

To express this in a more modern way: while we are doing, thinking and feeling, there is this identity of Zen and *Prajñā*. This spatial intuitive knowledge is not to be developed after the practice of Zen. *Prajñā* is where Zen is.

Prajñā is another difficult term to translate into English. We generally use "transcendental wisdom" or "intuitive knowledge" to express *Prajñā*. The Chinese, in spite of their dislike for foreign languages, used a term which is the Chinese translation of *Prajñā*. *Prajñā* is something which our discursive knowledge cannot attain. It belongs to a different category from mere knowledge. Buddhists emphasize this distinction very much; they say, not knowing, but knowing and seeing; these two must come together. To know there must be two—subject and object.

Now, seeing is not just knowing about something; seeing is directly seeing it. Knowing and seeing are generally coupled in Buddhist teaching; knowing is not enough; seeing must come with knowing. In the West you distinguish between knowing and seeing. Knowing is philosophical, knowing about; and seeing is seeing directly, personally, i.e., by personal experience. Knowing always requires a mediator but seeing is direct, yet in seeing we do not generally see things directly. When we think we see something, that seeing is not real from the Zen point of view. When you see a flower, for example, not only must you see it but the flower must see you also; otherwise there is no real seeing. Seeing is really my seeing the flower and the flower seeing me. When this seeing is mutual there is real seeing.

Certain scholars say that when we think we see the flower, we put our feelings into the flower. My thinking or seeing or your thinking or seeing is put into the flower and the flower is given life. But, to the Zen way of thinking, there is no transference of my imagination into the flower. The flower itself is living and, as a living thing, sees me. So my seeing is also the flower seeing. When this takes place there is real seeing. When this end is achieved, i.e., when my seeing becomes the flower seeing, then there is real communication or real identification of the flower with myself, of subject with object. When this mutual identification takes place, the flower is myself and I am the flower.

A Chinese scholar once asked a Zen master, "One of the earlier Buddhist philosophers said, 'Heaven and earth are of the same source; ten thousand things and I are one.'" He added, "Is this not a wonderful saying?" The master looked at a flower in the courtyard and said, "Men of the world see this flower as in a dream," meaning that their seeing is not real seeing, which implies that for real seeing it is necessary for me to see the flower and for the flower to see me. When this is mutual and identification takes place, then there is real seeing. Then we experience what the Buddhist scholar stated in the passage just quoted: "Heaven and earth are of the same source; ten thousand things and I are one."

But this is mere abstract talk and so long as we are dealing with abstractions there is no actual experience. The Zen master pointed out this fact to his disciple: "Instead of talking about abstractions or quoting what others have said, do look at this flower which is now becoming and identify yourself with it, not as if you are in a dream, but see in actual reality the flower itself. Then you see that the whole universe is nothing but the expression of one's own mind."

Before I left Japan I read in an English journal an interesting article by a Russian whose idea was this: "The objective world can exist only in my subjectivity; the objective world does not really exist until it is experienced by this subjectivity or myself." That is something like Berkeley's Idealism. One day this Russian was riding his bicycle and he collided with a lorry; the driver was very angry but the Russian kept on saying, "The world is nothing but my subjectivity." On another occasion when he was thinking in the ordinary way, there was no collision but something else happened and he was awakened to this truth: "There is nothing but my subjectivity." When he experienced this, he had quite an illumination and he said to a friend. "Everything is in everything else." That means that all things are the same but he did not say that; he said, "Everything, each individual object, is in each other individual object. So this world of multitudes is not denied, as each thing is in every other one." This is most significant. When he expressed this to his friend, the friend could not understand but later he attained the same experience. This is *Prajñā*; this is transcendental wisdom, and when this intuition is attained, we have Zen. Zen is no other than this intuitive knowledge.

I must say more about this intuitive knowledge, or direct seeing. For example, if we touch fire the finger is burned; I feel intuitively that fire is dangerous without having to reason about it. When people talk about intuition it is connected with individual objects. There is someone who has an intuition and something in regard to which he has it. There is nothing between subject and object. These intuitions may take place immediately, i.e., without any intermediary; nevertheless there are subject and object, though their relationship is immediate instead of being through an intermediate agent. This kind of intuition we talk very much about but the intuition that Zen talks about is identification-seeing. That is, when I see the flower and the flower sees me, this kind of intuition or mutual identification is not individual seeing; it is not individual intuition. "I see the flower and the flower sees me" means that the flower ceases to be a flower. I cease to be myself. Instead there is unification. The flower vanishes into something higher than a flower and I vanish into that something higher than any individual object.

Now when this leveling up takes place, this being absorbed into something higher than each relative being, it does not mean merely being absorbed; there is intuition, awakening; there is something that acknowledges itself to be itself, not annihilation or mere absorption into the void. This "annihilation" is accompanied by intuition and that is the most important point. When this takes place there is real seeing of the flower. Therefore we can say that this—my seeing the flower and the flower seeing me—takes place on a plane higher than that where the flower is seen as an individual flower and I am seen as an individual being. When there is absorption of the individual into something higher, there is intuition. This is most important. This is in accordance with the original teaching of Wei Lang. *Prajñā* is *Jhāna*.

Earlier teachers than Yeno had stated that when *Jhāna* was practiced all things vanished and there was nothing left. By this it was meant that no individual thing was left; but there is something which is not an individual object; there is a perception of something and this perception is intuition. This intuition is *Prajñā* or enlightenment and Yeno most strongly emphasized this.

Now it may not be quite clear what Zen is driving at. I have a book here which contains all the Zen sayings, starting with those of Bodhidharma. Bodhidharma may be a fictitious individual but that does not matter; Yeno is historical. From him down to the early part of the Sung Dynasty, about nine hundred years ago, this book contains all those Chinese sayings called *Mondo*. The mind revolves, i.e., works, operates as it faces ten thousand situations. When I see this lamp I see it illuminated; when I touch this table, it is hard; so my mind moves along; when I am struck, I feel. The mind moves in this way from one sense to another just as things come along. This moving of the mind is most subtle, obscure and mysterious.

When this table is struck I feel, but who is it that feels? What is it that feels? When you try to get that person or mind or soul or spirit out here and see it, you cannot. There is something you would like to get out of yourself but you cannot; soul or spirit moves on all the time and this moving on is subtle. When it is working in such a subtle way, when it is going on, you can get hold of that something which cannot be taken hold of. Then you have it. When you have that, then there is real wisdom or *Prajñā*. When you have this *Prajñā*, then you are entirely free from all sorrows, afflictions and all other things.

Now when I speak of being free from desires, tensions, fears, etc., you may think that the understanding of Zen will turn you into a piece of wood, insensitive, indifferent; but I do not say this. When I strike the table it feels pain as much as I would. You may say, "This is insane; it is not so." Everything is filled with sense, mind, heart. So when Buddha says to be free from desires and afflictions, this does not mean to become like a piece of wood; it means to make a piece of wood turn into a sensitive being. In a Chinese Zen monastery they have a heavy stick made of one piece of wood which they strike with a hammer and it is very sensitive. When a monk struck this, the master said, "I have a pain." That is not exaggerated; it really takes place. When they see a worm on the ground Buddhists try to avoid stepping on it. You may say that you cannot move an inch because something would be trodden on and die. True, you cannot move if you pursue this practice in its relative sense. But actually, when you have this intuitive understanding of things, you are like St. Francis of Assisi when he talked about "Our Brother Sun" and "Sister Moon" and befriended wolves and birds; he took everything as his own brother. His feeling was moving along the same lines, so there is no difference between the Christian and the Buddhist experience of final reality.

When Zen people talk about not having any feeling whatever, that does not mean no feeling on the relative plane, but no feeling based on selfish interests. To have no pain, no desires, does not mean to become cold ashes; it means to have no feeling in connection with selfish ideas. So long as we are individuals, we cannot but be selfish to some extent but this selfishness is not separate from that which is more than self. When self stays as self and does not expand to something higher than itself, that is the relative self. But when self finds itself enveloped, a component in something which is much wider and deeper, then it is not merely the relative self. When that kind of self is realized, enlightenment takes place. Zen Buddhism tries to make us attain that end.

Most Christians think that Christ was historically born at a certain place and time but, according to Eckhart, the great German philosopher of the thirteenth century, Christ is born in every one of us. When that is so, the relative self dies to itself and that relative self becomes empty. When the experience of uniformity, sameness and sensitivity takes place in our soul, it is then that Christ is born there. So every impediment or faulty particle of that which we call ourselves ought to be purged and the self ought to become really empty.

This is quite different from the ordinary Christian way of understanding the birth of Christ but Eckhart had no knowledge whatever of Buddhism and Buddha had no knowledge of him, yet their teachings coincide perfectly. When I read Eckhart, I seem to be reading a Buddhist text with but a different terminology; so far as inner comprehension is concerned, they are the same. This comprehension corresponds to intuition. Prehension is only grasping and touch is, I suppose, the most primitive sense, but this gives the purest feeling of identity; so prehension, taking hold of by the hand, is necessary. Sight is the most intellectual sense and hearing is next but there is a great distance between them and their object; whereas with touch there is an immediate coming together. We must experience that. It is the same as intuition, not just relative intuition but collective or total intuition. When this takes place there is real understanding of reality and the experience of Enlightenment. This is what constitutes the teaching of Zen as first taught by Yeno, Hui Neng or Wei Lang in the eighth century.

The Spirit of Zen

The late Dr. D. T. Suzuki first visited the Society on July 20th 1936. Before arriving in England for the first Meeting of the World Congress of Faiths he sent us an article which appeared in the January–February issue of *Buddhism in England,* later *The Middle Way.* When he visited the Buddhist Lodge, as it was then called, on July 20th, at our house at 37 South Eaton Place, he found "a full house" with distinguished visitors including Dr. G. P. Malalasekera, Miss Constant Lounsbery, founder of Les Amis du Bouddhisme in Paris, Count Wachtmeister, who had composed a Buddhist opera, and Mr. T. K. Ch'u, who translated our version of the Tao Te Ching, the first to be translated into English by a Chinese.

After introducing Dr. Suzuki, I asked him "to help us to understand something of the spirit of Zen." The following article, from *Buddhism in England,* is a slightly edited transcript of a full note taken in short-hand by a member present.—ED.

Seeing that we are endowed with the power of speech and understand one another by means of this power, we have to appeal to words. But words are such an intractable medium. If we become masters of words we are all right, but sometimes we are too willingly slaves to words, and when words enslave us we become perfect fools. Zen Buddhism tries to master words, but the means it uses to help us in mastering them are strange, though not so strange to those who are used to them. But to others, they seem extraordinary.

How did Zen come to use such extraordinary methods in its teaching? When we ask that question we have to trace the history of the human intellect, and when we have traced it to its very source we will understand that the methods of Zen were something inevitable in the development of our spiritual life. As I cannot give the whole history of Zen, you must be satisfied with a very brief outline of how it developed in China and Japan. The Indian mind was rich in imagination and wonderful in its capacity for speculation. Indian metaphysics are the deepest in the world, and their dialects are incomparable. All nations of the world have to bow to the Indians in this respect. To them, religion was philosophy and philosophy religion, for whatever religion there is in India is backed by philosophy. Intellect should always be backed by certain deeper understandings which we may call faith. Intuition is the affirmation of a certain fundamental belief on which and with which and by which we stand and live our life. This must be associated with the intellect, and when it is associated it becomes a certain philosophy. That is the reason why, in India, religion is always associated with philosophy.

In Christianity theology is separate from Faith, but when Faith is left to itself it is apt to go astray. It becomes superficial and superstitious, leading in the end to bigotry. Faith represents the emotional side of human life, while philosophy is its intellectual side. Faith and philosophy must always go hand in hand, for when they are separated the result is lame. In India this philosophy was well in its way, but it lacked something which was supplied by the Chinese mind, something which we may call a consciousness of practical life, of life itself. In China morality became the foundation of society, and the Chinese people are prone to things practical. That is where the true greatness of the Chinese lies.

When Indian philosophy came to China as Buddhism, the Chinese people took to it partly, but at the same time there was something that did not quite appeal to them, something against which they revolted. "Zen," said a Chinese scholar, "is the revolt of the Chinese mind against Buddhism," It is a revolt. Yet while it is not quite Buddhism, it still is Buddhism. It developed from Buddhism, and in fact it could not have developed from anything else. Zen has its origin in India, but when it came to China this revolt of the Chinese mind gave it a somewhat different form.

The Zen form of Buddhism is deeply imbued with a practical spirit. For while there was logic and metaphysics in ancient China, it was never highly developed. They had a very subtle way of reasoning, but we find little of it in the greatest era of Chinese culture—the T'ang Dynasty, which was some twelve hundred years ago. Certainly China has had its great philosophers, but Chinese philosophy was the result of Buddhist philosophy stimulating the Chinese mind. If China had to stand against Buddhism, it had to take Buddhist philosophy and assimilate it into its own body and make it its own blood. The result of this assimilation was Zen—and the work of assimilation was completed by the Sung Dynasty, which followed the T'ang.

The T'ang Dynasty represents the highest point of Chinese culture. With T'ang the Chinese mind developed to its fullest extent, and everything associated with this dynasty represents the flower of the Chinese mind—art, literature, poetry and religion. Zen is one aspect of that golden age.

In the early days of Buddhism in China the monks used to live in the monastery and devote themselves entirely to the practice of *Dhyāna*. They did not eat after midday, but because of its colder climate, this practice had to be changed. They considered it contrary to the spirit of the Buddha's teaching to refuse to adapt themselves to climatic conditions because of a blind reverence for mere formalities and rules devised for people living in the tropics. If we had to follow man-made rules which are only applicable to India, the result would be comic; things have to be adjusted in accordance with circumstances.

Thus while some monasteries adhered to the Indian rules and customs, these monks who desired a Buddhism more after the heart of the Chinese people formed monasteries of their own. These became the Zen monasteries. They undertake all kinds of manual work. They cultivate rice and vegetables and cut trees for fuel. Even now in Japan they follow that custom, and monks are seen doing all kinds of work which is usually left to laymen.

But teaching is carried on while they are engaged in manual work— not necessarily, however, by giving sermons or lecturing on abstruse subjects. Zen teaching is to be carried on in close connection with our daily life. As we walk in the fields, Zen teachings are to be demonstrated and understood—not outside the work, but with the work and in the work. One day a monk came to a master and asked him, "I have been here under you for many years, and my coming to you was expressly to study Buddhism. But so far you have not imparted to me any Buddhist teaching. If this continues, I shall have to leave you to my great regret." The master replied, "In the morning when you come and salute me with 'Good morning!' I salute you back, 'Good morning! How are you?' When you bring me a cup of tea I gratefully drink it. When you do anything else for me I acknowledge it. What other teachings do you want to have from me?"

There is no special teaching—the most ordinary things in our daily life hide some deep meaning that is yet most plain and explicit; only our eyes need to see where there is a meaning. Unless this eye is opened there will be nothing to learn from Zen. Another teacher said, "In Zen there is nothing special except our everyday thought (*shin*—mind-consciousness)." When we give something, someone receives it and is grateful. Everybody is called upon to do acts of kindness and to acknowledge them, and when it is done to forget all about it. That is the way we go on in this world! There is Zen!

If you say anything more about it—philosophical or ethical or anything else—you are not a Zen man or woman. In fact, when we carry on as we do in our everyday life, there is plenty of Zen in that. But an eye is needed—a third eye. We have two eyes to see two sides of things, but there must be a third eye which will see everything at the same time and yet not see anything. That is to understand Zen. Our two eyes see dualistically, and dualism is at the bottom of all the trouble we have gone through. This does not mean that dualism is to be abolished, only that there ought to be a third eye. The important thing is that the two eyes must remain, but at the same time there ought to be another. When I speak according to the ordinary way of talking, I have to say that a third eye is needed, but in fact this third eye is *outside* the two eyes we already have. But again, the third eye is not between or above the two eyes—*the two eyes are the third eye.* I am beginning to philosophize, and when we philosophize we are no more followers of Zen. Therefore Zen people always close their mouths when they are pressed. But that does not mean they cannot say anything.

That which is not mind nor matter is not Buddha nor anything else. The Absolute seems to be something beyond human understanding. But in discussing the Absolute it is no longer Absolute. We say God is everywhere, but we like to put God in Heaven. How can we conceive God as giving rules to us? If God is immanent, God is ourselves. But Zen does not say that God is transcendent or immanent. When you try to comprehend a fact by means of words, the fact disappears. When we use our minds we have to understand things dualistically—either transcendentally or immanently. When I have explained that, there is nothing more to say. All that is needed is the opening of the third eye. When we have a third eye, it does not annihilate the two eyes. So the world of dualities is not annihilated at all.

Let me tell you a Zen story about this. It is a sort of joke. Yejaku called on Yenen, and asked, "What is your name?" Yenen replied, "Yejaku." Yejaku said, "But that's my own name." Then Yenen said,

"My name is Yenen." Whereupon Yejaku gave a hearty laugh. You are I, and I am you; in oneness there is manyness, and in manyness there is oneness. The transcendental and the immanent God exist at the same time. When they exist at the same time, you cannot say anything about them (i.e., affirm or deny one or the other)—the only thing is to laugh.

You are you and I am I, but at the same time you are not me and I am not you. This particularization cannot be analyzed. So when things are brought to you, you just accept them and say thank you, but do not talk about it. This is the Zen attitude. Zen tries to make you accept things, and when you have accepted them you give a hearty laugh.

The Threefold Question in Zen

The question, "What is Zen?" is at once easy and difficult to answer.
It is easy because there is nothing that is not Zen. I lift my finger thus,
and there is Zen. I sit in silence all day uttering no words, and there too
is Zen. Everything you do or say is Zen, and everything you do not do
or say is also Zen. You see the flowers blooming in the garden, you hear
birds singing in the woods, and you have Zen there. No words are
needed to explain Zen, for you have it already before they are pronounced. The question is asked simply because you did not know that
you had Zen in you, with you, and around you; and therefore it is easy
to answer.

But from another point of view the very fact that it is easy to answer
makes it extremely difficult to give a satisfactory answer to the question, "What is Zen?" For when you already have a thing, and have it all
the time, and yet do not know it, it is hard to convince you of the fact.
To have a thing and yet not to know is the same as not to have it from
the beginning. Where there is no experience, there is no firsthand
knowledge. All you know is *about* it and not itself. To make you realize
that you have the very thing you are seeking, it will be necessary to get
that thing detached from you so that you can see it before your eyes and
even grasp it with your hands. But this is most difficult, for the thing
which is always with you can by no means be taken away from you for
inspection.

It is just like our not seeing our own eyes. We have to get a mirror to
do that. But this is not really seeing the eye as it is, as it functions. What
the eye sees in the mirror is its reflection, and not itself. According to
Eckhart, "The eye with which I see God is the same with which God sees
me." In this case, we must get God in order to see ourselves. This is
where the difficulty lies. How do we get God?

But this much I think we can say, that Zen is a kind of self-
consciousness. I see a table before me. I know that I am the one who

33

sees it, and I am fully conscious of myself experiencing the event. But Zen is not here yet, something more must be added to it, or must be discovered in it, in order to make this event of seeing really Zen. The question is now: what is this something? It is in all likelihood that which turns my eye inside out and sees itself, not as a reflection, but as a kind of superself which is hidden behind the moral and psychological self. I call this discovery spiritual self-consciousness. No amount of explanation will bring you to this form of self-consciousness. It unfolds itself from the depths of consciousness. No hammering at the door from outside will open it—it opens by itself from within.

In spite of this fact, we must do some hammering from outside, although this may be of no avail as the direct and efficient cause of opening. Yet it must be somehow carried on, for without it there will be no opening. Perhaps the door remains wide open all the time, open to welcome us in, and it is we who hesitate before it; someone is needed to push us in. The entering may not be due to the pushing, but when one sees somebody halting before the door, one feels like pushing him in. And I propose to do this kind of helping, and hope that you do your best to step in, that is, to understand what I am going to present to you as to the quiddity of Zen in the plainest and most direct way I can.

Oryo Yenan (Huang-lung-nan), a great Zen master of the Sung dynasty, was anxious to get his disciples to see into the secret of Zen, and proposed the following threefold question:

1. Everybody has his birthplace; where is yours?
2. How is it that my hands resemble those of the Buddha?
3. How is it that my legs resemble those of the donkey?

These perhaps, except the first, are trivial questions, and the last two are even nonsensical. What has Zen to do with my legs and hands? What does it matter if they resemble those of the Buddha or even those of the donkey? But there is no doubt about the master's seriousness and anxious concern for his pupils. What do these "puzzles" signify? When you understand them, you understand Zen.

The first one is trite if you answer, "I come from Tokyo or from London." But if you say, "I come from God" or "I know not whence, nor whither," the question assumes quite a religio-philosophical aspect. Though the master may have proposed it in a worldly way, the question no doubt acquires deep sense according to the frame of mind with which you approach it.

One of the pupils answered, "I had some rice gruel for breakfast and I feel hungry now." The master nodded his approval. In what relationship if any does this statement stand to the question, "Where is your birthplace"? In what way has the pupil's physiology to do with the philosophy of Zen as implied in the master's inquiry? Is the pupil merely making a fool of the master?

From another point of view, the pupil may be said to be just as serious-minded as the master in describing his bodily conditions, because however high-flying a man's idealism, he cannot escape his physics and physiology to which the spirit is most intimately wedded. The spirit, if it is to function at all, must implement itself in one way or another, while matter is not thought and thought is not matter and they are not to be conceived as self-identical; the one is always so inevitably associated with the other that we cannot cover them in our actual experience. The condition of the stomach decidedly affects the spirit. Did the pupil refer to this fact?

From whatever unknown region a man may have come to this world, the one most assured event is that he is here, and feels hungry at this moment. This experience we can say, therefore, is the sole reality; besides this absolute present there is no whence, no whither. In fact, all the past and the future are perfectly merged in this present moment, which is describable in human terms as hungry or thirsty or painful. Did the pupil survey the master's question from this point of view, and did the master appraise the pupil accordingly? Is this intended to explain what Zen is? Does this understanding of the present in its absolute aspect constitute Zen? I came somewhere in my recent reading across the phrase "the still point of the turning world" referring to the transcendental quality of the present. Does Zen stand at this still point where the past and the future converge? The ancient philosopher speaks of the "unmoved mover." Is the Zen student's consciousness of hunger this unmoved mover?

Everything in this world is subject to change, there is nothing here that is steady, permanent, and will retain its self-identity through its earthly career. This has been declared by the Buddha and other thinkers and is what we call experience. And yet, we all yearn after things immortal, things never moving, and never moved. Where do we get this idea of immovability or eternal quiescence if all that we see around us is forever changing? How do we solve this contradiction:

permanency and changeability, eternity and momentariness, immortality and dying every minute? There must be some way out.

One way we Buddhists think of it is this: Where we are experiencing the fleeting world, we are simultaneously experiencing "one moment, one and infinite"; that is to say, we are able to be conscious of a world of changes because those changes are the very thing that never suffers change. For this reason our consciousness of change and impermanency is deeply interfused with an unconscious consciousness of eternity, unchangeability or timelessness. This interfusion of consciousness and unconsciousness or, in Buddhist terminology, of the Many and the One, of Form *(rūpam)* and Emptiness *(śūnyatā)*, the Distinction (or Discrimination) and Non-distinction (or Non-discrimination) is, we can say, the philosophy of Zen.

If this be so, we may ask, how is it that none of us understand Zen even when we are hungry and conscious of the fact? The answer is that my just being conscious of hunger does not constitute Zen; there must be along with the physiological or psychological consciousness, another form of consciousness, which is a sort of unconsciousness but not in the ordinary sense of the term. For this unconscious consciousness we have no suitable logical or metaphysical term, for the terms used in the various fields of human understanding belong to the order of relativity, and when they are applied to the experience specifically Zen, Zen is liable to be grossly misunderstood. It is due to this reason that Zen literature abounds with superficially meaningless jargon as well as paradoxical and contradictory expressions.

Kokyu Shoryu (Nu-ch'in Shao-lung), was a great Zen master of the Sung dynasty. While still in his tutelage, he entered the master's room and the master said:

> When you say you see it,
> This seeing is not the (true) seeing;
> The (true) seeing is not seeing,
> Seeing can never reach it.

So saying, the master raised his fist and asked, "Do you see?"
Said the disciple, "I see."
"You are putting another head over your own."
Hearing this, the disciple became conscious of something inwardly awakened.

The master observed this and said, "What do you see?"

The disciple did not say this time, "I see," but quoted the poetic passage, "Even when the bamboos are growing thick, they do not obstruct the running stream."

What, let me ask, have they, master and disciple been talking about here? Evidently, speaking Zen-wise, seeing is not seeing, to be conscious is not to be conscious; when you say you have it, you miss it. But the reverse does not hold true, for not-seeing is not at all seeing. There must be actual seeing on the physical plane, and over and through this seeing there must be another sort of seeing, which makes the ordinary seeing a true seeing—which is seeing in the Zen sense.

Let me remark, *en passant,* that what distinguishes the Zen way of seeing or understanding experience from that of the Indian philosophers is generally that Zen speaks of it more in terms of time than those of space. Zen has no doubt developed from Indian thought and is deeply tinged with it, but the Chinese mind has added to it something of its own, and the result is Zen.

A modern thinker, Dr. Radhakrishnan, writes in *The Hibbert Journal* (July 1946):

The whole hierarchy of objective being is dependent on the primary reality, which is therefore both transcendent to it and immanent in it. It is consciousness of self and constitutive of what is other than self. It is the "unmoved mover," the immanent principle in the moving and the unmoving though himself is devoid of any movement. When we look upon the Supreme as the immanent Lord, he becomes the Divine Creator. When the Supreme Spirit objectifies itself thus, the essential unconditional freedom of the spirit becomes involved in conditions and limitations which contradict his freedom.

This is all well as far as it goes, but when he refers to "the Supreme" or "the Divine Creator," it is apt to make us think of something spatially extending. Of course, this is an illusion, and Radhakrishnan is anxious not to have us fall into this intellectual pit, for he says that "the inward self" is beyond the reach of discursive thought and the possibility of conceptual interpretation. In spite of this warning his terminology savors of spatiality. Zen avoids all argumentation; it simply raises a finger and asks, "Do you see?" When one says "Yes," Zen declares, "Don't put another head over the one you already have." When the master asks about the whence of one's being, he is dangerously near the battlefield of absolute reasoning. But the disciple knew how not to step into the hell-fire, and declares, "I had some rice gruel in early morning and am now hungry." He does not say, "I am a manifestation, however imperfect, of the absolute spirit which is above all distinctions." Nor does he say, "I am a concrete reflection of the eternal reason which is immanent in the endless variety of the physical world." Nor does he say, "I am one with the Supreme, the son of God, the only begotten son of God." If all religious teaching is meant to free us from ignorance and corruption, Zen must be said to point to the most direct way of emancipation.

We now come to the second and third question proposed by the Zen master at the beginning of this paper: "Why are my hands like those of the Buddha, and my legs like those of the donkey?" These two questions are practically the same. To the second the disciple put down this, "Under the moon I hear some one playing a lute"; and to the third, "A white crane is standing in the snow hardly distinguishable in color."

Superficially or intellectually judging, these statements have no internal or logical connection with the questions. When it is asked why my hands look like those of the Buddha, or why my legs look like those of the donkey, we may expect some biological or metaphysical or even spiritual analysis. The disciple's answer is no answer according to our every day way of thinking; there is apparently nothing that will satisfy one's intellectual curiosity. In fact, we detect a degenerating tendency in these poetical allusions to the lute playing under the moon, and to the standing crane in the snow, which has turned Zen into a kind of handbook of flowery literary diction. But to those who know what is really intended here, this is expressive enough; there is no ambiguity in them.

The questions in regard to my hands resembling those of the Buddha and my legs those of the donkey have deep metaphysical implications. The questioner does not just request the reason for resemblance in any outward form. He wants you to have attained a spiritual insight into the suchness of being. The main idea the questioner has in mind here is to make us look into our own self and perceive "the still point of the turning world," or lay hand on the moving of the unmoved mover.

When the second question is understood the third solves itself, and my statements hereafter will be confined to the hands. When man learned how to free the hands from supporting the body and began to walk the earth with a pair of legs only, he achieved epoch-making progress in the history of intellectual evolution. The free use of hands means our ability of working on environment. Man can now have his aspirations realized in the objective world. His hands or arms are the tools wherewith this wonder can be accomplished. Before he could swing his arms freely and grasp things with his hands for closer inspection and ready handling, he was a slave to the environment in which he happened to be. He had to make the best of his front paws, along with his locomotive facilities. He was hardly more than an automaton, with no means of expressing himself. Now that he has a pair of free hands with flexible fingers, he can gather up a bouquet of flowers and offer it to the Buddha; he can take up a lute and give vent to his emotion in the moonlight night; he can excavate a huge rock and carve it out into a form of beauty. Becoming an independent actor and creator, has he not now generated a consciousness altogether unique, which is, however, of the same order as the one possessed by the creator of the world? This consciousness or unconscious consciousness cannot be the mere consciousness of vitality, the pure feeling of joy, or anything connected with animality. For "acting" in the human sense and "creating" a new world as *homo faber* has something in it in communion with the working of the divine mind when it commanded, "Let there be light."

Some may remark, there is no comparison possible between divine work and human action, and it is highly sacrilegious even to think of such comparison. But this objection forgets the fact or rather the truth that man was made in the divine image and that this image has the remotest possible relation to outwardness, this-worldliness, or materiality. To be at all divine for an image bearing the name, it must be so in essence, in spirituality. God cannot be thought as being in the possession of hands, arms and legs. God did not mould this universe with all kinds of beings in it with his physical hands and fingers; he created all these things from "nothing," and in all probability our human way of regarding this world as objective reality is an illusion. It may be "nothing," mere "Emptiness" as Buddhists assert, reflecting the original "nothing" out of which God is said to have created the world. However this may be, I now take up the lute and strike on its strings and you hear a certain melody issuing from them. Is this sensuous hearing all that there is in our divine-human consciousness? If so, man as God's image cannot mean anything. Where is he to be distinguished from mere animality? Can there not be something more here, where our minds are attuned to the Divine Mind, a kind of superconsciousness transcending our ordinary sensuous limited consciousness which functions on the plane of psychology? Is this not a superconsciousness, which is frequently designated by Buddhists as "mindlessness" or "thoughtlessness" or "unconscious consciousness"! And is it not this that constitutes the divine-human mind?

The superconsciousness which is possessed by every human being as long as he is created in God's image cannot be separable from the relative sensuous consciousness which performs most useful functions in this world of particulars. The superconsciousness must be thoroughly and in the most perfect manner interfused with the one in daily use; otherwise, the superconsciousness cannot be of any significance to us.

It is indeed so interfused with our psychological consciousness that we are utterly unconscious of its presence. It requires certain spiritual training to be awakened to it, and it is Zen that has for the first time in the world history of mental evolution pointed out this fact. In a word, it is Zen that has become aware of the truth of superconsciousness in connection with the most commonplace doings in our daily life. People generally conceive of things spiritual as going beyond our prosaic everyday experience. But the plainest truth is that everything we experience is saturated, interfused, interpenetrated with spiritual signification, and for this reason my handling the lute, my standing in the snow, my feeling hungry or thirsty after a hard day's work, is surcharged with superconsciousness, with unconscious consciousness.

In conclusion, which is really no conclusion, I wish to quote three Chinese poems which purpose to interpret the meaning of the threefold question which was made the subject of this paper. They were composed by one of the disciples of Oryo Yenan, the author of the question.

> Oryo the old master
> Has the story of "birthplace";
> I know him thoroughly well.
> I'll show him up today,
> I'll show him up for you:
> The cat knows how to catch the old rat.

The Persian merchant arrives in China from the southern seas:
Wherever he comes across special treasures, he will assess them:
Sometimes he pays well, sometimes he gets them cheap;
[Thus trading] he watches the afternoon shadows lengthening as
   the sun reaches the western hills.

In summer days we all use the fan,
When winter comes charcoal is heaped in the fireplace to burn:
When you know well what all this means,
Your ignorance stored up for countless *kalpas* melts away.

Aspects of Japanese Culture

When we look at the development of Japanese culture we find that Zen Buddhism has made many important contributions. The other schools of Buddhism have limited their sphere of influence almost entirely to the spiritual life of the Japanese people; but Zen has gone beyond it. Zen has entered internally into every phase of the cultural life of the people.

In China this was not necessarily the case. Zen united itself to a great extent with Taoist beliefs and practices and with the Confucian teaching of morality, but it did not affect the cultural life of the people so much as it did in Japan. (Is it due to the racial psychology of the Japanese people that they have taken up Zen so intensely and deeply that is has entered intimately into their life?) In China, however, I ought not omit to mention the noteworthy fact that Zen gave great impetus to the development of Chinese philosophy in the Sung dynasty and also to the growth of a certain school of painting. A large number of examples of this school were brought over to Japan beginning with the Kamakura era in the thirteenth century, when Zen monks were constantly traveling between the two neighboring countries. The paintings of Southern Sung thus came to find their ardent admirers on our side of the sea and are now national treasures of Japan, while in China no specimens of this class of painting are to be found.

Before proceeding further, we may make a few general remarks about one of the peculiar features of Japanese art, which is closely related to and finally deducible from the world conception of Zen.

Among things which strongly characterized Japanese artistic talents we may mention the so-called "one-corner" style, which originated with Bayen (Ma Yüan *fl.* 1175-1225), one of the greatest Southern Sung artists. The "one-corner" style is psychologically associated with the

42

Japanese painters' "thrifty brush" tradition of retaining the least possible number of lines or strokes which go to represent forms on silk or paper. Both are very much in accord with the spirit of Zen. A simple fishing boat in the midst of the rippling waters is enough to awaken in the mind of the beholder a sense of the vastness of the sea and at the same time of peace and contentment—the Zen sense of the Alone. Apparently the boat floats helplessly. It is a primitive structure with no mechanical device for stability and for audacious steering over the turbulent waves, with no scientific apparatus for braving all kinds of weather—quite a contrast to the modern ocean liner. But this very helplessness is the virtue of the fishing canoe, in contrast with which we feel the incomprehensibility of the Absolute encompassing the boat and all the world. Again, a solitary bird on a dead branch, in which not a line, not a shade, is wasted, is enough to show us the loneliness of autumn, when days become shorter and nature begins to roll up once more its gorgeous display of luxurious summer vegetation.[1] It makes one feel somewhat pensive, but it gives one opportunity to withdraw the attention towards the inner life, which, given attention enough, spreads out its rich treasures ungrudgingly before the eyes.

Here we have an appreciation of transcendental aloofness in the midst of multiplicities—which is known as *wabi* in the dictionary of Japanese cultural terms. *Wabi* really means "poverty," or, negatively, "not to be in the fashionable society of the time." To be poor, that is, not to be dependent on things worldly—wealth, power and reputation—and yet to feel inwardly the presence of something of the highest value, above time and social position: this is what essentially constitutes *wabi*. Stated in terms of practical everyday life, *wabi* is to be satisfied with a little hut, a room of two or three *tatami* (mats), like the log cabin of Thoreau, and with a dish of vegetables picked in the neighboring fields, and perhaps to be listening to the pattering of a gentle spring rainfall. The cult of *wabi* has entered deeply into the cultural life of the Japanese people. It is in truth the worshiping of poverty—probably a most appropriate cult in a poor country like ours. Despite the modern Western luxuries and comforts of life which have invaded us, there is still an ineradicable longing in us for the cult of *wabi*. Even in the intellectual life, not richness of ideas, not brilliancy or solemnity in

[1]For pictures of a similar nature, see my *Zen Essays,* II and III.

marshaling thoughts and building up a philosophical system, is sought; but just to stay quietly content with the mystical contemplation of Nature and to feel at home with the world is more inspiring to us, at least to some of us.

However "civilized," however much brought up in an artificially contrived environment, we all seem to have an innate longing for primitive simplicity, close to the natural state of living. Hence the city people's pleasure in summer camping in the woods or traveling in the desert or opening up an unbeaten track. We wish to go back once in a while to the bosom of Nature and feel her pulsation directly. Zen's habit of mind, to break through all forms of human artificiality and take firm hold of what lies behind them, has helped the Japanese not to forget the soil but to be always friendly with Nature and appreciate her unaffected simplicity. Zen has no taste for complexities that lie on the surface of life. Life itself is simple enough, but when it is surveyed by the analyzing intellect it presents unparalleled intricacies. With all the apparatus of science we have not yet fathomed the mysteries of life. But, once in its current, we seem to be able to understand it, with its apparently endless pluralities and entanglements. Very likely, the most characteristic thing in the temperament of the Eastern people is the ability to grasp life from within and not from without. And Zen has just struck it.

In painting especially, disregard of form results when too much attention or emphasis is given to the all-importance of the spirit. The "one-cornered" style and the economy of brush strokes also help to effect aloofness from conventional rules. Where you would ordinarily expect a line or a mass or a balancing element, you miss it, and yet this very thing awakens in you an unexpected feeling of pleasure. In spite of shortcomings or deficiencies that no doubt are apparent, you do not feel them so; indeed, this imperfection itself becomes a form of perfection. Evidently, beauty does not necessarily spell perfection of form. This has been one of the favorite tricks of Japanese artists—to embody beauty in a form of imperfection or even of ugliness.

When this beauty of imperfection is accompanied by antiquity or primitive uncouthness, we have a glimpse of *sabi*, so prized by Japanese connoisseurs. Antiquity and primitiveness may not be an actuality. If an object of art suggests even superficially the feeling of a historical period, there is *sabi* in it. *Sabi* consists in rustic unpretentiousness or archaic imperfection, apparent simplicity or effortlessness in execution, and richness in historical associations (which, however, may not always be present); and lastly, it contains inexplicable elements that raise the object in question to the rank of an artistic production. These elements are generally regarded as derived from the appreciation of Zen. The utensils used in the tearoom are mostly of this nature.

The artistic element that goes into the constitution of *sabi,* which literally means "loneliness" or "solitude," is poetically defined by a teamaster thus:

> As I come out
> To this fishing village,
> Late in the autumn day,
> No flowers in bloom I see,
> Nor any tinted maple leaves.[2]

Aloneness indeed appeals to contemplation and does not lend itself to spectacular demonstration. It may look most miserable, insignificant, and pitiable, especially when it is put up against the Western or modern setting. To be left alone, with no streamers flying, no fireworks crackling, and this amidst a gorgeous display of infinitely varied forms and endlessly changing colors, is indeed no sight at all. Take one of those *sumiye* sketches, perhaps portraying Kanzan and Jittoku (Hanshan and Shi'h-tê),[3] hang it in a European or an American art gallery, and see what effect it will produce in the minds of the visitors. The idea of aloneness belongs to the East and is at home in the environment of its birth.

It is not only to the fishing village on the autumnal eve that aloneness gives form but also to a patch of green in the early spring—which is in all likelihood even more expressive of the idea of *sabi* or *wabi.* For in the green patch, as we read in the following thirty-one-syllable verse, there is an indication of life impulse amidst the wintry desolation:

> To those who only pray for the cherries to bloom,
> How I wish to show the spring
> That gleams from a patch of green
> In the midst of the snow-covered mountain-village![4]

[2]Fujiwara Sadaiye (1162–1241).

[3]Zen poet-recluses of the T'ang dynasty who have been a favorite subject for Far Eastern painters.

[4]Fujiwara Iyetaka (1158-1237).

This is given by one of the old teamasters as thoroughly expressive of *sabi,* which is one of the four principles governing the cult of tea, *cha-no-yu.* Here is just a feeble inception of life power as asserted in the form of a little green patch, but in it he who has an eye can readily discern the spring shooting out from underneath the forbidding snow. It may be said to be a mere suggestion that stirs his mind, but just the same it is life itself and not its feeble indication. To the artist, life is as much here as when the whole field is overlaid with verdure and flowers. One may call this the mystic sense of the artist.

Asymmetry is another feature that distinguishes Japanese art. The idea is doubtlessly derived from the "one-corner" style of Bayen. The plainest and boldest example is the plan of Buddhist architecture. The principal structures, such as the Tower Gate, the Dharma Hall, the Buddha Hall, and others, may be laid along one straight line; but structures of secondary or supplementary importance, sometimes even those of major importance, are not arranged symmetrically as wings along either side of the main line. They may be found irregularly scattered over the grounds in accordance with the topographical peculiarities. You will readily be convinced of this fact if you visit some of the Buddhist temples in the mountains, for example, the Iyeyasu shrine at Nikko. We can say that asymmetry is quite characteristic of Japanese architecture of this class.

This can be demonstrated *par excellence* in the construction of the tearoom and in the tools used in connection with it. Look at the ceiling, which may be constructed in at least three different styles, and at some of the utensils for serving tea, and again at the grouping and laying of the steppingstones or flagstones in the garden. We find so many illustrations of asymmetry, or, in a way, of imperfection, or of the "one-corner" style.

Some Japanese moralists try to explain this liking of the Japanese artists for things asymmetrically formed and counter to the conventional, or rather geometrical, rules of art by the theory that the people have been morally trained not to be obtrusive but always to efface themselves, and that this mental habit of self-annihilation manifests itself accordingly in art—for example, when the artist leaves the important central space unoccupied. But, to my mind, this theory is not quite correct. Would it not be a more plausible explanation to say that the artistic genius of the Japanese people has been inspired by the Zen way of looking at individual things as perfect in themselves and at the same time as embodying the nature of totality which belongs to the One?

The doctrine of ascetic aestheticism is not so fundamental as that of Zen aestheticism. Art impulses are more primitive or more innate than those of morality. The appeal of art goes more directly into human nature. Morality is regulative, art is creative. One is an imposition from without, the other is an irrepressible expression from within. Zen finds its inevitable association with art but not with morality. Zen may remain unmoral but not without art. When the Japanese artists create objects imperfect from the point of view of form, they may even be willing to ascribe their art motive to the current notion of moral asceticism; but we need not give too much significance to their own interpretation or to that of the critic. Our consciousness is not, after all, a very reliable standard of judgment.

However this may be, asymmetry is certainly characteristic of Japanese art, which is one of the reasons informality or approachability also marks to a certain degree Japanese objects of art. Symmetry inspires a notion of grace, solemnity, and impressiveness, which is again the case with logical formalism or the piling up of abstract ideas. The Japanese are often thought not to be intellectual and philosophical, because their general culture is not thoroughly impregnated with intellectuality. This criticism, I think, results somewhat from the Japanese love of asymmetry. The intellectual primarily aspires to balance, while the Japanese are apt to ignore it and incline strongly towards imbalance.

Imbalance, asymmetry, the "one-corner," poverty, simplification, *sabi* or *wabi,* aloneness, and cognate ideas make up the most conspicuous and characteristic features of Japanese art and culture. All these emanate from one central perception of the truth of Zen, which is "the One in the Many and the Many in the One," or better, "the One remaining as one in the Many individually and collectively."

2

That Zen has helped to stimulate the artistic impulses of the Japanese people and to color their works with ideas characteristic of Zen is due to the following facts: the Zen monasteries were almost exclusively the repositories of learning and art, at least during the Kamakura and the Muromachi eras; the Zen monks had constant opportunities to come in

contact with foreign cultures; the monks themselves were artists, scholars, and mystics; they were even encouraged by the political powers of
the time to engage in commercial enterprises to bring foreign objects of
art and industry to Japan; the aristocrats and the politically influential
classes of Japan were patrons of Zen institutions and were willing to
submit themselves to the discipline of Zen. Zen thus worked not only
directly on the religious life of the Japanese but also most strongly on
their general culture.

The Tendai, the Shingon, and the Jōdō[5] contributed greatly to imbue
the Japanese with the spirit of Buddhism, and through their icon-
ography to develop their artistic instincts for sculpture, color paintings,
architecture, textile fabrics, and metalwork. But the philosophy of
Tendai is too abstract and abstruse to be understood by the masses; the
ritualism of Shingon is too elaborate and complicated and consequently too expensive for popularity. On the other hand, Shingon and
Tendai and Jōdō produced fine sculpture and pictures and artistic utensils to be used in their daily worship. The most highly prized "national
treasures" belong to the Tempyō, the Nara, and the Heian periods,
when those two schools of Buddhism were in the ascendency and
intimately involved with the cultured classes of the people. The Jōdō
teaches the Pure Land in all its magnificence, where the Buddha of
Infinite Light is attended by his retinue of Bodhisattvas, and this
inspired the artists to paint those splendid pictures of Amida preserved
in the various Buddhist temples of Japan. The Nichiren and the Shin
are the creation of the Japanese religious mind. The Nichiren gave no
specifically artistic and cultural impetus to us; the Shin tended to be
somewhat iconoclastic and produced nothing worth mentioning in the
arts and literature except the hymns known as *wasan* and the "honor-
able letters" *(gobunsho* or *ofumi)* chiefly written by Rennyo
(1415–99).

Zen came to Japan after Shingon and Tendai and was at once
embraced by the military classes. It was more or less by an historical
accident that Zen was set against the aristocratic priesthood. The
nobility, too, in the beginning felt a certain dislike for it and made use of
their political advantage to stir up opposition to Zen. In the beginning

[5]These, with the Shin and the Nichiren, are the principal schools of Buddhism
in Japan.

of the Japanese history of Zen, therefore, Zen avoided Kyoto and established itself under the patronage of the Hōjō family in Kamakura. This place, as the seat of the feudal government in those days, became the headquarters of Zen discipline. Many Zen monks from China settled in Kamakura and found strong support in the Hōjō family— Tokiyori, Tokimune, and their successors and retainers.

The Chinese masters brought many artists and objects of art along with them, and the Japanese who came back from China were also bearers of art and literature. Pictures of Kakei (Hsia Kuei, *fl.* (1190–1220), Mokkei (Mu-ch'i, *fl. c.* 1240), Ryōkai (Liang K'ai, *fl. c.* 1210), Bayen (Ma Yüan, *fl.* 1175–1225), and others thus found their way to Japan. Manuscripts of the noted Zen masters of China were also given shelter in the monasteries here. Calligraphy in the Far East is an art just as much as *sumiye* painting, and it was cultivated almost universally among the intellectual classes in olden times. The spirit pervading Zen pictures and calligraphy made a strong impression on them, and Zen was readily taken up and followed. In it there is something virile and unbending. A mild, gentle, and graceful air—almost feminine, one might call it—which prevailed in the periods preceding the Kamakura, is now superseded by an air of masculinity, expressing itself mostly in the sculpture and calligraphy of the period. The rugged virility of the warriors of the Kwanto districts is proverbial, in contrast to the grace and refinement of the courtiers in Kyoto. The soldierly quality, with its mysticism and aloofness from worldly affairs, appeals to the willpower. Zen in this respect walks hand in hand with the spirit of Bushido ("Warriors' Way").

Another factor in the discipline of Zen, or rather in the monastic life in which Zen carries out its scheme of teaching, is this: as the monastery is usually situated in the mountains, its inmates are in the most intimate touch with nature, they are close and sympathetic students of it. They observe plants, birds, animals, rocks, rivers which people of the town would leave unnoticed. And their observation deeply reflects their philosophy, or better, their intuition. It is not that of a mere naturalist. It penetrates into the life itself of the objects that come under the monks' observation. Whatever they may paint of nature will inevitably be expressive of this intuition; the "spirit of the mountains" will be felt softly breathing in their works.

The fundamental intuition the Zen masters gain through their discipline seems to stir up their artistic instincts if they are at all susceptible to art. The intuition that impels the masters to create beautiful things, that is, to express the sense of perfection through things ugly and imperfect, is apparently closely related to the feeling for art. The Zen masters may not make good philosophers, but they are very frequently fine artists. Even their technique is often of the first order, and besides they know how to tell us something unique and original. One such is Musō the National Teacher (1275–1351). He was a fine calligrapher and a great landscape gardener; wherever he resided, at quite a number of places in Japan, he designed splendid gardens, some of which are still in existence and well preserved after so many years of changing times. Among the noted painters of Zen in the fourteenth and fifteenth centuries we may mention Chō Densu (d. 1431), Kei Shoki (fl. 1490), Josetsu (fl. 1375–1420), Shūbun (fl. 1420–50), Seshū (1421–1506), and others.

Georges Duthuit, the author of *Chinese Mysticism and Modern Painting,* seems to understand the spirit of Zen mysticism. From him we have this: "When the Chinese artist paints, what matters is the concentration of thought and the prompt and vigorous response of the hand to the directing will. Tradition ordains him to see, or rather to feel, as a whole the work to be executed, before embarking on anything. 'If the ideas of a man are confused, he will become the slave of exterior conditions.' . . . He who deliberates and moves his brush intent on making a picture, misses to a still greater extent the art of painting. [This seems like a kind of automatic writing.] Draw bamboos for ten years, become a bamboo, then forget all about bamboos when you are drawing. In possession of an infallible technique, the individual places himself at the mercy of inspiration."

To become a bamboo and to forget that you are one with it while drawing it—this is the Zen of the bamboo, this is the moving with the "rhythmic movement of the spirit" which resides in the bamboo as well as in the artist himself. What is now required of him is to have a firm hold on the spirit and yet not to be conscious of the fact. This is a very difficult task achieved only after long spiritual training.[6] The Eastern people have been taught since the earliest times to subject themselves to

[6]Cf. Takuan on "Prajñā Immovable."

this kind of discipline if they want to achieve something in the world of art and religion. Zen, in fact, has given expression to it in the following phrase: "One in All and All in One." When this is thoroughly understood, there is creative genius.

It is of utmost importance here to interpret the phrase in its proper sense. People imagine that it means pantheism, and some students of Zen seem to agree. This is to be regretted, for pantheism is something foreign to Zen and also to the artist's understanding of his work. When the Zen masters declare the One to be in the All and the All in the One, they do not mean that the one is the other and *vice versa*. As the One is in the All, some people suppose that Zen is a pantheistic teaching. Far from it; Zen would never hypostatize the One or the All as a thing to be grasped by the sense. The phrase "One in All and All in One" is to be understood as an expression of absolute *Prajñā*-intuition and is not to be conceptually analyzed. When we see the moon, we know that it is the moon, and that is enough. Those who proceed to analyze the experience and try to establish a theory of knowledge are not students of Zen. They cease to be so, if they ever were, at the very moment of their procedure as analysts. Zen always upholds its experience as such and refuses to commit itself to any system of philosophy.

Even when Zen indulges in intellection, it never subscribes to a pantheistic interpretation of the world. For one thing, there is no One in Zen. If Zen ever speaks of the One as if it recognized it, this is a kind of condescension to common parlance. To Zen students, the One is the All and the All is the One; and yet the One remains the One and the All the All. "Not two!" may lead the logician to think, "It is One." But the master would go on, saying, "Not One either!" "What then?" we may ask. We here face a blind alley, as far as verbalism is concerned. Therefore, it is said that "If you wish to be in direct communion [with Reality], I tell you 'Not two!'"

The following *mondo*[7] may help to illustrate the point I wish to make in regard to the Zen attitude towards the so-called pantheistic interpretation of nature.

A monk asked Tōsu (T'ou-tzu), a Zen master of the T'ang period: "I understand that all sounds are the voice of the Buddha. Is this right?" The master said, "That is right." The monk then proceeded: "Would

[7]This and what follows are all from the *Hekigan-shu,* case 79.

not the master please stop making a noise which echoes the sound of a fermenting mass of filth?" The master thereupon struck the monk.

The monk further asked Tōsu: "Am I in the right when I understand the Buddha as asserting that all talk, however trivial or derogatory, belongs to ultimate truth?" The master said, "Yes, you are in the right." The monk went on, "May I then call you a donkey?" The master thereupon struck him.

It may be necessary to explain these *mondo* in plain language. To conceive every sound, every noise, every utterance one makes as issuing from the fountainhead of one Reality, that is, from one God, is pantheistic, I imagine. For "he giveth to all life, and breath, and all things" (Acts 17:25); and again, "For in him we live, and move, and have our being" (Acts 17:28). If this be the case, a Zen master's hoarse throat echoes the melodious resonance of the voice flowing from the Buddha's golden mouth, and even when a great teacher is decried as reminding one of an ass, the defamation must be regarded as reflecting something of ultimate truth. All forms of evil must be said somehow to be embodying what is true and good and beautiful, and to be a contribution to the perfection of Reality. To state it more concretely, bad is good, ugly is beautiful, false is true, imperfect is perfect, and also conversely. This is, indeed, the kind of reasoning in which those indulge who conceive the God-nature to be immanent in all things. Let us see how the Zen master treats this problem.

It is remarkable that Tōsu put his foot right down against such intellectualist interpretations and struck his monk. The latter in all probability expected to see the master nonplussed by his statements which logically follow from his first assertion. The masterful Tōsu knew, as all Zen masters do, the uselessness of making any verbal demonstration against such a "logician." For verbalism leads from one complication to another; there is no end to it. The only effective way, perhaps, to make such a monk as this one realize the falsehood of his conceptual understanding is to strike him and so let him experience within himself the meaning of the statement, "One in All and All in One." The monk was to be awakened from his logical somnambulism. Hence Tōsu's drastic measure.

Secchō here gives his comments in the following lines:

Pity that people without number try to play with the tide;
They are all ultimately swallowed up into it and die!
Let them suddenly awake [from the deadlock],
And see that all the rivers run backward, swelling and surging.[8]

What is needed here is an abrupt turning or awakening, with which one comes to the realization of the truth of Zen—which is neither transcendentalism nor immanentism nor a combination of the two. The truth is as Tōsu declares in the following:

A monk asks, "What is the Buddha?"

Tōsu answers, "The Buddha."

Monk: "What is the Tao?"

Tōsu: "The Tao."

Monk: "What is Zen?"

Tōsu: "Zen."

The master answers like a parrot, he is echo itself. In fact, there is no other way of illumining the monk's mind than affirming that what is is—which is the final fact of experience.

Another example[9] is given to illustrate the point. A monk asked Jōshu (Chao-chou), of the T'ang dynasty: "It is stated that the Perfect Way knows no difficulties, only that it abhors discrimination. What is meant by No-discrimination?"

Jōshu said, "Above the heavens and below the heavens, I alone am the Honored One."

The monk suggested, "Still a discrimination."

The master's retort was, "O this worthless fellow! Where is the discrimination?"

By discrimination the Zen masters mean what we have when we refuse to accept Reality as it is or in its suchness, for we then reflect on it and analyze it into concepts, going on with intellection and finally landing on a circulatory reasoning. Jōshu's affirmation is a final one and allows no equivocation, no argumentation. We have simply to take it as it stands and remain satisfied with it. In case we somehow fail to do

---

[8]Seccho (Hsüeh-tou, 980–1052) was one of the great Zen masters of the Sung, noted for his literary accomplishment. The *Hekigan-shu* is based on Seccho's "One Hundred Cases," which he selected out of the annals of Zen.

[9]*Hekigan-shu,* case 57.

this, we just leave it alone, and go somewhere else to seek our own enlightenment. The monk could not see where Jōshu was, and he went further on and remarked, "This is still a discrimination!" The discrimination in point of fact is on the monk's side and not on Jōshu's. Hence "the Honored One" now turns into "a worthless fellow."

As I said before, the phrase "All in One and One in All" is not to be analyzed first to the concepts "One" and "All," and the preposition is not then to be put between them; no discrimination is to be exercised here, but one is just to accept it and abide with it, which is really no-abiding at all. There is nothing further to do. Hence the master's striking or calling names. He is not indignant, nor is he short-tempered, but he wishes thereby to help his disciples out of the pit which they have dug themselves. No amount of argument avails here, no verbal persuasion. Only the master knows how to turn them away from a logical impasse and how to open a new way for them; let them, therefore, simply follow him. By following him they all come back to their Original Home.

When an intuitive or experiential understanding of Reality is verbally formulated as "All in One and One in All," we have there the fundamental statement as it is taught by all the various schools of Buddhism. In the terminology of the Prajñā school, this is: śūnyatā ("Emptiness") is tathatā ("Suchness"), and tathatā is śūnyatā: śūnyatā is the world of the Absolute, and tathatā is the world of particulars. One of the commonest sayings in Zen is "Willows are green and flowers red" or "Bamboos are straight and pine trees are gnarled." Facts of experience are accepted as they are, Zen is not nihilistic, nor is it merely positivistic. Zen would say that just because the bamboo is straight it is of Emptiness, or that just because of Emptiness the bamboo cannot be anything else but a bamboo and not a pine tree. What makes the Zen statements different from mere sense experience, however, is that Zen's intuition grows out of Prajñā and not out of jñā.[10] It is from this point of view that when asked "What is Zen?" the master sometimes answers "Zen" and sometimes "Not-Zen."

[10] Prajñā may be translated "transcendental wisdom," while jñā or vijñāna is "relative knowledge." For a detailed explanation, see my Studies in Zen Buddhism, pp. 85 ff.

We can see now that the principle of *sumiye* painting is derived from this Zen experience, and that directness, simplicity, movement spirituality, completeness, and other qualities we observe in the *sumiye* class of Oriental paintings have organic relationship to Zen. There is no pantheism in *sumiye* as there is none in Zen.

There is another thing I must not forget to mention in this connection, which is perhaps the most important factor in *sumiye* as well as in Zen. It is creativity. When it is said that *sumiye* depicts the spirit of an object, or that it gives a form to what has no form, this means that there must be a spirit of creativity moving over the picture. The painter's business thus is not just to copy or imitate nature, but to give to the object something living in its own right. It is the same with the Zen master. When he says that the willow is green and the flower is red, he is not just giving us a description of how nature looks, but something whereby green is green and red is red. This something is what I call the spirit of creativity. *Śūnyatā* is formless, but it is the fountainhead of all possibilities. To turn what is possible into an actuality is an act of creativity. When Tōsu is asked, "What is Dharma?" he answers, "Dharma"; when asked "What is Buddha?" he answers, "Buddha." This is by no means a parrotlike response, a mere echoing; all the answers come out of his creative mind, without which there is no Zen in Tōsu. The understanding of Zen is to understand what kind of mind this is. Yakusan's meeting with Rikō will illustrate this.[11]

Yakusan (Yao-shan, 751–834) was a great master of the T'ang era. When Rikō (Li Ao), governor of the province, heard of his Zen mastership, he sent for him to come to the capital. Yakusan, however, refused to come. This happened several times. Rikō grew impatient and came in person to see the master in his own mountain retreat. Yakusan was reading the *sūtras* and paid no attention whatever to the arrival of the governor. The attendant monk reminded the master of the fact, but he still kept on reading. Rikō felt hurt and remarked, "Seeing the face is not at all like hearing the name." By this he meant that the person in actuality was not equal to his reputation. Yakusan called out, "O Governor!" Rikō echoed at once, "Yes, Master." The master then said,

[11] *Dentō-roku* ("Transmission of the Lamp"), fasc. 14.

"Why do you evaluate the hearing over the seeing?" The governor apologized and asked, "What is Tao?" Yakusan pointed up with his hand and then down, and said, "Do you understand?" Rikō said, "No, Master." Thereupon Yakusan remarked, "The clouds are in the sky and water in the jar." It is said that this pleased the governor very much.

Did Rikō really understand what Yakusan meant? Yakusan's is no more than a plain statement of facts as they are, and we may ask, "Where is Tao?" Rikō was a great scholar and philosopher. He must have had some abstract conception of Tao. Could he so readily reconcile his view with Yakusan's? Whatever we may say about this, Yakusan and Tōsu and other Zen masters are all walking the same track. The artists are also required to strike it.

Zen and Japanese Art

1

There must be something in Japanese character that harmonizes well with the spirit of Zen, for the latter has so readily and thoroughly been merged in the life and culture of the Japanese people that we can recognize its presence there, though not always in a uniform way. Its introduction into Japan took place in the Kamakura era.

Zen first united itself with the spirit of Samurai as soon as it gained its foothold in the Land of the Rising Sun. The Hōzyō family built several Zen temples in Kamakura, and their leaders most earnestly studied Zen under the teachers from China. Naturally the knights serving the Hōzyō government followed the example. Their resolute and almost reckless deeds of bravery are recorded in the annals of those days.

It was not, however, until the Asikaga era that Zen's spiritual influence permeated through the various fields of art so as to effect the general life of the people.

2

Among the most remarkable features characterizing Zen we find these: spirituality, directness of expression, disregard of form or conventionalism, and frequently an almost wanton delight in going astray from respectability. For instance, when form requires a systematic treatment of the subject in question, a Zen painter may wipe out every trace of such and let an insignificant piece of rock occupy just one corner of the field. Where absolute cleanliness is the thing sought after, a Zen gardener may have a few dead leaves scattered over the garden. A Zen sword-player may stand in an almost nonchalant attitude before the foe as if the latter can strike him in any way he liked; but when he actually tries his best, the Zen man would over-awe him with his very unconcernedness. In these respects, Zen is unexpectedness itself, it is beyond logical or common-sense calculation.

3

The main reason for Zen's unexpectedness or incalculability comes from its transcending conceptualization. It expresses itself in the most impossible or irrational manner; it does not allow anything to stand between itself and its expression. In fact, the only thing that limits Zen is its wanting to express itself. But this limitation is imposed upon everything human and indeed upon things divine as long as these are to be made intelligible.

The spirit of Zen is then the going beyond conceptualization, and this means to grasp the spirit of the most intimate manner. This in turn means the disregarding to a certain extent of all technique. The idea may better be expressed by stating that Zen holds in itself something which eludes all systematized technical skill but which is to be somehow grasped in order to come in the closest possible touch with Life, all-generating and all-pervading and all-invigorating.

4

The chief concern of the Japanese artist is to stand in an intimate relationship with this Life, this Spirit. Even when he has mastered all the technique necessary for the profession, he will not stop there, for he still finds himself wanting; he is still under the bondage of the technical restrictions and traditionalism; his creative genius he feels somehow clamped; he fails to give it the freest possible expressions. He has spent so many years to quality himself as a worthy heir to his profession, laden with a line of brilliant masters, but his works are not short of his ideals, they are not precipitating with Life, that is to say, he is not satisfied with himself—he is not a creator, but an imitator.

When the Japanese artist reaches this stage, he frequently knocks at the gate of a Zen master. He asks the latter to lead him to the inner sanctuary of Zen. When Zen is understood, the spirit takes varied form for its expression: the painter expresses it in paintings, the sculptor in sculptures, the Noh-dancer in dancing, the tea-master in tea-cult, the gardener in gardening, and so on.

5

One of the Kanō masters was asked to paint a dragon on the ceiling of one of the main buildings belonging to Myōsinzi. He wished to make it one of his masterpieces, for the temple lives long and is generally a repository of all kinds of great works of art. But he did not quite feel equal to the task. The dragon is of course a mythical creature, and the painter was naturally not ambitious to make his work look like a genuine one. His desire was to create it out of his own imagination full of life and spirit so that the animal however grotesque in appearance would be the painter himself living in a world of ideas. To achieve this was no easy task. The reality of sense incessantly worked against him as he wished to fly away to a heaven of artistic fantasies. The painter finally came to the abbot of the monastery who was a great Zen master of the day, and asked him how to proceed in his work. The master simply said, "You be the dragon yourself." The Kanō artist did not know how to take this advice, but after much cogitation the idea dawned on him. When he finally came back to the master, he was no more the plain painter who was trying to paint a dragon, he was the dragon himself. The master then told him to go ahead with his work. The work was the dragon painting himself, and not a human artist trying to portray the mythical creature. The work can still be seen on the original ceiling as the painter painted it in black and white.

6

An asymmetrical treatment of a subject is characteristically Zen as well as Japanese. One often comes across a square or circle cut off at one corner, a tea-cup quite disfigured, a dinner tray covered with dishes of varied shape, or a room with ceilings of different designs and with windows of various sizes and shapes cut into the walls. The typical example of asymmetry is the tea-room.

Asymmetry may be considered an imperfection, but in my view this is not true. A broken line is just as artistically perfect as a straight line or a curve. It all depends where one would fix a standard. A broken line or an irregular curve is perfect in its very "imperfection." If it is made to serve a utilitarian purpose a curve or line is to be perfectly formed, but art has no such teleology. This freedom from teleology is the spirit of Zen as well as of art.

7

A broken line or an imperfect representation of an object may be regarded as suggesting something regularly and therefore perfectly shaped; but from the Zen point of view which is also the Japanese way of feeling, a thing however misshaped is perfect and artistic in its being misshaped. What is needed here to make an imperfection perfect is the presence of the artist's spiritual love for the object—a love which is above egotism but which issues from Great Spirit.

8

The Japanese people are noted for their liking small things and making big things of them. This has a historical background but in reality it reflects the spirit of Zen, which turns the Buddha sixteen feet high into a single blade of grass and the latter into the former, and which also takes in a seed of mustard the great peak of Mount Sumeru. An insignificant green frog sits on a lotus leaf an early summer morning in a garden pond surrounded by some luxuriantly growing trees. A painter takes up this creature on a piece of silk and makes it sit on the lotus as if it were enjoying a life in the Pure Land. There it altogether loses is insignificance; it looks about it contented with itself; the leaf may occasionally be shaken by a gentle breeze, but it knows where it is and securely balances itself, taking all things in as if all belonged to it or as if it were one with them. It is after all not the frog that is rested there but the painter himself who is satisfied with himself and the world—no, it is not the painter himself, it is even the Great Spirit of the Universe. Not only the artist but the onlooker also is absorbed into the spirit pervading the picture.

This wonderful transformation realized through the agency of a little green summer frog has really taken place owing to the Zen-painter's loving spirit which embraces the world and all.

9

What a Zen-artist actually performs is not to suggest what is omitted, but to make the whole reality reflect itself in the small things before ourselves. For when the latter are understood they present themselves to be more than themselves. They are realities and not mere suggestions of them. Before Zen took hold of the Japanese soul, this was not possible however much of this proclivity there was in it. It will not express itself in this way. Zen made it eloquent and it ceased to be dumb. The primitive mind may harbor many virtues and possibilities deeply buried underneath, but it requires a touch of a higher spiritual culture which brings them out to the front through stages of historical development. Zen has fulfilled this requirement for the Japanese soul.

Rinzai on Zen

TRANSLATION FROM THE CHINESE

AND COMMENTARY

What follows is the first English translation of a sermon from the *Sayings of Rinzai (Lin-chi Lu).* Rinzai (Lin-chi), who died in 867, was a prominent master of the T'ang dynasty (618–905), and the school of Zen that started after him bears his name. His sermons and other material containing his "life" and *mondo* (questions and answers) were compiled after his death by a chief disciple, and the sermon reproduced here is probably one of Rinzai's first expository utterances on Zen. The *Sayings,* a book of about 14,800 characters, is considered one of the most remarkable documents elucidating the principles of Zen. Those who study Zen in one way or another cannot afford to neglect it.

The following points may be enumerated as characterizing the thought of Rinzai: (1) true understanding, (2) freedom, (3) not being deluded by others, (4) faith in self, (5) not craving for externalities, (6) "the one who is at this moment listening to my sermon," (7) nothing wanting in each of us, (8) a man of *buji,* and (9) not being different from the Buddha.

The master then said:

Those of you who wish to discipline themselves in Buddha's Dharma[1] must seek true understanding. When this understanding is attained you will not be defiled by birth and death.[2] Whether walking or standing still, you will be your own master.[3] Even when you are not trying to achieve something extraordinary,[4] it will come to you all by itself.

O Followers of the Way, from olden times each of my predecessors had his own way of training his disciples. As to my way of leading people: all that they need is not to be deluded by others. [Be independent] and go on your way whenever you desire; have no hesitancy.

Do you know where the disease lies which keeps you learners from reaching [true understanding]? It lies where you have no faith in your Self. When faith in your Self is lacking you find yourself hurried by others in every possible way. At every encounter you are no longer your master; you are driven about by others this way or that.

All that is required is all at once to cease leaving your Self in search of something external. When this is done you will find your Self no different from the Buddha or the patriarch.

Do you want to know who the Buddha or patriarch is? He is no other than the one who is, at this moment, right in front of me, listening to my talk on the Dharma. You have no faith in him and therefore you are in quest of someone else somewhere outside. And what will you find? Nothing but words and names, however excellent. You will never reach the moving spirit in the Buddha or patriarch. Make no mistake.

O Venerable Sirs, do not fail to take advantage of the present life we are enjoying. If you fail, this opportunity may never come again, even for as long as you go on transmigrating through the triple world, assuming one form of existence or another, for hundreds of thousands of *kalpas*. When you keep up your life of pleasures your incarnation in the body of an ass or a cow is an assured fact.

O Followers of the Way, according to my view, I see no difference between myself and Śākyamuni.[5] As I live this life of mine today in response to all kinds of situations, is there anything I am in want of? There is no interruption of light wonderfully emanating from my six senses.[6] When you see how this is, you will be no less than men of *buji*[7] all your lives.

O Venerable Sirs, there is no peace in the triple world, it is like a house on fire. It is not a place where you can stay for any length of time. When the devil of impermanence visits you, he does not differentiate between the humble and the noble, between the young and the aged. In no time they are all his prey.

If you desire to be like the Buddha or the patriarch, do not seek anything external. Radiating from the mind at every thought-moment, there is a ray of absolute purity—the *Dharmakāya*[8] in your body; there is a ray of non-discrimination[9]—the *Sambhogakāya* in your body; there is a ray of non-differentiation—the *Nirmāṇakāya* in your body. This triple body[10] is no other than your Self, who is listening at this moment in front of me to my talk on the Dharma. All these activities are revealed when your searching externally ceases.

For scholars of the *sūtras* and *śāstras*,[11] the doctrine of *Trikāya* is the final teaching of the Buddha. But from my point of view the *Trikāya* is nothing but a word—only a triple style of clothes a man may put on.

NOTES

[1]Dharma *(hō, fa)* has several meanings. Here it is used in the sense of reality, the ultimate, truth, absolute reason, etc.

[2]The cycle of birth and death is *saṃsāra* in Sanskrit. It stands against absolute reason or something that remains eternally in spite of all the vicissitudes that go in this world of relativity.

[3]"To be master of oneself" *(jiyū, tzu-yu)* is not to be understood in the sense of will power or self-control. According to the biblical account, God created the world out of his free will: he was his own master, nobody compelled him; he was then a free, independent, autonomous guest. Each of us has something of this in him, the same in essence as the divine will.

[4]"Extraordinary" does not mean supernatural or miraculous. When true understanding is attained, the ordinaries transform themselves into extra-ordinaries.

[5]"Silent sage of the Śākya clan," an epithet of the Buddha.

[6]Buddhist psychology counts the intellect or consciousness *(manovijñāna)*, a discriminating agency, as the sixth sense. "The light emanating from the six senses" simply refers to their dynamic quality or readiness to respond.

[7]*Buji (wu-shih)* is one of the most significant terms in the vocabulary of Zen, especially in that of the Rinzai Sect. The term, however, is liable to be grossly misinterpreted by those who are not used to the Oriental way of living and feeling. It is a key term in the teaching of Rinzai.

When the Dharma is truly, fully, and existentially (experientially) understood, we find that there is nothing wanting in this life as we live it. Everything and anything we need is here with us and in us. One who has actually experienced this is called a man of *buji*. *Buji* is one of those concepts whose equivalents probably cannot be found in any European language, because in the thought-structure of the West there is nothing corresponding to it. "Non-action" or "not-doing" may do for Lao-tsu's *mu-i (wu-wei)*, and "no-mind" for Eno's *mushin (wu-hsin)*, but "no-business" or "no-event" sounds very queer for Rinzai's *buji*. The trouble with *buji* (or *muji*) is that there is no good word in English expressing all the ideas implied in *ji*.

Ji (shih) generally means "business," "event," "matter," "concern," "engagement," "affair," etc. When all this is negated, we may have for "a man of *buji*" "one who has no business," or "one to whom no events happen," or "one who is unconcerned or indifferent or disinterested," or "one to whom nothing matters," and so on. But "a man of *buji*" is not any of them. He is the one who has a true understanding of the Dharma or Reality as is described in the sermon; he has an existential insight into the Self; he is the one who being freed from externalities is master of himself; he is a Buddha and a patriarch. He has the great business of trying to lead all his fellow-beings into a state of enlightenment. He cannot remain unconcerned and indifferent so long as there is even one being left unemancipated. He works hard, "covered with ashes and smeared with mud," as Zen people would say; he is really one of the busiest men of the world, and yet he has "no business," "no events are happening to him," he is "utterly unconcerned." What kind of a man can he be? One of the "aristocracy," to use Eckhartian terminology; Zen calls him a "man of *buji*."

⁸ *The Buddha is provided with a triple body (Trikāya): Dharmakāya,* the body of the Dharma; *Sambhogakāya,* the body of enjoyment; *Nirmāṇakāya,* the body of transformation. Rinzai's triple body has nothing to do with the Buddha's except in name. Rinzai thinks we can distinguish in our mind-activity these three aspects of the Buddha's Triple Body. The light of purity which is Aśvaghoṣa's *primary enlightenment* corresponds to the *Dharmakāya.* The light of non-discrimination may be regarded as the *Prajñā* (wisdom) aspect of the primary enlightenment, and the light of non-differentiation as the *Karuṇā* (compassion) aspect, whereby the *Dharmakāya* goes through all forms of transformation in order to deliver all beings from ignorance and its attendant fear and insecurity.

⁹Non-discrimination is intellectual, while non-differentiation is physical or objective. This is what I think Rinzai means.

¹⁰*Trikāya* in Sanskrit.

¹¹The *sūtras* and *śāstras* are the canonical texts and philosophical treatises elucidating the teaching of the Buddha.

Love and Power

A message read (in French and translated) by Dr. D. T. Suzuki in the Hall of the International Exhibition at Brussels on 28th May, 1958, at the Conference "In Defense of Spiritual Values in the Contemporary World."—ED.

Never in the history of mankind has there been a more urgent need for spiritual leaders and for the enhancement of spiritual values than there is in our contemporary world. We have achieved many wonderful things in this and the past century toward the advancement of human welfare. But, strangely, we seem to have forgotten that our welfare depends principally upon our spiritual wisdom and discipline. It is all due to our not fully recognizing this fact that we see the world at present being filled with the putrefying air of hatred and violence, fear and treachery. Indeed, we are trying to work all the harder for mutual destruction, not only individually but internationally and racially.

Of all the spiritual values we can conceive and wish to be brought out before us today, none is more commandingly needed than love.

It is love which creates life. Life cannot sustain itself without love. My firm conviction is that the present filthy, suffocating atmosphere of hatred and fear is generated through the suppression of the spirit of loving-kindness and universal brotherhood, and it goes without saying that this suffocation comes from the non-realization of the truth that the human community is the most complicated and far-reaching network of mutual dependence.

The moral teaching of individualism with all its significant corollaries is very fine indeed, but we must remember that the individual is non-existent when he is isolated from other individuals and cut off from the group to which he belongs, whether the group be biological or political or cosmological. Mathematically stated, the number one can never be one, never be itself, unless it is related to other numbers which are infinite. The existence of a single number by itself is unthinkable. Morally or spiritually, this means that the existence of each individual,

66

whether or not he is conscious of the fact, owes something to an infinitely expanding and all-enwrapping net of loving relationship, which takes up not only every one of us but everything that exists. The world is a great family and we, each one of us, are its members.

I do not know how much geography has to do with the moulding of human thought, but the fact is that it was in the Far East that a system of thought developed in the seventh century which is known as the Kegon school of philosophy. The Kegan is based on the ideas of interfusion, or interpenetration, or interrelatedness, or mutual unobstructedness.

When this philosophy of the interrelatedness of things is rightly understood, love begins to be realized, because love is to recognize others and to take them into consideration in every way of life. To do to others what you would like them to do to you is the keynote of love and this is what naturally grows out of the realization of mutual relatedness.

The idea of mutual relationship and consideration excludes the notion of power, for power is something brought from outside into a structure of inner relationship. The use of power is always apt to be arbitrary and despotic and alienating.

What troubles us these days is no other than a crookedly exaggerated assertion of the power-concept by those who fail to see into its true nature and therefore are not capable of using it for the benefit of all.

Love is not a command given us by an outside agent, for this implies a sense of power. Excessive individualism is the hot-bed in which power-feeling is bred and nourished, because it is egocentric in the sense that it asserts itself arrogantly, and often violently, when it moves out of itself and tries to overrule others. Love, on the contrary, grows out of mutuality and interrelationship, and is far from egocentric and self-exalting. While power, superficially strong and irresistible, is in reality self-exhausting, love, through self-negation, is ever creative, for it is the root of existence. Love needs no external, all-powerful agent to exercise itself. Love is life and life is love.

Being an infinitely complicated network of interrelationship, life cannot be itself unless supported by love. Wishing to give life a form, love expresses itself in all modes of being. Form is necessarily individualistic, and the discriminating intellect is liable to regard form as final reality; the power-concept grows out of it. When the intellect develops and pursues its own course, being intoxicated by the success it has achieved in the utilitarian fields of human activity, power runs amok and plays havoc all around.

Love is affirmation, a creative affirmation; it is never destructive and annihilating, because unlike power it is all-embracing and all-forgiving. Love enters into its object and becomes one with it, while power, being characteristically dualistic and discriminative, crushes any object standing against it, or otherwise it conquers it and turns it into a slavish dependent.

Power makes use of science and everything that belongs to it. As long as science remains analytical and cannot go beyond the study of infinitely varied forms of differentiation and their quantitative measurements it is never creative. What is creative in it is its spirit of inquiry, which is inspired by love and not by power. Where there is any co-operation between power and the sciences, it always ends in contriving various methods of disaster and destruction.

Love and creativity are two aspects of one reality, but creativity is often separated from love. When this illegitimate separation takes place, creativity comes to be associated with power. Power really belongs to a lower order than love and creativity. When power usurps creativity, it becomes a most dangerous agent of all kinds of mischief.

The notion of power as aforesaid grows inevitably out of a dualistic interpretation of reality. When dualism neglects to recognize the presence of an integrating principle behind it, its native penchant for destruction exhibits itself rampantly and wantonly.

One of the most conspicuous examples of this display of power is seen in the Western attitude toward Nature. Westerners talk about conquering Nature and never about befriending her. They climb a high mountain and they declare the mountain is conquered. They succeed in shooting a certain type of projectile heavenwards and then claim that they have conquered the air. Why do they not say that they are now better acquainted with Nature? Unfortunately, the hostility-concept is penetrating every corner of the world and people talk about "control," "conquest," "conditioning," and the like.

The notion of power excludes the feelings of personality, mutuality, gratitude, and all kinds of relationship. Whatever benefits we may derive from the advancement of the sciences, ever-improving technology, and industrialization in general, we are not allowed to participate in them universally because power is liable to monopolize them instead of distributing them equally among our fellow beings.

Power is always arrogant, self-assertive, and exclusive, whereas love is self-humiliating and all-comprehensive. Power represents destruction, even self-destruction, quite contrary to love's creativeness. Love dies and lives again, while power kills and is killed.

It was Simone Weil, I understand, who defined power as a force which transforms a person into a thing. I would like to define love as a force that transforms a thing into a person. Love may thus appear to be something radically opposed to power, and love and power may be regarded as mutually exclusive, so that where there is power there cannot be any shadow of love, and where love is no power can ever intrude upon it.

This is true to a certain extent, but the real truth is that love is not opposed to power; love belongs to an order higher than power, and it is only power that imagines itself to be opposed to love. In truth, love is all-enveloping and all-forgiving; it is a universal solvent, an infinitely creative and resourceful agent. As power is always dualistic and therefore rigid, self-assertive, destructive, and annihilating, it turns against itself and destroys itself when it has nothing to conquer. This is in the nature of power, and is it not this that we are witnessing today, particularly in our international affairs?

What is blind is not love but power, for power utterly fails to see that its existence is dependent upon something else. It refuses to realize that it can be itself only allying itself to something infinitely greater than itself. Not knowing this fact, power plunges itself straight into the pit of self-destruction. The cataract that blinds the eye must be removed in order that power may experience enlightenment. Without this experience everything becomes unreal to the myopically veiled eye of power.

When the eye fails to see reality as it is, that is, in its suchness, a cloud of fear and suspicion spreads over all things that come before it. Not being able to see reality in its suchness, the eye deceives itself; it becomes suspicious of anything that confronts it and desires to destroy it. Mutual suspicion is thus let loose, and when this takes place no amount of explanation will reduce the tension. Each side resorts to all kinds of sophistry and subterfuge, which in international politics go under the name of diplomacy. But so long as there is nowhere any mutual trust and love, and the spirit of reconciliation, no diplomacy will alleviate the intensity of the situation which it has created by its own machinery.

Those who are power-intoxicated fail to see that power is blinding and keeps them within an ever-narrowing horizon. Power is thus associated with intellection, and makes use of it in every possible way. Love, however, transcends power because, in its penetration into the core of reality, far beyond the finiteness of the intellect, it is infinity itself. Without love one cannot see the infinitely expanding network of relationships which is reality. Or, we may reverse this and say that without the infinite network of reality we can never experience love in its true light. Love trusts, is always affirmative and all-embracing. Love is life and therefore creative. Everything it touches is enlivened and energized for new growth. When you love an animal, it grows more intelligent; when you love a plant you see into its every need. Love is never blind; it is the reservoir of infinite light.

Being blind and self-limiting, power cannot see reality in its suchness; and, therefore, what it sees is unreal. Power itself is unreal, and thus all that comes in contact with it turns into unreality. Power thrives only in a world of unrealities and thus it becomes the symbol of insincerity and falsehood.

To conclude: Let us first realize the fact that we thrive only when we are co-operative by being alive to the truth of interrelationship of all things in existence. Let us then die to the notion of power and conquest and be resurrected to the eternal creativity of love which is all-embracing and all-forgiving. As love flows out of rightly seeing reality as it is, it is also love that makes us feel that we—each of us individually and all of us collectively—are responsible for whatever things, good or evil, go on in our human community, and we must therefore strive to ameliorate or remove whatever conditions are inimical to the universal advancement of human welfare and wisdom.

Buddhist Symbolism

Basho, one of the greatest *haiku*[1] poets in eighteenth century Japan, produced this when his eyes for the first time opened to the poetical and philosophical significance of *haiku*.

> *Furuike-ya!*
> *Kawazu tobi-komu*
> *Mizu-no oto!*

> Oh! ancient pond!
> A frog leaps in,
> The water's sound!

This is, as far as its literary sense goes, no more than the simple statement of the fact. Here is the ancient pond, probably partly covered with some aquatic plants and bordered with the bushes and weeds rampantly growing. The clear spring water, serenly undisturbed, reflects the trees with their fresh green foliage of the spring time, enhanced by a recent rainfall. A little green frog comes out of the grass and jumps into the water, giving rise to a series of ripples growing larger and larger until they touch the banks. The little frog jumping into the water should not make much of a sound. But when it takes place in a quiet environment it cannot pass unnoticed by Basho, who was in all likelihood absorbed in deep contemplation of nature. However feeble the sound might have been, it was enough to awaken him from his meditation. So he set down in the seventeen-syllable *haiku* what went through his consciousness.

Now the question is: What was this experience Basho, the poet, had at the moment?

As far as the *haiku* itself is concerned, it does not go beyond the matter of fact statement of the phenomenon of which he was the witness. There is no reference to what may be termed the subjective

[1] *Haiku* is the shortest form of poetic expression in Japanese literature.

aspect of the incident except the little particle, *ya*. Indeed, the presence of *ya* is the key-word to the whole composition. With this the *haiku* ceases to be an objective description of the frog jumping into the old pond and of the sound of the water caused thereby.

So long as the old pond remains a container of a certain volume of water quietly reflecting the things around it, there is no life in it. To assert itself as reality, a sound must come out of it; a frog jumps into it, the old pond then proves to be dynamic, to be full of vitality, to be of significance to us sentient beings. It becomes an object of interest, of value.

But there is one important observation we have to make, which is that the value of the old pond to Basho, the poet and seer (or mystic), did not come from any particular source outside the pond but from the pond itself. It may be better to say, the pond is the value. The pond did not become significant to Basho because of his finding the value in the pond's relationship to anything outside the pond as a pond.

To state this in other words, the frog's jumping into the pond, its causing the water to splash and make a noise, was the occasion—intellectually, dualistically, or objectively speaking—to make Basho realize that he was the pond and the pond was he, and that whatever value there was in this identification, the value was no other than the fact of this identification itself. There was nothing added to the fact.

When he recognized the fact, the fact itself became significant. Nothing was added to it. The pond was a pond, the frog was a frog, the water was water. The objects remained the same. No, it is better to express the idea in this way: no objective world, so called, at all existed with its frogs, ponds, etc., until one day a person known as Basho came suddenly to the scene and heard "the water's sound." The scene, indeed, until then had no existence. When its value was recognized by Basho this was to Basho the beginning or the creation of an objective world. Before this, the old pond was there as if it were not in existence. It was no more than a dream; it had no reality. It was the occasion of Basho's hearing the frog that the whole world, including the poet himself, sprung out of Nothingness *ex nihilo*.

There is still another way of describing Basho's experience and the birth of an objective world.

In their moment there was no participation, on the part of Basho, in the life of the old pond or of the little green frog. Both subject and object were totally annihilated. And yet the pond was the pond, Basho was Basho, the frog was the frog; they remained as they were, or as they have been from the beginningless past. And yet Basho was no other than the pond when he faced the pond; Basho was no other than the frog when he heard the sound of the water caused by its leaping. The leaping, the sound, the frog, and the pond, and Basho were all in one and one in all. There was an absolute totality, that is, an absolute identity, or, to use Buddhist terminology, a perfect state of Emptiness *(i.e., śūnyatā)* or Suchness *(i.e., tathatā)*. Intellectualists or logicians may declare that all these different objects of nature are symbols, as far as Basho is concerned, of the highest value of reality. That this is not the view I have tried to explain is quite evident, I believe.

Why did Basho exclaim, *"Furuike-ya!"* "Oh! Old pond!"? What significance does this *"ya!"*, corresponding to the English "Oh!" in this case, have to the rest of the *haiku*? The particle has the force of singling out the old pond from the rest of the objects or events and of making it the special point of reference. Thus, when the pond is mentioned, not only the series of events as particularly mentioned in the *haiku* but an infinite, inexhaustible totality of things making up the human world of existence comes along with it. The old pond of Basho is the *Dharma-dhātu* in the Kegon system of Buddhist philosophy. The old pond contains the whole cosmos and the whole cosmos finds itself securely held in the pond.

This idea may be illustrated by an infinite series of natural numbers. When we pick up any one of these numbers, for example, 5, we know that it is 1 (one) so many times repeated, that this repetition is not merely mechanical but organically related, and, therefore, that the series is an organic whole so closely and solidly united that when any one of the numbers is missing the whole series ceases to be a series (or group), and, further, that each unit thus represents or symbolizes the whole.

Take a number designated 5. 5 is not just 5. It is organically related to the rest of the series. 5 is 5 because of its being related to all the other numbers as units and also to the series as a whole. Without this 5 the whole is no more a whole, nor can all the other units (6, 4, 7, 8, 9, etc.) be considered belonging to the series. 5 then not only contains in it all the rest of the numbers in the infinite series, but it is also the series itself.

It is in this sense when the Buddhist philosophy states that all is one and one is all, or that the one is the many and the many the one.

Basho's *haiku* of "the old pond" now becomes perhaps more intelligible. The old pond with the frog jumping into it and producing a sound which not only spatially but temporally reaches the end of the world, is in the *haiku* by no means the ordinary pond we find everywhere in Japan, and the frog, too, is no common "green frog" of the spring time. To the author of the *haiku* "I" am the old pond, "I" am the frog, "I" am the sound, "I" am reality itself including all these separate individual units of existence. Basho at this moment of spiritual exaltation is the universe itself, nay, he is God Himself, Who uttered the fiat, "Let there be light." The fiat corresponds to "the sound of the water," for it is from this "sound" that the whole world takes its rise.

This being so, do we call "the old pond" or the water's sound or the leaping frog a symbol for the ultimate reality? In Buddhist philosophy there is nothing behind the old pond, because it is complete in itself and does not point to anything behind or beyond or outside itself. The old pond (or the water or the frog) itself is reality.

If the old pond is to be called a symbol because of its being an object of sense, intellectually speaking, then the frog is a symbol, the sound is a symbol, Basho is a symbol, the pen with which I write this is a symbol, the paper is a symbol, the writer is a symbol, indeed, the whole world is a symbol, including what we designate "reality." Symbolism may thus go on indefinitely.

Buddhist symbolism would therefore declare that everything is symbolic, it carries meaning with it, it has values of its own, it exists by its own right pointing to no reality other than itself. Fowls of the air and lilies of the field are the divine glory itself. They do not exist because of God. God Himself cannot exist without them, if God is assumed to be existing somewhere.

An old learned Chinese dignitary once said to a Zen master: "Chuang-tze announces that heaven and earth are one horse, the ten thousand things are one finger; is this not a wonderful remark?" The master without answering this pointed at a flower in the courtyard and said: "People of the world see the flower as if in a dream."

Zen Buddhism avoids generalization and abstraction. When we say that the whole world is one finger or that at the end of a hair Mount Sumeru dances, this is an abstraction. It is better to say with the ancient

Zen master that we fail to see the flower as it is, for our seeing is as if in a dream. We see the flower as a symbol and not as reality itself. To Buddhists, being is meaning. Being and meaning are one and not separable; the separation or bifurcation comes from intellection and intellection distorts the suchness of things.

There is another *haiku* giving the Buddhist idea of symbolization. This was composed by a woman poet of the nineteenth century. It runs like this:

> *Asagao-ya!*
> *Tsurube torarete*
> *Morai mizu.*

> Oh! the morning glory!
> The bucket seized away,
> I beg for water.

When the poet early in the morning went out to draw water from a well situated outdoors, she found the bucket entwined by a morning glory in bloom. She was so deeply impressed by the beauty of the flower that she forgot all about her mission. She just stood before it. When she recovered from the shock or trance, as it were, the only words she could utter were "Oh! The morning glory!" She did not describe the flower. She merely exclaimed as she did. No reference whatever to its beauty, to its ethereal beauty, did she make, showing how deeply, how thoroughly she was impressed by it. She was, in fact, carried away by it; she was the flower and the flower was she. They were so completely one that she lost her identity. It was only when she woke from the moment of unconscious identity that she realized that she was the flower itself or rather Beauty itself. If she were a poet standing before it and admiring its beauty, she would never have exclaimed, "Oh! The morning glory!" But as soon as she regained consciousness all that comes out of it inevitably followed, and she suddenly remembered that she was by the well because she wanted some water for her morning work. Hence the remaining two lines:

> The bucket seized away,
> I beg for water.

It may be noted that the poet did not try to undo the entwining vine. If she wanted to, this could have been easily done, for the morning glory yields readily to this process without being hurt. But evidently she had no desire to touch the flower with her earthly hands. She lovingly felt it as it was. She went to her neighbor to get the necessary water. She says the bucket was seized away by the flower. It is remarkable that she does not make any reference whatever to her defiling the transcendental beauty of the thing she sees before her. It was her womanly tenderness and passivity to refer to the captivity of the bucket.

Here again we see that there is no symbolism, for to the poet the morning glory does not symbolize beauty; it is beauty itself; it does not point to what is beautiful or of value; it is the value itself. There is no value to be sought outside the morning glory. Beauty is not something to be conceived beyond the flower. It is not a mere idea which is to be symbolized or concretized in the morning glory. The morning glory is the whole thing. It is not that the poet comes to beauty through or by means of what our senses and intellect distinguish as individual objects. The poet knows no other beauty than the morning glory as she stands beside it. The flower is beauty itself: the poet is beauty itself. Beauty recognizes beauty, beauty finds itself in beauty. It is because of human senses and intellect that we have to bifurcate beauty and talk about one who sees a beautiful object. As long as we cling to this way of thinking, there is symbolism. But Buddhist philosophy demands not to be blindfolded by so-called sense objects, for they will forever keep us away from reality itself.

We see, therefore, that there is something corresponding in Buddhism to what is ordinarily known as symbolism. Buddhism is, so to speak, thoroughly realistic in the sense that it does symbolize any particular object in distinction to something else. Buddhists would assert that if there is anything at all to be distinguished as a symbol bearing a specific value, the value here referred to has no realistic sense whatever. For there can be no such object to be specifically distinguishable. If anything is a symbol, everything is also equally a symbol, thus putting a stop to symbolism.

Symbolism in Buddhist philosophy may be said to be of a different connotation from what philosophers generally understand by the term.

Ignorance and
World Fellowship

1

According to the basic teaching of Buddhism which is accepted by all Buddhists, Hīnayāna and Mahāyāna, it is from Ignorance that there is Karma. In the Twelvefold Chain of Origination, we have *Saṃskāra* instead of Karma; but both terms are derived from the same root *kṛi,* which means "to do," "to act," or "to work," and practically they are equivalent to the English word, "action." To state that Action starts from Ignorance, or that, dependent on Ignorance there is Action, means that the world where we live and carry on our business is the product of Ignorance. For the world is our Karma, or the world is the stage for Karma to work out its destiny.

Ignorance is an epistemological term and Karma has a moral signification. They appear to belong to different spheres of thought, and we may well ask how it is possible for the one to issue from the other. In Buddhism, however, Ignorance has a more fundamental connotation, and points to the awakening of the intellect itself. This awakening is an act, and we can state that Ignorance is Karma and Karma is Ignorance; it is not, strictly speaking, quite right to establish a causal relation between the two terms, they are simply two aspects of the same fact. But because of the general intellectual tendency of Buddhism, Ignorance is mentioned first and spoken of as if Karma stands to it in the relation of dependence. In our practical life wherever there is Karma there is Ignorance and wherever there is Ignorance there is Karma. The two cannot be separated. To understand what they exactly mean is to have an insight into the Buddhist conception of the world and life. The aim of the Buddhist discipline is to overcome Ignorance, which is also freeing oneself from Karma, and all its consequences.

What, then, does it mean when we say that "the world is Ignorance and Karma"? It means that the world starts from discrimination, for discrimination is Ignorance and the beginning of dualism—dualism of all kinds. Before discrimination started there was no Ignorance, but as soon as we began to discriminate between that which knows and that which is known, between *noesis* and *noema,* the shadow of Ignorance fell over the entire field of knowledge—knowledge is always now accompanied by ignorance. Since that time, we have been deeply engrossed with dualism itself, and fail to become conscious of that which underlies it. Most people think that dualism is final, that the subject for its own reason ever stands contrasted to the object, and *vice versa,* that there is no mediating bridge which crosses over the chasm between the two opposing concepts, and that this world of opposites remains forever as such, that is, in a state of eternal fighting. But this way of thinking is not quite right and logical according to Buddhist philosophy; for the absolute antithesis in which "A" stands against "not-A" is only possible when there is a third concept, as it were bridging the two terms. When this third concept is not recognized, there is Ignorance. And we must remember that this recognition is more than merely epistemological.

Non-discrimination underlies the discrimination of an antithesis. So long as this non-discrimination is not intuited, Ignorance remains undispelled, and casts its dark shadow over life. To be shut up in the clouds of Ignorance means the acceptance of Karma as the supremely dominant power of life. We are then overawed by Karma; we subject ourselves to the dominance of matter; we are no more a free-willing and self-acting agent, but part of a grand machine of whose inner mechanism we are entirely ignorant; we move as the dead leaves are swept about by the autumn wind.

But how is it possible to rise above Ignorance, to free ourselves from Karma which is matter, and to have a glimpse into the realm of non-discrimination? The possibility of achieving this will mean the doing away with the world, which is tantamount to committing suicide. If Ignorance can be transcended only by death, what is the use, one may ask, of transcending it? Let us remain ignorant and continue suffering— this is probably then our conclusion. But in this conclusion there is no consolation, no happiness, only a despair of the deepest nature; and this was exactly what we desired to conquer at the beginning.

2

The world in which we find ourselves existing is, as I said before, the outcome of Ignorance, that is, of discrimination, and because of this, there is Karma. For Karma is possible only when there is the duality of subject and object in their mutual relationship, and this subject must be a conscious one, conscious of what it is doing. If it were unconscious, there would be no Karma, and therefore no world such as we live in. The mountains may be found towering towards the sky, the oceans filled with waves, the wind blowing over the trees, and the birds chirping in the early spring morning. With all these multiple phenomena, the world is not our own world; it may be the one for rocks, waters, trees, animals, and also perhaps for divine beings, but most assuredly not for us human beings. There are enough movements, of all kinds, indeed, but not such as are known as Karma, that is, those with moral and religious significance.

While consciousness was not yet awakened, the world had no meaning; there were no values in it intellectual, moral, and aesthetic, in short, there was no Karma. With the rise of consciousness, there is discrimination, and with discrimination Ignorance creeps along; for discrimination is double-edged, the one side of which cuts well whereas the other side is altogether dull. It is like a mirror; its bright surface reflects everything which comes before it, but the reverse side of it has no light whatever. It is again like the sun: where it is most brilliantly illuminating, its shadow falls the deepest. The appearance of consciousness in the world means the creation of an objective environment standing against and working upon a subjective mind. Superficially, everything is now well-defined and clarified, but there always hovers a dark cloud of Ignorance over the horizon of consciousness. As long as this cloud is not somehow swept away, Karma assumes a threatening aspect, and there is no peace of mind with us. We must somehow be enlightened thoroughly, and the overshadowing Karma must be understood and thereby overcome.

But is this possible? Does not enlightenment mean the negation of the world? Is not death the outcome of the whole procedure? Are not death and *Nirvāṇa* synonymous?

3

In short, there are two ways of dispelling Ignorance and attaining Enlightenment. The one is negative and the other positive. The negative way is to deny the world, to escape it, to realise Arhatship, to enter into *Nirvāṇa,* to dream of Heaven, to be reborn into the Western Land of Bliss. The positive way is to assert the world, to fight it, to be mixed in it, to go through birth and death, to struggle with tribulations of all kinds, not to flinch in the face of threats and horrors. The first way has been resorted to by most religionists and the second by people of the world— men of action; that is, by business men and statesmen and soldiers. But the latter classes of people are most deeply involved in Ignorance, in the assertion of egotistic passions, and far from being enlightened as to the meaning of life. The fact is not however to be denied that among them there have been quite a few who were really enlightened, masters of themselves as well as of the world.

The negative way is comparatively easier, but there is something about it not quite logical and it is inconsistent and antisocial. If the world is the outcome of discrimination and discrimination leads to Enlightenment, which is the dispelling of Ignorance, the world with all its evils—in whatever sense the term may be understood—must be accepted. If this is not done, we are led to dream of a Heaven where a state of absolute uniformity and mere inactivity prevails. Paradise is the death of all that makes up this world. There cannot be any community life in it, for there is no conflict in Heaven, and conflict is needed for a conscious being to have any feeling of himself and of beings other than himself. As long as discrimination is at the basis of our conscious life, we cannot consistently fly away from the world.

For this reason, the conception of an eternal life in the sense of a life beyond birth and death is untenable. Life means the struggle of birth and death. There can be no life where there is no death. Immortality is not a logical concept. It is no more than a dream. Life is a cloth woven of birth and death. The moment we are born, we are destined to die, in fact every moment means a constant succession of birth and death, of death and birth. To seek Enlightenment by negating the world, a world of birth and death, is really a deception. The negative way is not after all the solution of life.

The Buddhist way of solving the problem of life is a positive one. Buddhism accepts life as it is, faces its dualism, its evils, its struggles, its pains, in fact everything that makes it up. Life is Karma which is the outcome of discrimination; and there is no escaping this Karma inasmuch as discrimination is at the basis of all that makes up the world and life. To escape it is to commit suicide, but suicide is also a Karma and bears its fruit and the suicide is born again to a life of pain and suffering.

Enlightenment must come from truly recognizing the meaning of birth and death, and thereby transcending their dualism. Ignorance consists in regarding dualism as final and clinging to it as the basis of our communal life. This logically and emotionally ends in egotism and all the evils flowing from its assertion. Buddhism asks us to gain an insight into that which underlies all forms of dualism and thereby not to be attached to them as irreducively final.

4

What is this "that which underlies" the one and the many, birth and death, you and me, that which is and that which is not? It is not quite right to say "underlies," for it suggests the opposition between that which lies under and that which lies over—which is a new dualism; and when we go on like this, we commit the fault of infinite regression. According to Buddhism, this third term is designated *śūnyatā*, Emptiness. All opposites rise from it, sink into it, exist in it.

Śūnyatā is apt to be misunderstood by all of us whose so-called logical mind fails to conceive anything going beyond relativity. *Śūnyatā* is set against reality and understood as non-reality or nothingness or void. I generally translate it Emptiness.

Śūnyatā is not the Absolute as it is usually understood, when the Absolute is regarded as a something standing by itself. Such an Absolute is really non-existent, for there is nothing in this world which is absolutely separable from the rest of it. If there is such a one existent, we have nothing to do with it.

Śūnyatā is not God, for *śūnyatā* is not personal, nor is it impersonal. If it is at all personal, its personality must be infinitely different from what we generally conceive of personality. As long as human beings rise from *śūnyatā,* the latter must be regarded as to that extent personal and self-conscious. But it would be a grave error to try to find any parallelism between human personality and that of *śūnyatā.*

Nor is *śūnyatā* to be conceived atheistically, nor pantheistically, nor acosmistically. Therefore, Buddhism which upholds the idea of *śūnyatā* is not a godless religion, nor is it pantheistic as it is sometimes most incorrectly conceived. Nor is it acosmism.

Śūnyatā is sometimes identified with the Universal which is really non-existent. Devoid of all contents, the Universal is a mere logical concept and cannot be operative in this world of particulars.

5

The relation of *śūnyatā* to the dualism of existence will be illustrated by the following two Zen *mondōs.*

A monk came to Tōzan (T'ung-shan, 807–869) and asked: "Cold and heat alternately come and go, and how can one escape them?" The question has the same purport as this, "How can one transcend the dualism of birth and death, of being and non-being?" The Christian way of putting it may be, "How can one attain an immortal life?" As Zen does not follow an abstract, conceptualistic method of teaching, it is always in touch with the concrete facts of life.

The master answered: "Why not go where there is neither cold nor heat?" This may suggest the idea that Buddhism advocates the running away from the world, or its negation. Apparently, it does, if we do not go any farther than the bare statement by the master. But listen to what follows. The monk asked, "Where is the place where there is neither cold nor heat?" The questioner evidently took the master's answer for what we would generally do, i.e., a realm of absolute transcendence. The master however said, "When the cold season is here, we all feel cold; when the hot season arrives, we also all feel warm." This is where neither cold nor heat troubles us.

The actual outcome of Tōzan's answer is that where you suffer cold or heat is where there is neither cold nor heat. This is a paradoxical saying, but the ultimate truth of all religion is paradoxical, and there is no way to avoid it as long as we are sticklers to formal logic. To translate the idea in terms of regular Buddhist terminology, *śūnyatā* is to be found at the very seat of birth and death, or, more directly, *śūnyatā* is birth and death, and birth and death is *śūnyatā*. Yet they are not identical. *Śūnyatā* is *śūnyatā*, birth-and-death is birth-and-death. They are distinct, and are to be kept distinct when we desire to have a clear grasp of the fact itself.

A similar question was asked of Sōzan (T'sang-shan, 840–901), disciple of Tōzan: "The hot season is at its height, and how shall we escape it?" The experience of pain is universal, and all religion starts from pessimism, for without the experience of pain in one form or another there will be no reflection on life and without reflection no religion. Sōzan's answer was: "Escape into the midst of the seething waters, into the midst of a blazing coal." The Zen master's advice is like pouring oil into a fire; instead of being an escape in the ordinary sense of the word, it is aggravating pain, bringing it to its acutest point; and when there is thus no soothing of pain, where is the escape we are so earnestly in search of?

The monk has not stopped here, and, wanting to pursue the matter to its ultimate end, asks, "How shall we escape the seething waters and the blazing coal?" The point may be somewhat difficult to comprehend, but it means this. When life is accepted, with all its pains and evils, where is our salvation? Heaven has been created for this purpose, and if we go to Hell as advised by Sōzan, what is the use of our at all trying to escape, to save ourselves? Hence the monk's second question. The master's answer was, "No further pains will harass you."

When thought is divided dualistically, it seeks to favor the one at the cost of the other, but as dualism is the very condition of thought, it is impossible for thought to rise above its own condition. The only way to do this is to accept dualism squarely, and not think of it any further. When you are to suffer a pain for one reason or another, you just suffer it, and have no other thoughts about it. When you are to enjoy a pleasure you just enjoy it, and have no other thoughts about it. By thus experiencing what comes to you, you experience *śūnyatā* in which there is neither dualism nor monism nor transcendentalism. This is what is meant by the statement which makes up the basic teaching of the *Prajñāpāramitā,* that "when I thus talk to you, there is no talk, nor any hearing; nor is there any talker, and no audience either"—which is *śūnyatā.*

This conception of *śūnyatā* in relation to a dualistic or pluralistic world is expressed in Buddhist philosophy by the formula: *Byōdō in shabetsu* and *shabetsu in byōdō. Byōdō* literally means "evenness and equality" and *shabetsu* "difference and division." *Byōdō* is sometimes taken to mean identity, or sameness, or the universal, and *shabetsu* individuality, or particularity, or multiplicity. But it is more correct to consider *byōdō = śūnyatā =* "that which lies underneath pluralistic existences," or "that from which individuals rise and into which individuals sink." Individuals always remain individuals in a dualistically-conditioned world; they are not the same in the sense that you are I and I am you, for you and I are antithetical and their merging into each other is the end of the world. But this does not mean that there is no bridging between the two terms, for if there were no bridging, there would be no mutuality, and consequently no communal life. This discrete and yet continuous state of existence is described by Buddhist philosophers as *"Byōdō in shabetsu* and *shabetsu in byōdō."* Or, for brevity's sake, *"Byōdō soku shabetsu* and *shabetsu soku byōdō." Soku* is a copulative particle expressing equation or identity.

6

This being so, Buddhists frankly accept this world of pluralities with all its moral and intellectual complexities. They advise us not to try to escape it, because after all no escape is possible, wherever you go your shadow follows you. A monk asked a master, "How is it possible to escape the triple world?" Answered the master, "What is the use of escaping it?" The triple world of desire, of form, and of no-form is the place where we have our being and live our lives; our trying to escape it in order to find a land of bliss somewhere else is like a lunatic seeking his own head which he never lost. When the founder of the Myōshinji monastery was requested by a monk to help him get out of the cycle of birth and death, the founder roared, "Here in my place there is no birth-and-death." This answer in its final purport is not at all negativistic, it ultimately points to the same idea as given vent to by the other masters.

With consciousness once awakened, discrimination inevitably follows its steps, and on the reverse side of discrimination Ignorance is found. Ignorance shades our life as long as it is the ruling principle of the world, as long as we are unable to see behind a world of dualities and hence of pluralities. In short, if we hold up this dualistically-conditioned existence as finality, and altogether leave out the mediating notion of *śūnyatā* from which individual things rise and to which they return, and by which they are interrelated one to another while in existence, then we become incurably either crass materialists or dreamy idealists. Ignorance is dispelled only when we have an insight into *śūnyatā*.

Enlightenment may sound more or less intellectual, but in point of fact it illuminates life itself and all that makes up life is cleansed of its taints. Love now shines in its true life. Although differences are recognized and accepted, they cease to be the condition of antagonistic feelings—which latter is usually the case with us enlightened. Fellowship becomes an actuality. Here is the ideal of Bodhisattvahood.

Arhatship, which has been upheld by Buddhists as the supreme type of mankind, is not unconditionally countenanced by followers of Mahāyāna Buddhism. The latter recognize the dominating power played by the material world over the welfare for all beings, they endeavour to save them from all forms of misery, material and spiritual, and they are even willing to sacrifice their own welfare for others. In order to carry out their altruistic impulses, they are ever resourceful, they devise every possible means to attain the end they have in view— the work of universal salvation.

7

In the *Kwannon Sūtra,* Kwannon is made to incarnate himself in thirty-three different forms in order to realize his inexhaustible love-feeling toward all beings. According to Mahāyāna Buddhism, all enlightened ones are Kwannons and are able to manifest themselves in an infinite number of bodies when necessary. Kwannon is sometimes represented with eleven heads and one thousand hands. Eleven is ten plus one, symbolizing infinity, for Kwannon is infinitely capable of looking around and picking up those requiring his help; and one thousand arms mean Kwannon's utmost resourcefulness to carry out his mission of love.

It may not be out of place to refer in this connection to some aspects of Kwannon's, or any Bodhisattva's, love-activity. Love with him does not always mean mere apparent friendliness, for it may frequently take a form of hatred or any adverse feeling. Conditions in which the subject concerned may find himself may be externally unfavorable ones, at least humanly judging. They may even be to all appearances highly threatening and destructive. The Bodhisattva may sometimes appear to him in the form of an inanimate object—a piece of rock, a block of wood, etc., which, in a most mysterious way, afford him an opportunity to see into the secret sources of reality.

8

One of the greatest things religion has neglected in the past is the material aspect of life. Religion has emphasized too much its spiritual side, while spirit and matter are so intimately related that the one cannot go without the other. Since the rise of science, followed by the initiation of the machine age and capitalism, matter has come to assert itself at the expense of spirit, and religion which has been such a strong friend of the latter is at present steadily losing her power over mankind. In the face of modern armed nations ready to fall at one another's throat, religion is entirely helpless. Spiritual fellowship is closely related to material fellowship—we must not forget this fact.

It is in matter as well as in spirit that we feel fellowship and mutuality. Spirit often tends towards individualism, and matter towards communism. Matter is a world common to us all, for it is over matter that we exercise our spiritual power and feel our own existence. Matter resists our approach, and by this we grow conscious of ourselves, that is, of our own spirituality. In this respect, matter is our friend, not our enemy. Whatever resistance it may offer, it is to help us grow stronger in our spiritual power. When matter is attacked with any antagonistic feeling, the feeling reacts on us, and instead of really strengthening the spirit, sours its temper, and hatred is lodged in it.

Matter has hitherto been kept down too despisingly and it is revenging itself now upon the spirit—this is one way of explaining the present state of unrest all over the world. Matter has the just claim to be treated in a more friendly spirit.

From the Buddhist point of view, it is not right to keep matter from spirit and spirit from matter separated as fundamentally irreducible to each other. It is due to our intellectual discrimination that we have come to espouse dualism and hence the antagonism of matter and spirit. Ever since this separation, which is the outcome of Ignorance, the world knows no rest, no peace. As far as the Buddhist teaching is concerned, however, it stops with the wiping out of this Ignorance.

As to the management of the so-called material world, together with our communal life, national and international, which is based on matter, it is left to the best judgments of "worldly" wise people. The only direction Buddhism can given them is to remind them of the truth that as long as Ignorance, taken in its widest possible sense, has a firm hold of us, we are never able to rise above its most undesirable and most deplorable consequences. All these consequences are in fact the outcome of "love" wrongly directed by Ignorance. The removal of Ignorance has really far-reaching effects on human society.

9

Love *(karuṇā)* is the moving principle of all forms of fellowship. When this is misdirected, egotism results in every possible manner— individual egotism, national egotism, racial egotism, economic egotism, religious egotism, and so on. We are suffering at present most poignantly from all these various forms of egotism. Religion, which is supposed to combat the centripetal tendencies of egotism, is to all appearances entirely powerless to cope with the present situation.

Religion is never tired of teaching us to get rid of selfishness, but when the question concerns international or interracial or other world affairs, the teaching has no practical effects upon us. A corporation is noted for its being free from conscience, so is a nation. Legal subterfuges are liberally resorted to, to gain the object of its selfishness. Patriotism, or corporation spirit, differs from personal egotism in that the former is a congregation of individuals who are united with a common purpose. When it sustains a loss in one form or another, usually along the line of economy and political prestige, the loss is shared by the whole body. The directors feel, therefore, responsible for all their doings and also cherish a moral sense of public-spiritedness.

Public-spiritedness is all very well as far as it goes, but when it implies egotism of a fierce kind, and tends to exclusiveness at all costs, we know where it finally ends. We are just witnessing it practically demonstrated all over the world. And the saddest thing of all is that we are helpless to check its reckless progress towards an inevitable end. We have, perhaps, to submit to the logical working of our own Karma, which we have been accumulating since the beginningless past.

How can we rise from this almost hopeless state of affairs which we witness today everywhere about us? The easiest way is for us to become at once conscious of our own Ignorance and thereby to break off the fetters of Karma. But this is what is the most difficult task in the world to accomplish; we have been trying to do this all our lives throughout innumerable ages of the past.

If it is impossible for us, advocating the various faiths of the world, to stem the tide even when we know where it is finally tending, the only thing we can do is to preserve a little corner somewhere on earth, East or West, where our faiths can be safely guarded from utter destruction. When all the turmoils are over, if possible with the least amount of damage, material and otherwise, we may begin to think seriously of the folly we have so senselessly been given up to, and seek the little corner we have saved for this purpose.

If this sounds too negative, let all the large-hearted Bodhisattvas in the world get together and use their moral influence to the utmost of their abilities, and keep their spiritual fire, however solitary it may be, burning at its intensest. From the Buddhist point of view the main thing is to become enlightened regarding the signification of Ignorance and Karma, which, not being fully comprehended, darkens the purport of world-fellowship.

10

Let me suggest some practical methods of leading to Enlightenment, as proposed by all Buddhism. For individual Enlightenment, the six virtues of *Pāramitā* are recommended: Charity, Morality, Humility, Virility (or Indefatigability), Meditation, and Wisdom (or Transcendental Knowledge). In some schools of Buddhism, the last two *Pāramitās* are specially emphasized, but we must remember that Meditation and Wisdom have some well-defined connotation in Buddhism.

When individuals are enlightened, we are apt to think that the whole world too will attain Enlightenment, which means a millennium. But the fact is that universal Enlightenment is not the sum-total of individual Enlightenments, for individuals are always found connected, on account of Karma, which is to say, of history, with different communal groups such as races, nations, castes, etc. To rise above these Karma-hindrances it is necessary, at least as one of the practical methods of achieving the end—the world-fellowship of faiths—to have free communication of all kinds among religiously-aspiring people of different nations. This means free travelling—the establishment of various learned institutes for the understanding of different religions, or different cultures, the exchange of religious representatives corresponding to the exchange of ambassadors among nations, the summoning of a religious parliament which will consider various means of attaining world peace, etc., etc.

That at present no nations are willing to have a world religious conference, somewhat reminding us of a naval disarmament conference or of a league of nations, positively demonstrates the truth that our Karma-hindrance still weighs on us too heavily, and probably we have to wait patiently for our Karma to work itself out, although this does not imply that some enlightened individuals endeavour to work for universal Enlightenment in the best ways they can conceive and according to their vows, i.e., *praṇidhāna*.

Explaining Zen I

My way of explaining Zen may not be altogether the traditional way, but according to my understanding, the origin of Zen is traceable to Buddha's experience of Enlightenment about twenty-five hundred years ago in the northern part of India. Buddhism developed out of the Buddha's experience, and this experience is known as Enlightenment. In Sanskrit it is called *Bodhi,* and *Bodhi* and *Buddha* both come from the same root *budh. Bodhi* means Enlightenment and Buddha means the Enlightened One, so when we talk about Buddhism or Buddha, we have to connect what we are saying with the Enlightenment experience of the Buddha. Without Enlightenment Buddhism would have no meaning whatever, and when Zen claims to transmit the essential experience of Buddha we have to go up to the plane of that Enlightenment. When this is understood Zen will be understood.

To be a good Zen Buddhist it is not enough to follow the teaching of its founder; we have to experience the Buddha's experience. When we just follow the teaching, that teaching, however noble and exalted it may be, does not become our own. Buddha did not want his followers to follow his teachings blindly. He wanted his disciples to experience what he himself experienced, and to have his teachings proved by each follower's personal experience. Experience, therefore, counts much more in Buddhism than its teaching. In other religions the founder expects his teachings to be followed by his devotees, who do not necessarily repeat the experience of the founder. The founder gives instructions, and the followers follow those instructions; they do not necessarily experience the same experience. In some religions the repetition of such experience is even considered to be impossible because the founder's experience is divine, and we humans cannot have the same divine experience.

Buddhism, on the other hand, declares that so long as we can talk about the divine nature, whatever it may be, to that extent the divine nature must be our own. If it is our own, there is no reason why it cannot be experienced, and revealed within ourselves. This may be thought an ambitious aspiration. But to call it ambition is already degrading ourselves. Rather is it a most righteous aspiration, for all human aspirations come out of this divine nature. It is therefore natural for us all to reveal that divine nature in ourselves, instead of leaving it as something unexperienced.

Zen, therefore, aims to come in contact with that divine nature which is in us all, and this revelation of the divine nature in ourselves is what constitutes the Enlightenment experience of Buddha. This divine nature is what we may call the Absolute Self. When we talk about self it is generally confused with relative self, which is to be distinguised from the Absolute Self. When this distinction is not clearly made we are apt to take the individual, empirical, psychological self as the divine nature or Absolute Self. When we say "I am," this "I" is generally considered to originate from a relative "I." But the relative "I" cannot stand by itself; it must have something *behind* it which makes "I" possible, which makes this "I" really "I" in its deepest possible sense. If there is no real Absolute Self behind this relative, psychological "I," this psychological "I" will never achieve its I-ness. The relative "I" assumes something of the real "I" because it has at its back the real "I." When this "Absolute I" is taken away no relative "I" exists. But in our ordinary way of thinking this relative "I" is separated from "Absolute I," and we take this separated "I" as something absolute—something independent, something that can stand on its own right. When this notion is adhered to we have what we call egotism, the ego-centered notion which ordinarily governs our consciousness.

Now Buddhism talks about the *ātman* and *Non-ātman,* and Buddha taught the doctrine of *Non-ātman,* that is, the No-ego doctrine.

There is no ego, there is no *ātman.* When this kind of teaching is understood more or less superficially people judge Buddhism as something negative, or annihilistic. But, as we all know, nothing can stand on a negation. Negation can never stand by itself; it always implies something positive, something affirmative. The reason I can say "I am" is because this "I" stands on a great affirmation. "I am" is affirmation, and when this affirmation is understood in its positive sense we have the Enlightenment experience. When Buddhism denies the *ātman* this *ātman* is not Absolute *Ātman* but relative *ātman.* When this relative *ātman* is negated, the very negation implies that there is something affirmative behind it, and this affirmation is nothing but Absolute Self. Enlightenment brings out this Absolute Self in its original "Suchness." Buddhism, therefore, ought not to be understood in a negative sense.

In the same way, when Zen developed in China it took up the doctrine advanced by Nāgārjuna, the great Indian philosopher, who lived soon after the birth of Christ. His doctrine is based on the *Prajñā-pāramitā Sūtra,* which contains a famous series of negations in which everything is denied. This is quite natural, because our ordinary way of thinking is characterized by relativity, by bifurcation, dichotomy, the separation of subject and object. But this Enlightenment experience, the revelation of the Absolute Self, is beyond this dualistic way of thinking. We therefore naturally start by negating all those forms of dichotomy. But if we start with a negation, one negation not being enough, we go on negating continuously. This series of negations can never come to any conclusion; but when we realize that each negation implies in it an affirmation there is no need to repeat negations; one negation is enough.

A Zen Teacher in China used to hold up the stick which he carried, and say "If you call this stick a stick you touch," that is, you affirm. "When you do not call this stick a stick you turn against," that is, you negate. "So this stick—you cannot call it a stick, nor can you call it not a stick. So neither affirmation nor negation will do. Without negating, without asserting, make a statement!"

Zen teachers demonstrate ordinary every day truth in the same familiar way—by taking up a knife or fork, or picking up a book, or producing a hand with just one finger sticking up. "If you say this is a finger, that is assertion. If you do not call it a finger, that is negation. Then what do you call it?" Finger or hand or fist or stick, it does not make any difference. Whenever you say something it is either a negation or an affirmation. Apart from those two, we cannot say anything. But the teacher demands that you say something about it. What will you say?

One way of answering that kind of problem is recorded in a Zen book. A monk came out of the congregation, took the stick away from the master, broke it into two pieces and threw them away. But if we do the same as that monk did there is no Zen. That would be simply an imitation. Each individual must have his or her own original way of solving the problem. Someone may say, it is a stick just the same. Another may say it is not a stick. Whatever you say, that will also do; it all depends what inner experience you have had. Out of that experience assertion may come or negation may come or breaking the stick into several pieces—that may also come. Or you may ask the teacher: "What do *you* call the stick?" That will also do. All kinds of answers are possible, but if you imitate somebody else there will be no Zen. An individual original experience is needed, but backed by that experience you can swing the stick in any way you like. Otherwise your answers will be just dead things; there will be no life in them.

So this Absolute Self, unless it is most intimately, innerly experienced, will, when we say "I am that I am," be nonsense. When God appeared on Mount Sinai and pronounced his name to Moses as "I am that I am" he was right; for that was God's name. It was God himself. If we can really say "I am that I am," as Christ said, "I am before Abraham was," there is Absolute Self revealed. But this revelation is not just talking about it; it must be a real personal experience.

When the Buddha began to search for Self he wanted to find Self. What made him go through the cycle of birth and death? He wanted to know. When he knew what he was, he could really transcend this eternal cycle of birth and death, this flux of becoming. In modern terms we talk much about a stream or flux of becoming, but the Buddha's problem was to cross over this stream of becoming, to emerge out of becoming and see something in becoming itself. To do this he had first to divide himself. He had to analyze what his self was, to project a question out of himself. The analysis consisted in dividing himself, which is, from the ordinary point of view, impossible. To see what his self was, he projected himself as a second self and began to dissect that second self, to see what real Self was. That is an impossible task, but we all do that when we intellectualize—when we appeal to intellection. When he proposed a question, that was going out of himself. He projected himself as not-self, because the question went out of himself and he wanted by questioning to dissect himself. He could not apply his knife of dissection on himself. Intellectually he had to put himself out, that is, to negate himself. But this negation was killing himself. However precise, however logical that dissection may be, it is not he himself, but something projected out of himself. That is his second self, not the real Self. So however much he may analyze, he can never get at the real

Self, because real Self is himself. So it is altogether impossible, we might say, to dissect himself. To dissect himself is murdering himself. When he himself is murdered, nothing is left. The analyst himself and the subject he tries to analyze both disappear. Therefore, to understand what the Self is we must go back within the Self instead of having that self projected out of real Self—we must go back. Instead of intellectually trying to locate that self we must go deep within ourselves and take hold of it. That is impossible, but that is what we must all try to do, and unless we succeed we can never be rescued. And the Buddha succeeded.

The proof that he succeeded in taking hold of his Absolute Self does not come from the Buddha himself but comes out of ourselves. If the Buddha tried to prove his realization, that proof would naturally appeal to words, or to some kind of gesture. When it is expressed that way the expression is not the real one, but is only real in reference to the Buddha himself. When we try to take that reference, and to go back to its origin—Buddha himself—that can only be done by ourselves experiencing it. As long as we take up his intellectual reference as something real, that is taking the finger which points at the moon for the moon itself. When the moon is seen there is no need for the finger. The moon must be seen though the finger is needed to point at the moon. So long as the moon is not seen the finger is nothing but a finger. So with the Buddha's experience, we know that the Buddha's experience is true when we know it from our own experience.

A certain kind of reasoning used by an ancient master is recorded in one of the Zen books, and it reads like this:

Someone asked the master; "What is meant by seeing into the nature?" This nature means Buddha-nature, and everything is in possession of Buddha-nature, which is Absolute Self. So the monk's question is: What is the Absolute Self? What is the Self that makes us really say: "I am," that makes God say: "I am that I am"? This question, therefore, is most fundamental, for when we get into this nature we attain Buddhahood, we experience Enlightenment. And Zen starts from this. Therefore this question is the most fundamental one.

The master said: "The Buddha-nature (or Absolute Self) in its purity remains serene from the first and shows no movement whatever. It is free of all categories such as being and non-being, long and short, grasping and giving up, purity and defilement. It stands by itself in tranquility." Note that the Buddhist sense of purity is metaphysical, not merely ethical. Nature in its absoluteness remains serene, and serene means free from becoming. "And shows no movement whatever" means that there is no becoming when the nature remains in its absoluteness. This corresponds to the Western conception of Godhead. The Godhead remains serene, pure, unmoved and unmoving. It is not a creator; it is not created. Godhead exactly corresponds to this Buddha-nature, as explained by this Zen teacher.

All categories such as being and non-being, pure, defiled, long, and short, belong to this world. The world of relativity uses such standards of measurement, but these standards do not apply to the nature itself. To describe this state of being Buddhists say it is in tranquility, in this absolute state of tranquility. And where this nature is seen, it is called "seeing the nature." This nature is Buddha himself, and his Enlightenment. So to see the nature will be to see Buddha, to attain Enlightenment, to become cognizant of Absolute Self.

Now the question arises: when the nature is already pure, and does not belong to such categories as being and non-being, how can there be any seeing? When we talk about seeing, seeing implies one who sees and that which is seen. If nature is so pure and so absolute that there is no division of subject and object, how *could* there be any seeing? That is quite a natural question and the master's answer is: "In seeing there is nothing seen." We say that we see but there is nothing seen. Really, seeing is no seeing. When the stick is produced and we say it is a stick, it is not a stick. When we say it is not a stick, the stick remains just the same. This is what the master means. But this is hard to see unless one goes through a certain experience, unless one has a certain form of intuition. Now the question is: if there is nothing seen, how can one speak of seeing at all? This is also a natural question. The master replies: "Seeing is no seeing." This is no answer, you might say. But it is a most perfect answer when it comes out of one's real inner experience. But when it is just in the form of words it loses its real sense. It is mere parrot's repetition, or mere echoing.

When seeing takes place in this wise, who is it that sees? If seeing is no seeing who is the seer. When the question was asked in this way the master said: "There is no seer either." When we use the word to see or to hear or to do we think there is a seer, one who hears, one who acts, and so on. But the master says there is no seer. There is no hearer. There is no ego. There is no *ātman* that acts, feels, thinks, and so on. But whenever we assume something, there comes along this bifurcation of subject and object. That is inevitable.

Now you will remember a question was asked when a master produced that stick and said: "If you say this stick is a stick, that is an assertion, if you say it is not a stick, that is a negation. Beyond this negation and affirmation, make a statement." What is this one statement which goes beyond negation and assertion?

There was another master who was asked for the one statement that goes beyond assertion and negation, and he replied: "What do *you* say?" That was the answer given to this question. I wonder what *you* make of this! When you make an absolute statement which goes beyond the duality of negation and affirmation, the master asks, "What do *you* say?" When you understand this you will understand everything.

Now when you are facing reality this point of thought is dangerous. When you actually see Godhead face to face you will lose your life. This is a question of life and death, and is therefore most dangerous. Yet in Zen you have to face this thought. Just stand in front of the thought and grasp it. When the master answered: "What would *you* do?" he just raised his thumb. To this serious question he gave just a trifling answer. The monk, of course, did not understand what the master said. Please be merciful, he said, and explain it. The master said: "Why, you're far off. You are no more at the point of the thought. You're just running away from it!"

"I come here with the most urgent question. Will you be good enough to solve it for me?" When that question was proposed to the master, the master simply said: "Do you understand?" The Monk wanted to understand; therefore, he questioned. But the master asked: "Do *you* understand?" Of course he did not understand; that is why he came with the question to the master. It is a most absurd answer from the ordinary point of view. Then the monk replied, quite naturally "I do not, oh master!" Then the master said: "The arrow has passed away." All these things are not to be intellectually treated.

There was another monk who came to a master and asked: "What is myself?" That is the most absolute question one can ever ask. What is myself? You must surely know yourself, yet instead of doing that you come to somebody else and ask, "What am I?" I ought to know myself far better than all of you combined. Even God himself cannot understand me as well as I myself. Yet we all ask this kind of question. Who am I?

And the master said: "How many masters have you asked about this question?" This kind of search may go on for ever, but Absolute Self is to be perceived within oneself.

Explaining Zen II

In "Explaining Zen I" I talked about our wishing to go home—to go back to our original home, wherever it might be. Now in a well-known *mondo,* a dialogue between a monk and a Zen master, the monk asked the master: "What is Zen?" The Master said: "It is like seeking an ox while riding on it." Then the monk asked: "After I have ridden on the ox, what about it?" The master repeated, "It is like going home, while riding on the ox."

When Buddha attained Enlightenment he felt as if he had got home. He had found his own Self, the Self which he had had from the very beginning. But when he made an inquiry about it he lost it, for without losing it, without negating it, we cannot find it. It is of course unnecessary to try to find it if it has been with us from the very beginning, but the strange thing is that we have to lose it in order to find it, in order to be convinced that finding is not necessary at all. It is like the parable in the Bible of the prodigal son, who wanted to go home. In the *Saddharma Puṇḍarīka* we have the same theory of a son who ran away from his father's house, and after wandering about and going through all kinds of suffering, went back home. But the son was not able to identify himself as the heir to his father. He still thinks he is a stranger, and behaves as if he did not belong to his father. But the father, taking pity on him, uses all kinds of "expedients" or "methods" to make him feel at home. This story must have a common origin with that in the Bible, and this common origin may be traced back to our wishing for home—for we are all wanderers, wayfarers who have somehow lost our way.

Now when Christians deviate from the path which they are told by God to follow, this disobedience constitutes a sin, and because of this disobedience they feel the desire to be back in God. It is because they feel sinful that they wish to go back to God; it is the reminding themselves of their disobedience that makes them wish to go back to

98

their original home. But the original home is never found unless we first go out of the home for once at least—that is, unless we commit some kind of sin.

Now this is very interesting. Why have we deviated? Why was it necessary to deviate from God—to run away from our original home? Why did we not stay with God? Why did we deny God? This question cannot be solved intellectually, however much we use our present logic. We have to develop another kind of logic which is not revealed through the exercise of the intellect. But as soon as this experience, that is, Enlightenment, is experienced, the question "why" has no force whatever; it solves itself. We are what we are. Because we are not in reality we ask the question "why," but as soon as we are in reality itself we no more ask that question. But we are troubled with the sense of sin. We have lost ourselves, and deviated from the course that the Buddha or God indicated. We are lost and want to be back home. How do we manage it? Zen does not extend a helpful hand to take us into Zen itself. Rather it stands before us as an "Iron Wall' which we cannot scale, which we cannot break through. We just face it and do not know what to do.

We try, as the Buddha did in the beginning, an intellectual way of breaking through the wall. In the Buddha's time the problem was in the form of the cycle of birth and death. Nowadays we may formulate it in a different way, but the fundamental problem remains the same. How to break through this wall of dualism? Without dualism we should not have this world. But we are in the world, and want to get out of the world. Why are we not satisfied with this world? Why do we wish to transcend the situation in which we find ourselves? From the intellectual point of view, from the scientific point of view, the situation is not of our own making. In Christian terminology, God made *us*. As long as we are God's creatures, the responsibility must be placed on God himself; it cannot be said that we are responsible for what we are. But somehow we feel that we *are* responsible for it, and want to get away from it, or at least to ameliorate it.

Now intellect cannot solve the problem. It only involves us more desperately in the labyrinth in which we find ourselves. Before the Buddha had his Enlightenment experience he tried this intellectual method. He followed the most noted philosophers of his day, but he could not find a solution through discussing the problem with them. Then he tried the practice of asceticism, that is, a moral discipline. He trained himself morally, by reducing his natural or physical impulses to the minimum, so that his mind or *ātman,* whatever you may call it, might be as free as possible. But this excess of discipline acted unfavorably on his health, and he became so emaciated that he could not rise from his seat. So he quit this method too, and began to take milk. But taking milk and getting stronger left the problem still unsolved, and it hung before his mind like a threatening thought. He could not make that thought his own; it remained outside himself and threatened him.

This is the situation which modern man feels in his own way. The words that the Buddha used to express his situation may be different, but the situation is the same. And it is threatening. Yet we have created this situation for ourselves and it is an illusion that the thought or problem is standing before us threatening us and demanding solution. There is no such thing, objectively speaking, outside the person who puts the question. The question is not threatening at all. It is the questioner who asks that question who is really threatening himself, and this threat comes in the form of the question. The situation, then, is that we are all suffering from an intellectual illusion which is nowadays known as logic or science. Scientists try to solve the secrets of existence by means of scientific research, but after they have—as they think— found the secret, that secret leads to another secret, and the secrets never cease. Those scientists who realize this, who know that the secrets are endless and that we can never grasp the infinite, think that there must be something beyond human measurement. For all those scientific secrets are measured by human measurement, and they at least appreciate that this human measurement must itself be solved. For the implement with which the average scientist attempts to measure other things, itself requires another implement to measure it. Yet there must be some way of solving the riddle, for moral discipline is no more efficient than the intellect. As long as morality strives to acquire something, to attain something—some kind of perfection—we realize, as soon as we attain a certain degree of moral discipline, that there is still something that we have not attained. So the perfection recedes for ever, for there is no such thing as perfection as far as human measurement is concerned. The intellectual approach and the moral approach are, therefore, alike—of no avail. Yet, because we have put the question that question is solvable.

The very fact that we have set forth a certain problem which we may call the ultimate question of reality proves that the question is solvable. There is no question which can never be answered, and we have in Zen the saying: "Questioning is answering." You do not ask in order to get an answer from others; you just look within to see who asked the question. This measurement—who produced that measure? Instead of trying to evaluate a ruler by another ruler we return to the One who created the ruler itself. In theological terminology, we might say that as God created the world why not go to God himself? Instead of bothering with the created, why not go directly to the Creator? When God said, "Let there be light," the world came out. But where from? There is nowhere else but from God himself. In that case the world must have God in itself. God must be present in the world. If he stayed outside the world, if God stands against the world and the world against God, the world is no more a living world, and God is a dead machine. If God was able to create the world, the world must have something of God in it. In the same way, if we ask a question something of the answer that produced that question must be in us. So the solution of a problem takes place when question and questioner become one, that is when God and the world become one. When God created the world, that was God's question. God, by creating the world questioned himself. He wanted to know himself. When God created the world, he solved his question, and when he identified himself with the world, when the world was identified with God, the complete solution took place. God created the world out of himself; therefore, to solve the problem of the world God has to go back into himself. When this takes place God understands himself. Therefore God negates himself when he wants to know himself.

At the same time we want to go back to our original home where no negations, no affirmations ever existed, and no logic could ever apply. But if we seek that original home outside the world, and that original home is lost in the world itself, we shall have to seek another original home. So the original home must be in the world out of which the original home comes; that is, God must be in the world. Therefore, when the world is known, God is known, and when God is known, the world is known. This identification must take place before the final answer takes place.

So when the Buddha became enlightened, in his Enlightenment experience there was no question standing outside him, no questioner who produced that question. So the question dissolved itself into the question out of which the question came. And the questioner took the question into himself. When this identification took place the Buddha solved his question. Thereafter, his experience could not be demonstrated in any way except by saying "Oh," or "Ah," or "*Oṃ,*" or some such monosyllable which makes no articulate sense. In Zen teaching, words are therefore not used in the way they are generally used, for they have no relative sense. They all come out of the experience itself. Theologians say: "Believe first and you will be saved. Do not question about it, just believe it, and by believing you will be saved." But this believing is itself what those who have not attained faith are looking for. When faith is attained everything solves itself. But how to get that faith, that is the question, and we all ask it.

When we are told, "Believe and you will be saved," how to believe is the question, for faith is not a thing that comes from outside. Faith is what the Buddha experienced at the time of Enlightenment. Questioner and question must become one. When this one-ness is experienced, that is the state of faith.

Then what is faith and how can I be saved? As long as that question lingers outside oneself it will never be solved; that is, there will be no faith. Therefore, having faith is being saved, and being saved is having faith. Faith and salvation take place simultaneously. Faith *is* being saved; being saved is faith. So we must have faith first; otherwise, there will be no solution.

When psychology is used in its scientific or relative aspect it is just one of the sciences and will not apply to the Buddha's Enlightenment experience. But when it is understood in its broadest and deepest possible sense, the Zen approach to it concerns the *Ātman* or Self. But whether we talk of Self or Reality the main thing is to experience it, and experience concerns the Will. Now we *are* will, and God is will, and when will asserts itself, not in its relative sense of a craving for power but in its original sense, we may speak of God's will.

God wills to know himself, and this will, that is, God, moves, for God can never stand still. God moves and this movement is will. So what moves movement, what starts movement, is will. When God remains just as God, there is no world, there is indeed no God. Then God wills and when this motion or movement takes place, creation takes place. Each time I move my finger, the world is created. This is God's creation. Each time I utter a word this utterance is God's fiat. And this is will. To start from this will, to know what this will is, this is the psychological approach to Zen.

Now Eckhart has much to say about the saying, "Blessed are the poor in spirit," which is the most illuminating statement in the Bible. What does "poor" mean here, asks Eckhart. He replies: "The poor man, the one who is poor, is the one who wants nothing, knows nothing and has nothing. This exactly corresponds to the Zen idea."

"*Wants nothing*" means having no desire. When I said God wills, and that something comes out of the willing, it is already misstating reality as it is. But when we try to express reality in language, this contradiction and absurdity is inevitable. So I say that Will wills without willing or wanting anything. If God wills to create the world, something outside of himself, that kind of Will is no will. The divine will is just Will, and out of it the world comes. So God willed to create the world, as if he did not will at all. That's what Eckhart means by the poor man.

"*Knows nothing*" is another most expressive phrase. When we try to know something there is one who wants to know and something which is to be known; there is dichotomy. But God's knowing is not knowing at all.

And then there is "*not to have*." Eckhart says that if there is any one spot in the soul, however small, where God could be placed, God will never come into your soul. God does not want any place or point where he could set himself up. Within such a place you are God himself.

Of this *wanting nothing* he gives a fine example. Pious people continue their penances and external practices of piety, and are popularly considered of great importance. But Eckhart says "May God pardon it"! To all outward appearance these people are to be called holy, but inwardly they are fools, for they do not understand the true meaning of divine reality. By practicing penances, by looking virtuous, by saying prayers and attending Mass, and so on, they are quite religious people. But if they want something, if they are seeking something, they are really fools.

Compare this with the question of a Zen master: "Who is the teacher of all patriarchs?" or, we might say, all church fathers? His own answer was, "Cows and dogs." We think these are inferior to us, and this delusion troubles us all the time. The cat catches rats, and in that, the cat is performing his cat-ness. So long as he performs his cat-ness, he is divine. But we human beings deviate from the original nature which God intended us to have, and in that we are worse than cats, and we have something to learn from them.

There is another story. A monk asked a Zen master: "Everybody is supposed to have Buddha-nature. Have I got it?" The master replied, "No." Then the monk asked: "When the Buddhist scriptures tell us that everything is endowed with Buddha-nature, how is it that I don't have it? Trees and rocks, rivers and mountains, all have Buddha-nature. If so, why not I!" The master replied, "Cats, dogs, mountains, rivers, all have Buddha-nature; you do not." The monk asked, "Why not?" The master said: "Because you ask!"

But if we do not ask, how do we know it? That is the quandary. Eckhart says, do not want anything. Then he talks of *knowing*. Do not, he says, try to know anything. Each time I read Eckhart's sermons it strikes me how identical his thought is with Zen teaching, or with my own experience, I might say.

Back in the womb from which I came I had no God, and merely was myself. I did not will or desire anything. For I was pure being and knower of myself by divine truth. Then I wanted myself and nothing else. And what I wanted was, and what I was I wanted. And thus I existed untrammeled by God or anything else. But when I parted from my free will and received my created being then I had a God. For before there were creatures God was not God, but rather he was what he was. When creatures came to be and took on creaturely being, then God was no longer God, as he is in himself, but God as he is with creatures.

On the question of not knowing anything, he says: "Now the question is raised—in what does happiness consist most of all? Certain authorities have said that it consists in *loving*. Love is what constitutes happiness. Others say that it consists in *knowing* and *loving*. And this is a better statement."

But Eckhart says that happiness consists neither in knowledge nor in love, but that there is something in the soul from which both knowledge and love flow. To know this source from which love and knowledge flow is to know what blessedness depends on. This something has no before or after. It waits for nothing that is yet to come; it has nothing to gain or lose. Thus, when God acts in it, it is deprived of knowing that he has done so. So this kind of knowledge is not knowing anything.

The last of Eckhart's attributes of the poor man was not to have anything. There was a monk who studied Zen under a certain master. He took down every word the master said just as modern students do, and he kept his notebooks. One day the master called him in. "Now that you have been with me so many years you must know something about Zen. Tell me what you understand. So the monk said what he thought he understood, but the master did not accept his understanding. Whatever statement he made the master denied. He was so grieved, because he thought he understood Zen, that he went back to his own room and went over his notebook, page after page, trying to find a suitable word which would satisfy the master; but he could not find one. He was so disappointed that he thought it was not in him to understand Zen. So he departed from the master, and decided to devote himself to doing something pious. He went to a famous Zen master's grave and devoted himself to keeping the tombstone clean and the surrounding lawn well swept and in good order. One day, when he was cleaning around the tomb, he accidentally struck his bamboo broom against a stone. The striking caused a certain sound, and when he heard that he instantly understood all that his master had said, saying, "Last year my poverty" (note how this corresponds to Eckhart's idea of poverty) "was something like the point of a drill, a very small point. My poverty was such that I had nothing but the small point of the drill. This year my poverty is such that there is no drill, and there is no ground in which its point could be inserted. So I am entirely poor." This corresponds to what Eckhart means, for if there is any spot left in one's mind or soul God will never come in there; Christ will never be born in that soul. The mind must be entirely empty of the things we generally put into it. When this takes place there is real God, that is, real poverty—not to want anything, not to know anything, not to have anything.

Here is another story about not knowing. There was a master who studied Zen under another master, and he was noted for his understanding of Zen. There was a monk who came to that master whose name was Sekito, and the monk knew very well that he was a great master. But just to try how much he understood the monk proposed this question: "Eno, your master, taught you the Dharma, and you have taught many others. Do you understand that Dharma?"

Now everybody knew that Sekito was a great master, with perfect understanding of the Dharma taught by Eno, his predecessor, and the monk knew it too. Yet he purposely asked this question. Sekito replied, "I do not understand the Dharma." If he pretended to know something there would at once be knower and known. So not knowing—transcending this dichotomy of subject-object—is really to be in this dichotomy itself.

Another interesting remark which Eckhart makes is this: "If anyone does not understand this discourse let him not worry about that. For if he does not find this truth in himself, he cannot understand what I have said. For it is the discovered truth which comes immediately from the heart of God."

[Asked about the relationship between asceticism and Zen, Dr. Suzuki replied:] This is a point which invites misunderstanding. To understand Zen, asceticism is not needed; intellectual acuteness is not needed. If asceticism is practiced without any connection with attaining Enlightenment, this is all right. To discipline oneself in something, asceticism may be needed. But to try to reach Enlightenment by means of asceticism is wrong. That does not condemn asceticism, as ascetic discipline of the body or mind, but this distinction is most strongly to be made. The same with intellectuality. Zen experience itself needs some expression, and the experience, if it is a genuine experience, expresses itself. When it expresses itself it generally goes through the channel of intellection, but to attempt to reach Zen from the intellectual point of view is difficult, if not impossible.

The Supreme Spiritual Ideal

In July, 1936, Sir Francis Younghusband convened in London a World Congress of Faiths which, in a fortnight's hard work of discussions, punctuated by public meetings and ensuing questions, hammered out, with remarkable goodwill, the common ground of some seven religions.

At the Queen's Hall on July 9th, one of the speakers was Dr. D. T. Suzuki, and many who later discussed with me that memorable evening made the same remark, that all they remembered was his speech. The theme was no less than The Supreme Spiritual Ideal, and this would not do for a master of Zen with little liking for generalities. As I noted in my diary at the time, "he seemed to be dozing when roused by the Chairman for his contribution. Then with his soft and gentle voice he reached up, as it were, and brought the subject down to earth, where the heart may understand it and the hands make use of it." Here it is, taken from a large volume of the proceedings published by Watkins in 1937 as *Faiths and Fellowship* and republished by courtesy of the present Society in Norfolk Square—ED.

When I was first asked to talk about the Supreme Spiritual Ideal I did not exactly know what to answer. Firstly, I am just a simple-minded country-man from a far-away corner of the world suddenly thrust into the midst of this hustling city of London, and I am bewildered and my mind refuses to work in the same way that it does when I am in my own land. Secondly, how can a humble person like myself talk about such a grand thing as the Supreme Spiritual Ideal, and this before such a grand assembly of people, everyone of whom looks to me to be so wise and intelligent, knowing everything that is under the sun? I am ashamed that I have somehow been made to stand here. The first mistake was committed when I left Japan.

Let me tell you how I lived before I came to London. In my country we have straw-thatched houses. Japanese houses are mostly little. Well, still in the country you see many such straw houses, and mine is one of them. I get up in the morning with the chirping of the birds. I open windows which look right into the garden. Japanese windows are quite different from your English windows. English windows are somewhat like holes made in the walls, but Japanese windows are a combination of English windows and walls. So when Japanese windows are opened, one side of the house is entirely taken away. The house itself opens right into the garden. There is no division between the house and the garden. The garden is a house, a house is a garden; but here a house is quite separate. A house stands by itself, and so does its occupant. Its occupant is separated from his or her surroundings altogether. There is nature, here I am; you are you, I am I; so there does not seem to be any connection between those two—nature, natural surroundings, and the occupants of the house.

So by opening Japanese windows, the house continues into the garden. And I can look at the trees quite easily, not as I look from the English window—that is a kind of peeping out into the garden. I just see the trees growing from the ground. And when I look at those trees growing right from the ground, I seem to feel something mysterious which comes from the trees and from the mother earth herself. And I seem to be living with them, and they in me and with me. I do not know whether this communion could be called spiritual or not. I have no time to call it anything, I am just satisfied. Then there is the little pond, a little lower down the garden. I hear the fish occasionally leaping out of the pond as though they were altogether too happy, and could not stay contented swimming in the pond. Are they? I do not know, but I somehow feel they are very very happy indeed. Just as we dance when we are filled with joy, so the fish are surely dancing. Do they also get something from the element in which they live and have their being? What is this something, after all, which seems to be so stirred in my own self, as I listen to the dancing of the fish in the pond?

Then this is the time for the lotuses to bloom. The pond is filled with them, and my imagination travels far out to the other end of the globe. When I talk like this, do you think I am dreaming in the middle of this big city? Perhaps I am. But my dream, I feel somehow, is not altogether an idle one. Could not there be in these things of which I am dreaming something of eternal and universal value? These huge buildings I see about me are really grand work, grand human achievements, no doubt.

I had a similar feeling when I visited China and was confronted with the Great Wall, of which you have perhaps heard. Are they, however, of eternal duration, as I like to say my dreams are? Let the earth shake a little. Here in this part of the earth, fortunately, it does not seem to shake so frequently as it does in Japan. But let it shake for once. Well, I wonder what would be the result? I can see that result. I even refuse to think of it. But some time ago in an American magazine a certain writer wrote about the ruins of the city of New York when possible future explorers will try to locate where certain of the highest buildings in the world—they call them skyscrapers, don't they—which are now standing in New York would have been. But I will not go on any more with this kind of talk; I must stop dreaming, though it is very pleasant.

Let me awake and face actualities. But what are those actualities I am facing now?—not you, not this building, not the microphone, but this Supreme Spiritual Ideal, those high-sounding words. They come from me. I can't be any longer dreaming of anything. I must make my mind come back to this subject, the Supreme Spiritual Ideal. But really I do not know what Spiritual is, what Ideal is, what Supreme Spiritual Ideal is. I do not seem to be able to comprehend exactly the true significance of these three words, placed so conspicuously before me.

Here in London I come out of the hotel where I am staying. I see in the streets so many men and women walking—or rather, running hurriedly, for to my mind they don't seem to be walking; they seem to be really running. It may not be quite correct to say so, but it seems to me so. And then their expressions are more or less strained, their facial muscles are contracted intensely; they could be more easily relaxed. The roads are riddled with all kinds of vehicles, buses, cars, and other things; they seem to be running in a constant stream—in a constant, ceaseless stream—and I don't know when I can step into that constantly flowing stream of vehicles. The shops are decorated with all kinds of things, most of which I don't seem to need in my little straw-thatched house. When I see all these things, I cannot help wondering where the so-called modern civilized people are ultimately going. What is their destiny? Are they in the pursuit of the Supreme Spiritual Ideal? Are their intense expressions somehow symbolic of their willingness to look into the spirituality of things? Are they really going to spread this spirituality into the farthest end of the globe? I do not know. I cannot answer.

Now let me see, spirituality is generally contrasted to the material, ideal to actual or practical, and supreme to commonplace. If when we talk about the Supreme Spiritual Ideal, does it really mean to do away with what seems to be material, not idealistic but practical and prosaic, not supreme but quite commonplace—this our everyday life in this big city? When we talk about spirituality, do we have to do away with all these things? Does spirituality signify something quite apart from what we see around here? I do not think this way of talking, dividing spirit from matter and matter from spirit, a very profitable way of looking at things about us. As to this dualistic interpretation of reality as matter and spirit, I made some references to it in my little speech the other day.

In point of fact, matter and spirit are one, or rather, they represent two sides of one reality. The wise will try to take hold of the reality, the shield itself, instead of just looking at this side or that side of it, known sometimes as matter and sometimes as spirit. For when the material side alone is taken hold of, there will be nothing spiritual in matter. When the spiritual side alone is emphasized, matter will have to be altogether ignored. The result in either case is onesidedness, the crippling of reality, which ought to be kept whole and wholesome, too. When our minds are properly adjusted and are able to grasp the reality which is neither spirit nor matter and yet which is, of course, spirit and matter, I venture to say that with all its materiality London is supremely spiritual; and further, when our minds are crookedly adjusted, all the monasteries and temples, all the cathedrals and all the ecclesiastic orders in connection with them, all the holy places with their holy paraphernalia, with all their devout worshippers, with everything that goes in the name of religion, I venture to say again are nothing but materiality, heaps of dirt, sinks of corruption.

To my mind, the material is not to be despised, and the spiritual is not always to be exalted—I mean anything which goes in the name of spiritual; I do not mean anything that is really spiritual, but things that pride themselves on the name of spiritual. Such things are not always to be exalted. Those who talk about spirituality are sometimes men of violent nature, while amongst those who have amassed large fortunes and seem ever to be inclined towards things material we often find the highest and biggest souls, steeped in spirituality. But the main difficulty is how can I bring my straw-thatched house right into the midst of these solidly built-up London walls? And how can I construct my humble hut right in the midst of this Oxford Circus? How can I do that in the confusion of cars, buses, and all kinds of conveyances? How can I listen to the singing of the birds, and also to the leaping of the fish? How can one turn all the showings of the shop window displays into the freshness of the green leaves swayed by the morning breeze? How am I to find the naturalness, artlessness, utter self-abandonment of nature in the utmost artificiality of human works? This is the great problem set before us these days.

Again, I do not know about the Supreme Spiritual Ideal. But as I am forced to face this so-called materiality of modern civilization, I have to make some comments on it. As long as man is the work of nature and even the work of God, what he does, what he makes, cannot altogether be despised as material and contrasted to the so-called spiritual. Somehow it must be material-spiritual or spiritual-material, with the hyphen between these two terms—spiritual not divided from material, material not severed from spiritual, but both combined, as we read, with a hyphen. I do not like to make references to such concepts as objectivity and subjectivity, but for lack of a suitable term, just at this moment let me say this. If the spiritual-material, linked with a hyphen, cannot be found objectively, let us find it in our subjective minds and work it out so as to transform the entire world in accordance with it.

Let me tell you how this was worked out by an ancient master. His name was Yoshu, and the monastery in which he used to live was noted for its natural stone bridge. Monasteries are generally built in the mountains, and this place where Yoshu used to reside was noted for its stone bridge over the rapids. One day a monk came to the master and asked: "This place is very well-known for its natural stone bridge, but as I come here I don't see any stone bridge. I just see a rotten piece of board, a plank. Where is your bridge, pray tell me, O master?" That was a question given to the master, and the master now answered this way: "You only see that miserable, rickety plan and don't see the stone bridge?" The disciple said: "Where is the stone bridge then?" And this is the master's answer: "Horses pass over it, donkeys pass over it, cats and dogs. . . ." (Excuse me if I add a little more than the master actually said.) "Cats and dogs, tigers and elephants pass over it, men and women, the poor and the rich, the young and the old, the humble and the noble (any amount of those opposites might be enumerated);

Englishmen, perhaps Japanese, Muslims, Christians; spirituality and materiality, the ideal and the practical, the supreme and the most commonplace things. They all pass over it, even you, O monk, who refuse to see it, are really walking over it quite nonchalantly; and above all you are not thankful for it at all. You don't say, 'I thank you' for crossing over the bridge. What good is this stone bridge then? Do we see it? Are we walking on it? The bridge does not cry out and say: 'I am your supreme spiritual ideal.' The stone bridge lies flat and goes on silently from the beginningless past perhaps to the endless future."

I must stop here. Thank you for your kind attention to my Japanese English. I expect you have done your best to understand me. Then the kindness must be mutual, and in this mutuality of kindness, do we not seize a little glimpse of what we call Spiritual World Fellowship?

Dr. Suzuki, Christmas Humphreys, and Dr. Edward Conze outside the premises of The Buddhist Society in London, 1958.

Mr. G. Koizumi, Founder of the Budokwai in London, with Dr. Suzuki in the garden of Mr. and Mrs. Christmas Humphreys in London, 1958.

Index

Absolute, the, 31, 43, 54, 81, 95
Acitta. *See* Mushin
Affirmation, 92, 96
Agnosticism, 7
Amida, 48
Anātman, 4–5, 6, 15, 91, 96. *See also*
  Self
Anatta. *See* Anātman
An-hsin. *See* Anjin
Anjin, 15, 18
Arhat: Buddhism of, 1; ideal of, 2,
  12, 13, 80, 85
Asceticism, 99, 106
Asikaga era, 57
Aśoka, 3
Aśvaghoṣa, 6, 65
Atheism, 82
Ātman. *See* Ego-soul; Self
Awakening, 25
Awakening of Faith in the Mahā-
  yāna, 6

Basho, 71–74
Bayen, 42, 46, 49
Bodhi, 8, 90
Bodhicitta, 8
Bodhidharma, 14–20, 21; discourses
  by, 18; mission of, 19; teaching of,
  14–20, 25
Bodhisattva, 86, 88; Buddhism of, 1;
  ideal of, 2, 12–13, 85
Bodhisattvayāna, 12
Buddha(hood), 8, 55, 90–91, 94–95
Buddha-nature, 94–95, 104
Buddha, the, 3, 4, 21, 26–27, 34,
  38–39, 51–53, 62–63, 64, 93–94,

99–100, 102; and his triple body,
  65
Buddhism in England, 28
Buji, 62, 63, 64–5
Bushido ("Warrior's Way"), 49
Byōdō, 83–84

Cause and effect, 5
Ceylon, Buddhism in, 1, 3
Ch'an. *See* Zazen
Change. *See* Impermanence
Cha-no-yu, 46
Chao-chou. *See* Jōshu
Charity: practice of, 17; virtue of, 18,
  88
China, and Buddhism, 29–30
Chinese Mysticism and Modern
  Painting, 50
Chō Densu, 50
Christianity, 9–10, 26–27; the Bible,
  98, 103; theology of, 29. *See also*
  God
Chuang-tze, 74
Citta, 14
Concentration, 16, 22
Confucianism, 42
Contemplation, 16, 17, 22

Daruma. *See* Bodhidharma
Deliverance. *See* Enlightenment
Dentō-roku, 55
Dharma, 4, 6, 17, 18, 55, 62, 63, 64,
  65, 105–106; to be in accord with,
  18
Dharmadhātu, 73